Zachariah Black's Quest for Truth

Robert S. Baker

Paperback Edition First Published in the United Kingdom in 2024 by Robert S. Baker

Copyright © Robert S. Baker 2024

Robert S. Baker has asserted his rights under 'the Copyright Designs and Patents Act 1988' to be identified as the author of this work.

All rights reserved.

No part of this book may be reproduced or transmitted in any form or by any means, electronic, mechanical, photocopying, recording, or otherwise, without prior written permission from the Author.

Disclaimer

This is a work of fiction. Names, characters, businesses, places, events and incidents are either the products of the author's imagination or used in a fictitious manner. Any resemblance to actual persons, living or dead, or actual events is purely coincidental.

Cover Image: Robert S Baker

ISBN: 9798333576248

Typeset by aSys Publishing 2024

CHAPTER 1

The Unseen Threads

The house, once filled with the warmth of shared dreams and laughter, now felt like a mausoleum preserving echoes of a life that was. Each room held a ghost of the past, a fragment of a shared memory with Hazel that I clung to desperately.

I ran my fingers over the spines of books we had collected over the years, each title a chapter in our own story. But now, the narrative had taken an unexpected turn, and I was the sole author of the remaining pages.

The envelope lay on my desk, an anomaly in the otherwise meticulous order Hazel had always enforced. It was her handwriting, no doubt, but how? She had been gone for weeks, and I had been through her things more times than I cared to admit, searching for some semblance of solace.

With trembling hands, I opened it, half-expecting to find her familiar scrawl detailing mundane tasks or a shopping list we would never complete. Instead, I found a single sheet, a cryptic message that read: "Look beyond the mirror, where the truth lies hidden in plain sight."

The words sent a shiver down my spine. It was a riddle, a puzzle that Hazel knew only I could solve. But why leave this now? What truth was so important that it had to be concealed until after her departure?

I stood before the mirror, the one that had reflected our lives together, now just a man with a grizzled beard and tired eyes. I looked beyond my reflection, focusing on the frame and the glass, searching for anything out of place.

And there it was, a slight discrepancy in the corner of the mirror, almost imperceptible—a hidden compartment. My heart raced as I pried it open, revealing a small velvet pouch.

Inside was a flash drive, unmarked and innocuous, yet it felt like I was holding the key to Pandora's box. This was Hazel's final message, her last act in a play that had been cut tragically short.

I inserted the drive into my computer, the soft whir of the machine a stark contrast to the thundering of my pulse. What secrets would it unveil? Was I ready to face the revelations it held?

The screen flickered to life, and I was met with a password prompt. Hazel's voice echoed in my mind, "Always remember our anniversary." Of course, the password. It was so simple, yet so intimate.

I typed in the date, holding my breath as I hit enter. The files began to load, and I braced myself for the journey of discovery that lay ahead.

The grey sky seemed to mirror the turmoil within me, a canvas of my inner storm. The world outside moved on, indifferent to the void Hazel's absence had left in my life. I sipped my tea, the warmth a stark contrast to the chill that had settled in my bones.

I returned to my desk, the blank screen of my computer a daunting challenge. Writing had always been our shared passion, Hazel my muse and harshest critic. Now, her silence was louder than any words she had uttered.

The mirror caught my eye again, and my reflection was a stark reminder of the passage of time. I wasn't the young man who could charm with a smile or the secret agent who could navigate the shadows. I was just... me, a writer with a story that had taken an unexpected twist.

But Hazel had always said, "Every ending is just a new beginning." Perhaps this was mine. I opened a new document and began to type, not the fiction I was known for, but our story, our truth. It was time the world knew the woman behind the man, the hero behind the spy.

As I typed, I found a rhythm and a purpose. The words flowed, a tribute to Hazel and to us. With each sentence, a piece of my heart began to mend. This was more than a book; it was a journey of discovery, a path to healing.

The chapter of Hazel may have ended, but our story was far from over. It was time to move on, to embrace the legacy she left behind. And maybe, just maybe, I could find peace in the memories we created and the love that would never fade.

The words echoed in my mind, a chilling reminder of the dark undercurrents that had always been a part of our lives. Janet, Annabella, Agnes—names that meant nothing to the outside world, but to me, they were the harbingers of a plot that had taken Hazel from me. But who are they?

I sat in the dim light of my study, the shadows casting long fingers across the room as if trying to grasp the truth that was just out of reach. The new variant—it wasn't just a random stroke of fate; it was orchestrated, a targeted strike to remove Hazel, the one person who knew too much.

The realisation hit me like a physical blow, and I staggered back, the weight of betrayal heavy on my shoulders. How deep did this conspiracy go? And why Hazel? She was the heart of our operation, the one who could navigate the treacherous waters of espionage with grace and precision.

I knew then that my retirement was a farce, a mere illusion of safety. The game was still on, and the stakes were higher than ever. I had to act to uncover the truth and expose the ones responsible for this heinous act.

With renewed determination, I reached for the phone. It was time to call in old favours, to rally the allies I still had. Janet, Annabella, and Agnes were not the masterminds, but they would have to answer for their actions. And I, the retired spy, would be the one to bring them to justice.

I would move heaven and earth for Hazel, for the love we shared, and for the peace she deserved. The journey of discovery was far from over; it had just taken a turn into the shadows.

The world seemed to tilt on its axis as I processed the scene before me. My car, once a symbol of freedom and escape, now lay in ruins, a casualty of the chaos that had descended from above. The metal monstrosity that had crushed it was alien in this quiet suburban street, a harbinger of the pandemonium unfolding.

The distant explosions were like the drumbeats of an advancing army, each one sending ripples of dread through my already shaken frame. I retreated to the sanctuary of my living room, the flickering images on the television painting a picture of devastation that my mind struggled to comprehend.

London, the heart of the nation, was reeling under an assault from the sky. The reporter's face, usually so composed, was a mask of terror and disbelief. The bodies, the rubble, the despair—it was like a scene from the very books I wrote, but this was no fiction.

As the screen went blank, a cold realisation washed over me. This was no mere accident, no natural disaster. It was an attack, precise and catastrophic, a message written in fire and steel.

I stood frozen, the cup of tea in my hand now forgotten. A hundred miles away, yet the danger felt as close as my own shadow. Hazel's warnings, her fears—they all made sense now. She had known, somehow, that our world was on the brink.

I had to move, to act. But first, I needed to understand. I turned to my computer; the messages I had sent to friends were now trivial in the face of this new threat. I began to search, to dig for information, for any clue that could shed light on this dark day.

The journey of discovery was no longer just a personal quest; it was a race against time to unravel the threads of a conspiracy that had just shown its hand. And I, the reluctant hero, had been thrust back into the game.

The street outside was a tableau of uncertainty, my neighbours' faces etched with concern as they peered skyward. The facemasks they donned seemed almost superfluous now, a feeble shield against a threat far greater than any virus. The roar of the jet's overhead was a stark reminder that the world was teetering on the brink of chaos.

Yet, amidst the turmoil, a laugh escaped me. It was a sound I hadn't heard from myself in a long time, a remnant of a past where the weight of the world didn't rest on our shoulders. The memory of that book, written in a time of whimsy and adventure, seemed like a message from a former self—to find levity even in the darkest of times.

The shed at the end of the garden was a time capsule, housing relics of a life once lived to the fullest. The electric bicycle and its companions, the trailer and generator, were symbols of freedom, of journeys taken and those yet to come. The flat tyres and the dust-covered surfaces were minor obstacles, easily overcome with a bit of care and the surprising resilience of technology.

The generator's rumble was a comforting sound, a heartbeat in the stillness, and the batteries, still holding a charge, were a testament to the enduring spirit of adventure. The YouTube tutorial that had once inspired a trip was now a guiding light for the journey ahead.

My old camping gear, the teepee that had been a haven for Hazel and me, brought a smile to my face. They were more than just equipment; they were memories, tangible pieces of a life shared. And in that moment, I made a decision.

Life is for living, not for waiting for the end, whether it comes in an hour or in years. The open road called to me, promising new horizons and the chance to honour Hazel's memory by embracing the world she loved. With the summer stretching out before me, I chose the path of adventure; the road less travelled, carrying with me the legacy of a love that would always guide my way.

The sirens' wail was a jarring interruption to my reverie, a stark reminder that the world was not as it should be. The rush towards Long Marston Airfield, now a skeleton of its former self, hinted at hidden dangers from a bygone era. The unexploded bomb theory seemed plausible, a silent threat lying dormant until now, much like the secrets I harboured.

With the dawn came a sense of urgency, a need to move, to flee not just the physical dangers but the ghosts that haunted me. The small trailer hitched to my bike was a modest vessel for my escape, carrying the essentials for survival and the remnants of a life once lived.

The cash, a crisp reminder of emergency plans made at a different time, felt almost alien in my hands. The credit cards, symbols of a society that might no longer exist as we knew it, were tucked away as an afterthought. Locking the door to the house, I couldn't help but wonder if it was a final farewell. The thought should have pained me, but instead, there was a hollow acceptance, a detachment from the material world I was leaving behind.

Meon Hill loomed in my memory, a beacon of childhood innocence. The mansion where my mother worked and the horse chestnut tree that stood as a testament to time—they were landmarks of a simpler time. The destruction of the tree for the sake of progress was a bitter pill to swallow, a microcosm of the greater devastation that seemed inevitable.

As I pedalled away, the weight of my past and the uncertainty of the future battled within me. Yet, there was a strange comfort in the motion, in the act of moving forward. The road ahead was uncertain, the destination unknown, but the journey was mine to make. And perhaps, in the act of journeying, I would find the purpose that had eluded me since Hazel's passing. The world might be crumbling, but I was still here, still breathing, still capable of shaping my own path.

The resilience of the old electric bike was a testament to the craftsmanship of its makers, a reliable companion on this unexpected journey. Its 750-watt motor hummed with a quiet strength, defying the years of neglect with every turn of the wheels.

As I approached Meon Hill, the familiar landscape greeted me like an old friend. The gate, the lush fields, and the steady climb were all part of a ritual from a time when life was simpler when Hazel's laughter was a constant melody in the air.

The summit of Meon Hill was a vantage point not just over the countryside but also over my past. I had only covered five miles, but each one was a step away from the life I had known. There was no rush, no need to prove anything. This journey was not about distance; it was about discovery, about finding a new rhythm in the aftermath of loss.

The bike's performance was reassuring, a sign that I could rely on it as I navigated the route laid out in the pages of my book. The hills ahead would be a challenge, but one that I and the bike were ready to meet.

As I stood at the summit, the world stretched out before me, a tapestry of green and gold under the open sky. It was a moment of peace, a brief respite from the chaos that had engulfed the world. And in that moment, I knew that no matter what lay ahead, I had made the right choice. The road was calling, and I was ready to answer.

The act of setting up the teepee was a dance with the past, each movement stirring memories of adventures with Hazel. The structure, once a symbol of our shared wanderlust, now stood as a solitary figure against the backdrop of Devil's Drop. The name, whether a childhood creation or a darker history remembered by my mother, added a layer of mystery to the hill that had been a playground of my youth.

The spring's melody was a soothing counterpoint to the distant chaos, its clear waters a lifeline in the midst of uncertainty. As I made my tea, the simple act took on a ritualistic significance, a moment of normalcy in a world that seemed to be unravelling at the seams.

The explosion shattered the calm, a violent reminder of the dangers lurking beneath the surface. My gaze turned towards the old airfield, now shrouded in smoke and flame. The unexploded bombs, relics of a war long ended, were asserting their presence, a deadly legacy that refused to be forgotten.

As the fire consumed the excavators, I couldn't help but feel the fragility of our constructs, both physical and societal. The world was changing, and I, with my teepee and electric bike, was a witness to the turning of an era. Yet, in the midst of it all, there was a strange sense of clarity. The path forward was uncertain, but it was mine to tread, with the spirit of Hazel as my guide and the open sky as my canvas.

The evening's embrace was a solitary one, the natural symphony of birdsong a stark contrast to the silence of my thoughts. The machete, a tool of both survival and protection, lay within reach, a reminder of the primal instinct to defend oneself against the unknown.

The night was a restless entity, every rustle and whisper magnified by the solitude. It was a dance with shadows, a test of the senses honed by years of experience and the cautious wisdom that comes with age. Trust was a luxury, one that the current state of the world could not afford.

The news on my mobile was a grim lullaby, tales of accidents and catastrophes that seemed to unravel the fabric of society thread by thread. The incident at Long Marston, the horror in London—they were not just headlines; they were harbingers of a new reality, one where the Specter of terror loomed large.

Sleep, when it came, was a fleeting visitor, disrupted by the slightest touch of the unknown against the canvas of my teepee. Adrenaline was a swift companion as I emerged, machete in hand, ready to confront the intruder. But it was not a foe that awaited me; it was nature itself, a stag caught in a moment of curiosity.

The encounter was a dance as old as time, a confrontation between man and beast that ended not in conflict but in mutual retreat. The plastic bag, a trivial human artefact, became a token of the encounter, carried off as a trophy by the retreating stag.

As I watched the animal disappear into the night, I couldn't help but reflect on the absurdity of it all. The world was on the brink of war, yet here I was, a man with a machete facing down a stag. It was a moment of clarity, a realisation that life, in all its forms, would continue to challenge, surprise, and inspire wonder, even in the darkest of times.

The morning ritual of cooking outdoors brought a simple joy. The Flavors of bacon and eggs were enriched by the open air, and the hint of adventure lingered with the dawn. The sky, a tapestry of moods, held the promise of rain, but I was prepared. There's something about food cooked in the great outdoors that awakens the senses, a reminder of the primal connection to the elements.

With breakfast savoured and the remnants of my meal cleansed by the spring's bounty, I turned my attention to the map. The route was a thread through the heart of England, from Warwick's historic bounds to Lichfield's spired skyline.

The A46 would be my guide, leading me to the arteries of the A4177, A452, and A446, each road a step further in my odyssey.

The field that awaited me, a mere mention in my book, now beckoned as a real destination. It was a race against the setting sun, a challenge to reach the haven just beyond the A38's bridge before night's curtain fell.

The spring's cold embrace was a baptism of sorts, a cleansing of both body and spirit. As the water trickled down my beard, the last vestiges of sleep were washed away, leaving behind a clarity of purpose. The road called, the journey beckoned, and I answered with the turn of my bike's wheels, ready to embrace whatever lay ahead.

The morning's urgency was a familiar companion, the overcast sky a blanket that mirrored my mood. The descent from Meon Hill was cautious, and the back roads were a labyrinth that eventually spilt me onto the A46, Warwick's roundabout, a beacon in the distance.

The A4177 was a river of metal and motion, a stark contrast to the quiet expectation of empty roads. My electric bike, with its inconspicuous number plate and the trailer laden with life's necessities, was an anomaly amidst the rush. The encounter with the police was a moment of levity, their laughter a fleeting connection in a world that seemed increasingly disconnected.

The ache in my legs was a testament to time's passage, a reminder of the days when such exertions were commonplace. The garage stop was a respite, the tangerines and grapes a makeshift sustenance for the journey ahead. The absence of a prepared flask or sandwich was a minor oversight, a chuckle-worthy moment when I thought of Hazel. Her spirit, I felt, was with me, a silent affirmation of my choices and a comforting presence on the road to Lichfield.

As I pedalled on, the landscape unfurled, a tapestry of the English countryside that Hazel and I had once explored together. Each mile was a step further into the unknown, yet there was a sense of coming home. The road was both a challenge and a charmer; its whimsy was a reflection of the life I was now navigating—alone, yet not entirely so.

The journey across the A38 bridge was a testament to the resilience of my neglected bike, its performance a small miracle that brought a chuckle as I reminisced about the field from my book. The farmer's wave was a silent acknowledgement of shared history, a connection rooted in the land and the stories it held.

The Rolls-Royce, with its smoked windows and air of mystery, was an enigma that briefly crossed my path, its occupants a fleeting question mark in my narrative. But my focus was on the familiar—the generator humming in the background, the teepee rising against the sky, and the simple pleasure of a cup of tea that tasted like victory.

Sleep came easily, a deep slumber accompanied by the generator's drone, only to be broken by the morning's agricultural symphony. The scent of manure was a harsh alarm, urging me to pack up and move on, leaving behind the field and its olfactory memories.

The aches in my body were a chorus of protest, a reminder of the physical toll of my adventure. Yet, the aroma of pasties cooking was a siren call, luring me to the open cake shop. The pasties and strawberry milkshakes were not just sustenance; they were comfort, a balm for the weary traveller.

As I set off towards the A515, the road ahead was more than a route; it was a journey through time, a path Hazel and I had once travelled together. Ashbourne and Buxton awaited, each pedal stroke a step closer to the next chapter, each mile a memory of the love that propelled me forward.

The journey unfolded with each pedal stroke, the simple pleasure of a hot pasty on the move a delightful challenge. Leaving Lichfield behind, I eased into a rhythm, the road ahead a familiar friend from the pages of my story.

Yoxall's local shop was a snapshot of the times, my surgical gloves and face mask now as commonplace as the groceries I carried. The added weight was a reminder of the practicalities of travel, a balance between preparedness and the burden it brings.

April's skies, heavy with the threat of rain, mirrored the transformation of the landscape. The encroachment of concrete upon the countryside was a sign of changing times, a testament to policies and progress that often forget the beauty of green spaces.

The sudden downpour was almost poetic justice for my musings, a drenching reality that had me scrambling for waterproofs. The passing vehicles seemed to conspire with the weather, each puddle a splash of cold reality, making me long for the shelter of a motorhome.

The A50 was a brief interlude before rejoining the A515, my electric bike and I battling the elements and the inclines. The impatience of lorries and the close calls with motorists were a stark reminder of the vulnerability of a cyclist on these wet and winding roads.

Yet, there was a resilience within me, a determination fuelled by memories of journeys past and the spirit of adventure that Hazel and I had always shared. Ashbourne and Buxton were not just destinations; they were chapters yet to be written, stories waiting to be told through the lens of my journey.

The silence was a stark contrast to the steady hum I had grown accustomed to. The generator's stillness sent a ripple of concern through me, but it was the oil, not the fuel, that had betrayed my trust. The dipstick, almost dry, was a reprimand for my oversight.

In a near-panicked search, I found salvation in the form of a nearly spent oil bottle. It was a gamble, pouring the last of it into the engine, hoping it would suffice. The engine sputtered to life, a mechanical sigh of relief that mirrored my own. I whispered my apologies to the faithful machine, vowing to be more attentive in the future.

The journey resumed, the rain's retreat leaving behind a landscape dotted with puddles like mirrors reflecting the tumultuous sky. Ravensdale appeared sooner than expected, a familiar sanctuary from a time when Hazel's presence made every place feel like home.

The small brick-arched bridge was a gateway to memories, leading me to a grassy verge that offered respite for the night. Here, under the watchful eye of the Tissington Trail, I pitched my camp, surrounded by echoes of laughter and love that once filled such spaces. As night fell, the past and present merged, and I found comfort in the continuity of life's journey.

The night had wrapped its cloak around the campsite as I secured my teepee, the darkness a shroud for the day's end. Tucked away behind the canvas was my equipment, a cache of modern-day treasures, their value far beyond their monetary worth.

The generator's hum was a lullaby of sorts, its rhythm a counterpoint to the induction hob's sizzle and the wind's wild serenade. The meal, though not gourmet, was a feast in its simplicity, a reminder of the road's rough-hewn comforts.

As I lay cocooned in my sleeping bag, the world outside seemed to fade into insignificance. The news, or lack thereof, was a void that mirrored the emptiness of my homecoming. The decision to leave my laptop behind was a conscious, unburdening release from the chains of creation that no longer held meaning.

Dawn's light was obscured by the abrupt departure of an unknown vehicle, sounding like a transit van. Its haste was a harbinger of ill tidings. The fresh air did little to quell the rising tide of panic as I discovered the theft of my generator. Anger was a fire within, burning with the injustice of the act.

The bicycle and batteries, spared from the thief's grasp, were small consolations. Yet, the generator's absence was a significant blow, its presence vital for the journey's continuation. The pandemic's shadow loomed large, a spectre of desperation that made such acts of survival all too common.

The road to Buxton seemed daunting without the assurance of electrical aid. The hope of a garage, a beacon in the uncertainty, was all that propelled me forward. Until then, the simple pleasure of a cup of tea remained a luxury just out of reach, a symbol of the normalcy that had been so abruptly stolen.

In the distance, I could see a vehicle. Could this be poetic justice? A suspicious white van succumbed to a breakdown, and a nervous young man hesitated, his eyes darting between me and the open road. "It's the engine," he muttered, "can't seem to figure it out." I nodded, understanding the frustration that comes with mechanical failures. "Let's take a look together," I noticed a knife in his hand and without thinking, I removed my machete and severed his head. I wiped my machete blade on his grubby grey jumper, removing as much blood as possible and dragging through the grass to ensure no evidence was left on the blade. I quickly opened the van's back door using my sleeve, discovering my generator. I removed it and placed it on my trailer, cycling off. I thank my lucky stars for my agent training.

The road to Buxton was a blur, each mile marker a reminder of the distance I was putting between myself and the deed. The generator's hum was a constant companion, a mechanical heartbeat that seemed to sync with my own erratic pulse. As the adrenaline faded, the tremors took over, a physical manifestation of the turmoil within.

I pulled over, the vast expanse of the Peak District stretching before me. The rolling hills were a stark contrast to the chaos of my thoughts. I sat there, the weight of what I had done pressing down on me. Murder was a word that seemed too clean, too detached from the reality of taking a life. It was an act that couldn't be undone; a line crossed that forever altered the course of my existence.

The silence of the countryside was a stark reminder of my isolation. I had become an island, cut off from the mainland of morality and law. The machete, now clean and hidden away, was a symbol of my transgression, a secret I would carry with me.

As I continued on the A515, the picturesque scenery of Buxton in the distance, I knew that my life had irrevocably changed. The person who had set out on this journey was not the same one who would arrive. I was a fugitive now, from the law and from myself. The road ahead was uncertain, but one thing was clear: there was no turning back.

The A515 stretched before me, a familiar yet distant memory of journeys past. The potholes, like scattered memories, jolted me back to a time when life was simpler, shared with a companion whose presence was now just an echo. The detour toward Hope, where history whispered tales of daring and precision, lingered in my mind, a stark contrast to the mundane reality of the present.

The woman in the tracksuit, a spectre from another life or a mere coincidence, jogged on, her gaze locked with mine in a silent acknowledgement of shared existence. The possibility that she might be Jennifer, a fragment from my school days, teased my thoughts, yet the differences were clear as day. The past was a puzzle, and she was a piece that didn't quite fit.

Seeking solace, I found a bench, a temporary anchor in the fluidity of life. Here, I could pause, a spectator to the world's continuous motion. The Rolls-Royce, a symbol of a life far removed from my own, rolled past, and I found a game in its rarity, a distraction from the pressing weight of reality.

As I sat, the possibility of a reencounter with the mysterious jogger loomed. A simple greeting could bridge the gap between strangers, or it could widen it, especially in these cautious times. The risk of misinterpretation was high, and the last thing I needed was trouble with the law.

So, there I waited, counting luxury cars, pondering the threads of fate that weave our lives together, and contemplating the next move in a game that had no clear rules or outcomes.

The lanes of Millers' Dale, with their twists and turns, seemed to mirror the winding thoughts in my mind. The woman in the tracksuit, a puzzle piece from a past life, jogged on, her presence a constant question mark that trailed my every move. The local's words about her echoed in my ears, adding layers to the mystery she embodied.

As I settled into the rhythm of the road, the generator's hum a steady backdrop, I found solace in the simplicity of the task at hand—topping up the oil, a small but necessary act to keep moving forward. The encounter with the mower repairman was a brief interlude, a snippet of local gossip that painted the jogger in a different light. Yet, her fleeting glance held no answers, only the silent acknowledgement of two lives briefly intersecting.

The decision to stop and set up camp was instinctual, a need to ground myself amidst the chaos of recent events. The teepee, a temporary haven, rose against the backdrop of the English countryside, a solitary silhouette against the fading light. The kettle's whistle and the batteries' quiet charge were comforting constants in a world that had shifted beneath my feet.

As the day waned, I pondered the roads not taken, the miles left untraveled. Hope, with its historical echoes and personal significance, would have to wait. For now, the verge was my domain, a place to rest and reflect on the journey that had brought me here and the path that lay ahead, shrouded in the mists of uncertainty.

In a strange but welcome event, the jogger in her Range Rover came into view, stepping out with arms folded. "Why are you following me?" she asked abruptly.

I shrugged my shoulders. "I'm not following you." We continued to converse, for several minutes before the woman in her pink and brown tracksuit climbed into her Range Rover. The silver Range Rover's engine faded into the distance, and with it, the woman in the tracksuit disappeared from view, leaving behind a cloud of dust and a lingering sense of mystery. Her identity remained out of reach, a puzzle piece from a life I once knew but could no longer place.

The quiet that settled was a stark contrast to the flurry of activity that had just occurred. I was alone again, with only my thoughts and the news of the tragedy in London for company. The world felt heavier with the knowledge of such loss, and I couldn't help but feel a twinge of guilt for the relief that washed over me at being so far removed from it all.

My neighbours' messages were a reminder of the life I had left behind, even if just for a while. Their concern was touching, and I was grateful for the technology that allowed me to reassure them without revealing my whereabouts. The decision to turn off my tracker felt like the right one, granting me a semblance of control in a world that seemed increasingly chaotic.

As the last light of day gave way to the darkness of night, I settled into my teepee, the generator humming softly in the background. The kettle's whistle had long since quieted, but the warmth of the tea lingered, a small comfort against the chill that was beginning to set in.

I pondered the woman's words, her recognition of me, and the mention of my wife. The pain of loss was still fresh, and her absence was a void that no amount of time on the road could fill. The new variant had taken her from me, and now I was left to navigate this new reality alone.

The day had been full of unexpected encounters and revelations, each one adding a layer to the story of my life. As I lay there, the fabric of the teepee fluttering gently in the breeze, I knew that tomorrow would bring its own challenges and perhaps more answers. For now, though, I would rest and let the mysteries of today wait for the light of a new day.

***

The tapestry of hidden agendas and clandestine operations. Janet, now revealed to be of significant lineage, is entrusted with a mission that could shape the destiny of an ancient bloodline. The '12', a group shrouded in secrecy, have placed their trust in her to guide Zachariah Black on a path that serves their enigmatic purposes.

Annabella, a figure of authority and knowledge, advises Janet with a blend of caution and strategy. The conversation between them reveals layers of manipulation that span decades, involving Zachariah's unsuspecting family and his late wife. The mention of Anna and her children adds a personal dimension to the plot, highlighting the ruthless criteria the '12' impose on their legacy.

As Janet prepares to engage Zachariah with her acting prowess, she must navigate a minefield of potential recognition and the sharp intellect of a man who is more observant than anticipated. The Rolls-Royce, a symbol of their watchful presence, has already caught Zachariah's attention, indicating that their plan is not as foolproof as they had hoped. They would watch and listen, and each play their part.

***

As the nightlight cast its glow, the unexpected sound of a vehicle approaching sent a jolt of alarm through me. The sight of Janet, with her offering of Bacardi and Coke, was both a surprise and a puzzle piece falling into place. Her connection to a past encounter, one that had left its mark on both our lives, was now coming full circle.

Janet's revelation about her mother and the life she had led brought a sense of clarity to the mystery. Her decision to live a life of solitude, away from the complications of her family's history, resonated with my own desire for escape. Yet, here she was, in my teepee, bridging the gap between our worlds with a shared drink and a shared past.

Her laughter and candid admission of curiosity were a welcome reprieve from the weight of my thoughts. In this unexpected visitor, I found a kindred spirit, someone who understood the value of privacy and the allure of the unknown.

As we sipped our drinks, the barriers of time and circumstance seemed to melt away. Janet, no longer just a memory or a name from a bygone era, was a tangible presence, a reminder that the past is never truly behind us. And as the night deepened, so did our conversation, weaving the threads of our stories into a tapestry of shared confidences and revelations.

The morning after Janet's unexpected visit, I found myself alone once more, the silence of the dawn punctuated only by the hum of my generator. The remnants of last night's encounter—a half-empty Coke can and an empty Bacardi bottle—were the only evidence that Janet had been here at all.

As I prepared my breakfast, the events of the previous evening replayed in my mind. Janet's arrival with alcohol in hand, her confession of a shared past, and her subsequent collapse were a whirlwind that had disrupted the quiet trajectory of my journey. Her presence had brought a momentary respite from the loneliness that had become my constant companion since my wife's passing.

The concern I felt for Janet, despite her assurance of being able to drive home in any state, was a reminder of the care that still lived within me despite my cynical outlook on life and its end. Her collapse and the way she sought comfort in my arms were a stark contrast to the solitude I had chosen.

Now, as I faced the day ahead, I couldn't help but wonder about the paths we both had taken. Janet, with her life of privacy and her choice to remain unattached, and I, with my bicycle and my thoughts of a final destination, were two souls adrift in a world that seemed increasingly alien.

The Range Rover's departure marked the end of an interlude, and as I watched it disappear, I knew that my journey was far from over. There were still miles to travel, decisions to make, and perhaps more encounters to come. For now, though, I would enjoy my breakfast and the peace of the morning, taking each moment as it came.

***

"Janet, observe him closely. We need to understand his motivations and capabilities. If he is indeed of the bloodline, his actions will reveal it in time. Be patient and cautious; remember, subtlety is key in these matters."

Janet nodded, understanding the weight of her task. "I'll do my best, Annabella. He's a complex man, full of surprises. I won't underestimate him again."

"Good," Annabella replied with a nod. "Keep me informed of any developments. And Janet, be careful. We can't afford any mistakes."

The call ended, and Janet sat in silence, contemplating her next move. Zachariah Black was more than just a target; he was a man with a past that intertwined with her own in ways she was only beginning to understand. The game was on, and she was a player, whether she liked it or not.

***

I cycled to the top of Snake Pass, setting up my teepee in horrendous rain and wind, preparing to fall asleep, too lazy to cook or make a drink, surprised by the teepee flap opening.

She smiled, "Finding you is easy; you only have to look out for a teepee. I thought you might like some fish and chips with me, Zachariah Black, a peace offering. I'm somewhat ashamed of how I behaved, and you never took advantage of the situation."

"I might have if you were dressed like that yesterday. Is that how you dress for work?"

"Sorry," Janet stood after entering the teepee; she must have realised with her bent forward that I could see down her blouse, and her mini skirt wasn't hiding much either.

"Don't apologise! That's the most excitement I've had for weeks," I laughed, accepting the fish and chips. "I presume you've just finished work, Janet?"

She nodded, eating her chips: "I shouldn't be eating this; it's not good for my figure." I discovered your books online some time ago, which was rather a surprise. I'd never considered you a writer.

The revelation that Janet had been aware of my books, and by extension, parts of my life, for over a decade was a jolt. It was as if she had been a silent observer, watching the narrative of my life unfold from the shadows.

"Life is full of unexpected chapters, isn't it?" I mused, taking another bite of the fish and chips. "Sometimes, it feels like we're characters in a story, our paths written by an unseen hand."

Janet nodded, her eyes reflecting a depth of understanding. "We all have our secrets, Zachariah. Sometimes, they're the only things that keep us going."

Her words hung in the air, heavy with truth. We were two souls, each with our own burdens, finding solace in a shared moment of vulnerability. The storm outside raged on, but inside the teepee, there was a sense of calm.

"I never thought my books would bring someone from my past back to me," I said, the reality of the situation settling in. "But I'm glad it did. It's comforting to know that even as we journey alone, our stories can still touch others."

Janet smiled, a genuine warmth in her expression. "I may not have read your books before, but I'm starting to see why people are drawn to them. You have a way with words, Zachariah. They're more than just stories; they're reflections of life."

The moment lingered on the soft press of Janet's lips, a whisper of goodbye or perhaps a promise of more to come. Her silence, punctuated by the grin and the kiss, spoke volumes more than words could. As she drove away, the Range

Rover's taillights a fading beacon in the twilight, I was left with a mix of emotions—surprise, curiosity, and an unexpected flutter of anticipation.

Janet, the enigmatic figure from my past, had re-entered my life with the subtlety of a storm, leaving just as quickly but not without altering the landscape of my journey. Her parting gift, a simple kiss, was a signature on an unspoken contract, one that hinted at future encounters and conversations yet to be had.

As the night settled around me, the solitude of my teepee felt different, as if the air itself had been charged with the potential of what lay ahead. I tucked away her phone number, a tangible connection to the woman who had, in a few short visits, become a compelling character in the story of my life.

The road ahead was still uncertain, but now it seemed less daunting, less lonely. Janet's presence had brought a spark of something unexpected, something that made me look forward to the miles yet to travel. For the first time in a long while, I found myself eager to see what the next chapter would bring.

The storm outside mirrored the turmoil within as I sat in my teepee, the warmth of the tea offering little solace. Janet's departure had left a void, her presence a fleeting comfort now gone. The news on my mobile cast a shadow over my solitude, the grim reminder of the van and its gruesome discovery weighing heavily on my mind.

As the wind howled, I pondered the notion of companionship, the idea of marriage at this juncture of life. It seemed like a distant possibility, a path not taken that led to a place where the heart might once again find a companion. Yet, doubts clouded this thought—age, desire, and the ability to connect with another soul.

The rain lashed against the canvas, a relentless drumming that matched the beat of my thoughts. The weather had made the decision for me; today, I would not travel. Instead, I would sit with my memories and the questions they raised, the what-ifs and the maybes that danced at the edge of consciousness.

In the solitude of the teepee, with the storm as my only companion, I closed my eyes and let the sound of the rain wash over me, a natural symphony that soothed the restless thoughts and offered a moment of peace amidst the chaos.

The rain's persistence seemed to underscore the unexpected turn my life had taken. Janet's arrival, with her thoughtful offering and half-day reprieve from work, was a welcome interruption to the solitude of my journey. Her presence brought a sense of normalcy and companionship that I hadn't realised I'd been craving.

"Janet, you've managed to turn a dreary day into something quite special," I said, accepting the plate she offered. "And as for payment, consider it an investment in our shared adventure."

Her laughter filled the teepee, a sound that seemed to push back against the drumming of the rain on the canvas. "Adventure is one way to put it," she replied. "But really, Zachariah, it's no trouble. It's nice to have someone to share a meal with, even under such ... unique circumstances."

As we ate, the conversation flowed as easily as the wine. Janet's candidness about her attraction was both flattering and disarming. It was a dance of words and glances, a delicate balance between the past and the present.

"You're far from boring, Zachariah," Janet said, her eyes sparkling with mischief. "And as for looking at you...well, let's just say some habits are hard to break."

The afternoon passed in a blur of stories and laughter, the storm outside forgotten. In that teepee, with Janet's company, I found a moment of peace amidst the chaos of my thoughts. It was a reminder that life, even in its most unexpected moments, could still offer warmth and connection.

In the quiet of the teepee, with the storm raging outside, Janet's presence was a tempest of its own. Her confidence and forwardness were disarming, and her mention of her mother's fond memories brought a bittersweet nostalgia.

"Janet, life is a complex tapestry of moments and memories," I said, meeting her gaze. "Some threads are vibrant with passion; others are sombre with regret. But every thread is essential, weaving the story of who we are."

Her smile was a challenge, a silent question of whether I would rise to meet her expectations. "You're right; I am a bit weird and crazy," I admitted with a chuckle. "But isn't that what makes life interesting? The unexpected turns, the surprises, the moments that take our breath away?"

Janet's laughter joined mine, filling the space between us with an understanding that went beyond words. "You have a way with words, Zachariah Black," she said, her voice tinged with admiration. "And maybe that's what my mother saw in you—a man who can paint with words, who sees the world in a different light."

As the evening wore on, the wine flowed, and the conversation deepened. We spoke of dreams and desires, of the paths we'd taken, and the roads still ahead. And in those shared confidences, I found a connection that transcended time and circumstance.

Janet's visit, once an intrusion into my solitude, had become a welcome interlude, a reminder that even in the twilight of life, there can be moments of warmth and intimacy.

The teepee flap violently opened, and a man brandishing a handgun stepped in, grabbing Janet's hair without hesitation. I thrust my machete into his chest, pushing him out of the teepee. Janet screamed and fainted.

I left him outside the teepee, wiping my machete on wet grass, leaving the gun with him for now. I entered the teepee holding Janet, tapping her face gently; she regained consciousness with a startled expression. I assured her: "He won't hurt you again." She sat up, taking a drink from her wine glass, starting to cry and tremble. I realised I was now in trouble up to my armpits.

She asked hesitantly, "Is he."

I paused, my words measured and deliberate. "Janet, you must collect yourself. Drive home and erase this afternoon from your memory," I urged with a calm yet firm tone. "We are strangers, you and I. Do you understand?"

Her nod was faint, almost imperceptible, as she shakily donned her jacket and pulled on her Wellington boots. Clutching the carrier bag she had brought with her, she cast one last, lingering glance at her father's lifeless form.

The rain had begun to fall, a fine mist that turned the ground beneath our feet treacherous. I offered my arm for support, guiding her through the slick grass to her Range Rover. Behind us, her father's Bentley stood as a silent sentinel.

Janet's lips parted, a whisper of words ready to spill forth, but I cut her off. "Leave now before another car comes by. Trust me to handle the rest," I said, my voice a low whisper against the patter of rain. "Forget me, Janet. And when the news of your father's passing reaches you, let your shock be genuine, your grief palpable. Otherwise, we may as well face the gallows ourselves."

With a fleeting kiss that spoke of gratitude and fear, she climbed into her vehicle and sped off towards Glossop, leaving only the echo of her departure and the weight of our secret hanging in the damp air.

***

Upon reaching the safety of Rose Cottage, Janet wasted no time in contacting Annabella. "Your plan was flawless," she whispered into the phone, her voice a mix of relief and trepidation. "My father, in his fury, came after me, but Zachariah...he didn't flinch. It's done."

"Exquisite news," Annabella purred, satisfaction lacing her tone. "I had my suspicions about his heritage. Tell me, has he pledged his allegiance to you?"

Janet exhaled, the weight of the day's events pressing down on her. "Zachariah is a man of honour, or so he claims. He insists that he could never satisfy me, that he won't even attempt such a feat. Yet, I believe him. One glance into his eyes, and it's as though he's undressing me with his thoughts alone. He may require a nudge in the right direction."

Laughter bubbled through the line, a momentary reprieve from the gravity of their conspiracy. "Ease into it, Janet. We can't afford to arouse his suspicions. You're adept at persuasion; use it wisely when the moment presents itself," Annabella counselled.

A dangerous glint in her eye piqued Janet's curiosity. "To be frank, Annabella, he fascinates me. I still recall the echoes of my mother's cries; whatever power he held, it was enough to bring her to her knees. I'm determined to uncover his secrets." With a promise to reconnect soon, she ended the call, her mind racing with possibilities.

***

I dashed back to the shelter of the bushes, the damp earth clinging to my boots. With hurried movements, I dismantled the makeshift teepee, a silent promise to leave no trace behind. My hands fumbled through the contents of my rucksack until they found the refuge bag I used to obscure his identity. It felt morbid, a shroud for the dead.

His pockets yielded the keys after a frantic search, my pulse racing with each passing second. Moving his body was a gamble under the broad daylight, but necessity overruled caution. I glanced both ways, my ears straining for the sound of approaching cars. None came.

The driver's door creaked open, and I heaved his substantial form into the seat, the refuge bag tossed carelessly onto the back seat. For once, the absence of traffic felt like a small mercy granted by fate.

I retrieved the petrol tin, its contents sloshing within, from the depths of the Bentley. With a swift motion, I released the handbrake, struck a match, and watched as flames began to consume the interior. The car, now a burgeoning inferno, rolled backwards with a mind of its own.

My escape was a blur of motion as I pedalled furiously towards Glossop, the descent aiding my swift departure. A sudden, chilling thought halted me—my DNA, left behind in a moment of human need, now buried but not beyond discovery. I shook off the fear, convincing myself of the improbability of its discovery. After all, why would they search there when the fiery wreckage lay a mile distant, a beacon of misdirection?

The road to Glossop was a treacherous ribbon of asphalt; each bends a potential dance with death. I gripped the handlebars, my knuckles white, as I navigated the serpentine path. The scent of burning brakes filled the air, a pungent reminder of the gravity that pulled at the trailer—and at my conscience.

Ahead, a garage emerged, its lights a beacon of normalcy in the chaos of my escape. I veered in, and the final turn was a sharp challenge to my resolve. Donning my facemask and plastic gloves, I transformed from fugitive to surgeon, my movements precise as I filled the petrol container to its limit.

Inside, the mundane act of purchasing groceries felt alien, my hands mechanically transferring items to the counter as if in a dream. Payment made, I slipped back into the night, pedalling towards Hadfield on the B6105, the fading light a race against time.

By the time 7 o'clock drew its curtain, I was concealed within the embrace of trees, my teepee a makeshift fortress against prying eyes. The machete, a grim companion, showed no trace of its recent use, its blade and sheath cleansed in the forgiving waters of a nearby stream.

As I settled with a cup of tea, the distant dance of car lights played out a few yards away. The noose of fate seemed to tighten with each passing headlight, and yet, fortune favoured me still—no blue sirens, no inquisitive police. For now, I remained a ghost on the periphery of their world.

I drew the teepee flap closed, and a shiver of concern ran through me for Janet. Her ability to maintain composure under the inevitable police scrutiny would be crucial. My mobile's glow revealed the latest news—a burnt-out husk of a vehicle teetering on Snake Pass. The image was stark; the car was reduced to nothing more than a charred skeleton, and its tyres surrendered to the inferno. The open boot suggested a violent end, likely the fuel tank's last defiant act. A grim smile touched my lips; the macabre scene mirrored a tale I once penned, where premeditated plots of murder proved useful. Yet, the reality of my involvement weighed heavily on my conscience.

The decision was made—I would divert to Keighley come morning, altering my initial path to stay ahead of suspicion.

Sleep, if it came at all, was a fleeting visitor. The morning chorus of a blackbird heralded a new day and, with it, the urgency to depart. I tended to the generator, its oil checked, its belly filled, and allowed myself the small comfort of a steaming cup of tea before embarking at 7 o'clock sharp. By noon, Hebden Bridge was nearly within reach, and I found solace in a secluded spot, away from curious eyes that might scrutinise my unconventional attire.

Dawn's light barely had a chance to stretch across the sky when the rain unleashed its torrent. Clad in my wet weather gear, I stood resolute, sipping my tea amidst the downpour. The journey thus far had been a tapestry of human encroachment; landscapes I yearned to see returned to their natural glory. A part of me wondered, with a tinge of dark irony, if the new viral variant would be the great equaliser, allowing Mother Nature to reclaim her dominion from the grasp of humanity.

With a weary exhalation, I mounted my electric bike, the downpour reducing visibility to a mere blur through my rain-streaked glasses. The relief of dismounting was palpable as I found refuge on the A6034, just shy of Addingham. There, I pitched my teepee, a temporary haven from the relentless storm. As darkness enveloped the sky, my aching legs were a testament to the day's arduous journey.

The soft glow of my mobile screen cut through the night as I perused the news. The police had stumbled upon cannabis remnants in the charred remains of the Bentley, its false plates a silent accusation of underworld dealings on Snake Pass. A turf war, they surmised, and the driver—gone. A smile crept across my face at the thought of their misguided conclusion; it would be a stroke of luck if they were content with that narrative.

My gaze drifted over the map, plotting the next leg of my escape to Ripon, then Thirsk—a day's travel, no doubt. But then, an unexpected message from Janet jolted me: "I'm marrying." The words were a bolt from the blue, contradicting everything she had professed. Yet, I had to feign joy for her sudden change of heart.

"Lucky fellow, I wish you every happiness," I replied, though reluctance laced every letter.

Her response was immediate, unsettling: "I have a few days off work. Switch on your locator, and I'll find you."

Against my instincts, I activated my locator, sending a cautionary message in return: "You should stay away from me and enjoy your life with your new partner. Remember, the government's travel restrictions. You'll be prosecuted. Stay away!"

The risk was immense, but the die was cast. Now, all I could do was wait and hope that Janet would heed my warning.

Nestled in my sleeping bag, thoughts of Vicky, an echo of a past life, drifted through my mind. Yet, it was Hazel who had filled my years with joy, a chapter I wouldn't trade for the world. Slumber must have claimed me, for I awoke to the pastoral symphony of a cow's call. Emerging from my teepee, I found myself mere inches from a Highland cow, its shaggy visage a gentle reminder of the world's simple wonders.

After a modest breakfast, I set off into the stream of traffic, the hum of civilisation a stark contrast to the morning's tranquillity. The A6055 stretched before me, leading towards Scotch Corner, with Catterick but a stone's throw away. The miles had taken their toll, leaving me weary to the bone.

A suitable spot beckoned, a respite from the road and the rain. There, I erected my teepee and savoured a cup of tea, a moment of peace amidst the chaos. That's when I saw it—a silver Range Rover, sleek and out of place, pulling up before my makeshift abode.

Janet emerged, her smile wide and mischievous, a Cheshire cat come to life. She breezed past me, a woman on a mission, her arms laden with a flask and the promise of a warm meal. Inside the teepee, she handed me a container of sweet-and-sour chicken fried rice, the aroma mingling with the earthy scent of canvas and rain.

"What's that?" I inquired as she doctored my coffee with a mysterious powder.

"Sweetener," she assured, her grin never faltering. "I'm not poisoning you."

As we settled in, Janet recounted her encounter with the police, her voice a mix of relief and resignation. They had questions about her father, his life shrouded in shadows and suspicion. Her answers had been enough, it seemed, to satisfy their curiosity—for now. The mention of a solicitor loomed on the horizon, a harbinger of revelations yet to come.

Janet's smile didn't waver as she stirred the coffee, her movements deliberate. "Life is full of unexpected turns, Zachariah. As for the man I'm to marry, he's...an old acquaintance whose path crossed mine again under unusual circumstances."

I sipped the coffee, its bitterness tempered by the sweetener, and pondered her cryptic words. "And yet, here you are, sharing coffee and secrets with me instead of basking in the glow of your newfound love."

She leaned back, her gaze fixed on the canvas ceiling as if it held the answers. "Let's just say he's not the only one with a past that's best left unexplored. Besides, I owe you for...everything."

The weight of her gratitude was a tangible thing, heavy and uncomfortable. I wanted to dismiss it, to tell her that no debt existed between us, but the words caught in my throat. Instead, I changed the subject.

"Tomorrow, I'll be heading towards Ripon. It's time I put more distance between myself and...all of this." I gestured vaguely, encompassing the teepee, the Range Rover, and perhaps, our shared history.

Janet nodded, her expression unreadable. "I understand. Just remember, Zachariah, no matter where you go, you're not alone. Not anymore."

As she packed away the remnants of our meal, I couldn't shake the feeling that her words were more than mere comfort—they were a warning.

Janet looked at her wristwatch, removing her jacket. I finished my meal and coffee, leaning back on one elbow, becoming aroused, which I considered odd; the more I studied Janet, the more wicked things I thought I could do with her. Janet leaned forward, kissing me softly. Somewhat concerned, I suggested: "So much for your future husband and faithful, Janet; I was sure you'd be different from your mother."

As Janet's presence enveloped me, a warmth I hadn't felt in years ignited within. Our connection deepened, transcending the mere physical as we made love. In those moments, a whirlwind of scenarios danced through my mind. A twinge of guilt surfaced—after all, it wasn't Hazel—but a gentle reminder settled in my heart: I am single now. Life, with its shades of joy and sorrow, must go on. And so, I embrace this new chapter, however bittersweet, with open arms and a resolve to find happiness in the days to come.

The generator's hum gently pulled me from sleep. Janet, already dressed, entered the teepee with two steaming mugs of tea, her smile wide and victorious. "Great night, don't you think, Zachariah Black?"

I couldn't help but agree. "What was in my coffee last night, Janet?"

"Does it matter? It got us what we wanted," she teased, a playful glint in her eye. "Now I understand my mother's obsession with you. But don't worry, I won't repeat her mistakes."

Her words sparked a fantasy, but reality's weight soon settled in. "Janet, I'm flattered, truly. But let's be realistic. I'm not getting any younger, and you...you have your whole life ahead."

She laughed, her confidence unwavering. "Oh, Zachariah, age is just a number, especially for someone as fit as you, thanks to that electric cycle of yours. I'm not chasing fairytales. I've seen enough heartache with my mother's escapades. Let's just see where this goes; there is no pressure. Just enjoy the ride."

Her laughter was infectious, and I found myself joining in. "And what if I run off with some wild woman?"

"You won't, Zachariah Black," she said with certainty. "You're a man of integrity. I've done my homework."

With a final kiss, she turned to tidy up, her movements efficient and caring. She tossed the trash into her Range Rover, then returned with another kiss. Slipping on her coat, she winked. "See you soon. Keep your tracker on, and don't fret about me. I'm a keyworker, after all."

***

Janet, after a brief drive, found solitude in a lay-by. Her mobile in hand, she couldn't contain her mirth. "Annabella, I must confess, the Viagra was a stroke of genius. He was...invigorated, to say the least," she said, her laughter a soft echo in the quiet morning.

Annabella's response crackled through, her amusement evident. "Splendid work, Janet. If he's still potent, we might just get our heir. Tell me, was it as dreadful as you feared?"

A chuckle escaped Janet, her voice tinged with unexpected admiration. "Far from it. In the dark, age becomes just a number, and he...he was like a stallion reborn. His experience spoke volumes, and for two whole hours, he was nothing short of spellbinding."

The line buzzed with Annabella's delighted laughter. "Scandalous! Well, I do hope your efforts bear fruit. And don't forget, a £1 million bonus awaits you—and a son would double it."

***

With the dawn barely breaking, I hastily stowed my belongings, eager to resume my journey. Scotch Corner beckoned, and from there, the B6275 would lead me towards Bishop Auckland. My start was sluggish, my zest for travel unusually dim. Perhaps Janet's vibrant energy had overshadowed my own. Yet, amidst the languor, a serene calm enveloped me.

The wind was capricious, gusting with a force that demanded respect. I rode with my lights ablaze, their glow a beacon against the tempest, a shield against becoming an imprint on a lorry's tyre. Along the way, curious motorists captured my image while others greeted me with friendly waves.

The countryside unfolded before me, a familiar tapestry of green that I cherished. Upon reaching Scotch Corner, I veered onto the B6275, a solitary ribbon of road where the wind's fury softened to a whisper. It was then that my trusty generator began to falter, its steady hum marred by a sudden misfire. Concerned, I pulled over, my hands working deftly to diagnose the ailment. The spark plug, long neglected, was promptly tended to—a simple act of care that breathed new life into the weary machine.

With the generator's heartbeat restored, I ventured onto the A68, a thoroughfare bustling with life, leading me towards Edinburgh's storied Forth Bridge—a crossing shared by taxis, buses, and the rhythmic dance of cyclists and pedestrians. My attire, I hoped, would not draw ire.

As twilight approached, I sought refuge beyond Rowley, hidden from prying eyes. The day's grime called for a cleansing ritual. Boiling water transformed into a makeshift bath, my flannel scrubbing away the day's adventures. The thought of submerging in a water trough teased my mind, a chilling prospect that could very well stop my heart.

Nourished and nestled in my teepee, I reached for my phone. There, a message from Janet awaited, three simple words that spoke volumes: "I love you."

A wry smile played upon my lips as I pondered the whirlwind that had swept me up. Janet's declaration of love came swiftly, a mere week into our reacquaintance. I, a man who peers through spectacles, sports a wiry beard, and boasts a boldly barren crown—save for the dental woes that have plagued me since the accident—found it all rather bemusing. To the world, I might not be a prized catch but to a crocodile. Perhaps a feast. With these thoughts, I extinguished my nightlight, surrendering to the lullaby of the wind through the silver birch trees.

Disillusionment with my journey's purpose crept in, a shadow cast by Janet's unexpected entrance into my life. My once-clear mission now seemed shrouded in fog. Yet, as I drifted into slumber, I harboured hope for a kinder morning, free from the tempest's chill.

The chirp of my mobile broke the silence of dawn. It was 7:30 a.m., and Janet's message awaited: "A cheque for 2.5 million from my late father's estate has arrived."

I replied with a hint of caution, "Invest wisely. Money is a fleeting guest."

Breakfast was a simple affair: two rashers of bacon, a fried egg, and the last of my crusty buns, a local delight. The overcast sky mirrored my contemplative mood. I mused on the irony of life's twists—sometimes, it seemed, a touch of roguery paid dividends. Janet's inheritance was a testament to that.

Her following message arrived amidst the hedge's cacophony: "Two million invested, half a million liquid for easy access."

"Smart move," I texted back, my thoughts with her. "Stay safe. Let's not rush; the journey back can wait. And remember, key worker status might not hold much sway beyond the Forth Bridge."

With my belongings packed, I gazed skyward, a smile tugging at my lips. Sometimes, life's script holds more surprises than one could ever pen.

CHAPTER 2
The Adventure Continues

As I emerged from the shadow of the Forth Bridge, the Scottish skies greeted me not with a warm embrace but with a foreboding growl. Thunderstorms loomed as if the land itself was questioning my presence. A thunderclap jolted me awake, its roar almost sending my heart leaping from my chest.

The thought of navigating my electric bike through this tempest was less than appealing; it felt like a dare against nature itself. Breakfast was an afterthought as I donned my waterproofs, hastily dismantled my teepee, and shielded everything with plastic against the relentless rain. With visibility nearly nil behind my rain-streaked glasses, I set off into the storm.

The heavens unleashed their fury, sheet lightning casting ghostly shadows on the road, while thunderbolts struck with precision near the path I tread. My reliance on the bike's electrical system was absolute—without its assistance; I'd be stranded, a mere spectator in this electric ballet.

By the time I reached Loch Leven, my resolve was drenched. Enough was enough. I sought refuge in a secluded spot, my hands trembling as I pitched my teepee against the howling wind. The cold bit at my bones, and I burrowed into my sleeping bag, seeking solace in its meagre warmth.

In the quiet that followed, a realisation crept in—I might have overestimated my readiness for such an undertaking. Age, it seems, is more than just a number when pitted against the raw power of nature.

The patter of rain on canvas was a familiar serenade, a reminder of the many days spent under open skies. A smile crept across my face, dismissing the absurdity of my earlier fears. After all, a lifetime of braving the elements had surely granted me some immunity to the common cold.

As the wind toyed with the teepee, a distant thunderclap rolled across the Scottish highlands, a dramatic welcome to a land I had come to know well. Memories of Hazel and our travels in the comfort of a motorhome, the ease of a car, and the adventure of towing a caravan filled my mind. Those were simpler times, times of companionship and predictable paths.

But now, as I lay alone, the world outside a maelstrom of nature's making, my phone pierced the silence. It was Janet, her concern reaching through the digital ether: "Are you okay? The weather forecast where you are is terrible; you need my help?"

4 a.m. blinked back at me from my wristwatch. Why was she awake? My fingers danced across the screen, reassuring her: "Don't worry about me. I'm nice and cosy in my teepee; it's a shame you're not with me! I'm only joking. Stay where you are; I'm thinking of you."

Her reply came swiftly, a mix of affection and anxiety: "Why do you think I'm up? I can't sleep. I'm worried about you, Zachariah Black. I love you; be careful."

"Okay, boss!" I typed back, a chuckle escaping me as I settled deeper into my sleeping bag, the storm outside a stark contrast to the warmth within.

The morning greeted me with the quacking of ducks, a soothing symphony to rouse me from slumber. Clad in my last set of dry garments, I ventured out to find the aftermath of the storm had given way to a sky of brilliant blue. The world was drenched, yet the promise of the sun's warmth filled me with hope.

With a sputtering start, my generator came to life, allowing for a modest breakfast and a comforting cup of tea. Once my belongings were secured, I set my sights on Perth, a mere seventeen miles away, where the A9 awaited. A spontaneous decision led me to choose the scenic route along the A-82, with the legendary Loch Ness in my sights.

The journey resumed with a newfound lightness, the bike gliding beneath me as if buoyed by the clear skies. We soared along, occasionally flirting with seventeen miles per hour, a testament to the day's benevolence. A pit stop on the outskirts of Perth yielded fuel, savoury pies, sandwiches, and the indulgence of my favoured milkshake. Not to be forgotten, a tin of three-in-one oil to tend to my trusty steed and its companion trailer.

Back on the A9, a brief pause in a lay-by allowed me to lavish care upon my bike and trailer, their joints now moving with ease. The generator hummed contentedly, a stark contrast to the day's earlier fury. As I resumed my ride, a Rolls-Royce glided by, its occupants shrouded in mystery, sparking a flicker of curiosity within me.

The journey's narrative took a turn as I veered off the A9 onto the A85, making my way to Crieff. The day's travel ended in a secluded spot, perfect for my teepee. The landscape here was a feast for the eyes, a stark contrast to the previous leg of my trip. Yet, as I watched the clouds gather with a suspicious eye, I braced myself for another night's deluge.

My culinary skills were put to good use; a hearty meal of grilled sausage, mashed potatoes, and baked beans was my reward for the day's toil. The garage's coffee was a luxurious touch to the simple feast. As I savoured the last bite, the skies opened up, sending me scurrying back into the shelter of my teepee.

Dawn broke with mercy, and the rain ceased. Cycling in dry conditions is a joy, allowing one to truly appreciate the splendour of the surroundings. The road ahead was clear, and my spirits lifted.

Then, the familiar chime of a text message: Janet's news of her promotion to branch manager. Her words conveyed a sense of fortune linked to our encounter. I responded with light-hearted well-wishes, masking the concern that her surprise might involve an ill-advised journey to Scotland.

Her cryptic reply did little to ease my mind. Despite the humour I found in the thought, the possibility of her pregnancy sent a chill through me. At my age, the likelihood seemed remote, yet the seed of worry had been planted.

In the solitude of my teepee, I journeyed through a digital album of memories, each image a portal to a life once lived. Jason's smile, forever young, paused my heart—a son lost to the unforgiving waters. Anna's absence echoed in the silence, her life unfolding beyond my reach, her happiness a silent wish upon my lips. The scars of past skirmishes lingered, words cast in anger, now etched in regret.

A deep breath ushered in the night's embrace, my mobile's glow fading into darkness. The rain's rhythmic dance upon the canvas lulled me into slumber, a solitary lullaby for the weary traveller.

Dawn's chorus heralded a new day, the sun's rays piercing the remnants of the storm. With a cup of tea to warm the spirit, I packed my world into bags, setting forth once more. The Bridge of Orchy beckoned, and with Loch Ness in my sights, the adventure continued, each pedal stroke a step towards redemption.

The journey's pace was unhurried, the weather's gentle caress a stark contrast to the tempests of days past. I revelled in the present, a traveller content with the road beneath and the sky above. The past, with its shadows and whispers, could not be altered; the future was a canvas in the hands of fate.

Lost in thought, the tranquillity shattered as a majestic and untamed stag charged across my path. The world spun, and I found myself cradled by the earth's soft verge—a merciful reprieve from the unforgiving asphalt. My intact glasses were a small blessing as I steadied myself, grateful for unbroken bones and the helmet that shielded my thoughts.

With my bike upright and the generator's heartbeat steady, I assessed the damage. A wing mirror, bent but not broken, was a simple fix—a reminder of the fragility of our plans against nature's will.

Pedalling resumed, my senses heightened to the possibility of wildlife's sudden whims. Rabbits darted, their games of chance a blur against the landscape. Fortune favoured me with clear skies and dry roads as I sought solace by Loch Fulla, a haven from the world's

The loch's tranquil waters mirrored the sky as I settled beside it, my teepee standing sentinel. With a coffee in hand and a Mars bar, slightly worse for the warmth of my pocket, I savoured the quietude of this newfound spot. It was then that the stillness was broken by an approaching figure, a gamekeeper, his presence marked by the gun resting on his shoulder.

His stance was firm, his words sharp as the Scottish brogue cut through the air. "You have no business here! Be on your way," he commanded, leaving no room for debate.

The heat of indignation rose within me, yet my response was measured. "I shan't move until the morning. I don't need your permission; I won't leave any rubbish or damage," I asserted, standing my ground.

His eyes narrowed, the ginger beard barely moving as he spoke. "You're not from these parts; you have no business in Scotland," he challenged.

The encounter, unwelcome as it was, could not dampen my spirit nor my right to be. With a respectful nod, I turned away, my resolve unshaken. The journey was mine to make, and Scotland's beauty was not his alone to gatekeep.

The gamekeeper's retreat was as swift as it was unexpected, his belief in my ruse a testament to the power of persuasion. Alone once more, I found solace in the routine of sharpening my machete, the evening's calm restored. As the sky blushed crimson, a harbinger of fair weather, I allowed myself a moment of quiet reflection.

The abrupt arrival of a blue Jeep shattered the peace, its skid a stark contrast to the serene loch. From it emerged a figure of fiery hair and fierce demeanour, her presence commanding despite her youth. Her words were as direct as her approach: "You're on my property; I don't care if you're a solicitor!"

Yet, as quickly as the confrontation arose, it dissipated, her departure as brisk as her entrance. Her father's troubles, it seemed, were a burden she was keen to avoid.

In the wake of this encounter, I couldn't help but chuckle at the day's unexpected turns, especially about my comment concerning her posterior. The loch, a silent witness to these human dramas, reflected the last rays of the sun as I settled in for the night, the promise of a new day on the horizon.

***

Agnes parked her blue Jeep a discreet mile away before reluctantly dialling Annabella's number. She hoped against hope that Annabella wouldn't end up marrying her brother. "I can confirm he's here. The gamekeeper wasn't mistaken," she reported.

"Excellent. I'll inform the others. Keep an eye on him; we can't afford any slip-ups now. We're on the brink of achieving our goal," Annabella responded with a tone of urgency.

Agnes hesitated, recalling the recent encounter. "He had the audacity to comment on my posterior, Annabella. Are we certain he's the one?"

"Absolutely. Janet's report is conclusive, and she's already expecting, which is a promising start. We're just awaiting confirmation," Annabella assured her.

"I'm surprised he's still potent at his age, though we do need to confirm Janet's pregnancy," Agnes mused, scepticism lacing her voice.

"The 12 have made their intentions clear. A million pounds is a compelling incentive for anyone," Annabella reminded her.

***

As the night enveloped the loch, I found comfort in the steel embrace of my machete, the day's events weighing heavily on my mind. Sleep, when it came, was a fleeting escape until the morning light nudged me awake at 7:30 a.m. A brisk dip in the loch's icy waters was a jolt to the system, a stark reminder of nature's indifference to human bravado.

Refreshed, albeit chilled, I dressed and prepared to face the day's journey toward Glencoe. The absence of Janet's usual text was a silence that spoke volumes, her new responsibilities as a bank manager no doubt consuming her time. I braced myself for the possibility that our paths might diverge, our fleeting connection becoming a mere footnote in my story.

The abrupt halt of a blue Jeep shattered the tranquillity of the morning ride. The driver, the same young woman from the previous evening, confronted me with a demand for an apology. Her attempt to mask a smile betrayed her stern facade.

"Whatever gives you that impression?" I inquired, my tone light, the bike now resting safely on its stand.

"Your rude comment regarding my posterior," she accused, though her stance softened slightly.

"I thought it was quite the compliment; most would be flattered," I retorted with a cheeky grin, observing her reaction. Her shock was evident, a mix of indignation and surprise playing across her features. With a huff, she retreated to her Jeep, leaving me to ponder the curious encounters that seemed to punctuate my Scottish adventure.

The day's trials had taken a toll, but fortune favoured me with no more than a jolt and a bent mirror bracket as I was unceremoniously dismounted from my bike by an impatient blue Jeep driver intentionally reversing. The hope that this would be our final encounter lingered as I gathered my wits and continued on.

The campsite at Glencoe offered a welcome reprieve—a chance to wash away the grime of the road and the tension of the day. My generator, too, enjoyed a well-deserved rest as I tapped into the campsite's amenities. The quiet was notable, the new variant casting a long shadow over travellers' plans.

Janet's message broke the silence, and her concern was evident even through the digital distance. "Broken mobile purchased a new one. Are you okay?" she inquired.

I couldn't help but recount the day's adventures with a touch of dry humour. "Apart from a gamekeeper wanting to shoot me and a redhead woman in a Jeep trying to run me over, I'm still here to tell the tale," I replied.

Her response came with a hint of possessiveness, tinged with humour. "I can see on the map you're at Glencoe; leave the women alone. You're spoken for, and I don't share!" It seemed Janet had pieced together the day's events, her smile almost palpable through the text.

I assured her with a light-hearted jest, "Don't be silly; she's twenty, barely out of nappies, just a hot-headed individual who thinks she owns the world."

The exchange brought a moment of levity to an otherwise taxing day, and as I settled in for the night, I found comfort in the thought that, despite the chaos, there were still those who cared.

The comfort of clean clothes and the security of a campsite's civilised embrace afforded me a night of undisturbed rest. Come morning, the world was a canvas of possibilities, and I set off towards Fort William with the sun as my companion. The A85, with its notorious curves and hurried travellers, demanded respect and caution.

Fort William soon lay behind me, a bustling town I bypassed for fear of prying hands eyeing my gear. A mile beyond, I found a haven among fellow nomads, a communal sanctuary by the roadside.

As I settled in, the blue Jeep reappeared, its driver, the fiery-haired enigma, alighting with an unexpected offering—two glasses and a bottle of whisky. Her smile, a rare sight, hinted at a ceasefire. Mask in place, I rose to meet her, the machete at my side, a silent guardian of past and present.

Her admission hung in the air, a rare vulnerability on display. "I shouldn't have reversed into you—a childish act, stupid and dangerous; I'm surprised you haven't phoned the police."

The invitation to sit was silent but clear, and as we faced each other across the worn logs, a sense of understanding began to bridge the gap between us. "At least you had the courtesy to apologise; that goes a long way," I acknowledged the warmth in my voice genuine. "I wouldn't have expected a woman in your position to concern herself with an old codger like me."

Her response was tinged with a weariness I recognised all too well. "Normally, I wouldn't. I'm usually confined to the estate office, wrestling with my father's accounts." Her gaze lingered on the amber liquid as if seeking answers in its depths.

Curiosity coloured her tone as she inquired about my origins. "Where are you from?"

I shared a piece of my heart with her, "Miles away, on my final journey to the places I've cherished over the years. My wife recently passed; she would have been by my side now. Scotland has always been a special place for us."

In that shared space, two strangers found common ground, our stories unfolding with each sip of whisky, under the vast Scottish sky.

The whisky flowed once more, a liquid bond between two solitary souls. "Be careful; you have to drive home. You don't want to be prosecuted," I cautioned, but she only smiled, her life steeped in the spirit's warmth from her father's distillery.

"You are the most popular girl in the area," I remarked, the whisky's burn a rare sensation on my tongue.

She sighed, a weight in her words. "Men are only interested in what I'm worth, not me as a person; I'm treated as a commodity, especially by my father."

"Then it's time to chart a new course," I suggested. "There's always someone for someone somewhere."

She confessed to feeling trapped by time and circumstance, her youth shadowed by the pandemic's isolation. "I'm twenty-three and feel like ninety-three."

Her laughter was a rare melody as we exchanged names and tales—Agnes, the heiress with the world at her feet, yet confined by golden chains. And I, Zachariah Black, a writer by trade, retired by choice, united by a shared sense of being adrift.

Her chuckle turned into a cough as the whisky took her by surprise. "I haven't laughed for ages, Zachariah; you certainly made a lovely ending to my day," she said, her grin genuine.

I offered a compliment, a hope for her future. "Not every man's a bastard, although most are. You will have to be selective and take your time. You have many years ahead of you."

At that moment, under the fading light, our laughter mingled with the whispers of the glen, and for a brief spell, the world seemed a little less daunting.

"I'm pleased I met you, Zachariah Black; I feel more confident. You are a total stranger and have no reason to speak anything but the truth."

"I suggest you stop drinking, Agnes and carefully drive home. Don't worry; Mr Right will come along. Here's a secret: I married twice before I found the perfect wife and would be together now if it wasn't for the pandemic."

Agnes stood smiling, approaching me. I rose to my feet; she carefully removed my facemask and kissed me lovingly. She stepped back, lifting her red Aran jumper and exposing her bra, asking bright-eyed, "The front is as good as the back, your opinion?" She smiled, pulling her jumper down over her pink bra.

I smiled warmly, "Absolutely perfect. Can I book an appointment, please?" I watched her walk off, giggling towards her Jeep; she'd left me the bottle of whisky and two glasses. She glanced back, blowing a kiss, "Don't worry, Zachariah Black. Alcohol and the variant don't mix; you're perfectly safe." She climbed in her Jeep and drove away.

***

Using hands-free, Agnes contacted Annabella, her voice a whisper against the Scottish winds, "Annabella, he's on the other side of Fort William. I'm plotting my next move to ensnare him."

"Excellent, Agnes," Annabella's voice crackled through the line, a blend of approval and caution. "Proceed with care, but do not arouse his suspicions. He is a pivotal piece in our grand design."

Agnes's eyes narrowed, a spark of determination igniting within. "How far should I entwine him in our web?"

There was a pause, the kind that stretched seconds into eternities, as Annabella weighed the gravity of the situation. "The 12 have decreed—the more, the merrier. The extent of your engagement is at your discretion, Agnes. Resources are plentiful; they expect full participation unless one can justify abstention."

***

With a contented smile, I retreated into the sanctuary of my teepee, the events of the evening swirling in my mind like a gentle brook. Sleep claimed me swiftly, a merciful reprieve from the day's exertions. Dawn's light brought with it the remnants of last night's revelry, a slight hangover that clouded my thoughts. As I pondered the enigmatic nature of human behaviour, I realised some mysteries were not meant to be unravelled.

Breakfast was a solitary affair, after which I embarked on my journey toward Strone. The road was a familiar friend, and after several hours, I found solace on the serene banks of Loch Ness. Amidst the whispering scotch pines and birch trees, I erected my temporary abode, a teepee that stood as a testament to my wanderlust.

Scarcely had I savoured my meal when Janet's message chimed through, a playful warning that stirred a chuckle from within: "Mind the Loch Ness Monster doesn't bite you!"

My fingers danced across the screen in response, "I hope you are well; how are you enjoying your new position as bank manager?"

Her reply came swiftly, a mix of exhaustion and affection, "Hectic. I fell asleep; I didn't text you last night. Don't worry, I love you. Don't be away too long, or I'll come and find you."

Settling into the evening, I perused the weather forecast, strategising my route through Inverness and onto the A9. A small whisky, courtesy of Agnes's bottle, warmed my insides, the water a mere whisper in the robust spirit.

As twilight deepened, an unexpected visitor graced my teepee. Agnes stood at the entrance, her smile a beacon in the dimming light. "I see, drinking my whisky without me; shame on you, Mr Black," she teased, her presence a welcome intrusion.

She joined me, her glass clinking softly against mine, the amber liquid reflecting the last rays of the sun. "You're desperate to know how I found you?" she mused her grin a mixture of pride and mischief. "On the way home from Inverness, my father mentioned an 'idiot' on a bicycle by Loch Ness. I surmised you sought seclusion, and this spot, shrouded by nature's embrace, was the only logical haven."

Her smug satisfaction was palpable, a shared secret between two souls intertwined by fate and a bottle of whisky.

"I must admit, I'm surprised," Zachariah mused, his gaze lingering on the horizon. "I wouldn't have expected your father to take kindly to you mingling with a wanderer like me, Agnes. What brings you here? Not that your company isn't appreciated."

Agnes's smile was a sliver of moonlight in the dimming twilight. "I sought your presence, Zachariah. Yesterday, you looked beyond my wealth and status; you saw me for who I am," she said, her grin widening. "I find myself in need of your unique perspective, especially on days when the clouds hang heavy. Might I have your mobile number? Your words have a way of parting the skies."

"If it brings you solace," Zachariah replied, his fingers deftly displaying his number on the screen. Agnes captured it with swift precision, her own phone now a bridge between their worlds. "Thank you, Zachariah," she whispered, tucking the device back into the folds of her tweed jacket.

As the last of the whisky kissed the bottom of their glasses, Agnes's inquiry was gentle, yet laden with curiosity. "What's your next destination, Zachariah?"

He pondered, the question stirring memories of a past intertwined with another. "I was contemplating that very thought. Tain seems a fitting waypoint, a place where memories of my wife still linger. And then, Inverewe Gardens beckons. Beyond that, the path is unwritten."

"Settle down again?" Zachariah echoed the question, his voice tinged with a wistful scepticism. "Doubtful. I lack the wealth of a tycoon or the looks of a silver-screen idol. At this juncture in life, I'm far from a prized catch. Should fortune smile upon me, I fear it would only attract those with eyes for my coffers, not my heart," he sighed, the weight of his words hanging in the air like mist.

Agnes nodded her expression a mirror of understanding. "You see the quandary of my station. The suitors my father parades before me are nothing more than glorified fortune hunters."

Zachariah's gaze met hers, earnest and unflinching. "You're ensnared in an antiquated game, Agnes. Why must your father chart your course? You possess the strength to navigate your own destiny."

"The rules of our circle are ironclad," Agnes replied, a note of resignation threading her voice. "We're bound by standards, by lineage. It's akin to the meticulous selection of breeding stock, tracing the family tree to its affluent roots."

"I recall my days on a dairy farm," Zachariah mused, "where the union of heifer and bull was a careful choice. It seems your father seeks a similar match for you. If that's the life you choose, so be it."

Agnes's eyes held a glimmer of rebellion. "Tradition is a chain, but not unbreakable. An ancestor of mine dared to defy it two centuries past, and her happiness was the stuff of legend. My brother shall carry on the Montague name; my path remains my own." Her voice trailed off as Zachariah choked on his drink, a name from a bygone tale biting at his memory.

Agnes's hand was gentle on his back. "What ails you, Zachariah? You look as though you've seen a spectre."

Zachariah's voice held a note of sombre reflection. "The book 'Secret Obsession' might shed light on my reaction. But to the matter at hand, Agnes, it's only you who stands in the way of your happiness. The aristocracy's days, including the Royal Family's, are numbered. With the Queen's passing, the monarchy's future is uncertain."

Agnes's eyes widened in recognition. "Zachariah Black, it's you! Father was incensed over a book about the Montagues last year. The author unveiled a secret lineage tied to the Royals."

"You've mistaken me for someone else," Zachariah chuckled, a twinkle in his eye. "My book is a work of fiction, though I confess, you do bear a striking resemblance to Maggie, one of my characters."

"Your presence is a breath of fresh air, Zachariah," Agnes confessed, her guard down. "With you, I can shed the mantle of my title and just be myself."

Glancing at his watch, Zachariah noted the time. "It's 8:30, Agnes. Perhaps it's time you returned to the safety of your estate."

Her smile was playful, a challenge in her gaze. "And if I choose to stay, what then, sir? What becomes of the fair maiden?"

Zachariah's laughter was a soft rumble. "Alas, the knight's days of gallantry are behind me. The spirit is willing, but the flesh is . . . well, less so."

As Agnes stepped out, her touch was light on his cheek. She returned swiftly, mischief in her eyes. "Close your eyes and open your mouth. Trust me," she urged.

With a mix of trepidation and curiosity, Zachariah obeyed. A small object landed on his tongue, followed by her command to drink. The whisky's warmth spread through him, a liquid courage.

His eyes snapped open. "Was that a drug?" he asked, a hint of alarm in his voice.

Agnes looked at her wristwatch, "In about fifteen minutes, you'll feel a new man, and shortly after, I should feel a new woman if all goes to plan. In the meantime," She paused and removed my glass from my hand, laying me down on my sleeping bag, kissing me softly; she sat up momentarily, removing her tweed coat. Within fifteen minutes, we were making love. Is she intense? I realised she'd given me a stimulant; there was no way I could perform otherwise; why she would be carrying Viagra with her, I don't know. Still, I'll find out; curiosity is killing me. We finally relented, lying beside each other. I looked at my wristwatch at 12:30 a.m. "What did you give me, Agnes," I asked calmly, not receiving an answer.

We kissed goodbye in the cold morning air, our breaths mingling and forming a transient cloud of warmth in the chill of dawn. I returned to my teepee, the silence of the early hours enveloping me like a comforting shawl. Exhaustion weighed heavily on my eyelids, and I surrendered to sleep's sweet embrace. Agnes, with her fiery spirit and insatiable zest for life, certainly knew how to sap a man's strength. Yet, as I drifted into dreams, I pondered the enigma that she presented. Why would a vibrant twenty-three-year-old woman find an interest in a man like me? I was a wanderer, a drifter, with nothing to offer but stories and time.

Morning arrived too soon, its light a stark contrast to the soft darkness of my slumber. I dressed in the dim glow of dawn, the fabric of my clothes whispering against my skin as I moved. Breakfast was a simple affair, but the act of making coffee felt like a sacred ritual. The rich aroma filled the air, promising a much-needed jolt to my weary senses. I needed something potent to wake my brain after the night's escapades.

With my equipment secured, I moved to the lay-by, checking each item with meticulous care. The road beckoned, and I set off towards Inverness, bracing myself for the usual cacophony of horns and the near-misses that turned the tarmac into a treacherous dance floor. Motorists and lorries seemed to conspire in their attempts to turn me into strawberry jam.

By lunchtime, I had conquered the ascent to Inverness, my muscles protesting each pedal stroke across the Moray Firth bridge. The A9 stretched before me, a ribbon of constant motion that didn't ease until Inverness was but a speck in my rearview mirror. I pressed on, the landscape unfurling around me, a tapestry of greens and browns stitched together by the road.

I finally came to a halt just before the road bridge over the Cromarty Firth. It was not one of my brightest ideas to stop for the night, as the area offered little privacy. I found myself taking a minor side road, seeking a secluded spot away from the prying eyes of the world. There, amidst the whispering grass and the distant call of seabirds, I pitched my tent. As the sun dipped below the horizon, painting the sky in hues of fire and gold, I reflected on the day's journey and the mysterious allure of Agnes. The night promised rest, and perhaps, in the quiet hours, I would find the answers that eluded me.

I'd barely set up my teepee when I noticed a blue Jeep winding its way down the dusty junction. It had to be Agnes. With her signature precision, she parked well off the road, her silhouette framed by the setting sun. Stepping out, she carried a large picnic basket, her smile as warm as the evening glow. "I thought you might fancy something different tonight," she said, unveiling an array of meats and a bottle of wine from beneath the chequered cloth.

As we settled inside the teepee, Agnes leaned in for a kiss. "That's for last night... or this morning," she whispered, her grin infectious. "I haven't felt this alive in ages."

Her words stirred something within me. "Agnes, your kindness is as boundless as the prairie sky. What we shared... it's etched in memory. You're remarkable, not just for your grace or that enchanting accent, but for your spirit."

A blush bloomed on her cheeks, a rare sight. "I've been reading some of those books I downloaded," she confessed. "They're fascinating."

I chuckled a hint of pride in my voice. "I have a secret to share. I'm dyslexic. Without technology, my stories would remain untold whispers in the wind."

Agnes's eyes softened, her admiration clear. "Then it's a good thing we live in an age where technology bridges gaps, not just in our stories, but between us."

"Why should I shatter her illusion?" I pondered, eyeing the sandwiches sheathed in cling film. "What's special about these?" I inquired, gesturing towards the neatly packed meal.

Agnes' smile was a beacon in the dimly lit teepee. "I made those for your journey tomorrow. Wrapped them myself to keep them fresh," she said, her eyes twinkling with a mix of mischief and care.

The wine seemed to unravel the years between us as if they were mere threads in the fabric of time. Agnes, now without her tweed armour, appeared more vulnerable, yet there was a playful challenge in her gaze. "I suppose it's time to interrogate you, Mr Black," she teased, her voice a soft lilt. "Unless you're ready to divulge your secrets about the Montagues?"

Laughter erupted from my chest, genuine and unguarded. "My dear Agnes, the only Montagues I know are the ones trapped within the pages of my book."

Her grin was a silent acknowledgement of our game. A soft kiss, a whispered challenge. "Will you talk now?"

"Never," I declared the word a vow. "I have nothing to confess."

The night unfolded like a dance, each step measured, each glance an invitation. Agnes' laughter was the melody to which my heart kept time. "Crumbs," she exclaimed amidst a passionate embrace. "If tomorrow's interrogation is half as successful..."

Her determination was a flame, and I was merely a moth drawn to its warmth. I gave all that I was, hoping my weary heart could endure the exhilaration. And as the thought crossed my mind—what a way to depart this world, in the throes of such passion—I bid farewell to Agnes in the small hours of the morning.

As I glanced at my mobile, the glow of unread messages from Janet pierced the dawn's tranquillity. "Are you okay? I haven't heard from you." Guilt gnawed at me, a reminder of the tangled web I'd woven. My reply was a half-truth, a bandage over a wound yet to heal. "Bad signal. I just received your message. Don't worry, I'm okay missing you. Stay safe."

The situation was of my own making, a dance on the edge of commitment's blade. Janet and Agnes, two stars in my sky, equally luminous and alluring. What would my late wife think, her celestial gaze upon me? A chuckle from the heavens, perhaps, branding me a 'dirty devil.'

Sleep was a fleeting visitor, chased away by the anticipation of the road ahead. Agnes's sandwiches, a testament to her thoughtfulness, paired well with the bitter tang of coffee. The A9 beckoned, a ribbon of possibility stretching towards Dingwall. The journey, some 80 or 90 miles, to Inverewe Gardens promised solitude and reflection.

The Scottish roads were alive with the blare of Klaxon horns, a symphony of impatience. Yet, the journey was mine to savour. A text from Agnes broke the silence: "Wait for me at Garve; I'll join you at 5 o'clock." The message hung in the air, a decision deferred, as the sun's warmth and the tailwind propelled me along the A835.

The hills demanded effort, a physical echo of my emotional climb. The landscape, a canvas of beauty, offered moments of respite from the chaos within. Garve was a crossroads in more ways than one, leading to the A832 and the serene Inverewe Gardens. What awaited me there, only time would tell.

I arrived with time to spare, the anticipation of Agnes's arrival a steady hum in my thoughts. Her Jeep appeared on the horizon, a familiar sight in the unfamiliar terrain. With a casual wave, she signalled me to follow, leading me down the A832 to a secluded property nestled among the whispering pines.

"We own this," Agnes said, her voice carrying a hint of pride as she gestured to the quaint house with its welcoming garden. "It's usually for tourists, but with the travel restrictions..." Her voice trailed off, leaving an unspoken understanding between us.

The door swung open, and she moved with purpose, her bag landing with a thud on the kitchen table. She was back in a flash, wrestling with a hamper that seemed to contain a small feast. "Planning a banquet?" I joked, raising an eyebrow.

Her grin was enigmatic, a secret dancing behind her eyes. "No, just a few days' worth of provisions," she replied, stocking the fridge with an assortment of necessities.

The coffee brewed, and I caught a glimpse of her adding a mysterious powder to my cup. It was a move reminiscent of Janet, sparking a curiosity about the connection between these two formidable women.

"Make yourself at home, Zachariah," she said, her tone light yet commanding. "I'll be down shortly, and then we can enjoy a quiet evening."

As the sound of the shower echoed from upstairs, I settled in, the television's chatter a backdrop to my racing thoughts. Agnes's presence was a catalyst, stirring a whirlwind of emotions and desires. The evening promised a respite, a momentary pause in the journey that was both literal and metaphorical.

I navigated my way into the living room, the familiar weight of unease settling in my chest as I sank into the couch. The television flickered to life for the first time in weeks, its glow casting shadows across the room. I was there in body, but my mind was adrift, caught in the turbulent sea of Agnes's intentions. Her fixation was becoming unsettling—a single night's encounter, I had presumed, would quench her fleeting curiosity. Yet, here she was, weaving herself into the fabric of my days with unnerving persistence. There had to be an underlying current to her actions.

Agnes descended the staircase; the sight of her halted my breath. She wore an air of nonchalance as if the morning's events were but a wisp of fog, quickly dissipated by the sun. "It's your turn; I've left towels by the shower," she announced, her voice devoid of inflexion. She breezed past me into the kitchen, her demeanour undisturbed by the storm she'd stirred within me. The offer of a shower was a siren's call I couldn't resist—my attire had become a second skin over the weeks, save for the brief respite at Glencoe's campsite laundry.

With haste, I ascended the stairs, the bathroom a sanctuary at the journey's end. Shedding my garments, I surrendered to the embrace of the warm cascade. Fifteen minutes dissolved into the steam, and as I emerged, I reached for a towel, only to find a void where my clothes once were. "Agnes, my clothes?" I called, a note of vulnerability in my voice.

"They're taking a spin in the washing machine," she replied, her tone casual. "Don't fret; I've safeguarded your wallet and phone. You're welcome to join me downstairs." I lingered, the towel now a makeshift garment, my thoughts drifting to the other clothes nestled in my rucksack—soon to be refreshed.

Descending the stairs was a tentative affair, each step a reminder of my discomfort. In my youth, such exposure might have been a trifle, but the years had draped me in modesty. Agnes waited in the kitchen, my rucksack emptied and its contents succumbing to the whirl of the wash—consent an afterthought. I inhaled deeply, seeking solace in the mundane. "Your efforts are appreciated, Agnes, truly. But now I'm bereft of attire. Might you have a robe to lend while my clothes embark on their cleansing journey?"

Agnes chuckled, "You have nothing I haven't seen before."

"There's a chasm between us, Agnes. You're twenty-three, and I'm...well, let's just say I've seen more seasons," I confessed, the awkwardness of the situation settling like dust on an old bookshelf. "I could give a wrinkled rug a run for its money."

Before I could react, Agnes whisked the towel from my waist with a playful flick of her wrist. Her grin was impish as she teased, "Wrinkled? Hardly," she chuckled. "Zachariah Black, if I didn't desire your company, I wouldn't be here. Your words these past days have sparked a plan in me—one that's a perfect fit and solves a certain quandary. But hold your horses; I'll reveal all in good time, depending on how gracious you are to me," she said, her eyes twinkling with mischief. As she prepared another cup of coffee, I caught a glimpse of her slyly adding what I assumed to be more Viagra to the brew.

With a heavy sigh, I retreated to the living room, the settee offering a refuge as I shielded my dignity with a cushion, disheartened by the turn of events. Agnes soon appeared, setting down my coffee with a peck on the cheek, and chirped, "I'm whipping up a bite to eat. Any requests?"

"Surprise me," I replied, my appetite as indifferent as my mood.

The familiar ringtone from the kitchen snagged my attention. Agnes offered a knowing glance as she handed me my phone. Retreating to the solitude of the front room, I found a message from Janet: "You, okay? I'm missing you."

"I'll be at Inverewe Gardens by tomorrow; missing you too," I typed back.

From the kitchen, Agnes's voice floated in, "Zachariah, sandwiches are ready; come and join me."

Stepping into the kitchen, I settled onto a chair with a cold plastic seat and leaned against its steel frame. Agnes was seated opposite me, and despite my efforts to maintain eye contact, my gaze involuntarily wandered. It's either a natural inclination, or I'm just a relic of a bygone era, I mused. Her smile was enigmatic, a stark contrast to the prim image she had projected just days prior. "Will you share your plans with me, Agnes?" I inquired, curiosity piqued.

"Perhaps in the morning," she teased, her eyes alight with mischief. "But for now, you're as red as a beetroot and brimming with anticipation—why postpone what's bound to happen?" With a gentle tug, she led me to the living room. There, she reclined on the carpet, and the ensuing hour became a blur of passion. Agnes, though young, possessed an uncanny ability to stoke the fires of desire. Eventually, we found ourselves entwined in the sheets upstairs, where the night enveloped us until dawn. The memories of our fervour were as hazy as the morning light filtering through the curtains.

Upon waking, I caught sight of Agnes, a serene figure atop the bed. A fleeting, irrational thought crossed my mind, quickly dismissed as I noticed a fresh set of clothes neatly laid out for me. She approached, her lips meeting mine in a tender kiss. "What a night," she exclaimed before dashing off, leaving modesty behind. The clatter from the kitchen hinted at breakfast preparations. Dressed in my new attire, I joined her downstairs. She served up a simple yet satisfying meal of egg on toast. As she nibbled on her toast with marmalade, her gaze held a youthful infatuation that felt oddly out of place.

Breakfast concluded, I shouldered my rucksack, ensuring my wallet and phone were secure. At the door, Agnes's farewell kiss lingered with a promise of more. "See you later," she whispered. I returned the gesture, a peck on her cheek, and mounted my bicycle, eager for the escape. In my haste, I had neglected the generator; only a mile out did I start it, relishing the engine's steady hum. A glance in the rearview mirror confirmed my unchanged visage—no signs of a Travolta transformation or a miraculous return to youth. The reasons behind these events remained an enigma.

***

Agnes picked up the ringing phone with a practiced ease. "Annabella, what a pleasant surprise," she greeted.

Annabella's voice was tinged with urgency. "Agnes, I'll cut to the chase. Is your brother stepping out on me?"

Suppressing a smirk, Agnes replied, "Annabella, he's as much a mystery to me as he is to you. Men will be men, after all."

There was a heavy exhale on the other end. "I get it. And how's the situation with Zachariah Black? Any developments?"

A chuckle escaped Agnes. "Let's just say he's surprisingly resilient. A little pharmaceutical assistance, and he's anyone's guess. But rest assured, he's en route to Inverewe Gardens as we speak."

"I must admit, I'm baffled, Agnes. Your eagerness to...engage with him seems out of character for someone of your upbringing."

Agnes's laughter was light and untroubled. "Oh, he's no sports car, but rather a reliable SUV—robust and unwavering. You might consider giving him a chance; he could surprise you."

Annabella's laugh held a note of shock. "Agnes, you're full of surprises. But thanks for the update."

***

The journey to Inverewe graced me with fair weather; a welcome reprieve as I veered off at Gairloch. Exhaustion had set in, demanding a brief respite. I parked near the quaint shop, 'Buddha by the Sea,' a place that held memories of past visits with my wife. A keepsake crossed my mind, a token for the possibility of a return home. The village hinted at a nearby campsite, an ideal spot to rest for the night. But fatigue won over, and I opted for a patch of waste ground instead.

My teepee became a sanctuary as I settled with a cup of coffee, the solitude a shield against Agnes's persistent presence. Laughter bubbled up at the thought of my recent escapades—more action in three weeks than in years, akin to running marathons back-to-back. Gratitude mingled with disbelief; the attention from someone as young as Agnes was unexpected, to say the least.

A ping from my phone broke the silence—a message from Janet: "You'll soon run out of land, then you'll have to head home to your loving girlfriend and future wife!"

I replied with a tease: "Hey, crazy woman, are you on happy pills? Missing you. I'm about one hundred and sixty miles from John O'Groats. Skipping it this time—it's always too windy."

Her response was swift: "Why shouldn't I be? I have the perfect job and the perfect boyfriend. Stay safe."

Janet's words were clear; she was committed to our relationship. I had hoped the distance might bring clarity, perhaps encourage her to find someone closer to her age. Yet, as 8 p.m. approached without a word from Agnes, I found myself torn between concern and relief. The prospect of another night fuelled by passion seemed overwhelming. With a wry smile, I nestled into my sleeping bag.

Dawn brought the cacophony of a seagull, its cries as loud as a megaphone. Opening my teepee, I was greeted by the sight of it perched on my handlebars, leaving a mess worthy of a canine. Breakfast was a quiet affair under the grey, overcast sky, the sea breeze brisk and refreshing. Coffee finished, I packed up and hit the A832, bracing myself for the steep ascent out of Gairloch, knowing the road would lead me to Poolewe and the local shop below.

The wind sliced through the open spaces, a relentless force as I descended the hill, my eyes fixed on the distant village. The trailer behind me was a wild beast, threatening to overtake me at any moment. I whispered a silent prayer for my disc brakes, hoping they would spare me from a chaotic tumble.

Reaching the village shop, I exchanged wary glances with the shopkeeper as I gathered supplies. No words were exchanged—only the unspoken acknowledgement of my journey.

Leaving the village behind, I pedalled towards the old Russian Anchorage, the narrow track hugging the side of Loch Ewe. The decaying emplacements from World War II stood as silent sentinels, a headstone among them speaking of lives lost for freedom. The wind's howl reminded me of the area's untamed nature, and the 'no camping' sign confirmed my decision to move on.

I pressed forward, past the old camping site, climbing the steady gradient in search of shelter for my teepee. As Ullapool loomed ahead, I questioned my sanity—this road was a cyclist's nightmare.

A glance in my wing mirror revealed a familiar sight—a blue Jeep towing a horsebox. Agnes's grin was unmistakable as she pulled alongside. "Zachariah Black, you're even crazier than I thought," she laughed, offering sanctuary and a ride past Ullapool. "Load up; you can thank me later."

Gratitude led me to accept her offer. I secured my bike and trailer inside the horsebox and settled into the passenger seat. The journey revealed the daunting gradients I had avoided, and within an hour, we arrived at Agnes's rental property—a lavish house that spoke of wealth and privilege.

Agnes's voice broke the silence, "Carry the hamper, Zachariah; I'll see to the door." The hamper was suspiciously heavy, but I managed to place it on the kitchen table without incident.

As Agnes brought the house to life, her plan for the morning hung in the air, a promise laced with conditions. I chose not to engage, instead taking in the grandeur of the Montague estate. It wasn't my place to question their fortune.

A shower was all I desired, and Agnes directed me upstairs. "Towels are on the way," she assured me. To my surprise Agnes stepped into the shower and the rest is history as they say.

Agnes faced me, her expression tense. "Zachariah Black, I must confess, I haven't been completely truthful with you. After our gamekeeper's encounter with you, I recognised your name. Previously, my father had chanced upon your book, 'Secret Obsession,' under rather salacious circumstances. He shared his discovery with me, particularly your mention of the Montagues. It piqued our curiosity, especially since you'd discerned our ties to the Royals."

Her admission captivated me. "Do go on," I urged. "While I can assure you that my writing stemmed from pure creativity, I sense there's more you wish to disclose. Rest assured, the narrative is purely a work of fiction."

Settling down with two freshly brewed cups of coffee, Agnes let out a sigh. "Our initial interactions were rather chilly. Later, driven by curiosity, I delved deeper into your background. During our second meeting, when I rather boldly revealed myself, you seemed interested solely in me, not my lineage or social standing. Reflecting on that, I revisited the role of Christine Gibbs in your novel. It struck me as ingenious—unable to possess Donald Selwyn, she opted for the next best thing: his offspring."

I probed further, "What exactly are you implying, Agnes?"

Agnes shared with a sly grin, "You might recall my mentioning my brother's upcoming nuptials to a rather vexing, yet wealthy woman. The more I pondered over your novel, the more enticing the concept became. Should I bear a son, he would be heir to my father's estate. Moreover, if I were to conceive prior to my brother's bride-to-be, I believe the law would favour my son to inherit the estate and our family businesses."

I countered, "That strategy is flawed. Any child of ours would be labelled illegitimate. I've experienced that stigma firsthand—constantly tormented by circumstances beyond my control."

Agnes persisted, "I disagree, Zachariah. There must be another way! It's unjust that my gender should bar me from inheriting the estate, especially when I'm the one effectively managing it. Without me, my father would face financial ruin."

I proposed half-jokingly, "The simplest solution might be to remove the competition altogether—an unfortunate hunting mishap or a tragic fall from a cliff, perhaps? Your estate seems rife with such hazards."

Her eyes widened in shock. "You're suggesting we do away with my brother?"

"If you're truly determined, you'll go to great lengths, as you've done in your attempts to conceive with me. But there are many more capable men out there," I pointed out.

Agnes' smile was mischievous. "Others might complicate things, unlike you. Your calm nature appeals to me; it reminds me of my cherished pony, whom my brother spitefully shot."

I suggested, "Perhaps a temporary fix for your dilemma would be to let his fiancée catch wind of his indiscretions—either with a servant or someone from the village. Planting a seed of doubt might just send her packing."

Agnes' eyes sparkled with intrigue. "And how would I orchestrate that without her suspecting me?"

"With a simple trip to Tesco's for a burner phone, you could anonymously send her the sordid details," I said, amused by her growing excitement.

"Would you assist me, Zachariah Black? There's a Tesco open all night here. I'll get the phone now. And instead of cooking, I'll grab fish and chips, leave the horsebox here—it'll make navigating Ullapool's narrow roads easier."

After a quick kiss on her cheek, we unhitched the horsebox, Agnes beaming like never before. She sped off towards Ullapool, while I settled in at home, flicking through the channels, half-listening to the news. The government's reassurances about the new virus variants didn't convince me. Nature has its ways of dealing with what it deems an infestation, and humanity, with its disregard for the planet, fits the bill. The ongoing migrant crisis only adds to the chaos.

Agnes burst in, breathless, with two servings of fish and chips. She placed one on my lap and quickly set up the new mobile phone to charge. After fetching plates and cutlery from the kitchen, she sat next to me, her smile brimming with anticipation.

"You know, Agnes, if your brother were out of the picture, you'd have a wider selection of suitors," I remarked casually.

She scoffed lightly. "Suitors or gold diggers? My plan to have a child remains. It's a child I can raise on my terms, ensuring the future of the estate and our businesses. There's always the risk of illegitimate heirs from my father, but I blame my mother for his indiscretions—she's withheld affection since my birth."

I chuckled. "And here I thought you were the innocent type. You're quite the schemer."

Agnes didn't miss a beat. "My father would be overjoyed with a grandchild, especially a Montague. He's well aware of my dedication to our estate, unlike my frivolous brother."

I raised an eyebrow. "But there's no certainty in conception, especially given my age."

She was confident. "After the passion we shared, I have no doubts about your ... potency."

As we finished our meal, I pondered Agnes' true nature—a woman as calculating as any. She then took the charged phone, inserted the SIM card, and topped it up with credit, ready to send a message that could change everything.

Agnes slid the phone across the table with a conspiratorial glint in her eye. "Your turn, wordsmith. Craft the perfect message."

"Names?" I asked, poised to weave a web of deception.

"Annabella and James," she replied.

I pondered for a moment, crafting a message both convincing and irrefutable. With a steady exhale, I began to type: "Dear Annabella, it has come to my attention that James Montague, the man you intend to marry, has been less than faithful. While I labour on an oil rig, contributing to your father's fortune, James has entangled himself with my wife back in the village. A tale ripe for the press, don't you think? Especially for your father's eyes." With a tap, the message was sent.

Almost instantly, a reply buzzed in: "This is news to me; thank you."

Twenty minutes ticked by before Agnes' phone erupted into a jingle. "It's James," she whispered, her voice a mix of nerves and excitement. She answered, putting him on speaker.

"Agnes, are you there? I'm in a spot of bother," James' voice crackled through. "Some scoundrel tipped off Annabella about me and...well, you know. How did they learn about the oil rig? It's a mess. Annabella's family has wealth, and I've got to smooth things over. If she reaches out, tell her it's all poppycock, will you? Cheers, sis."

"You're a genius, Zachariah Black. What's our next move?" Agnes asked, her eyes alight with schemes.

I couldn't help but smile at the unfolding drama. "Start with a coffee," I suggested. "It's fortuitous, your brother's entanglement in the village. Seems he's inherited more than just the family name."

As Agnes hurried to the kitchen and returned with our coffees, her phone erupted with Annabella's ringtone. "It's her! What do I do, Zachariah?"

"Play the innocent," I advised.

With a click, Agnes put the call on speaker. "Hello, Annabella! What a pleasant surprise. How may I assist you today?" she said, masking her anticipation.

Annabella's voice was strained. "I've just learned of James's affair. I'm devastated. Trust is shattered; I can't marry him now."

Agnes nodded in feigned sympathy. "I understand, Annabella. Betrayal is a bitter pill. If he's been unfaithful, it's best to know now rather than face a scandalous divorce later. Let's catch up soon, maybe at Aintree or over drinks at the castle."

Agnes, her voice a delicate quiver, reached for me in a sudden flurry, nearly toppling my coffee in her haste. Her lips met mine in a desperate kiss as she whispered urgently, "Zachariah Black, you're a genius; what's my next move? I'm carrying a child; there's no doubt in my mind. What steps should I take? I can't afford to err." The tremor of uncertainty in her words lent a profound gravity to her predicament.

I could only offer a sombre reflection, "James, burdened by despair, might seek solace in the abyss, an unforeseen tragedy that would, by fate's cruel hand, ensure your ascension to the Montague inheritance should he vanish."

The evening waned, and we retired prematurely, Agnes seemingly propelled by an unseen urgency. Our connection remained untouched; not a whisper of intimacy graced the night. Come dawn, we rose and adorned ourselves in haste, her eagerness for my departure hanging heavy in the air. After a swift breakfast of coffee and toast, I was ushered to the horsebox, where I reclaimed my bike and trailer. Agnes bestowed upon me a fleeting kiss, a mere brush of lips.

Pedalling with resolve along the A835 towards Elphin, the incline tested my resolve, but the generator hummed faithfully, sustaining my journey. The landscape unfolded majestically, a tapestry of nature's grandeur, despite the nipping chill. Distant hills, crowned with snow, stood sentinel on the horizon.

A turn of the handlebars and I merged onto the A837, steering towards Bonar Bridge. By the juncture for Rose Hall, weariness had seeped into my bones, mirroring the gloom that Agnes' demeanour had cast upon our parting. Seeking solace, I nestled my teepee within a hidden alcove, brewed a comforting cup of tea, and there, nestled among my provisions, I found Agnes' silent offering: sandwiches. Perhaps her heart harboured care, veiled beneath a brusque exterior.

Glancing at my wristwatch, it was just past 3 p.m. I sat in contemplative silence, pondering the crossroads of my future. The options lay before me: board a local train beyond Bonar Bridge to Scotland's far reaches, pedal onwards to meet Janet in Buxton or return home to a life of stagnant waiting. The latter thought struck a chord of self-pity.

My introspection was interrupted by Janet's texts, a mix of concern and mystery. "I see you're on the way back. Why the silence?" she inquired, followed by a more alarming, "I'm coming to find you!" I hastily reassured her, blaming the poor signal, a common scapegoat in the Scottish wilds.

Her reply brought a tentative smile, "Worried sick, but I've got a surprise for you. You'll be thrilled!" I responded with affection, urging her to stay put.

With a relieved exhale, I settled into my makeshift abode. The last thing I needed was Janet risking her career for my sake. As I sipped my coffee, the local radio broadcast a chilling update: James Montague's suicide, discovered by Agnes in a stable, no foul play suspected. The news sent a shiver down my spine. Could Agnes target me next, the sole confidant of her dark musings?

I decided to go dark, disabling my locator to sidestep potential legal entanglements, and texted Janet my intentions. Her understanding response came with a cautionary note about the First Minister's current disillusionment. It seemed everyone was on thin ice.

With the locator off, I hoped to become a ghost to Agnes. The thought that she might not flinch at my demise sent a chill through me, and I clutched the machete tighter as I drifted into a restless slumber. Dawn's chorus, led by a pheasant's call, roused me from uneasy dreams.

The morning's light was a balm to my wary soul. I broke camp with swift hands, eager to put distance between myself and yesterday's shadows. The road to Bonar Bridge unfurled before me, and soon I was weaving through the familiar routes of A836 and A949, the memories of past visits to Dornoch with my wife playing in my mind like an old film.

A pit stop at a garage to refuel the generator, and I was back on the road, skirting Dornoch, the A9 under my wheels. The day's ride was a marathon, ending only as the Calamity Firth Bridge receded behind me. Exhaustion claimed me as I collapsed into my teepee, the simple fare of pork pies and milkshake my feast.

Then, an unexpected visitor shattered the solitude. Agnes emerged from a blue Jeep with a smile that didn't reach her eyes. "Zachariah Black, your face is an open book of displeasure," she taunted. Her words hinted at dark deeds, and my heart raced. "You think I'd harm you, the co-architect of our plan?" she mused.

Her challenge hung in the air, "Prove I'm unarmed." I rifled through her jacket, half-expecting to find a weapon, but found none. "So, you followed through with my grim advice," I said, handing back her tweed shield.

"No need for such drastic measures," Agnes declared, her tone laced with a mix of relief and disdain. "My dear brother, in his misguided quest for sympathy, met his end by his own hand—a tragic rehearsal gone awry. You were right, Zachariah; the grisly outcome was confined to the stable walls, his own fingerprints the sole witness on the shotgun. And that note, meant to be a token of undying affection for Annabella, now serves as his final, ironic testament."

I perched on the trailer's edge, the weight of her words pressing the air from my lungs. Agnes continued, her voice tinged with a hint of offence, "Mr Black, I find it rather insulting that you'd suspect me of foul play, especially towards the one who secured my estate's future. Do you truly trust no one?"

"Trust is a luxury I can seldom afford," I confessed. "And forgive my bluntness, but your lack of sorrow for your brother's demise is . . . unsettling."

Agnes scoffed, "Sorrow? For a brother who brought nothing but turmoil and theft into my life? No, Zachariah, I shed no tears for him. And now, these opportunistic suitors emerge, feigning sympathy while eyeing my inheritance. They underestimate me, but thanks to you, I have all I need," she gestured to her belly with a knowing smile.

Her lips met mine with favour, a seal of shared secrets and survival. "Let's brew some tea and toast to life," she proposed, her eyes dancing with a rare joy. "I'll abstain from spirits until I'm certain of my little one's safekeeping."

Zachariah Black's Quest for Truth

The generator's hum was a gentle backdrop as I prepared two cups of tea, the aroma mingling with the earthy scent of the tepee. Agnes settled beside me, her glance fleeting, a playful smirk dancing on her lips. "I can read your thoughts clear as day, Zachariah, and the answer is a firm no. You've had more than your fair share of my affections of late."

Her refusal sparked laughter within me, a genuine amusement that felt foreign after such a long absence. It was ironic, really, how desire ebbed and flowed, leaving us chasing after the unattainable.

Agnes' voice cut through my mirth, practical as ever. "What's your plan from here, Zachariah Black? Will you take the A9, traverse Edinburgh, then venture cross-country towards home?"

I shrugged, the future a murky river of possibilities. "My path is yet undecided. But you have my number—let's keep the lines open. I'm curious to see how your story unfolds."

Her lips brushed my cheek in a parting kiss, a whisper of warmth before she disappeared into the world beyond my canvas walls. Alone, I let the tears come, a deluge born of relief, sorrow, or perhaps a blend of both. In that moment, I wished for an end, a swift conclusion to the saga of Zachariah Black.

***

Upon returning to the manor, Agnes dialled Annabella's number, a triumphant smile gracing her lips. "The estate is secure, and Zachariah Black has played his part. He's all yours now, Annabella."

Annabella's voice, tinged with both anticipation and trepidation, came through. "Agnes, any advice on how I should approach him?"

Agnes, ever the pragmatist, replied, "Your beauty alone is a formidable weapon. Employ a touch of allure, a hint of skin, but maintain your grace."

A light laugh escaped Annabella. "I'm willing to bear a little if it sways him. But intimacy? The very thought chills me to the bone."

With a knowing sigh, Agnes reminisced, "Oh, Annabella, you're unaware of the pleasures you're foregoing. Seize the moment and savour the experience. Fear not; our secret is safe within these walls, far from the prying eyes of your metropolitan circle."

***

Dawn's light crept over the horizon as I packed away my temporary home, the tepee, without the usual ritual of breakfast. The road ahead, the A9 towards Inverness, seemed to mirror my mood—downhill yet daunting, with the Murray Firth bridge marking the transition from the familiar to the uncertain.

The gradient out of Inverness was a physical challenge, but it was the expanse of the road—some one hundred and fifty miles—that weighed heavily on my mind. Seeking a semblance of connection, I activated my locator, a silent beacon for Janet to find me in this vast Scottish landscape.

The journey led me to the slip road for Aviemore, where I sought the solitude of seclusion to pitch my teepee once more. It was here, amidst the quiet, that loneliness and despondency found me, uninvited guests on my solo expedition. My bank balance, viewed on a small screen, was a number that reassured yet confined me, a reminder of the pensioner's life I led.

Janet's text was a lifeline, a reminder of the world beyond these roads. "Be cautious with your locator," she warned, her words laced with concern. My reply was swift, a reassurance for her peace of mind.

Her promise to find me once I crossed back into England was a beacon of hope, a future meeting to anchor my drifting spirit. Yet, there I was, wallowing in self-pity, contemplating the absurdity of ending it all under the wheels of a lorry. A sharp slap brought me back to reality—the risk of survival was far greater than the certainty of death.

My morose reflections were interrupted by the sight of luxury—a Rolls-Royce parking nearby. The occupant, a woman who bore a striking resemblance to Kate Moss, approached with an air of nonchalance. Her attire spoke of wealth and taste, and the pearl necklace at her throat was a siren's call to a life of ease in distant, sunnier climes.

As she neared, her blue eyes captivated me, and I stood, uncertain of the protocol. Was she royalty, or merely the embodiment of grace and affluence? To bow or not to bow—that was the question that danced in my mind as I awaited her approach.

Annabella halted a mere two metres away, her voice a gentle murmur. "I'm Annabella, and Agnes, our mutual friend, guided me to you."

My following words were a blend of condolence and dismissal. "I've heard about your fiancé's fate." "It's a relief, really.

You've spared me a scandal and preserved my family's dignity. Agnes mentioned your role in unveiling James's deceit."

I was puzzled by Agnes's motives and my inadvertent involvement. "My apologies," I offered, "but it seems any man would brave the highest peaks for your companionship."

Her smile was fleeting, and she gave a subtle nod acknowledging my compliment. "There's no need for concern; I'm vaccinated, and you're safe with me. Let's continue this conversation in my Rolls-Royce, away from the cold."

I trailed behind her, a mix of apprehension and curiosity guiding my steps. The chauffeur, a silent sentinel, opened the door for her, and she slipped into the car with an elegance that seemed almost otherworldly. I followed suit, enveloped by the car's luxurious interior as the windows tinted at the press of a button, cloaking us in privacy.

Annabella's coat fell open, revealing a pink blouse strained against the confines of propriety. "What's your preference?" she inquired, her tone smooth as silk.

"Bacardi and coke," I replied, watching her deftly mix our drinks from a hidden compartment. The clink of glass against glass punctuated the beginning of an unpredictable encounter.

Gratefully accepting the glass, I offered a simple "Thanks," my mind racing with questions. Annabella's intent gaze suggested a purpose beyond courtesy, a mystery yet to unfold.

"I'm flattered by your effort to find me," I ventured, breaking the silence. "But I sense there's more to this encounter than gratitude. My writer's intuition tells me there's a deeper plot at play."

Annabella's response was measured, her trust in me hanging by the thread of Agnes's assurance. "If you're seeking advice, I'm here to listen," I assured her, "on a journey of my own, destination unknown."

Her question was unexpected, veiled in hypotheticals yet hinting at a dark reality. "A brother ... disappearing permanently?" she echoed, my smile faltering as I pondered Agnes's involvement.

Annabella's grin was conspiratorial, revealing a bond forged in secrecy and sisterhood. "Agnes believes you could help, as you did with her brother," she confided.

The confines of the Rolls-Royce felt suddenly too close for such clandestine talk. "I'd rather not discuss this here," I admitted.

Understanding my caution, Annabella commanded her chauffeur away and followed me through the rain to my humble teepee. As the downpour intensified, she sought refuge inside. I hurriedly started the generator and plugged in a small heater, offering her a semblance of comfort amidst the storm.

Securing the teepee's flap, warmth enveloped us as the heater hummed to life. The soft glow of the internal light casts a cosy ambience. "Let's get down to business," I suggested, my gaze drifting to the kettle's gentle steam. "Tea?" I offered, but she declined with a smile.

Her bluntness caught me off guard. "He's quite the charmer then," I mused, sipping my tea thoughtfully. "Does that stir any envy within the household?"

Annabella's frustration was palpable. "The staff dare not show it, but his indiscretions are an open secret. And his taste for gambling is bleeding our estate dry."

I pondered her predicament. "High-stakes games in shadowy corners are his hunting grounds then."

She sighed, her distress clear as she toyed with her golden locks. "This conversation weighs heavily on me," she confessed.

The solution she hinted at was dark and desperate. "Luring him into a trap could be an end to your troubles," I said cautiously, "but it requires a confidant of unshakable loyalty."

"He's currently on the estate, then?" I inquired, steering the conversation carefully.

Annabella nodded, her expression grim. "Jonathan has a penchant for...excesses, away from our parents' watchful eyes."

"I see," I replied, understanding the delicate nature of her situation. "I'll help coordinate a meeting for him—strictly business. Send me a message, and I'll have your contact."

As time pressed on, I opened the teepee flap, signalling it was time for her to depart. Annabella sealed our agreement with a grateful kiss before stepping out into the night. Her perfume lingered as I watched her silhouette glide back to the waiting Rolls-Royce, a mix of elegance and urgency.

With a final glance at her retreating figure, I shut down the heater and generator, plunging the teepee into silence and darkness—a necessary precaution to ensure our conversation remained ours alone.

As the quiet hour passed, I poured over the map, pinpointing the perfect spot for Annabella's request. I sent a text to confirm: "Tomorrow, 9 p.m. at Loch Tummel. There might be a reward for your troubles."

Her reply was succinct: "Understood."

Despite the storm's fury outside, I found solace in sleep, waking to a Scottish morning of stark contrasts. After a leisurely breakfast, I journeyed to Loch Tummel, scouting the landscape under the guise of an early arrival.

I surveyed the terrain with a tactician's eye, seeking the ideal spot—for harm an encounter that would dispose of Jonathan.

As dusk settled, I prepared my ruse—a bag filled with harmless moss. The roar of a Ferrari engine broke the silence. I waved my makeshift signal from behind foliage as Jonathan approached.

The convertible halted beside me, its top invitingly open. I stepped forward with caution, splitting his head with my machete. His foot hit the accelerator, and the Ferrari plunged into the water.

With every ounce of speed my years would allow, I made my escape, ensuring the paper bag and stick was securely in my grasp. Once I reclaimed my bicycle and trailer, I pedalled along the A9, my lights piercing the darkness. Veering onto the A 8524, I sought a secluded spot to camp until dawn's light. An early departure was imperative; by morning, someone might stumble upon an abandoned car, a mystery unfolding with the sunrise.

7 a.m. on the A-9, travelling as fast as I could, desperately trying to gain some distance. Once I reached Perth, using side roads, I made my way to Kinross, staying beside Loch Leven.

Zachariah's mind was a tempest, each thought colliding with the next in a relentless storm. He grappled with the weight of his actions, the gravity of decisions made in moments that now seemed to stretch and warp the fabric of his conscience. There was a gnawing in his gut, a relentless whisper that echoed with every beat of his heart—a reminder of the line he had crossed, the irreversible step into a chasm of moral ambiguity.

He wrestled with the duality of his nature; the part that craved the thrill of the clandestine and the part that yearned for redemption, for a return to innocence that he knew was forever out of reach. The cold touch of metal and the flicker of flames haunted him, not for their physical sensation but for what they represented—the extinguishing of a path once walked in the light.

As he stood by Loch Leven, the chill of the water seeping into his bones, Zachariah pondered the cost of secrecy, the price of survival. He was caught in a web of his own making, each strand a choice that led him here. The solitude was both a balm and a poison, offering respite from prying eyes while amplifying the cacophony within.

In this moment of reflection, Zachariah understood that he could never outrun himself. No matter how far he travelled or how deep he buried his past, it would always be there, lurking beneath the surface like the dark waters of the loch—still, silent, and impenetrable.

Zachariah was taken aback by Annabella's sudden appearance, her silhouette a stark contrast against the backdrop of the dense trees. Her arrival was as unexpected as a gust of wind on a still day, stirring a mix of emotions within him. There was an initial surge of relief at the sight of a familiar face, quickly followed by a ripple of anxiety—why was she here now, and what did it mean?

Her presence was both comforting and disconcerting; she was a link to a life he once knew, yet her arrival could also signify change—perhaps even danger. As she walked past him with purpose, her coat billowing like the sails of a ship braving uncertain seas, he couldn't help but feel a sense of foreboding.

Inside the teepee, her hesitant voice only added to his inner conflict. Her words were measured, and her actions deliberate. She had taken steps to protect their shared secret, but the very fact that she had to do so reminded him of the precariousness of their situation.

As he sat there on his sleeping bag, watching her in the dim light, Zachariah realised that her sudden appearance was both a balm and a burden. She was an ally in this tangled web they had woven, yet her presence also amplified the stakes. He pondered what her next move would be and how it would affect their intertwined fates.

Annabella's voice was tinged with hesitation, a clear sign of the inner turmoil she was experiencing. "No one can contact Jonathan. Mother and father have reported him missing; obviously, I said nothing. I've rebooted my mobile, removing the text message you sent me. Even if you sent it in a code, I thought it could be incriminating."

"I tried to be vague. Why have you come to see me, Annabella? The police could be following you discreetly."

Annabella's response was hesitant, a reflection of the uncertainty that shrouded her actions. "I shouldn't think so. I've come to pay my debt," she said, her voice barely above a whisper.

The notion of debt between them was ambiguous, and his surprise was evident. "I don't recall asking you for payment, Annabella; you're a friend of Agnes."

Her next words were laced with a complexity that went beyond monetary transactions. "I think I should pay for your services. I've seen the way you look at me like most men."

The conversation had taken a turn, touching upon unspoken understandings and the intricate dance of human interactions. "And you are quite happy to oblige?" he asked, his tone neutral yet probing, aware of the myriad implications their exchange held.

"I don't have any choice other than to surrender," she said, a note of resignation in her voice.

Holding her hand gently, he offered her an out, his gaze earnest. "Don't if you're not interested in me as a person. The way you're glaring at me gives me the impression that you're disgusted with the whole idea. Call it quits. You go home, I'll continue my journey, and we'll never meet again." His smile was reassuring, an attempt to ease the tension, even as he questioned his own sanity.

Her shock was palpable, and her eyes were wide as she processed his words. "Are you serious? I can walk and leave without a worry."

"Exactly," he affirmed. "What is the point of engaging in something you don't want to? I'm sorry if I've made you uncomfortable; that was never my intention."

Annabella's smile was one of relief, a tension easing from her shoulders as she spoke. "You risk your freedom for no reward, Zechariah Black. Agnes is right about you. You are kind and considerate," she said, her words carrying a weight of sincerity.

Her admission revealed a complex web of emotions and plans, a testament to the intricate dance of human relationships. "She expressed her plan and what she'd performed with you. I couldn't imagine performing with you," Annabella continued, her honesty stark and unfiltered.

"Agnes remarked it was marvellous and well worth the adventure. She's waiting for final confirmation that she's pregnant. I must admit it's a clever idea on her part," Annabella shared, a mix of admiration and intrigue in her voice.

"You had better go, Annabella," he suggested with a gentle firmness. "You are the prettiest woman on two legs I've ever seen. James wanted his head examined. If I were him, I'd have married you."

Her response was a soft kiss, a gesture of gratitude and perhaps farewell. She patted his cheek and left the teepee with a smile that spoke of relief and resolution. As he sat there, the scent of his unwashed clothes lingering in the air, he heard the familiar sound of her mini starting up. She drove away, leaving behind a chapter in his life that perhaps was now closed.

***

Annabella pulled over to the roadside, dialling Agnes: "It's Annabella."

Agnes' voice crackled through, tinged with curiosity. "Heard about Jonathan. Did you settle your dues? I can only imagine his reaction, given your allure."

Exhaling a weary breath, Annabella confessed, "No, it's over. He sensed my reluctance and proposed we part ways—a relief, frankly. The mere thought of intimacy with him is revolting. I can't fathom what drove you to it."

Agnes paused, her tone serious. "Remember the mandate from the 12, tread carefully. I shared your sentiments once, but trust me, one taste, and you'll see things differently."

Annabella's response was a heavy sigh. The idea of Zachariah's hands on her was repulsive. Yet, she mused, if he had taken care to groom himself and possessed a fortune, perhaps her disgust would wane.

***

Dawn broke as I set my resolve to traverse Edinburgh's outskirts today. Retracing my entry route, I crossed the Forth Bridge, skirting Edinburgh to join the A68 towards Oxton and Jedburgh.

A pit stop at a garage allowed me to refuel, and I snagged a pack of sausages and a crusty loaf along the way. Soon after, I found the perfect spot to pitch my teepee. Now, beyond Edinburgh's reach, I slice my bread with my machete, the sausages hissing on the grill.

Janet's text arrives: "Your current location—where to next?"

I reply: "Might veer towards Cumbria's mountains, but Derbyshire's my aim. There's someone I need to see."

Her response comes swiftly: "You mean 'we', don't you?"

Puzzled, I type back: "What do you mean?"

Her next message hits like a thunderbolt: "You're not shooting blanks!"

A mix of shock and delight prompts my fingers to dance across the screen: "Well, that's news to brighten my day!"

As I bite into my sausage sandwich, too eager to wait for it to cool, her words sink in. Despite the surprise, a smile finds its way onto my face. With Janet's financial security, our child would want for nothing—a stark contrast to her own upbringing.

A black mini pulls up on the verge, and I can't help but suspect Annabella's arrival spells trouble—likely some dark errand involving her parents. Yet, as I savour my sandwich, I can't suppress a chuckle. The only thing missing from this peculiar evening is a bottle of my favourite tomato sauce.

Annabella navigated the damp grass, weaving between the trees in her familiar drizzle bone coat, carrying a hamper of moderate size. She set it down beside me with a gentle thud. "I've brought something a bit more hearty, Mr Black," she announced, unfolding a portable chair and settling down. With a flourish, she produced a bottle of wine and two glasses, uncorking the bottle with a satisfying pop and pouring.

Curiosity piqued, I couldn't help but ask, "This is unexpected, Annabella. What brings you here? Though I must admit, your company is a pleasant surprise."

She took a tentative sip from her glass; her demeanour tinged with unease. "Please, help yourself to the sandwiches. I can't fathom how you manage this nomadic lifestyle—a teepee without any comforts! Oh, and I've brought something; just a moment."

I watched as Annabella hastened back to her mini, retrieving a sizable plastic bag from the boot. Returning to me, she paused with an air of anticipation and presented a new sleeping bag. "I thought you might appreciate something fresh and more comfortable," she said with a hopeful smile, silently wishing for him to accept this token of cleanliness.

Gratefully, I accepted. "Thank you, Annabella. My old one has certainly seen better days."

Annabella perched on her collapsible stool, her voice laced with concern. "My brother's still missing. Can you shed any light on his whereabouts?"

Puzzled, I replied, "I'm afraid you're mistaken, Annabella. I don't know your brother."

With a swift motion, Annabella stood, unfastening her drizzle bone coat and removing her hat to reveal she was unarmed and unencumbered by wires. "See? No tricks, Mr Black. I'm not here to deceive," she said, rebuttoning her coat before sitting back down.

"You can never be too cautious," I admitted. "Trust is a luxury that often leads to a cell or a coffin."

She nodded solemnly. "Zechariah Black, your actions shielded my family's reputation from my brother's disgrace. His eventual discovery will stir some trouble, but we'll weather that storm."

"I suspect your brother and his Ferrari are at the bottom of Loch Tummel."

"A deep place indeed," she mused. "Without knowledge of his destination, it could be months before he's found."

"You've yet to say why you're here, though the provisions are welcome," I noted with a hint of suspicion. "You remind me of Agnes; there's always a motive behind your kindness."

. Annabella's grin was knowing, a spark of mischief in her eyes. "You see right through the façade, Zachariah Black. Agnes and I have shared quarters in one of her many estates. It's hard to imagine, given our past indifference towards each other. She never did fancy me with her brother, and now I understand her reasons. You, at least, had the decency to alert me to his duplicity. Frankly, my affection for him was never fervent; our union was more a matter of convenience than passion. His lineage may be notable, but our wealth far surpasses theirs. Agnes and I are members of the same clandestine circle, unlike our brothers—they lacked the fidelity required for such trust."

My laughter broke the tension. "Doesn't the notion of love ever cross your mind, Annabella? Or is your world solely woven from threads of wealth and status?"

Annabella's smile widened, a hint of intrigue in her tone. "I've digressed, haven't I? Our conversation should be about you and why I'm here. Over a few glasses of Chardonnay, Agnes confided in me about her fleeting liaison with you. Her revelations were quite unexpected. She reminisced about a particular night in the teepee, describing it as a remarkable encounter she wouldn't trade for the world. Yet, she conceded that your most memorable moments weren't confined to traditional settings."

Her eyes danced with curiosity. "It's curious, isn't it? How certain experiences can leave such a lasting impression."

Annabella's expression turned contemplative as she produced a small packet from her purse. "Agnes was quite insistent that I'd be remiss not to seize the same opportunity she had with you," she said, her voice laced with a mix of amusement and challenge. "She spoke of experiences that were transformative, and I must admit, I'm intrigued by the prospect."

Annabella slipped a pill on my tongue. "You have already admitted, Zachariah Black, that I'm attractive. Your eyes tell me exactly what you'd like to perform with me; perhaps within half an hour, you will."

I was taken aback by Annabella's meticulous scheming, with Agnes as her co-conspirator. Curiosity piqued, I asked, "Might you shed some light on why Agnes was so keen on me for her plan? There's no shortage of willing participants out there."

Her reply was swift and matter-of-fact. "You possess a certain steadiness, an unflappable nature that's rare to find. The men in our circles tend to be...less reliable."

I pondered her words, unsure whether to feel flattered or slighted. As I sipped my wine, I caught Annabella's self-satisfied smile and extended my glass towards her. "A top-up, if you please, Annabella. And perhaps another pill, just to ensure your evening isn't wasted." Her look of astonishment was almost comical—it would make for quite the tale if I ever decided to recount this encounter. It was clear that Agnes and Annabella were driven by their own agendas, with little regard for others.

Observing Annabella as she fulfilled my request, I felt a subtle warmth from the wine coursing through me. I drained my glass and proceeded to replace my old sleeping bag with a new, superior one inside the teepee. With a serene tone, I inquired, "Will you be joining me, Annabella?"

Annabella stepped into the teepee, her usual confidence replaced by a hint of hesitation. She sat next to me on the sleeping bag, carefully removing her hat. With deliberate movements, she unbuttoned her drizzle bone coat, slid it off her shoulders, and set it aside, a silent question hanging in the air between us.

Annabella's lips were hot and passionate, and she was determined to sample what she'd come for; she wasn't taking any prisoners. She made passionate love to me. Her skin was like silk to the touch there was no blemish to be seen.

Annabella paused, her gaze softening as she turned to me. Her kiss was tender, a whisper of understanding. "I see now what Agnes meant," she murmured. "You may not boast the vigour of youth, but there's a warmth and gentleness in you, an intensity that's both surprising and profound." With those words, she swiftly gathered her belongings, her departure as sudden as her arrival. The fading sound of her Mini's engine was the only goodbye.

Clad in the day's attire, I stepped out into the crisp morning air. Annabella's hasty departure was evident; her hamper remained, untouched except for the few sandwiches I consumed with my tea. Her petite seat, too, was left behind. Puzzlement washed over me as I pondered her swift exit.

I decided against burning the old sleeping bag, its memories too significant to reduce to ashes. Instead, I secured the hamper to my trailer and set my sights on Melrose, planning to traverse the country until reaching Loch of the Lowes by nightfall. The journey was serene, with narrow lanes offering passage mostly unobstructed by traffic, save for the occasional farm vehicle and wandering sheep.

The warmth of the weather was a welcome companion as I arrived at 6 pm. Without haste, I erected my teepee and savoured a coffee in the evening solitude. A ping from my mobile broke the silence—a text from Janet inquiring about my day.

I replied with a message of contentment, describing the steady ride and picturesque views. Her response came swiftly, a note of discomfort laced with the undertones of early pregnancy.

"Rest well," I texted back. "Do you need me to return and assist you?" Her situation weighed on my mind as I awaited her reply.

Janet's text arrived with a touch of humour amidst her discomfort: "You mean, hold a bucket for me to be sick in? I can manage that much; you go on and enjoy your adventure!"

Her words, though light-hearted, carried an undercurrent of strength and independence. It was clear she wanted me to continue my journey without worry.

Stepping out of my teepee, the crisp morning air greeted me with a silent hush. The loch lay still, a mirror reflecting the awakening sky. Not a soul in sight, I seized the moment of solitude. Shedding my garments, I dashed into the embrace of the loch's icy waters. The chill was a jolt, a vivid reminder of life's rawness.

I retreated hastily to the warmth of my shelter, drying off with brisk rubs that set my skin aglow. Clothed and cosy, I savoured the last bites of my sandwich, a remnant from yesterday's feast. As I scrolled through my mobile for news, one headline snagged my attention: "Car found by fishermen in Loch."

The loch's waters held no judgment, and as I put distance between myself and its depths, I felt a sense of liberation. The machete, my loyal companion through thick and thin, was the last tie to a past I was eager to leave behind. It was more than a tool; it was a symbol of survival, of choices made in moments where life hung in the balance.

Annabella, with her beauty that could turn the coldest heart warm, was now just a memory. A memory laced with the bitter aftertaste of her calculating nature. She saw the world through the lens of profit and loss; her affections doled out with the precision of an accountant. Love, that elusive alchemy of the soul, was foreign to her—a language she chose not to speak.

As I pondered over my next move, I couldn't help but wonder if our paths would ever cross again. Would she even notice my absence? Or would she simply calculate it as another transaction completed? With each step away from the loch, I felt the weight of these thoughts lessen. I was free from the chains of her expectations, ready to carve out a new path with my trusty machete by my side.

Nestled within the cocoon of my new sleeping bag, I was on the cusp of surrendering to sleep's embrace when the elements conspired to keep me awake. The weather report's promise of rain played in my mind like a foreboding lullaby, accompanied by the wind's symphony through the trees.

The sudden intrusion jolted me from my reverie. The harsh glare of a torch cut through the darkness, and instinctively, my hand found the machete's handle. But it was her voice that halted me—a voice that stirred memories of warmth and laughter. "It's me, silly," Agnes said, her presence in this remote place as surprising as a bloom in winter.

As she nestled beside me, her kiss banished all questions for a moment. Yet curiosity bubbled up like a spring. "I can't wait to discover why you have ventured this far from home, Agnes; I thought I'd never see you again," I whispered, my voice tinged with a mix of wonder and apprehension.

Her eyes held stories yet to be told, and as she settled into the curve of my arm, I knew that her arrival heralded a new chapter—one where past and present would intertwine in unexpected ways.

Agnes' eyes flickered with a hint of mischief as she recounted Annabella's hasty departure. "She was quite the sight, all flustered and dishevelled. Left her hamper and all," she chuckled softly. "But no, I didn't come for the hamper. It's just a basket, after all."

Her casual mention of her properties in Edinburgh and the plight of those less fortunate painted a stark contrast that wasn't lost on me. "The world's in a bit of a state, isn't it?" I mused aloud, thinking of the vagrants she spoke of.

The conversation took a darker turn with the mention of the news. A head found—such grim tidings seemed out of place amidst our secluded retreat. "Yes, I saw that headline, too," I replied, my voice lowering instinctively. "Makes you wonder what kind of world we're living in."

Agnes nodded solemnly, her playful demeanour replaced by a sombre reflection. "It does. But let's not dwell on it tonight," she suggested, her hand finding mine in the dim light. "We have this moment, and that's enough for now."

As we lay there, the world outside seemed to fade away, leaving only the sound of our breaths and the beating of our hearts—a reminder that life, with all its mysteries and chaos, was still capable of moments of peace.

Agnes' revelation about Annabella's brother added a layer of complexity to the already tangled web of events. The discovery of his car in the loch was a piece of the puzzle that seemed to connect Annabella, Agnes, and myself in ways I hadn't anticipated.

Her grin held a hint of irony as she spoke of Annabella's predicament. It was clear that Agnes had stepped into the fray willingly, yet her playful banter suggested she had her own reasons for coming.

As the night unfolded, Agnes and I found solace in each other's embrace, a quiet storm of passion that was as much about connection as it was about desire. Her whispered confession about a possible pregnancy brought a new gravity to our encounter. The thought that our union could have created life was both exhilarating and daunting.

We lay together as dawn approached, wrapped in the warmth of shared secrets and unspoken promises. The world outside, with its mysteries and dangers, felt distant, as we clung to the serenity of our shared sanctuary.

The first light of dawn cast a soft glow as Agnes made her swift departure, leaving behind a kiss and a promise of future encounters. I watched her silhouette against the morning sky, a fleeting presence in my now solitary world.

With her exit, the silence of the morning weighed heavily. I busied myself with breakfast, the ritual of coffee making a comforting routine amidst the chaos of recent events. As I sipped the steaming brew, contemplation took hold.

Months ago, my life was a predictable pattern, loneliness an unwelcome shadow since Hazel's passing. But life, it seemed, had other plans. The solitude I had once dreaded had become a crucible for transformation. My body and spirit had grown stronger, more resilient.

As I gazed out at the loch, its surface a mirror to the sky above, I realised that change was the only constant. And perhaps, in this ever-shifting tapestry of life, loneliness was simply another thread—one that could be woven into something new and unexpected.

The newfound strength in my legs was a testament to the journey I had embarked upon, both physically and emotionally. My upper body, too, had borne the brunt of exertion, shaping into a testament to my resolve.

As I pondered over the enigmatic allure that drew Agnes and Annabella to me, I couldn't help but feel a sense of bewilderment. My roots were humble, my life far removed from their world of privilege and calculation. Yet, they had both sought something in me—a raw authenticity, perhaps, or an escape from the gilded cages of their existence.

Agnes' desire to bear a child with me was the most startling revelation of all. The thought that I would be a father in genetics alone was both comforting and disconcerting. The child would lead a life of luxury, one I could never offer—a stark contrast to my own upbringing.

Annabella's motives remained shrouded in mystery. Our encounter had been a transaction of sorts, yet there was an undercurrent of curiosity in her actions. She had willingly entered my world if only for a fleeting moment, seeking an experience far removed from her own.

As I sat alone with my thoughts, I realised that some truths might forever remain elusive. And perhaps that was for the best—for in mystery lies the essence of life's endless possibilities.

The road to Moffat was a familiar one, each pedal stroke a rhythmic meditation that carried me away from recent complexities. St Ann's provided a serene backdrop for my teepee, a solitary sentinel amidst the whispering trees.

As night fell, I sought solace in routine, checking the news with no mention of Annabella's brother—a curious silence in an otherwise clamorous world. The sausages, a remnant of provisions, sizzled on the grill, their fate sealed by my adventurous palate. The crusty loaf, too, was on the brink of surrender to time.

Dinner under the stars was a simple affair, yet rich with the flavours of freedom and self-reliance. The crisp air hinted at frost's touch, nature's gentle reminder of the changing seasons.

Then came the abrupt end of my generator—a companion on this journey of solitude. Its sudden failure was a stark reminder of life's impermanence. I buried it with respect, crafting a makeshift cross from twigs—a humble monument to its service.

As I stood there in the silence, a tear escaped. It was not just for the generator but for all that it represented—the end of an era, the loss of Hazel, and the relentless march of time. Yet, as I gazed at the stars above, I knew that with each ending came a new beginning. And with my trusty bicycle by my side, I was ready to pedal into tomorrow's unknown.

Nestled within the confines of my teepee, I turned to my mobile for a semblance of connection in the quiet night. Dumfries was not far, and with it, the promise of a new generator to fill the void left by my old one.

Janet's message was a beacon in the darkness, her words tinged with distress. My reply was a matter of fact, reflecting my current predicament. Her offer to help was touching, yet I couldn't bear to impose on her, especially given her condition.

The night was restless, and my thoughts were entwined with memories of the generator—such a small thing to cause such turmoil. Dawn's arrival brought the habit to the forefront, and my hand reached for a machine that was no longer there.

Janet's concern was palpable through her texts, her affection woven between the lines. My response aimed to reassure her, to let her know that despite the setback, I was capable and determined.

As I prepared for the day ahead, I felt a sense of resolve. The journey would continue, powered by my own strength and the support of those who cared from afar. And perhaps in Dumfries, among its streets and shops, I would find not just a new generator but a renewed sense of purpose.

The morning air was crisp as I dismantled my temporary abode, my wristwatch marking the start of a new day. Dumfries awaited, and with it, the hope of a new generator to ease my journey.

The search was methodical, garage by garage until success greeted me in the form of a sleek Honda two KVA generator. It was a significant expense, but necessity often outweighed the cost. With groceries in tow, I set my sights on Gretna Green, amused by the romantic connotations it carried.

My detour to Rekik Point was a quiet affair. The gentle lapping of water provided a soothing soundtrack as I erected my teepee once more. The new generator hummed to life, a symphony of efficiency as it powered my evening's endeavours.

Dinner was a feast fit for a king, each sizzle and crackle from the pan a promise of satisfaction. The sandwich I crafted was a monstrous creation, challenging the limits of appetite and mouth capacity alike.

As night fell, I followed the salesperson's advice, changing the oil to ensure my new companion's longevity. The task was simple yet grounding—a reminder that even amidst luxury, maintenance is key.

With my mobile in hand, I reached out to Janet. It felt right to share my small victory with her and inquire about her well-being. The connection we shared was not just through messages but through shared experiences and mutual concern.

Janet's message was a jolt, her words laced with frustration and a hint of resentment. My advice was practical, yet it seemed to do little to ease her discomfort or her growing animosity towards me.

The silence that followed was telling, and I couldn't help but feel a pang of guilt. The situation was complicated, and while blame was shared, it did little to mend the rift that was forming.

Morning brought with it a new direction—Longtown beckoned, and then Haltwhistle. The spontaneity of my travels was liberating, each turn of the wheel a step further into the unknown.

The weather was kind, a gentle companion on my May journey. Breakfast was indulgent, perhaps overly so, as I found myself grateful for the electric bike's assistance. Without it, the journey would have been a struggle against the weight of my own appetite.

The road unfurled before me, leading through Brampton and onto the A69. It was there I chose a detour, drawn by a desire to connect with history at Hadrian's Wall. The ancient stones stood as silent witnesses to time's passage—a poignant reminder of humanity's enduring spirit.

As I paid my respects to Adrian's Wall, I felt a kinship with those long gone. Their legacy was etched in stone and memory, and for a moment, I was part of something greater than my solitary journey. I mourn the loss of a tree that has stood the test of time only to be destroyed by a chainsaw.

Not only had I indulged beyond measure this morning, but a creeping suspicion gnawed at my insides, whispering that I'd unwittingly embraced the new variant that was rampant here. The news had been clear: it was all around us.

With a heavy heart, I ceased my grocery hoarding, anticipating solitary confinement within my canvas walls.

Erecting my teepee became a Herculean task; each movement was met with protest from my overburdened limbs. My breaths were shallow and laboured, and when I sought solace in the minty refuge of a lozenge, it dissolved into nothingness—a telltale harbinger of the variant's cruel touch.

I burrowed into my sleeping bag's cocoon, seeking respite from the relentless ache that had commandeered my body. Paracetamol was no magic bullet, but it dulled the throbbing in my skull just enough to let the world fade away.

The next three days were lost to me, a void where time and memory refused to tread. It wasn't until I lay there, swaddled in down and isolated, that the ping of my phone pierced the silence. My wristwatch betrayed the passage of days with its unyielding march of hands. Janet's texts were a lifeline, pulling me back to reality.

I mustered what little strength remained to send a warning across the digital expanse: "Stay away. I may have succumbed to the new variant or some vile affliction. I've been entombed in this sleeping bag for three days."

Her reply came swift and fierce: "You can't perish on me, you old curmudgeon! You owe me years of nappy duty for this ordeal. Rest up; we'll tackle moving Zachariah Black when you're back on your feet. Love you."

My fingers danced across the screen with newfound vigour: "Your love is my anchor."

The flap of my teepee snapped open, revealing the imposing silhouette of a burly police officer. His voice, devoid of empathy, cut through the still air: "What do you think you're doing camping here?"

With every fibre of my being screaming in protest, I mustered a feeble defence. "I probably have the new variant. I wouldn't be here otherwise; I'm isolating, I can't move." The flap fell shut with a thud, casting me back into shadow. The officer's presence receded without another word—his silent departure as chilling as the illness itself.

Desperation clawed at my throat, a thirst only tea could quench. Crawling from the confines of my sleeping bag, I coaxed the generator to life. The hum was a comforting companion as I brewed a simple cup of tea. The sun, now at its zenith, showered me with rays that felt like an apology for the cold nights past.

Cradling the mug, I pondered over my condition. Was it merely a cold or flu? Escaping the clutches of COVID-19's new variant seemed too fortunate a fate. Yet there I was, basking in sunlight and solitude.

Hunger gnawed at me, but only faintly—a distant echo of normalcy. Remembering the emergency rations tucked away, I rummaged through my rucksack to unearth a chicken and mushroom hotpot. With the last drops from the kettle, I summoned life into the meal and clutched my favourite spoon like a lifeline.

As I waited for the hotpot to transform from rations to comfort food, patience became my meditation. The first bite was tentative, but as the flavours melded on my tongue—a hint of chicken here, a whisper of mushroom there—I allowed myself to believe in magic, if only for a moment.

My phone's ping shattered the midday calm, a harbinger of news. Expecting Janet, I was met instead by Agnes' name flashing on the screen: "You haven't moved for three days. Why?"

Fingers trembling, I typed back, "I may have caught the new variant and am unwell. I won't be moving for another two days unless I'm arrested."

Her reply was succinct, a bolt from the blue: "Confirmed pregnant. Stay safe."

Before I could process this revelation, another ping demanded my attention. Annabella's name glowed accusingly. Her message echoed Agnes': "You haven't moved for three days, why."

"I'm unwell," I texted back, "possibly contracted a new variant, and I won't be moving from this location for at least two more days."

The situation was bizarre. Two women of high society, both keeping tabs on me? Our shared history was rich with indulgence; memories of our encounters brought a fleeting warmth to my chilled bones.

Lost in reverie, I was jolted back to reality by the scorching heat of the hotpot against my tongue. I wrestled with the fiery mouthful, determined not to surrender to the pain. Once conquered, I approached each subsequent spoonful with caution.

The pot was now empty, and a semblance of strength returned. I nestled back into my sleeping bag's embrace, succumbing to sleep's erratic rhythm—awakening to shivers, then sweating in feverish fits.

As I lay there, drifting between consciousness and delirium, a stark realisation dawned: survival was not guaranteed. Either I would emerge from this ordeal reborn or not at all—and in the depths of my solitude, I wondered if it truly mattered.

The next day, as the sun climbed to its zenith, a sound stirred me from my restless slumber. Glancing at my wristwatch, I realised it was nearly lunchtime. The teepee flap creaked open, and to my utter shock, Annabella slipped inside, a hamper in tow, boldly venturing into what could be a viral lair.

"Are you out of your mind?" I exclaimed, annoyance lacing my words.

Her laugh was carefree as she retorted, "Quite possibly! But you've been there for me, Zachariah Black. This new variant is no match for me; I've had an exclusive vaccine," she said with a wink.

Before I could protest, she produced a syringe from the icy depths of her hamper. "You don't have the variant—just a common chill. Now roll up your sleeve; it's your turn for protection." Her movements were swift, leaving no room for argument as the needle pierced my skin.

"That never hurts!" she declared with a triumphant smile. "Did you hear about Agnes? She's expecting and couldn't be happier."

"Yes," I replied warily. "I'm pleased for her if that's her desire. Surprised she didn't opt for some genius donor from a sperm bank."

Annabella chuckled. "With her resources, Agnes could turn anyone into a prodigy. But it's not just about intellect—it's temperament too. You reminded her of her childhood pony—steadfast and gentle."

Her laughter filled the space as she teased, "And you, Zachariah Black, with those captivating eyes—you remind me of a charming rogue."

She then unveiled a bottle of brandy from the hamper, pouring two generous glasses. Handing one to me, she quipped, "This will either be your undoing or your salvation."

Next came a container of warm food which she placed on my lap with care. "Venison stew—nourishment from my estate. And don't bother asking for my last name; 'Annabella' will suffice for now."

I devoured the exquisite meal before me, each bite a testament to a chef's skill. Annabella sat close, her presence a puzzle. Her high-society air contrasted sharply with our current surroundings, and yet she seemed at ease beside me. I pondered her motives; my task for her was complete, yet here she remained.

"Zachariah," she began, her tone sombre, "the police believe my brother got entangled in a drug deal gone awry. It's a murder investigation now, but they're grasping at straws for leads."

I eyed her cautiously. "Don't let your guard down, Annabella. The police aren't fools. They could be tracking your car or tapping your calls. Safety is often an illusion."

She scoffed lightly. "My family's influence runs deep. The authorities wouldn't dare cross us without just cause—not without risking their careers."

A silence fell between us before I ventured a personal question. "How old are you, Annabella? You seem to share Agnes' youthful glow."

Her smile was enigmatic as she replied, "Take a guess. If you're wrong, you owe me a favour in the future—should I require it."

"Twenty-five," I answered after a moment's hesitation.

Her laughter was light and genuine. "Damn, spot on."

"I'm here for you, Annabella," I said, my voice softening. "Your presence alone is a balm to my weary spirit. You bear a striking resemblance to Kate Moss, but it's your blue eyes and golden locks that truly captivate."

She brushed off the compliment with a graceful tilt of her head. "I've heard such comparisons before. But tell me, Zachariah Black, why don't you seek to uncover my wealth or identity? Doesn't it pique your curiosity?"

I shook my head, sincerity in my gaze. "No, I'm grateful for the moments you've graced my life. Today, you've shown me kindness without expectation. True companionship can't be bought—it must be earned. And so, I'll always be here to support you with what little I have."

"Our bond is an unusual one," she mused, her eyes reflecting a mix of fondness and regret. "I can't bring you into my world; it wouldn't accept you. So instead, I come to you. Agnes says it's rare to find someone genuine like you—someone without hidden agendas, except perhaps a desire that flatters rather than offends me."

Her voice softened as she continued, "You don't see age; you see me. And in your embrace, I feel cherished—a sensation new and precious. Many have showered me with gifts, but none have sought to cherish me for who I am rather than what I have."

"Don't elevate me to sainthood just yet," I warned her with a wry smile. "I've been through the wringer—three marriages, a son lost to the waters, and a daughter who despises me. Maybe age has mellowed me, or perhaps it's this journey of self-discovery that's changing me. And in this journey, you, Agnes, and Janet have been unexpected guides."

Annabella's grin was knowing as she mentioned Janet. "Ah, Janet! Her mother, Vicky, was quite the sensation in London, a favourite among my father's acquaintances. She left that life behind after marrying a man with...let's say, a colourful reputation."

Her words left me reeling. Annabella knew far more about my life than I had ever shared. "Your knowledge of my history is unsettling," I admitted. "My mother's Canadian roots, her troubled marriage, her affair that led to my birth—all true. I've dabbled in agriculture, survived a near-fatal accident, and yes, I've had my share of ventures before settling into education."

Her smug smile widened. "I've done my homework on you, Zachariah Black. But fear not, for I seek only understanding, not leverage."

"Should I assume Agnes is equally informed?" I asked, a hint of unease threading my voice.

Annabella's grin didn't wane. "Naturally. We wouldn't involve ourselves with someone without due diligence. And despite how some may perceive you, we know better. Dyslexia doesn't equate to a lack of intelligence—in fact, many of the world's most successful individuals share the trait."

Her words did little to quell my apprehension about her extensive knowledge of my life. As she tidied away our meal remnants, she offered me another brandy, her smile never faltering. "I'll be back next week with your second vaccine dose," she promised. "Then you'll be as protected as Agnes and I."

I raised an eyebrow at her indulgence. "Two brandies might impair you're driving," I cautioned.

She chuckled softly. "Worry not, Zachariah. My chauffeur awaits in the Rolls-Royce outside." With that, she gathered her hamper and exited my humble abode.

Left alone with my thoughts, I marvelled at the day's revelations. Agnes and Annabella had done their homework on me, uncovering more than I'd ever expected.

In the quiet that followed Annabella's departure, I found solace in the solitude, my mind turning over the recent events. With my health regaining its footing, I took to my mobile, scouring for any clues about Annabella's brother, Jonathan Goldstone. The silence from the police on his case was deafening—no leads, no news, nothing that connected to me in any discernible way.

Janet's texts were a constant, a lifeline of concern that tethered me to a sense of normalcy. Her care was a comfort I hadn't realised I'd needed.

When strength returned to my limbs, I felt the call of the road beckoning. With methodical precision, I dismantled my teepee, securing it to my trailer with a practised hand. My rucksack, filled with essentials, felt lighter than before—perhaps a reflection of my unburdened heart.

The journey to Penrith was set before me—a path winding through Whitefield along the A686. Eighty-six miles lay ahead, but I was in no rush. The world could wait for Zachariah Black.

Aiston's outskirts offered a resting place for the night. There was no need to push my limits; recovery was still fresh on my mind. The injection Annabella had provided was a shield against unseen threats—a kindness I didn't take lightly.

As I settled in for the night under a sky sprinkled with stars, I pondered my newfound guardians—Annabella and

Janet. They had entered my life unasked but not unwelcome. As I drifted into sleep, I couldn't help but feel a sense of gratitude for their unexpected presence.

The spam was a touch on the dry side, but it served its purpose, filling the void left by a day of travel. I washed it down with a mug of strong coffee, its bitterness a welcome jolt to my senses. As I settled in for the night, my mobile buzzed with Janet's concern. Her words brought a smirk to my face, and our banter was a small slice of ordinary in an otherwise tumultuous time.

But the tranquillity was short-lived. A call from an unknown number pierced the silence of my teepee. "Mr Black," the voice on the other end spoke with an air of finality, "I regret to inform you that your car is beyond repair."

The news of my car's demise at Long Marston Airfield, crushed beneath the wreckage of an exploded lorry, was a stark reminder of the chaos I had left behind. The offer of compensation was cold comfort, but practicality won out. "Deposit the funds," I instructed, already thinking ahead to when I would choose a new vehicle—a decision for another day.

With the call ending and the night pressing in, I reflected on the strange turns my life had taken. From a simple journey of self-discovery to being embroiled in mysteries and accidents, it seemed fate had more in store for Zachariah Black than he could have ever anticipated.

The revelation about my car lifted a weight, but it left room for other musings—particularly about Janet. The age difference between us was a chasm I wasn't sure how to bridge. Did she envision a life together, or did she prefer to love from a distance? The thought of being seen as an old man chasing youth was unappealing, yet here I was, caught in the affections of two wealthy women who seemed to see past my empty pockets.

Dawn broke, bringing with it the stark reminder of my limited wardrobe. A stop at Tesco was in order—new jeans, tops, and shoes were essential if I were to avoid turning noses wherever I went.

Sunday's tranquillity was a balm as I pedalled toward Penrith. The roads were mine alone, save for the occasional gust that hinted at an impending storm. Tesco loomed ahead, a beacon of modern convenience in the rural expanse.

Mask in place, I navigated the aisles with purpose, selecting garments with the urgency of a man on a mission. But at the till, my plans unravelled. "I'm sorry, sir," the cashier said, her eyes apologetic above her mask. "Clothing isn't considered essential under the new restrictions."

I pleaded my case, gesturing to my bike visible through the window. "I'm not indulging in retail therapy—I'm in dire need," I insisted. "Surely there's room for compassion in these extraordinary times?"

The cashier hesitated, her gaze shifting between me and the clothes. After a moment that stretched too long, she nodded. "I'll make an exception this once," she conceded.

Relief washed over me as I paid for my items. It was a small victory, but it felt monumental—a reminder that even in a world constrained by rules and regulations, human kindness could still find a way.

The manager's nod was all the permission I needed. With a swift transaction, I was out the door, my new possessions in tow. The A66 to Keswick beckoned, its roads nearly deserted—a rare luxury in these times. The landscape unfolded like a painting, each turn revealing another stroke of natural beauty.

Off the B5322, I found a spot that seemed made for me—a hidden nook where I could set up camp. The ritual of changing into new clothes was like shedding old skin, and I felt renewed in my fresh attire. My old garments, now just a reminder of the past few days' trials, were soon reduced to ashes, their smoke mingling with the creeping mist.

The generator hummed to life, and soon, the aroma of pork chops filled the air. As I prepared my simple meal, the mist enveloped me, a blanket of white that made my secluded spot seem a world away.

With my meal ready on paper plates—a small but significant upgrade—I sat down to dine. The solitude was complete, save for the sizzle of chops and the whistle of the kettle. Moments like these reminded me of the simple joys of life on the road—self-sufficiency amidst nature's embrace.

The undercooked pork chops were a minor inconvenience compared to the hunger gnawing at me. I devoured them with a side of Jaffa cakes, and my makeshift dinner was a mix of necessity and indulgence. The mist outside my teepee turned the world into a shrouded mystery, urging me to seek refuge in sleep.

Morning greeted me with a persistent mist, a gloomy companion for my breakfast. My equipment was soaked, but my spirits remained undampened as I sipped my tea. Annabella's text was a spark in the dreariness, her playful banter a reminder of the connections that still tethered me to a world beyond the fog.

Her jest about Viagra was met with a chuckle, and as if on cue, the mist lifted, revealing a world draped in dewy cobwebs. It was as though Annabella's message had chased away the fog; her presence felt even in her absence.

Packing up took longer than usual; the wet gear was stubborn and uncooperative. But by midday, I was on the move again, Keswick behind me and Cockermouth ahead. The lake I passed was a serene sight, its calm waters tempting me to pause my journey.

Yet, as I veered towards Lowes Water on the B5289, I couldn't shake the feeling that my adventure had lost its direction. The roads seemed to loop back on themselves, and I wondered if I was truly seeking something or merely riding in circles.

A stop at a garage for petrol and provisions brought practical concerns back into focus. Fresh food was a luxury I couldn't afford on this journey—not with mild weather spoiling any chance of natural refrigeration.

As I continued on, the road ahead seemed both familiar and foreign—a path leading both towards and away from discovery.

By the tranquil shores of the lake, I pitched my teepee, a sanctuary amidst nature's splendour. Yet, within me, a storm brewed—a tempest of doubt and despondency that no serene view could quell. The thought of returning home surfaced, but it was swiftly dismissed; there was nothing for me there but walls to echo my own brooding.

Laughter broke through my gloom, a surprising sound in the silence. It was my own. The absurdity of my spiralling thoughts struck me, and for a moment, I found respite in humour. The steak before me—its origins questionable—promised a simple pleasure, a reminder that not all was lost.

As the peas warmed on the grill and the steak sizzled, memories of past journeys and past lives seeped into my mind. France, with its unfamiliar tastes and experiences, was a lifetime away. Those days were tinged with naivety and trust long since eroded by life's harsh lessons.

Trust is such a fragile thing, shattered by youthful love and marital betrayal. The pain of those betrayals lingered as a dull ache that time had dulled but never truly healed.

And then there were the losses too profound for words—the kind that leaves scars on the soul. My daughter, once so close, is now just a whisper of what could have been. My son's loss was a wound that no amount of time could mend.

In these moments of solitude, I confronted my life's tapestry—a mosaic of joy and sorrow, triumphs and tragedies. The thought of surrendering to despair loomed large, yet something within me rebelled against it.

I am still here, still breathing, still capable of laughter amidst tears. Perhaps that is enough—for now.

The sizzle of the steak was a comforting sound until it betrayed me, spitting hot fat onto my hand. I cursed under my breath, juggling the bubbling peas and the preparation of my makeshift meal. Despite the minor burns, the food tasted like a small victory—a well-earned feast after days of monotony.

As I sat by the lake, utensils cleaned and body still tingling from the icy swim, I pondered over my solitude. The absence of my wife's voice was a void no amount of nature's beauty could fill. Yet, in this silence, I found a strange kind of freedom.

Janet's text was a lifeline back to a world I felt increasingly detached from. Her struggles at the bank, her resilience in the face of discrimination—it all reminded me of battles fought and sometimes lost. Her strength gave me a semblance of hope, a spark in the fog of my own despondency.

"That's my girl!" I replied with pride, though I knew her battles were her own.

The map before me held both promises and regrets. My route had been aimless, but tomorrow would bring direction. Windermere awaited—a place tethered to dreams of speedboats and escapades on the water.

As night fell, I settled into my teepee with a plan forming in my mind. The road ahead was uncertain, but it was mine to travel—a path leading towards new memories to overlay the old.

CHAPTER 3

Cycling on to God knows where

The morning air was crisp, carrying the scent of impending rain. I set off after breakfast, my spirits buoyed by the promise of a new day's journey despite the brooding clouds overhead. The weather forecast had become a mere suggestion, its accuracy as fickle as the wind.

As I approached Ambleside, the skies made good on their threat, unleashing a downpour that sent me seeking refuge. I found solace down a narrow lane, a hidden nook perfect for my teepee. There's a certain peace that comes with surrendering to the elements and accepting the rain as an inevitable companion on this journey.

Inside my canvas haven, I watched rivulets of rain carve paths in the earth, their steady flow a soothing counterpoint to my restless thoughts. My mobile became a window to the world beyond, its screen glowing with possibilities—a poor substitute for my laptop, which I regretted leaving behind.

Perhaps this adventure deserved to be chronicled, its tales woven into a narrative that could capture the essence of solitary travel—the introspection it invites and the unexpected encounters it brings.

But for now, I was content to let my mind wander through cyberspace, seeking connection in a world that felt increasingly distant. As the rain tapped its rhythmic dance upon my teepee, I found a strange comfort in the solitude it enforced.

Taking me by surprise, a well-built man approached, appearing possessed, wearing waterproofs and a mask, wielding a baseball bat, swinging wildly, appearing out of control, and taking a wild swing at me. Thankfully, the bat only grazed my shoulder. Using my left hand, I reached for my machete, thrusting, pushing him away; he screamed in agony. I severed his head to silence him. I never caused this problem, but I will finish it. Thank God for the rain, washing the evidence away. I slipped on my waterproofs, looking over the gate behind my teepee. I smiled, seeing a manure heap steaming in the field by the hedge.

I quickly opened the gate; thankfully, no cars had travelled this narrow lane since I pitched—my teepee. I dragged the body across the grass, and using my camping spade, I carefully removed sufficient manure to conceal the body, grabbing his head by the hair I buried with the body. I made sure his waterproofs were damaged, enabling worms and other organisms to consume his corpse.

I packed away swiftly, the rain a relentless companion as I rejoined the road. Ambleside was a blur of wet stone and fleeting figures, all seeking shelter from the deluge. The road led me to a secluded spot by the side of Lake Windermere, a serene escape from the day's earlier chaos.

The rain, though torrential, was a curtain that shielded me from prying eyes. In my teepee, I found a moment of peace, the bruise on my shoulder a dull reminder of the day's trials.

The baseball bat, now discarded into the lake's depths, was an unwanted burden released into the water's embrace.

With my generator humming in the background, I braved the indoor elements to cook—a couple of eggs sizzling in the pan, their aroma mingling with the earthy scent of rain. The sandwich I assembled was simple but satisfying, complemented by the comforting warmth of freshly brewed coffee.

As night fell and the storm raged on outside, I found solace in my small sanctuary. The tempest outside mirrored the tumult of my thoughts, but here, at this moment, there was tranquillity.

Zachariah's thoughts meandered through the past and present, the stark contrast of his childhood memories with his current predicament. Sugar sandwiches—a symbol of simpler times, yet tinged with the pangs of poverty—were a stark reminder of how far he'd come and the struggles he'd overcome.

The ping of his phone cut through the silence, and a message from Janet brought him back to the now. Her concern was a warm embrace in the cold, damp world outside his teepee. Zachariah's reply was light-hearted, an attempt to bring a smile to her face despite the dreary forecast she mentioned.

Janet's response, playful yet firm, was a testament to their bond. Zachariah chuckled at the thought of twins, the idea both exhilarating and terrifying. But her sign-off, "Loves you," was enough to dispel any lingering unease from the day's events. It was a reminder that no matter what uncertainties lay ahead, they faced them together.

As Zachariah settled into his sleeping bag, the world outside continued its tempestuous dance. Yet inside, wrapped in warmth and the knowledge of Janet's love, he found a haven—a place where the storm could not reach.

Zachariah's morning greeted him with a rare gift—the warmth of the sun, a stark contrast to the previous day's downpour. The whims of the weather were as fickle as fate itself, and he couldn't help but muse over the irony as he pedalled toward Kendal.

The sunlight was a balm to his spirit, and as he cycled, his thoughts drifted to Agnes and Annabella. Distance had stretched between them, both physical and emotional, and he wondered if their paths would ever cross again. Yet, there was a sense of finality in that thought, a silent acceptance that some ties were meant to be left behind.

The sudden loss of power in his electric bike jolted him from his reverie. He coasted to a stop; his mechanical skills put to the test. The search for the culprit—a blown fuse—was a minor ordeal, but finding the spare was a victory that brought a smile to his face.

With the bike purring back to life, Zachariah resumed his journey, the road to Sedbergh stretching before him. The challenge of the terrain was a welcome one; it was in overcoming these small battles that he found his strength.

As the miles unfolded beneath him, Zachariah couldn't shake off the feeling of gratitude for the journey's lessons—the resilience born from solitude and the unexpected joys found in the simplest of victories.

With the teepee standing proud against the backdrop of Fairfield Mill and the River Ure, Zachariah settled in with a cup of tea, his thoughts drifting to Janet. The lack of response to his text was unsettling, a knot forming in his stomach as he sent another message into the void.

The arrival of the silver Range Rover shattered his worries, revealing a surprise that brightened his world. Janet's presence was like a burst of sunshine on a cloudy day, her playful scolding music to his ears. The kiss was a reaffirmation of their bond, a moment of tenderness amidst the wild.

Zachariah's compliment was genuine, his eyes reflecting the admiration he had for her—unchanged, unwavering. Her retort about the food and her overnight bag brought a chuckle; her practicality was one of the many things he loved about her.

As they settled in for the night, the new generator's hum was a lullaby that promised comfort. This makeshift misery, as Janet called it, was transformed into a cosy retreat by her mere presence. Together, they found contentment in simplicity, their shared laughter echoing into the night.

Zachariah's question was met with Janet's quick wit, and her humour was a testament to their easy rapport. The mention of deckchairs brought a smile to his face; comfort was a luxury he hadn't realised he missed until now.

As he set up the chairs, he couldn't help but admire Janet's preparedness, her attire a stark contrast to his own well-worn clothes. Yet, in her eyes, he saw the same warmth that had drawn him to her in the first place.

The sudden appearance of the Rolls-Royce was a curveball he hadn't anticipated. Annabella's grand entrance, complete with a chauffeur and her unmistakable presence, was as baffling as it was concerning. Zachariah's mind raced for an explanation, but words failed him.

Caught between two worlds—one of rugged survival and the other of opulent luxury—Zachariah stood at a crossroads. Annabella's arrival promised to unravel the simple peace he had found with Janet. As he faced the two women, each significant in their own right, Zachariah knew that the tranquillity of the day was about to give way to a storm of explanations.

As the sharp sensation of the needle subsided, he felt a peculiar warmth spread through his arm. "There, all done," Annabella said with a reassuring nod. "You're now as protected as one can be in these tumultuous times."

Janet's eyes met mine, filled with a mixture of gratitude and something else—perhaps a hint of the ambition that Annabella's patronage had ignited within her. "Yes, Zachariah," she echoed. "Protected and prepared for what's to come."

I rubbed my sleeve down, still processing the rapid turn of events. "And what exactly is to come?" I inquired, my curiosity piqued by their cryptic assurances.

Janet and Annabella exchanged a glance before Janet replied, "Opportunity, my dear Zachariah. The kind that could change our lives forever."

Before I could press for more details, Annabella interjected, "But let's not dwell on the future just yet. For now, enjoy the peace of mind this vaccine brings."

I took a moment to absorb Janet's words, the weight of our shared history with Annabella hanging between us. "Yes, our future," I echoed, setting my tea aside. "It seems we're at a crossroads, with more paths open to us than ever before."

Janet nodded, her expression serious. "With the baby on the way, we need to think about what's best for our family. And with Annabella's support, it seems we have more options than we might have dared hope for."

I considered this, the reality of impending fatherhood and the shifting tides of our fortune intertwining in my mind. "We do," I agreed. "But whatever path we choose, we must ensure it's one that brings us happiness and security."

Janet reached across her hand, finding mine. "I have no doubt that together, we can navigate any challenge that comes our way," she said confidently.

As we sat there, united in our resolve, I felt a sense of peace settle over me. The future was uncertain, but with Janet by my side and friends like Annabella in our corner, I was ready to face it head-on.

The gravity of Janet's proposal hung in the air, a tangible force that seemed to press upon my chest. Her logic was sound, yet the thought of abandoning my own home, my sanctuary, was daunting.

"Janet," I began, my voice steady despite the turmoil within. I understand the practicality of your suggestion. But it's not just about convenience or financial security. It's about us and our relationship. Can we truly blend our lives together in such a way?"

Janet set her tea down, her gaze unwavering. "I believe we can," she said firmly. "But it will require trust, Zachariah. Trust that I won't cast you aside; trust that we can adapt to living together as a family."

I pondered her words, the risk of vulnerability against the backdrop of our shared future. "And if we find that we're incompatible under the same roof?" I asked.

"We'll cross that bridge if we come to it," Janet replied with a hint of determination. "But I have faith in us. And I think deep down, you do too."

Her confidence was infectious, and slowly, a resolve began to form within me. "All right," I said at last. "I'll move in with you on a trial basis. We'll see how it goes."

Janet's face broke into a smile, one that promised new beginnings and shared dreams. "That's all I'm asking for," she said as she reached for my hand once more.

As we sat there, plans for the future slowly taking shape, I realised that this was more than just a compromise—it was a leap of faith into a life we would build together.

The idea of a motorhome brought a sense of adventure to my mind, a way to maintain some independence while embracing the changes ahead. "A motorhome could be our little escape," I mused, watching Janet as she busied herself with the hotpots.

Janet laughed, her eyes sparkling with mischief. "An escape, or perhaps a mobile extension of our home," she suggested. "And you're right about the facilities. With a baby on the way, we'll need all the convenience we can get."

The kettle whistled, and Janet poured the water with practised ease. The steam rose in gentle curls, mingling with the warmth of our conversation.

"And as for our...experiments," I continued, matching her grin, "I think we can find ways to be adventurous without any pharmaceutical assistance."

Janet's laughter filled the teepee, a sound that eased the lingering doubts in my heart. "I'll hold you to that promise, Zachariah," she said playfully.

As we shared the hotpot meal, the future seemed less daunting. With each laugh and tender glance, I felt more certain that together, we could face any challenge and find joy in even the simplest of moments.

As Janet's Range Rover disappeared into the distance, I stood there for a moment, the silence of the evening wrapping around me like a familiar blanket. The brief interlude of intimacy had been a poignant reminder of our connection, and her parting words echoed in my mind—a promise of closeness despite the physical distance.

I turned back to my teepee, contemplating the evening's revelations and the unasked questions that lingered. The mystery of Annabella's involvement in our lives was yet another thread in the complex tapestry of our relationship. But for now, it was a puzzle for another day.

With a sigh, I began to tidy up the remnants of our shared meal, my thoughts drifting to the motorhome Janet had promised. It symbolised a bridge between my past independence and our future together—a tangible commitment from her that bolstered my confidence in our shared path.

As night fell and the stars began to twinkle overhead, I felt a sense of contentment. Our journey together was just beginning, and though it would undoubtedly be filled with challenges, it was a journey I was ready to embark on—with Janet, our child, and a motorhome that would carry us toward new horizons.

***

Janet's call with Annabella concluded she felt a chill despite the warmth of the car's interior. The conversation had been brief, but it was laden with unspoken meaning. The potential birth of a male heir was more than just a family matter; it was a chess piece in a game that spanned generations.

Janet knew her role in this game was crucial. The child she carried could be the key to securing a lineage, and with Agnes also expecting, the stakes were higher than ever. She couldn't help but wonder about the man at the centre of it all—the father of these future heirs. Annabella's comments had painted a picture that was both vivid and unsettling.

Driving through the darkening roads, Janet's thoughts turned back to Zachariah. He was unaware of the larger forces at play, the silent battles being waged in whispered conversations and behind closed doors. She felt a twinge of guilt for keeping him in the dark, but she also knew it was for the best—for now.

The road ahead was uncertain, and Janet understood that the coming months would test her in ways she couldn't yet imagine. But she was determined to navigate these treacherous waters with care, for the sake of her child and the legacy they would inherit.

***

As I lay in the cocoon of my sleeping bag, the weight of Janet's gesture settled over me. The motorhome was more than a mere convenience; it was a testament to her dedication to us and to our unconventional relationship that defied norms and expectations.

It was a stark contrast to my own indecisiveness, my reluctance to fully commit despite the love I felt for her. But as I drifted off to sleep, I resolved to change that. Janet deserved more than half-hearted promises; she deserved all of me, just as she was willing to give all of herself.

The morning brought with it a renewed sense of determination. The rain had eased into a gentle patter, a soothing backdrop to my contemplations. As I packed away my belongings, I made a mental note to discuss the motorhome with Janet in detail—to make it not just a symbol of her commitment, but of ours.

The drizzle was a constant companion as I made my way towards Hawes, each droplet a reminder of the dreariness that seemed to mirror my mood. The mist on my glasses was like a veil, obscuring the path ahead and forcing me to peer over them in search of clarity.

By the time I reached Swinithwaite, my patience had worn thin. The allure of the open road had lost its sheen under the relentless grey sky. I found a spot to set up camp, and the hum of the generator was a comforting sound against the pattern of raindrops.

As I watched the steam rise from where rain met the exhaust pipe, I couldn't help but feel a sense of isolation. The warmth of the steam was a stark contrast to the cold dampness that surrounded me. It was in this moment of solitude that I realised how much I missed Janet's presence, her laughter, her warmth.

I settled into my teepee with my tea, contemplating my next move. The journey had been mine alone, but perhaps it was time to share it—to share all of it with Janet. The thought brought a small smile to my face, a flicker of warmth in the coolness of the day.

The collapse of the teepee was like the last straw, a physical manifestation of the turmoil I felt within. As I sat there, drenched and dishevelled, Janet's text was a lifeline—a reminder that no matter how far I roamed, her thoughts were with me.

I couldn't help but chuckle at her response. "Only you could find humour in my misfortune," I texted back. "But it's your love that keeps me going."

The exchange with Janet was a balm to my weary soul. It was moments like these that made all the hardships bearable—the knowledge that someone cared deeply for me, even when I was miles away, battling the elements.

I took a deep breath, letting the warmth of Janet's love fill me. The rain outside continued to fall, but inside the teepee, I felt a sense of peace. Tomorrow was another day, and with Janet in my heart, I knew I could face it head-on.

The news was unsettling, to say the least. The thought of another murder, executed in the same manner as Jonathan Goldstone's, sent a shiver down my spine. It was a stark reminder of the dangers lurking in the shadows, dangers that I had been all too eager to leave behind.

I lay back on my sleeping bag, my mind racing with the implications. If the authorities were to connect the two murders, it could spell trouble for anyone even remotely associated with Goldstone. And that included me.

The idea of changing my electric bike to an electric trike seemed more appealing by the minute. Not only would it serve as a disguise of sorts, but it would also ensure I stayed on the right side of the law—assuming no one decided to check the wattage.

I resolved to visit the garage in Leyburn first thing in the morning, weather permitting. It was time to sever ties with my current ride. Sentimentality had no place in a situation like this. If changing cycles could help me evade detection and keep the police at bay, then so be it.

As I drifted off to sleep, I couldn't help but feel a twinge of sadness at parting with my bike. But survival was paramount, and if a new set of wheels was what it took to stay free, then I was ready to make that change.

The morning sun was a welcome change from the previous day's gloom. I savoured my coffee and breakfast, feeling a sense of urgency to get to the garage before anyone else. The sight of the red trike in the window sparked a mix of emotions—excitement at the prospect of a new beginning, and apprehension about being more visible on the road.

The realisation that my bicycle's number plate could link me to my past actions hit me hard. I removed it with haste, discarding it in a skip, hoping it would be lost among the refuse.

As I watched the shop owner approach, his cautious gaze made me self-conscious. I donned my mask, trying to appear as inconspicuous as possible. The closed sign in the window made my heart sink, but his subsequent offer to help reignited a flicker of hope.

"I'm looking for a new ride," I said, trying to keep my voice steady. "Something reliable and...less conspicuous than my current setup."

His eyes flicked to my bike and then back to me. "I might have just what you need," he replied, motioning for me to follow him inside.

As we entered the showroom, I couldn't help but feel that this was a pivotal moment—one that could very well determine my fate in the days to come.

I listened intently as the sales rep listed the features and necessities for the trike. The idea of a fresh start with a new set of wheels was becoming more appealing by the second.

"The 500-watt motor should be sufficient for my needs," I mused aloud. "And I agree, looking road-legal is half the battle won."

I walked around the trike, inspecting it from all angles. The fat tyres promised stability and comfort, and with the additional accessories, it would indeed make for a smooth ride.

"I'll take your advice on the saddle and the mobile holder," I said, nodding in agreement. "Spare inner tubes are a must, and wing mirrors for safety. Let's make sure that trailer bracket fits snugly too."

The sales rep's smile widened as he sensed a sale was imminent. "Excellent choice," he said, clapping his hands together. "Let's get you set up and on your way."

As we worked through the details of the purchase, I felt a sense of relief wash over me. This trike would not only serve as my new mode of transport but also as a symbol of my determination to move forward, to outpace the shadows of my past.

I nodded in understanding as the sales rep explained the logistics of the sale. Considering its condition and the circumstances, the offer for my old bike was more than fair.

"£500 sounds reasonable," I agreed, trying to mask my reluctance to part with my old companion. "And £3500 for the new trike is a deal."

As I handed over my credit card, I couldn't help but feel a pang of nostalgia for the journeys my old bike and I had shared. But progress demanded change, and this was a necessary step.

The sales rep's workaround for the sale was clever, and I appreciated his efforts to protect both of us. The backdated receipt was a thoughtful touch, ensuring that I would have warranty coverage without any complications.

"Thank you," I said sincerely as he handed me the receipt. "I'm sure the 500-watt motor will serve me well."

Watching the mechanics dismantle my old bike was bittersweet, but as they worked on fitting my new trike with all the necessary gear, I felt a growing sense of excitement. This was more than just a new vehicle—it was a new beginning.

The sales rep's kindness, coupled with the mechanics' efficiency, made me feel grateful as I sipped coffee and watched them work. The all-weather cover was an unexpected bonus, and I thanked him with a genuine smile.

Riding away on the trike was a novel experience. The stability was reassuring, but it lacked the familiarity of my old bike. As I made my way towards Thirsk, taking the less-travelled roads, I couldn't shake off the feeling that I was riding something meant for someone else.

The trike's electric motor hummed along competently, but as I approached the hills near Pickhill, I realised that it lacked the raw power of my previous 750-watt motor. Pedalling harder to compensate, I couldn't help but question my decision.

Resting at Pickhill, I weighed the pros and cons of my new purchase. The trike allowed for more storage and stability against the wind—a definite plus. Yet, its bulkiness made it less manoeuvrable than a two-wheeled bike.

It was too late for regrets now. This trike was part of my new reality, and I had to make the best of it. The journey ahead would be different, but perhaps that was exactly what I needed—a change in pace and perspective.

Covering the trike felt like tucking in a new member of the family. The cover's snug fit promised a dry seat for the morning's journey. My teepee, now a familiar refuge, stood proud against the backdrop of the North Yorkshire Moors.

As I sipped my tea, Janet's text brought a smile to my face. Her teasing words were a reminder of our easy banter, and I retorted in kind, feeling a warmth that only an old friend could provide.

The farmer's arrival was unexpected, but his request was not unreasonable. The countryside had its own set of challenges, and rustling was a serious concern. I assured him of my vigilance, feeling a sense of duty to help protect his livelihood.

With the farmer gone and my role as an unofficial guardian established, I returned to my pasty with a renewed appetite. Making coffee seemed like the next logical step—a simple pleasure to cap off an eventful day.

As dusk settled over the moors, I felt content. The day had brought changes, some welcome, others less so. But as I sat there, with my new trike safely covered and my responsibilities as a temporary shepherd set, I couldn't help but feel that this journey was exactly where I needed to be.

The sudden flurry of activity was a stark contrast to the peaceful evening I had been enjoying. As I watched the vehicles speed past, I felt a mix of adrenaline and anxiety. My intention was to help, not to become entangled in a police matter.

The farmer's call was a relief. His words of gratitude were reassuring, and I appreciated his quick thinking in explaining my presence to the police. It was comforting to know that my actions had helped prevent the further loss of his farm stock.

As I settled down for the night, I reflected on the day's events. It had been a day of new beginnings, unexpected roles, and unforeseen heroics. Despite the initial doubts about my trike purchase and the unforeseen role as a 'sheep bodyguard,' everything had turned out well.

I drifted off to sleep with a sense of accomplishment. My journey had taken an unexpected turn, but it was these moments of unpredictability that made life interesting.

The howling wind was a lullaby that sang of the wildness of North Yorkshire, and I surrendered to its song, cocooned in my teepee. The morning brought with it a deluge that transformed the landscape into a transient river, but my spirits remained undampened.

As the sun broke through, banishing the rain, I was greeted by an unexpected but pleasant sight—two horse riders approaching. Their acknowledgement of my small part in thwarting the rustlers warmed me more than the emerging sunlight. It was a reminder that even the simplest acts can ripple outwards, touching lives and weaving new connections.

Their words left me with a sense of belonging—an honorary member of this close-knit community. As they trotted away, I pondered my next move. The beauty spot might be a cliché, but perhaps clichés exist for a reason—to be experienced and appreciated.

With a newfound sense of purpose and acceptance, I decided to continue my journey into the heart of Yorkshire.

There was beauty to be found, not just in places but in moments and in the people who made them memorable.

The smile lingered as I packed up my teepee, a silent companion to my thoughts. The A61 was a familiar friend, leading me to sustenance in the form of groceries that promised a hearty meal later. The A170 beckoned, and I heeded its call, finding solace in Wass, away from the relentless wind.

Today's journey was measured not in distance but in the ease with which I settled into my new routine. My teepee stood once more, a testament to my nomadic existence, as I set about cooking with a determination born from past culinary mishaps.

The pork chops sizzled, their aroma mingling with the earthy scent of peas warming in their tin. As the meal came together, I prepared my Cadbury smash with an almost ceremonial reverence. With a paper plate laden with food, I sat back and indulged in the simple yet profound pleasure of a meal cooked under the open sky.

Each bite reminded me of the freedom this journey afforded me—the freedom to roam, explore, and savour life's simple joys.

Janet's text was a surprise that sparked a mixture of emotions. The picture of the motorhome was a statement of intent, a grand gesture that spoke volumes of her feelings. Her playful message about testing the bed brought a hearty laugh from me, and I played along with equal jest.

Agnes' message was a stark contrast, filled with news of life blossoming. The thought of twins brought a sense of pride and a pang of longing. Her assurance that we would meet again was a balm to my nomadic soul.

As I sat there, amidst the fading light, I realised that my journey was not just about the places I'd see or the roads I'd travel. It was also about the people who touched my life, however briefly. Janet's spontaneity and Agnes' warmth—were waypoints on my map, guiding me as much as any road sign.

With a heart full of laughter and a mind at peace, I looked forward to whatever tomorrow would bring.

The unexpected sight of Annabella emerging from a black mini was like a scene from a film, surreal and yet vividly real. Her smile was infectious, and it was impossible not to be drawn in by her confidence and the air of victory that seemed to surround her.

Her attire was a bold statement; the Driza-bone coat was left open to reveal the daring choice of a miniskirt and corset-style top beneath. It was clear she had dressed with intention, and as she approached my teepee with that knowing grin, I felt a mix of anticipation and admiration.

There was an unspoken understanding between us, a mutual recognition of the attraction that had simmered beneath the surface. As she stood before me, stunning and unapologetic in her desires, I knew I would be more than happy to oblige.

In that moment, with the twilight as our backdrop, we embraced the spontaneity of life and the unexpected encounters that make it all the more thrilling.

She entered my teepee, removing her Driza-bone and hat casting to one side; she lay in my sleeping bag. I'm making love to her in seconds; we have not spoken a word; I'm struggling to control my excitement. I can imagine her walking around London looking like that; half the place would follow her with their tongues dragging on the pavement. I don't know what possessed her to find me, but at this precise second, I didn't care. I watched a pleasing smile come over her expression, and she rolled to one side. She dashed outside, coming back moments later. Not bothering to fasten her corset, slipping a Viagra tablet on my tongue and passing me my drink, she was far from finished with me. "Why are you like this, Annabella? I'm not complaining. You are a dream for anyone."

Annabella's candid admission was a revelation, a glimpse into her desires that were as raw and real as the untamed landscape around us. Her request for coffee was almost mundane in its normalcy, a grounding act that brought a sense of domesticity to our wild encounter.

As I busied myself with the generator, her transformation was not lost on me. The layers of societal expectations seemed to have fallen away, leaving a woman who sought authenticity over pretence. Her smile was genuine, and her teasing comment about my new trike and the unfortunate fate of a man in a manure pile hinted at a shared secret, a complicity that went beyond words.

Her confidence was magnetic, and I found myself drawn to this new Annabella who defied expectations and embraced her desires without apology. It was a reminder that people could surprise us, revealing depths we might never have suspected.

She placed her cup to one side, making herself comfortable, with the casual comment: "I'm waiting." She didn't need to ask twice. I was glowing like a beetroot; the more I surveyed her beautiful figure, the more I couldn't believe my luck. I'm still puzzled why she finds me enjoyable when there are eighteen-year-old men out there who would chase her with the enthusiasm of a stallion. We lay beside each other. I glanced at my wristwatch: midnight; Annabella was going nowhere.

The morning brought a softness between us, a tenderness that lingered in her kiss. It was a contrast to the fiery passion of the night before, showing another facet of our connection.

Annabella's decision to stay for coffee and share a moment of normalcy before the day began was a small but significant gesture. It spoke of a desire for something more than just fleeting encounters—a hint of longing for shared time, however brief.

Her words as she prepared to leave were laced with the reality of our situation. The need for discretion, the outside world with its prying eyes, was a reminder of the delicate balance we maintained. I felt the weight of her kiss as she left, a promise and a goodbye all at once.

Watching her drive away, I was struck by the complexity of human connections—how they can be both simple in their intensity and complicated by circumstances. As her car disappeared from view, I was left with memories of the night and a quiet hope for what might come.

As I packed up my teepee, my thoughts were a tangle of emotions and questions. The open road ahead was both a path to new adventures and a chance to reflect on the complexities of my relationships with Agnes and Annabella. The realisation that they both sought my company was flattering, yet it left me pondering the intricacies of human connections.

The B1257 stretched before me, a ribbon of possibilities, and I let the steady hum of my trike's engine soothe my contemplative mood. The countryside offered a sense of freedom, a place to set up camp away from the scrutiny of the world.

The sight of Janet's motorhome was unexpected, her smile a beacon of warmth in the open expanse. Her invitation was a welcome one, and I stepped into the comfort of her luxurious motorhome with a sense of curiosity. The offer of a meal and a shower was tempting, the promise of simple comforts after days on the road.

Janet's practical request to plug in my generator reminded me of the self-sufficiency required by life on the road. It was a different kind of intimacy, one born out of shared experiences and an understanding of this nomadic lifestyle.

As I settled into the rhythm of this new encounter, I couldn't help but marvel at the unexpected turns life could take. Each person I met along the way added another layer to my journey, each moment a story in itself.

The practicalities of life on the road were made easier with Janet's thoughtful preparations. The generator hummed to life, infusing the motorhome with energy, a small but significant luxury. The space was cosy, a testament to efficient living and the joy of simplicity.

The shower was a refreshing respite, washing away the dust of travel. Janet's casual demeanour and the comfort of the motorhome made it easy to relax into this new routine. The meal she prepared was hearty, a shared pleasure as we sat together, the world outside our window.

Janet's suggestion sparked a vision of future adventures, and her idea of a baby trailer became an intriguing possibility. It was a blend of our individual passions—a way to merge the freedom of my rides with the companionship of shared journeys.

As the evening unfolds, Zachariah and Janet find themselves wrapped in the comfort of the motorhome. Their conversation is a blend of playful jests and earnest plans for the future. The warmth of the space around them is matched only by the warmth in their hearts as they envision a life of shared adventures and new beginnings.

The motorhome, with its promise of mobility and comfort, stands ready to carry them across the landscapes of their dreams. From the rugged beauty of Scotland to the rolling hills of Wales, each destination holds the potential for discovery and the creation of cherished memories.

Janet's suggestion of adding a baby trailer for their cycling excursions is met with Zachariah's thoughtful consideration. The idea of family outings, complete with picnics and laughter, fills him with a sense of anticipation. It's a vision of a life that balances freedom with togetherness, exploration with homecoming.

Their dialogue continues, a delicate interplay between jest and sincerity, as they navigate the contours of their relationship. Each word, each glance, each shared smile is a step further into a future they are crafting together—a future that holds as much promise as the open road before them.

The motorhome's cosy interior enveloped us as we sat together, sipping our coffees. Janet's smile held a mix of satisfaction and mischief, and her comment about the drive from Buxton hinted at a deeper connection—one that seemed to involve Annabella, a force to be reckoned with.

Her mention of the letter from senior management piqued my curiosity. It was clear that Janet was no ordinary bank manager; her competence and influence extended beyond the branch. Annabella's involvement added an intriguing layer to the story—a reminder that relationships could shape our professional lives as much as our personal ones.

As we sat there, the motorhome cocooning us in warmth, I wondered about the complexities of their interactions. Janet's warning about not crossing Annabella echoed in my mind. It was a puzzle—one that I was eager to unravel as our journey continued.

Having experienced both passion and practicality during his encounters with Janet and Annabella, Zachariah finds himself at a crossroads. The motorhome adventure with Janet has opened new possibilities, and he contemplates the delicate balance between yielding and asserting in their relationship. As he watches Janet drive away, he wonders how this unexpected chapter will shape his journey. Perhaps the road ahead holds more surprises than he could have imagined.

Zachariah, torn between practicality and Janet's determination, contemplates the future of his trike. The hills and the extra-large motor weigh on his mind, but Janet's vision of family outings tugs at his heart. As he envisions a baby trailer attached to the trike, a chilling thought crosses his mind—a juggernaut threatening their idyllic plans. The road ahead holds both promise and uncertainty, and Zachariah must navigate this new chapter with care.

I decided to head toward Hornsea. The narrow track led me to a secluded piece of coastline—a hidden gem where the sea whispered secrets and the wind danced with the grass. The traffic noise faded, replaced by the rhythmic waves and the distant cries of gulls. I pitched my teepee, its canvas a shelter against the elements.

As I settled in, I couldn't help but feel a sense of freedom. Here, far from the bustle of civilisation, I was a speck on the edge of the world. The police cars that had passed me earlier were forgotten; their suspicion was lost in the vastness of the horizon.

The wind picked up, tugging at the teepee's guy ropes. I secured them, knowing that the lullaby of crashing waves would accompany tonight's sleep. The kettle whistled, and I made my first cup of tea, savouring the warmth against the chill of the evening.

The coast held its secrets—of shipwrecks and lost souls, of storms and sunsets. I sat there, mug in hand, and wondered what stories this secluded spot would tell me tonight. I watched a woman approach without a swimsuit, her attributes plain to see, taking me by surprise with her boldness.

The woman's words hung in the salty air, a mix of curiosity and caution. Her knowledge of my drone-assisted sheep-rustler-catching exploits surprised me. I wondered how far those pictures had travelled, how many eyes had scrutinised my actions from afar.

As she dried herself, her gaze never wavered. There was an intensity to her scrutiny as if she were assessing me beyond the surface. The offer of tea or coffee was a polite gesture, but her guarded demeanour hinted at deeper motives.

I stood, brushing sand from my trousers. "Zachariah Black," I confirmed, "and you are?"

She hesitated, then offered a name. "Evelyn. Evelyn Hartley."

The pieces fell into place—the secluded coast, the private ownership, and now the enigmatic woman before me. Evelyn Hartley was no ordinary stranger. Her presence held secrets, and I wondered what role she would play in my unfolding journey.

Evelyn Hartley, the enigmatic woman with a penchant for cold sea swims, revealed herself. Her knowledge of my past exploits—both literary and explosive—left me momentarily speechless. As we sat there, sharing coffee and guarded smiles, I wondered what other secrets she held.

Her cliffside abode and the fierce loyalty of her two dogs added to the intrigue. Evelyn was no ordinary recluse; she was a puzzle waiting to be solved. As the waves crashed against the shore, I realised that our chance encounter might lead to more than just conversation—it could be the beginning of another unexpected chapter in my journey.

"I must take my leave now. As much as I relish the tranquillity of this spot, the prospect of an encounter with two irate canines is less than appealing. Allow me a quarter of an hour to gather my belongings, and I shall depart. You will not see me again unless fate decrees otherwise—either through the unlikely success of my literary endeavours or an untimely demise beneath the wheels of a juggernaut."

"Remain as my guest," she offered, her voice carrying a note of unexpected kindness. "You've caused no harm, and your presence is merely a whisper in the night. Age has rendered you inconspicuous, a benign visitor in this secluded haven." With that, she turned away, her figure receding along the path that snaked away from the cliff's edge—the very path I had descended earlier. The towels she clutched hinted at her destination or perhaps her lifestyle. I watched her go, pondering the possibility that she belonged to the free-spirited fold of naturists.

As the twilight deepened, I crafted a humble supper—a sandwich layered with fried egg and bacon, its texture punctuated by an unexpected sandy crunch. Settling into the embrace of the night, I pondered the day's peculiar exchange. The notion of a drone had been alien to my thoughts, yet it seemed my trusty bicycle had dispersed across the nation, piece by piece. This newfound notoriety was evident in the waves of passersby—a silent acknowledgement of my existence.

Why, then, amidst this quiet recognition, had the authorities not descended upon me? My trike's legality was dubious at best, yet the police had spared me their attention. Could it be indifference, or was there something more? Each unanswered question wove itself into the fabric of a grander enigma, transforming my reality into the pages of a mystery novel yet to be written.

Awakened by the raucous cries of seagulls, I greeted the dawn with a brisk concoction in lieu of breakfast, keen to avoid a repeat of last night's unintended crunchy fare. With my belongings swiftly stowed, I embarked on the arduous ascent from the beach to the promise of solid ground. The tarmac of the road to Doncaster was a welcome sight, and I merged onto the A161 with a sense of purpose, setting my sights on Worksop.

The day's ride was a testament to endurance; sixty miles of pedalling that etched a new record in my cycling chronicles. As dusk approached, I sought refuge in a hidden grove, where I erected my teepee—a solitary sentinel amidst the quiet of the countryside. My only pause had been a pragmatic one, to replenish supplies and partake in the simple luxury of a proper lavatory. Refreshed, I rejoined the A620, my wheels carrying me steadily to my current haven beyond Saundby.

Laughter bubbled up within me as I spotted the gleaming silver Range Rover pulling up. Janet emerged, a plastic bag in hand, wafting the unmistakable aroma of fish and chips. "Come along, Zachariah, let's savour these in the warmth of my Range Rover," she beckoned.

We nestled into the back seat, the comfort of the car amplifying the enjoyment of our quintessentially British feast. Between bites, Janet mused with a playful twinkle in her eye, "You're nearly there, Zachariah. By tomorrow, you'll be at my doorstep, discovering my world. Perhaps you'll even stay the night and indulge in a bit of mischief," her grin widening.

I chuckled, feigning ignorance. "But Janet, your abode remains a mystery to me; your visits have always been to my humble teepee for moments of delightful indiscretion."

She tapped her forehead in mock realisation. "Ah, how silly of me! I assumed you knew. Rather than navigating a maze of directions, let's meet in Buxton, just past the cement works. You can trail me from there."

I nodded, a hint of jest in my voice. "Just bear in mind, Janet, my trusty steed only gallops at a stately pace of fifteen miles per hour."

"Recall the place where you replenished your generator's oil. That's where we'll rendezvous," Janet suggested with a gentle smile. "Navigating the labyrinthine village to find my house is a task even I dread. It's easier if I just show you the way."

In the quiet that followed her departure, I brewed a pot of coffee, the rich aroma mingling with the crisp morning air. We shared a cup, our hands brushing, a silent acknowledgement of the connection we'd forged. A kiss, a fleeting embrace, and then she was gone, her vehicle a fading speck on the horizon.

Alone in my teepee, I wrestled with my desires. The thought of cohabitation with Janet stirred a mix of anticipation and trepidation. She was an enigma, her trustworthiness a stark contrast to the duplicity I'd known. Yet, the prospect of sharing a life with her painted a picture both alluring and daunting.

The morning greeted me with a deluge, a relentless downpour that seemed to mock my awakening. Donning my waterproofs, I brewed a steaming cup of tea, the warmth a stark contrast to the rain's chill. With practised motions, I dismantled my teepee, tucking away my transient home into the confines of my pack.

The day's journey was a marathon of persistence, six hours of unyielding pedalling that brought me to the departure from B6049. As the clock's hands aligned at 5, I couldn't help but wonder if Janet's thoughts were tracing my route. My concerns were unfounded; there she was, her Range Rover a beacon of certainty in the rain's haze. Her wave was a signal to follow, and I caught the glint of her smile in the mirror—a silent reassurance.

The lane we took was a ribbon of seclusion, barely accommodating her vehicle. It led us to a period cottage, its grey slate roof a testament to time. This was Janet's domain, a revelation far removed from my expectations. She navigated her Range Rover with precision, parking behind a motorhome as I found a spot on the verdant lawn. She dashed to the door, keys at the ready, and I followed suit, seeking shelter from the storm in what promised to be a haven of stories yet to unfold.

The cottage's interior was a tableau of meticulous order, each item a testament to Janet's dedication to cleanliness. Not a speck of dust dared to settle, not a cushion out of alignment—it was a sanctuary sculpted by an unwavering hand.

Janet's movements were a dance of efficiency as she peeled away my layers, drenched from the day's trials. My waterproofs were first to go, followed by the rest until I was down to my essentials. Her command was gentle yet firm, "Shower, Zachariah. Our bedroom is just to the right. I've procured new attire for you; they await your fitting. Should there be any discrepancies, my sewing machine and I shall attend to them. Proceed, cleanse away the journey's grime. I shall tend to the aftermath here. Discard the damp towels on the shower floor; I'll collect them post haste."

With a nod, I retreated to the warmth of the shower, the water cascading over me, washing away the remnants of the road. The promise of fresh clothes and a new beginning lingered in the steam, an unspoken vow of change at Janet's hand.

I stood in the sanctuary of Janet's home, a realm so immaculate it bordered on the surreal. The shower was a gleaming oasis, its tiles so pristine that they could have doubled as dinner plates. Refreshed and wrapped in the warmth of a towel, I ventured into the bedroom—a realm crowned by a majestic four-poster bed that whispered tales of bygone luxury.

The wardrobe doors swung open to reveal a treasure trove of garments, a collection so vast and varied it could only be the result of a generous heart and a lavish hand. Jeans that fit as if tailored for me, a shirt that felt like a second skin, socks that embraced my feet with the softness of a morning breeze, and trainers that marries style with comfort—each item a silent testament to Janet's thoughtful care.

Clad in these new vestments, I felt a transformation—not just of attire but of spirit. The trainers, a symbol of a path I seldom walked, now carried me forward into a world reshaped by kindness and unexpected companionship.

The sound of Janet's footsteps on the plush carpet was a prelude to her presence, a soft herald of her approach. She entered the bedroom, her movements a blend of purpose and tenderness, and her kiss was a seal of affection that promised more to come. "That's where passion will unfold later," she said with a playful grin, her eyes alight with anticipation.

Her question about the house hung in the air, but before words could form, she whisked me away to another room—a sanctuary of potential, bathed in neutral tones and furnished with every conceivable comfort for a child. I stood there, breathless, taking in the meticulous care she had poured into every corner. "You have been busy, Janet," I managed to say. "And these clothes, they're wonderful. How can I ever repay you?"

Her gaze fixed on me, a flicker of annoyance crossing her features. "Me future wife, you future husband; we share," she declared, her voice a mix of admonishment and affection. "Or are you getting cold feet, Zachariah?"

A heavy sigh escaped me as I grappled with the rapid pace of change. "Give me time to catch up with you, Janet. I'm rather set in my ways. You are 30 and look 20. I'm waiting to wake up from this dream."

The room, with its promise of new beginnings, seemed to echo my sentiments—a blend of hope and hesitation, of dreams and the daunting reality of stepping into a shared future.

Janet's offer was a testament to her understanding, a gentle concession to my comfort. "If the familiarity of your motorhome or the teepee calls to you, Zachariah, take refuge there," she said. "But know that my bed will feel all the emptier without you. And remember, as my pregnancy progresses, our moments of intimacy will become memories. Seize the joy we have now."

Descending the stairs, the living room welcomed us with its rustic charm. The oak beams stood as silent guardians of history, their presence a perfect complement to the cottage's character. Not a single cobweb marred the corners, each space a reflection of Janet's meticulous care. The open fire crackled its glow a bastion against the evening chill.

We nestled into the couch, enveloped by the luxury of Janet's choices—a surprising indulgence given her penchant for perfection. As we sat entwined, the world outside faded, and I surrendered to the comfort of the moment, drifting into slumber.

Awakening to Janet's voice was like emerging from a dream. "Dinner is served, Zachariah," she announced, her silhouette framed by the kitchen's warm light. The day's journey had led me here to a place of unexpected solace and the promise of a shared future, however uncertain it may be.

The smile on my face was a mirror to the warmth that filled the room. I stepped into the kitchen, where history lay etched into the flagstone floor, each stone a silent witness to the lives that had passed before. The table was a canvas of Janet's affection, dishes arrayed like a constellation of culinary delights, candles flickering their approval, and cutlery aligned with ceremonial precision. It was a setting that transcended the ordinary, elevating our meal to a celebration.

"Is this a nightly tradition for you, Janet?" I inquired, half-expecting tales of daily grandeur.

Her response was a symphony of sincerity. "No, this is but a glimpse of my gratitude for you, Zachariah. You've turned the tides of my once sombre existence into a sea of joy. In the brief span of our acquaintance, fortune has smiled upon me—wealth, advancement, and new life blossoming within. Had someone prophesied such a future a year prior, I would have met it with disbelief. But here we are, and I need you to understand—you are cherished, you are desired. Accept the gifts of the present, and cast aside the shadows of doubt. There is no deception here, only the truth of my heart."

Janet's vision for our future was as expansive as the feast laid before us. I savoured each bite, the vegetables a vibrant medley, the turkey breast succulent, and the gravy—a culinary embrace. The wine, far from ordinary, complemented the meal with its refined bouquet. As we concluded with strawberries and cream, a dessert of simple elegance, I found myself immersed in the ritual of tidiness that followed, a dance of dishes and dishwasher.

Later, ensconced in the living room's embrace, coffee in hand, I pondered the life that unfurled before me. It was a tapestry of comfort and precision, woven by Janet's exacting standards—a stark contrast to the simplicity of my own existence.

Janet's suggestion broke through my reverie. "Why not journey home in the motorhome from here, Zachariah? Your gear can rest in the garage; it's yours to use." Her plan unfolded further, a shared adventure on wheels for the summer days ahead. "I'll acquire a trike just like yours, complete with a trailer for our little one. There's a world out here we've yet to discover."

Her enthusiasm was infectious, yet I hesitated, a confession on my lips. "My trike isn't exactly within the legal bounds. It's meant to have a 250-watt motor, but mine boasts 500 watts."

The admission hung between us, a cloud of concern in the otherwise clear skies of our aspirations. Yet, in Janet's company, I felt the possibility of resolution, of finding a path that adhered to both our dreams and the letter of the law.

Janet's laughter was a gentle chiding, a playful nudge at my unconventional ways. "Zachariah Black, you're full of surprises," she said with a twinkle in her eye. "But now, the night beckons us to rest. Tomorrow's duties await—your journey to Long Marston and my return to the daily grind."

As I ascended the stairs, the sight of pyjamas by my bedside was a quaint reminder of domesticity. Across the room, Janet donned her nightie, a fortress of fabric that seemed to challenge any would-be intruder. I slipped into the pyjamas, their fabric a soft whisper against my skin, and settled into the embrace of the bed.

Janet nestled close, her voice a murmur in the dim light. "A trip to the bathroom, Zachariah. Clean teeth are happy teeth." I couldn't help but smile, noticing the personalised cups, each holding a toothbrush and paste, ready for use. It was a small gesture, but it spoke volumes of her care.

As I stood before the mirror, the bristles of the brush sweeping across my teeth, I pondered the cost of dental perfection. The accident had left its mark, and the failed attempts at dentures were a testament to that struggle. The thought of spending a fortune on implant surgery—drilling into the bone for the sake of a smile—was a price too steep for me to pay. Yet, at this moment, in the comfort of Janet's home, such concerns seemed distant, like shadows chased away by the light of newfound hope.

The veneer of civility, the mantle of 'Mr Nice Guy,' began to fray at the edges as contemplation gave way to a burgeoning resolve. Why should I continue to don this guise? The question echoed in the silence of the room. I returned to bed, my back to Janet, a silent statement of the turmoil within. Somewhere in the night's embrace, sleep claimed us, only to be chased away by the shrill call of the alarm at dawn's first light.

With haste, I adorned myself in the new garments Janet had gifted, their fabric a reminder of the life she envisioned for us. Descending the stairs, I manoeuvred my trike and trailer into the sanctuary of the garage, retrieving my rucksack—the repository of my past life.

Breakfast was a quiet affair, the air thick with unspoken words and lingering doubts. Janet's Range Rover retreated, making way for my departure. I guided the motorhome onto the lane, its passage a careful negotiation with the encroaching hedges—a metaphor, perhaps, for the delicate balance of our relationship.

As the motorhome inched forward, I couldn't help but reflect on the path ahead. The journey promised freedom, yet the thought of what I was leaving behind—a home, a future, a partner—lingered like the morning mist. The road to Long Marston awaited, a canvas for the next chapter of my story.

The motorhome's engine hummed a low farewell as I wrapped my arms around Janet, her smile a blend of joy and disappointment. "Have a nice day," I whispered, sealing the sentiment with a kiss.

"And you," she replied, her voice a soft echo of our parting. She lingered for a moment, her wave a delicate thread connecting us as I pulled away. The lane behind me felt like a cocoon shed, the open road a canvas of possibilities.

The fuel gauge's reassuring fullness was a silent ally, and the hands-free feature of the motorhome was a nod to modern convenience. Then, Janet's call—a tether to the life I was navigating away from.

"Hi Janet, you okay?" I pressed the button, my voice steady.

Her concern was palpable. "No, you are upset with me, aren't you?"

A chuckle escaped me, a mix of affection and reassurance. "Not really, you silly girl. We're just two souls learning to dance in step. How about we continue the dance at Long Marston this weekend?"

Her hesitation was a whisper of societal norms. "What about the neighbours seeing me? Remember your wife hasn't been dead that long, Zachariah?"

I laughed, a sound that carried the weight of our shared secret. "Let them talk. They won't bite you—I might, though."

Her laughter was the sweetest of replies. "That would be lovely. See you Friday night. I love you. Bye."

And with that, the road stretched out before me, a path leading to a future where the past was a memory, and the present was a promise waiting to be fulfilled.

***

Annabella's voice came through the speaker, warm yet edged with concern. "Janet, conning someone is delicate. It's about trusting your instincts. Maybe it's time to step back and let him come to you."

"I pray our sacrifices are worthwhile. I have to confess I'm surprised you allowed him?"

As the miles passed, Janet's grip on the steering wheel loosened. By the time she reached the crest of the hill, with the sunset painting the sky in hues of gold and purple, she had made a decision. She would think of the money, the million pounds, and forge ahead with the 12's instructions.

***

The steam from the tea rose in gentle swirls, mingling with the late afternoon light that filtered through the kitchen window. Zachariah held the warm mug between his hands, the familiar scent of Earl Grey grounding him in the present. Zachariah took a deep breath, turning to his neighbour,

"Your kindness is a comfort, Susan," Zachariah said, his voice soft with gratitude. "Hazel's things going to those in need would have pleased her greatly."

Susan nodded, her eyes reflecting a shared sorrow. "She was always thinking of others. It's what made her so special."

Zachariah glanced towards the staircase, where the box sat like a silent testament to Hazel's absence. The decision that loomed over him felt heavier now, the weight of memories anchoring him to this place, yet the possibility of a new beginning with Janet called to him like a siren's song.

He set the mug down, resolution hardening within him. "I think it's time for a change, Susan. Time to embrace the future, however uncertain it may be."

Susan reached out, placing a reassuring hand on his shoulder. "Whatever you decide, Zachariah, you won't be alone. We're all here for you."

With a nod of thanks, Zachariah watched as Susan was about to leave, her figure receding into the golden hue of the setting sun. Alone with his thoughts, he knew the road ahead would be fraught with challenges, but it was a road he was ready to travel. Only time would tell whether it led to the open road in a motorhome or to a shared life with Janet.

Susan returns, hugging Zachariah. "Life's journeys are rarely straightforward, and love's paths even less so," she said thoughtfully. "But it sounds like this woman has brought a spark back into your life. That's precious, especially after all you've been through."

Zachariah nodded, the uncertainty in his eyes betraying the calm he tried to project. "It's just... everything's happening so fast. And with such a big age difference, I worry about what people will think."

"Let them think what they will," Susan replied firmly. "What matters is how you feel, and how she makes you feel. If there's joy, if there's a connection, then age is just a number. The heart doesn't count the years."

He chuckled, a sound tinged with both nervousness and relief. "You always know what to say, Susan. I suppose I'm just afraid of making the wrong choice."

"There's no right or wrong choice here, Zachariah," Susan assured him. "There's only the choice that makes you happy.

If being with her, moving to Buxton, starting anew gives you happiness, then that's the path you should take."

Zachariah took a deep breath, the resolve building within him. "You're right. I'll have her stay for the weekend and see how things go. And if it feels right, I'll take that leap."

"That's the spirit," Susan said with a smile. "And remember, whatever happens, you've got a friend in me, and a community that cares about you."

With a grateful nod, Zachariah watched Susan walk away, her figure gradually blending into the evening shadows. He turned to look at the motorhome, its presence a symbol of new beginnings. The weekend would be a test to see if the past could blend with the future and if memories could make room for new dreams.

Susan paused at the door, her laughter subsiding into a smile that held a world of understanding. "Zachariah, you've always been one for surprises," she said, her voice tinged with affection. "But remember, life's too short for regrets. You've got a chance at happiness, and that's worth exploring, no matter the age difference."

Zachariah nodded, his heart buoyed by her words. "I know, Susan. It's just... all new to me. I never expected to feel this way again, especially not after Hazel."

"Life has a funny way of throwing us curveballs," Susan replied, stepping back into the house. "And sometimes, those curveballs are blessings in disguise. Janet sounds like she could be one of those blessings."

He watched as Susan carefully placed the box of Hazel's clothes in her hallway. "I'll take good care of these, Zachariah. Until the charity shop collects."

CHAPTER 4

Where to go from here

The musty air began to clear as the warmth from the heating mingled with the fresh breeze from the open windows. Zachariah stood there, momentarily lost in the unexpectedness of the moment. Janet's presence was like a jolt to the quiet monotony of his life.

"Janet," he said, his voice a mix of surprise and delight. "I wasn't expecting you until tomorrow. What a pleasant surprise."

Janet smiled, her eyes scanning the modest interior of Zachariah's home. "I just couldn't wait," she admitted, setting down her night bag. "I wanted to see where you've been living, to understand all parts of you."

Zachariah watched as she moved through the space, taking it all in. The place was nothing like her own; he knew that much. It was smaller, older, and filled with the remnants of a life he had shared with Hazel. But now, it was also a canvas for new memories.

"I hope you don't mind the sudden change of plans," Janet continued, her gaze settling on a photograph of Hazel. "I thought we could use the extra time to really talk, to plan, to be together."

He nodded, the initial shock giving way to a warm sense of anticipation. "Of course, I don't mind. I'm glad you're here."

They spent the evening sorting through the mail, dealing with the overdue bills, and talking about everything and nothing. Janet listened as Zachariah shared stories of Hazel and their life together, and in turn, she opened up about her own past.

As the night deepened, they cooked a simple meal together, laughter and the clinking of dishes filling the space. The rented accommodation, with its peeling wallpaper and creaky floorboards, felt alive again.

When they finally settled on the couch, a comfortable silence enveloping them, Zachariah realised that this was more than just a visit. It was a beginning. Janet had come early not just out of curiosity but out of a desire to be part of his world and weave her life into his.

"Where to go from here?" Zachariah mused aloud, glancing at Janet.

She leaned in, her hand finding his. "Wherever we want, Zachariah. Together."

And in that moment, with the heating warding off the evening chill and Janet's hand in his, Zachariah felt a sense of direction. The road ahead was still uncertain, but it was one he was ready to travel, with Janet by his side.

The kettle whistled softly in the background as Zachariah poured the steaming water into two mugs, the tea bags bobbing gently. He turned to Janet, who was perched at the breakfast bar, a soft smile playing on her lips.

"I'm getting the hang of it," Zachariah replied, handing her a mug of tea. "It's different. But you're right, the hands-free feature is a godsend, especially on the longer drives."

Janet took the mug, her fingers brushing against his. "I'm glad you like it. I wanted to make sure you had all the comforts, even on the road."

They sipped their tea in companionable silence, the warmth from the mugs seeping into their hands. Zachariah couldn't help but feel a sense of contentment. Here was Janet, making herself at home in his simple kitchen, talking about motorhomes and future adventures.

"Susan's been a great support," he continued, breaking the silence. "She's seen me through some tough times. And now, with you here, it feels like... like I'm starting a new chapter."

Janet's eyes met his, and he saw the same hope reflected in them that he felt in his heart. "We are starting a new chapter, Zachariah. Together."

As they finished their tea, the conversation turned to plans for the weekend, to the places they could visit in the motorhome, to the life they could build. It was a new beginning, one that Zachariah had never anticipated, but now that it was here, he couldn't imagine it any other way.

Zachariah's eyes twinkled with amusement as he watched Janet navigate her phone with such deft precision. "It's just... I'm not used to this level of efficiency," he admitted with a chuckle. "You handle that phone like a maestro conducts an orchestra."

Janet's smile widened, and she tucked a strand of hair behind her ear. "Well, we can't have our first proper evening together spent on cooking and cleaning, can we? This way, we get to relax and enjoy each other's company."

He nodded, appreciating her thoughtfulness. "You're right, as always. A takeaway it is, then. And sweet-and-sour chicken sounds perfect."

As they waited for the food to arrive, Zachariah found himself marvelling at the ease with which Janet had slipped into his life. Her presence turned the mundane into something special, and he couldn't help but feel grateful for this unexpected turn his journey had taken.

"You might be right," Zachariah admitted with a sheepish grin. "But every item has a story, a memory attached to it."

Janet leaned against the doorframe, her frown softening. "Memories are important, but sometimes we need to make room for new ones," she said gently.

Zachariah nodded, understanding the truth in her words. "Perhaps it's time for a clear-out. A fresh start," he mused, glancing around at the accumulated years.

Janet's expression brightened. "Exactly! And I'll help you. We can sort through it together this weekend."

The prospect of tackling the clutter with Janet turned the daunting task into an opportunity for bonding. Zachariah felt a surge of gratitude for her presence, her willingness to dive into his life, clutter and all.

"Let's do it," he said, determination in his voice. "But first, let's enjoy our evening together."

Janet's voice was tinged with urgency as she ended the call, her eyes meeting Zachariah's with an apologetic glint. "I'm so sorry, Zachariah. I didn't expect this, but I have to go. It's an emergency at the bank."

Zachariah's heart sank, but he masked his disappointment with a supportive nod. "Of course, you must handle it. Don't worry about me; I'll be fine."

She grabbed her anorak and hesitated at the door, her hand on the knob. "I'll make it up to you, I promise. We'll have our weekend, just a little delayed."

With a swift move, she was out the door, leaving Zachariah in the quiet aftermath. He stood there for a moment, processing the sudden change. The house felt empty, the echoes of their earlier laughter now a distant memory.

He glanced at the clock. It was nearing 5:30 p.m., and the food would be arriving soon. A meal for two that would now be a solitary affair. With a heavy heart, he prepared the table, setting out plates and cutlery for one.

***

Janet's laughter echoed through the phone as she spoke to Annabella, "He's all yours now. I've ordered a Chinese meal and told him I had to rush back to the bank."

Annabella let out a weary sigh, "I appreciate it, Janet, but the 12 are far from pleased. We might need to resort to more extreme measures. Our instructions were to lead him to the castle, not to let him go back to his house."

"I don't see why that's such a big deal, Annabella. He's already shown his worth. It's time we confirmed the bloodline once and for all, though it seems pretty obvious at this point."

"Well, at least he'll be clean and dressed in fresh clothes; that's something," Annabella conceded. "The 12 are adamant that I fulfil my role. It doesn't make sense to me; you're expecting, and so is Agnes."

Janet's tone turned serious, "Don't cross the 12, Annabella. Remember our oath of allegiance. I, for one, have no desire to end up adrift at sea—and I'm sure you don't either."

Annabella responded with a heavy sigh, "I do love my figure, and so do my suitors. This whole situation is quite unpalatable. But then again, if one wants to maintain a life of luxury and have everything, I guess some sacrifices are necessary."

"You've got all the resources you need, Annabella," Janet reassured her. "You'll be back to your usual self in no time."

"Thanks for the vote of confidence," Annabella replied with a breath of relief. "Talk to you soon, Janet."

***

Peering out the front room window, I felt a chill run down my spine as I watched a familiar black Mini pull up. Annabella emerged with her usual boldness and made her way to my front door. I hurried to open it, hoping no one noticed her enter.

"You just missed Janet," I said, a sense of relief in my voice. "She had to rush back to the bank because of some issue."

Annabella shrugged off her sheepskin coat with a nonchalant air. "It's not about luck, Zachariah. I make it my business to know where people are," she stated confidently.

As I busied myself making coffee, Annabella took a leisurely tour of my home. Returning to the kitchen, she commanded, "Open your mouth," as if I were a servant. Without thinking, I obeyed, and she placed a tablet on my tongue. I quickly washed it down with coffee, avoiding the taste.

Checking her diamond-encrusted watch, Annabella announced, "It's nearly 5:30, and the food will be here soon.

We don't have much time. I want to make the most of our evening together," she said with a hint of urgency.

Puzzled, I asked, "How did you know about the Chinese meal Janet ordered?"

Her grin widened, "Zachariah, let's just say I have my ways. Now, let's focus on enjoying our meal and the time we have."

The knock at the door was swift, a brief interruption to the evening's unfolding drama. Zachariah opened the door to find the delivery person, face obscured by a mask, holding the fragrant dishes they had been awaiting. With a quick exchange, the food was his, and the delivery boy disappeared into the night.

Zachariah set the sweet-and-sour chicken on the breakfast bar, the steam rising invitingly from the containers. Annabella wasted no time, tucking into her portion with an eagerness that betrayed a hunger for more than just the meal. She ate with a gusto that seemed out of place amidst the evening's earlier tension, yet it was a moment of normalcy in an otherwise abnormal situation.

As Annabella savoured the flavours, Zachariah watched, his mind racing with questions and doubts. The tablet she had given him, her cryptic comments, and the sudden departure of Janet—all these elements swirled in his thoughts, a maelstrom of uncertainty.

The meal was a brief respite, a chance to gather his thoughts before the night resumed its mysterious course. Zachariah knew that the story was far from over, and as Annabella finished her meal, he braced himself for what was to come. The narrative of his life had taken a turn into uncharted territory, and he could only hope to navigate it with care.

Zachariah's thoughts were a whirlwind as he pondered the evening's events. The food was indeed excellent, a small comfort in the midst of the unfolding mystery. How did Annabella know about Janet's absence and the Chinese food order? It seemed too coincidental to be mere chance. The logical explanation was communication between Janet and Annabella, but the purpose behind it remained shrouded in secrecy.

As for Annabella's interest in him, Zachariah could only speculate. Perhaps it wasn't what he had but who he was or the role he was destined to play in a larger scheme that drew her to him. Her allure was undeniable, reminiscent of the iconic Kate Moss, and her confidence in taking what she wanted was both intimidating and intriguing.

Zachariah's musings about Annabella's past were natural, given the circumstances. Her experience and decisiveness were clear, but they also added layers to her enigmatic persona. What was clear was that Annabella was a force to be reckoned with, and Zachariah was caught in the current of her intentions, whatever they might be.

Zachariah pondered the complexities of attraction and the enigma of his situation. The beach memory lingered a reminder of his perceived age and worth in the eyes of others. Yet here he was, caught in a web woven by younger women with motives as mysterious as their actions.

Patience, indeed, would be his ally in this game. The truth, he hoped, would unravel in time, revealing the reasons behind Janet's and Annabella's interest in him. For now, he chose to embrace the moment, to savour the unexpected company and the intrigue that surrounded him.

Annabella's nonchalance at the text message was telling; her presence was no accident. Janet's orchestration of the evening's events spoke of a plan in motion, one that Zachariah was only beginning to glimpse. Annabella's father's approval of Janet, her prowess at the bank, and the bold insinuation of the night's promise all hinted at a larger narrative at play.

With a twinkle that hinted at secrets untold, Annabella excused herself, her voice trailing off, "I shan't be a moment." Her swift footsteps echoed as she ascended the stairs, leaving Zachariah in a state of anxious anticipation. The brief sound of running water signalled her return was imminent.

When Annabella reappeared, the sight of her left Zachariah breathless, his heart racing at the vision before him. She was flawless, her presence overwhelming, and in that moment, all words failed him. They came together with a fierce urgency, their embrace a tangle of fervent passion that brought them to the floor.

Annabella's resolve was clear, her actions driven by a purpose beyond the grasp of the moment. She was on a mission, one ordained by the enigmatic group known only as the 12, and she would not be swayed. Zachariah, caught in the intensity of their connection, was swept along by the current of her determination, the implications of their encounter hanging in the air, unspoken yet understood.

As the first light of dawn crept through the curtains, Zachariah lay in bed, the remnants of the night's intensity still clinging to his consciousness. He turned to look at Annabella, her features softened by sleep, and he marvelled at the transformation. The woman who had been a whirlwind of passion and mystery now seemed serene, almost vulnerable in the quiet of the morning.

The events of the night played back in his mind like a vivid dream, leaving him to wonder if the person beside him was indeed the same Annabella he thought he knew. She had revealed layers of herself that were both exhilarating and confounding, challenging his every perception.

Together, they rose and stepped into the shower, the warm water cascading over them, washing away the lingering doubts and questions. It was a moment of renewal, a silent agreement to embrace the new day and whatever it might bring.

As they dressed and prepared for the day ahead, Zachariah realised that life with Annabella would never be predictable. Each day promised new revelations and experiences, a journey of discovery.

I held Annabella around her waist, gently kissing her neck and lips: "Won't you enlighten me on what's going on, Annabella? You know so much about everyone's movements. Why are you sleeping with a wreck? I'm well past my sell-by date. There must be a reason?"

"You must remember Zachariah. The bank employs Janet, and I'm privileged to have certain information because of my father's position. Janet's tracked for security, as am I on occasions; of course, you must never divulge that secret to anyone. In Janet's case, if an attempt is made to persuade her to open the bank vault, I only have to look on my mobile, and I know where she is at any time of day," Annabella smiled.

"Oh, I suppose it makes sense. A lady of your position should be tracked, and Janet holds the key to millions of pounds."

"Exactly! Every vehicle I use can be tracked if I should go missing," Annabella smiled.

The morning after their intense night, the house was quiet except for the sound of Annabella's footsteps as she descended the stairs. Her hair was neatly tied in a bun, a stark contrast to the wildness of the previous evening. Zachariah handed her the cup of coffee he had prepared, a small gesture of domesticity in the midst of their complicated entanglement.

"I needed this," Annabella said, taking a thoughtful sip. "You've kept me awake all night, Zachariah. I'm still tingling from it; you truly are dangerous."

Her words were a mix of accusation and affection, and Zachariah couldn't help but feel a twinge of pride. He watched her finish her coffee, her soft kiss a promise of more to come, and then she was gone, her departure as sudden as her arrival had been.

Zachariah stood at the door, the taste of her kiss lingering on his lips, and he pondered the enigma that was Annabella. She was a tempest, a force of nature that had swept into his life and left him reeling. As her Mini disappeared down the street, he realised that whatever game they were playing, whatever secrets lay between them, he was inextricably drawn to her.

Exhausted, Zachariah had barely hit the pillow before sleep claimed him. The loud banging at the door jolted him awake, and through the window, he saw Janet. A wave of panic washed over him as he dashed downstairs and flung open the door. Without a word, Janet brushed past him, her movements quick and purposeful as she inspected each room.

When she returned to the kitchen, her shoulders dropped, and the tension seemed to leave her body. "I had this awful thought that you might be with someone else," she admitted, her voice betraying a mix of relief and lingering doubt.

Zachariah, realising the depth of Janet's concern, sought to reassure her. "Janet, there's no one else," he said earnestly. "You're the only one I want to be with."

Zachariah's attempt at humour did little to quell Janet's suspicions. As she inspected the bed with the scrutiny of a detective, her accusation was half-hearted, her punch playful. It was clear that despite her jesting, there was an undercurrent of genuine curiosity and perhaps a hint of jealousy.

"Tea sounds perfect," Zachariah replied, trying to steer the mood towards something more light-hearted. "And I'll get the groceries for you."

As he made his way to Janet's Range Rover, he couldn't help but reflect on the tangled web of relationships he found himself in. Annabella's visit, the mysterious tablet, and now Janet's teasing about "Lover Boy"—it was all becoming a complex narrative that Zachariah was struggling to navigate.

Returning with the groceries, he found Janet in the kitchen, the kettle already boiling. "You know, Annabella and I are just friends," he said, addressing her earlier comment. "There's nothing to worry about."

Janet looked at him, a smile tugging at the corners of her mouth. "I trust you, Zachariah. But remember, I'm the one you're marrying," she said, her tone a mix of jest and earnest.

Zachariah's playful banter with Janet filled the house with a light-hearted energy. "Ye of little faith," he teased, a smile in his voice as he playfully suggested the handcuffs. His laughter echoed through the stairwell as he made a dash for the lower level, with Janet in hot pursuit.

Her playful thump on his shoulder was met with mock indignation. "You do realise, Janet, that you're not supposed to beat your boyfriend," he said, turning to face her with a grin.

Caught off guard by Janet's playful accusation that he's a pirate, Zachariah could only stand in silence. His name, which he had always found peculiar, now took on a new meaning. Was there truth to Janet's teasing, a lineage traced back to the high seas and swashbuckling ancestors?

Janet's laughter broke the silence, her jest about his pirate heritage a light-hearted attempt to make sense of their undeniable attraction. "It must be the pirate blood in you, Zachariah, that draws me in," she said with a wink. "And as for not firing blanks—well, that's a story for another day."

Zachariah's tone held a mix of bemusement and reflection as he considered Janet's playful theory. "You know, Janet, it's a unique name, that's for sure. Maybe there's a bit of pirate charm in it after all," he mused, the corners of his mouth turning up slightly.

Janet's curiosity about his past marriages brought a sombre note to the conversation. "Three," he answered quietly. "The last one... it was tough. The virus took her, and somehow, I was spared. It's one of life's mysteries, I suppose."

The room filled with a silent understanding. Zachariah's history was marked by love and loss, a journey that had shaped him into the man he is today. Janet reached out, her touch a wordless comfort, acknowledging the shared vulnerability between them.

Zachariah pondered Janet's words, the coffee in his hands a comforting warmth as he considered his past. "You know, Janet, I've always just lived in the moment, never really stopped to think about why things happen the way they do," he said thoughtfully.

Janet nodded, her gaze softening. "Maybe it's not just about looks or names, Zachariah. There's a certain charm about you, something that draws people in. It's in the way you carry yourself, your resilience, and yes, maybe even a bit of that pirate's allure, if we're to believe the tales."

They sat in silence for a moment, the history of Zachariah's name hanging between them like a question mark. Was it merely a coincidence, or was there a deeper story behind the name Black, one that tied him to a lineage of adventure and romance?

"Perhaps it's time I did a little digging into my family history," Zachariah mused, a spark of curiosity lighting his eyes. "Who knows what I might find? Maybe there's a treasure map hidden in the attic, or a secret legacy waiting to be uncovered."

Janet laughed, the sound bright in the quiet room. "Whatever you find, I'm sure it'll be an adventure, Zachariah. And I'll be right here, ready to embark on that journey with you."

She paused, her confession hanging in the air like a delicate but dangerous mist. "I was afraid," she continued, her voice barely above a whisper, "afraid that the truth would push you away. But here we are, standing on the precipice of a future neither of us planned for."

He looked at her, his eyes reflecting a storm of emotions. "I won't lie and say I'm not shocked, or scared," he admitted. "But this... this child," he placed his hand gently over hers, "is a part of us. And I may not know much about the future, but I know I want to face it with you."

Together, they stood in silence, the weight of their shared secret binding them closer than ever before. It was a moment of vulnerability, of unspoken promises and quiet resolve. They were in uncharted waters, but they were together, and somehow, that made all the difference.

"A night I will remember," he reflected. "I never realised I could manage; after years of abstinence, the very act of taking charge seemed foreign to me."

Janet's gaze held a mixture of gratitude and resolve as she spoke. "I decided after watching my mother that I would never find a trustworthy man. I had a couple of men before I met you. The relationships went sour." She sighed, the memories bitter on her tongue. "I don't know why I couldn't trust them, and if it weren't for you now, I'd be hiding from my father."

Her smile then broke through the clouds of her past, warm and bright. "Thank God you dealt with the situation, proving beyond a shadow of a doubt that you cared for me." She reached out, her hand finding his, a silent symbol of their shared journey. "Forget your age; it's not important," she continued her voice firm. "It's how we look after each other! You have many good years ahead of you; you only have to keep fit," she smiled reassuringly, her eyes sparkling with a blend of hope and certainty.

Their connection was a testament to the power of understanding and support, a beacon for both of them in the uncertainty of life's vast ocean.

The early morning light filtered through the curtains, casting a soft glow on the scene. "I think we've talked enough, don't you?" His voice was gentle, an invitation rather than a question. Janet's grin was the only answer he needed as he held out his hand, and together, they retreated to the sanctuary of the upstairs room.

Dawn broke, and with it came the realisation of the night's passion. He awoke to find Janet, her movements laboured but her spirit undiminished, making her way to the bathroom. She caught his gaze, a playful frown on her face. "You're an animal. I'm crippled," she declared, her grin betraying the satisfaction behind her mock complaint.

He dressed quickly, the echoes of laughter still warming the air. Descending the stairs, he called out to her, "Stay in bed; I'll bring you breakfast." Silence was his only reply, but he knew she heard him. In the kitchen, he prepared eggs on toast, the familiar motions a comforting rhythm, and brewed a pot of tea, its aroma a promise of the day ahead.

Returning upstairs, he found Janet sitting up in bed, her smile as radiant as the morning sun. He placed the tray before her, the clink of China a soft symphony. The pot of tea found its place on the bedside table, and he poured her a cup, the steam rising like a prayer.

A soft kiss, a whispered "I'm going downstairs; enjoy your breakfast," and he left her to savour the moment. It was a simple act, a breakfast in bed, but it was also a declaration, a commitment to care for each other, to cherish each moment, and to face whatever the future held together.

The computer screen flickered to life, a digital portal to a world of unsolicited sympathy. Condolence messages flooded his inbox, a parade of names he hadn't seen in years. With a cynical chuckle, he typed out his thanks, labelling them all hypocrites in his mind. Yet, as he scoured the Internet for clues to his name and origin, the search yielded nothing but the echoing void of uncertainty.

Janet's offhand comment lingered in his thoughts, a potential piece of a larger puzzle. He suspected she held secrets close to her chest, and Annabella—Annabella was the enigma at the heart of it all. Agnes, too, was entwined in this web, her connection to Annabella undeniable. The more he pondered, the more he saw Annabella as the central kingpin, with the others orbiting her mysterious gravity.

And then, amidst his musings, a sudden warmth enveloped him. Janet's arm slid around his neck, her presence a welcome jolt from his reverie. "How's my lovely pirate this morning," she whispered, her lips grazing his neck in a kiss that sent shivers down his spine. Her gratitude for the breakfast he had served her was genuine, a moment of pure affection that cut through the complexity of their situation.

"That's the first time anyone's ever done that for me except Mother when I was ill with chickenpox," she beamed, a statement that spoke volumes of the simple yet profound act of care he had shown her.

In that instant, the tangled threads of doubt and suspicion were overshadowed by the undeniable truth of their connection. Whatever the mystery of his past, whatever the machinations of Annabella and the others, the reality of the present was Janet's smile, her gratitude, and the undeniable bond that had formed between them.

Zachariah's suggestion hung in the air, a playful nudge towards normalcy. "I suggest you put the kettle on, Janet. We'll have a cup of tea and decide what we plan for the day other than lying in bed together," he said with a smug grin.

Janet's response was swift and light-hearted, her energy undiminished despite her protest. "You can forget that Zachariah; it will take me a day to recover from last night." With that, she dashed off into the kitchen, leaving Zachariah to switch off his computer and follow her lead.

Perched on a stool at the breakfast bar, he watched as she moved with a familiar grace, the morning light casting a warm glow on her face. She passed him a cup of tea, her smile an unspoken conversation between them. Then, with a sip of curiosity, she asked, "Have you ever checked your family tree, Zachariah, and seen your ancestry?"

Zachariah pondered the question, the steam from his tea curling up like the tendrils of his thoughts. "I can trace my family back to my mother's parents. I haven't investigated further than that. It never bothered me; the name seems to fit with a Canadian background. My mother came over with her parents when they sold the farm in Canada."

The conversation was a gateway to the past, an invitation to explore the branches of his family tree that extended beyond the known. It was a moment of connection, not just between him and Janet, but between him and the generations that had come before—a lineage waiting to be discovered.

Janet's words were a playful challenge, a reminder that assumptions often lead one astray. "I'm afraid you're so wrong, Zachariah Black; as the saying goes, you're barking up the wrong tree." But her tone was light, the banter between them easy and familiar. "Anyway, change the subject. Where are you taking me today? I don't want to push my luck too far, Zachariah; using my position coming here is quite risky."

Zachariah's suggestion was a glimpse into his childhood, a piece of his history offered to her. "If you fancy a hike, I can take you up Meon Hill, where I played as a kid?"

Her response was immediate, the prospect of a shared adventure sparking a gleam in her eye. "Why not? I have to keep in shape; that reminds me, I've ordered my trike and child trailer," she said with a smug grin. "I selected the 500-watt motor, the same as yours, having the extra lighting supplied, and I also ordered two new batteries, one for your trike and one for mine. They should be here next month."

The plans they made were more than just for a day's outing; they were preparations for a life of shared experiences, of journeys taken together. The trikes and trailers were symbols of their commitment to each other, to their child, and to the adventures that lay ahead.

The world outside the window was awash with the promise of a clear day. Zachariah donned his anorak with a sense of anticipation, assisting Janet with hers, a silent dance of preparation for the day ahead. Together, they approached her Range Rover, the vehicle that would carry them to the foot of memories and the peak of new experiences.

He directed her to the other side of Mickleton, where Meon Hill rose gently against the horizon. It was the easier path, one that welcomed all who sought its heights. She parked on the generous grass verge, the car coming to rest like a faithful steed after a long journey. Janet retrieved her walking boots from the boot, a ritual of readiness, while Zachariah, already clad in his own, awaited her readiness with a patient smile.

The pedestrian gate yielded to his touch, an old friend greeting them into the embrace of the hill. Hand in hand, they ascended, their fingers intertwined like the roots of the ancient trees that witnessed their ascent. The easy route unfolded before them, a path well-trodden by the feet of a younger Zachariah, who once knew the hill as a playground of endless winters and joyous abandon.

Memories cascaded like the snowballs he once rolled down these slopes, each one growing with the momentum of the past. The steel serving trays that served as sledges, the laughter that mingled with the chill of the air, and the wetness that seeped through layers of clothing—all were part of the tapestry of his childhood.

Now, with Janet by his side, Meon Hill was not just a canvas of memories but a landscape of possibilities. Each step was a shared journey, each breath a shared moment, as they climbed towards the summit, where the past met the present and the future was a view that stretched beyond the horizon.

The peak of Meon Hill greeted them with a panoramic view that took their breath away. As they reached the summit within an hour, Janet's eyes scanned the horizon, a silent signal that there was more to this hike than met the eye. Suddenly, she seized Zachariah's hand, guiding him with a determined "This way."

They walked along the crest where horse chestnut trees once stood tall, now reduced to stumps and memories. It was there, amidst the ghosts of fallen giants, that Annabella appeared as if conjured by the land itself. The two women embraced a meeting that seemed orchestrated by fate or perhaps something earthlier.

"Don't look so shocked, Zachariah," Annabella chided with a playful grin. "My father has investments all over England, and this happens to be one of them. I'm merely surveying on his behalf; I have to work occasionally." Her words were casual, but the undercurrent of significance was palpable.

The conversation shifted to the recent past, to an excellent Chinese meal shared, and a crisis at the bank averted.

"Excellent Chinese, Janet, I sampled with Zachariah. I hope all is well with the bank, whatever the problem was?" Annabella inquired, her tone light but probing.

Janet's reply came with ease, the issue at the bank dismissed as "Quickly resolved, Annabella, thank you." She then turned the focus back to Zachariah; her voice tinged with affectionate humour. "I'm pleased you were in the area to help Zachariah with the Chinese meal. I know what he'd have attempted trying to eat both portions."

At that moment, the summit of Meon Hill transformed from a childhood playground into a nexus of connections, old and new. The felled trees bore witness to the intertwining of lives, to secrets shared and kept, and to the unfolding drama that Zachariah, Janet, and Annabella were a part of.

Zachariah's jest about the weirdos was met with blush and reassurance from Annabella. "Zachariah, your concern for my welfare is charming. Don't worry. I'm a black belt in judo, and so is Janet, bank policy," she stated with a confidence that spoke of hidden depths. Her departure was swift, leaving behind a trail of intrigue. "I must continue my report. I'll leave you two lovebirds to enjoy the rest of your weekend. We'll meet up soon, Janet. We have plans to prepare, as you are aware."

As Annabella disappeared from view, Zachariah was left with a realisation that sent a shiver down his spine. Both Janet and Annabella possessed skills that could easily overpower him. The question that gnawed at his mind was poignant: Why hadn't Janet disposed of her father? She had the means, the training, and, presumably, the motive. Yet, she had not acted. And what of that fateful moment? Had Janet truly fainted when he had taken matters into his own hands?

The answers were veiled, obscured by the complex web of their relationships. Janet's actions, or lack thereof, suggested layers of strategy and emotion that Zachariah had yet to fully comprehend. The truth was a puzzle, each piece a revelation, each revelation a step closer to understanding the enigmatic figures of Janet and Annabella.

Annabella's wave was a silent farewell, her figure diminishing towards Quinton. Zachariah's gaze then swept over the landscape, the Long Marston Airfield in the distance, a canvas of his childhood now dotted with the signs of progress—or so it was called. The houses under construction were like an advancing army, relentless and unyielding.

To his left, the old army camp had surrendered to the same fate; its barracks and parade grounds were now foundations for a future where history was buried under layers of brick and mortar. "Will people never realise you can't keep building; eventually, you will run out of ground to grow food," he mused, the thought a heavy stone in his stomach.

The proliferation of humanity was a topic that often troubled him. "Why do we have to breed so prolific? We are worse than rabbits," he lamented his words not just a question but a cry for mindfulness. The world was changing, and not always for the better.

His thoughts darkened as he considered the new variant, a spectre that loomed over the vulnerable. "The new variant is artificial to thin out the population," he pondered, a theory that many whispered but few dared to voice. And there he was, "an old bugger," as he put it, in the crosshairs of an unseen enemy.

It was a moment of vulnerability, of facing the fragility of life and the inexorable march of time. Yet, in the midst of these reflections, there was a glimmer of resilience, a determination to question, to challenge, and to seek truth amidst the tumult of existence.

Janet's voice cut through Zachariah's reverie, a gentle anchor to the present. "Hey Zachariah, stop daydreaming," she chided with a playful tug on his hand. They descended the hill, the old pine trees standing as silent sentinels to their passage. At the Range Rover, Janet's practicality was a reminder of the mundane yet necessary rituals of life. "Sit on the seat and remove your boots, Zachariah. Otherwise, you can clean my Range Rover carpet."

With a resigned sigh, he complied, leaving the boots in the boot, and they set off towards the familiarity of home. It was Zachariah who broke the silence with a thoughtful suggestion, one that promised ease and a break from the day's exertions. "Hey Janet, turn to Quinton chip shop. It will save cooking," he proposed.

The chip shop was a beacon of warmth and the promise of a hearty meal. In his haste and sock-clad feet, Zachariah braved the damp pavement, his determination rewarded with a bounty of fish and chips, curry sauce, mushy peas, and pickled eggs—a feast to sate any hunger.

Back in the Range Rover, Janet's grin was a silent conversation, one of shared understanding and unspoken affection. They returned home, the journey marked by the savoury aroma of their takeaway and the comfort of each other's company.

At home, the ritual of unwinding began. Socks discarded, plates gathered, and the breakfast bar became a tableau of contentment as they settled in. Zachariah devoured his meal, each bite a testament to the day's joys and the simple pleasures that awaited.

"You're annoyed with me again, Zachariah?" Janet's question was laced with a hint of amusement, her eyes searching his for the truth.

"Whatever gave you that idea, Janet!" Zachariah retorted with feigned indignation. "I enjoy walking outside in my socks. I'm purchasing a car. At least when I travel in my vehicle, I can do what I like and not be bossed around by a woman who has a phobia."

Janet's laughter was a melody that filled the room, her response quick and sharp. "I don't have a phobia; I like cleanliness more than you do. If you had your chance, Zachariah Black, you would sleep in a pigpen!"

The silence between them was a canvas, each unspoken word a stroke of colour on the complex painting of their relationship. Zachariah savoured his meal, a small act of independence, while Janet's declaration hung in the air—a decision that spoke of distance and contemplation. "I have decided, Zachariah. I'm returning home this evening. I need time to think."

His agreement was swift, a reflection of his own need for space. "I think you're right, Janet; I'll accompany you. I'll cycle my bike home and use it here." The words were simple, but the subtext was rich with meaning.

The routine of tidying up and packing was a familiar dance, each movement a step towards their temporary separation. Zachariah's resolve not to apologise was a silent affirmation of his dignity, a refusal to take blame where none was due.

As they arrived at Janet's house, the reality of their parting set in. Zachariah's trike, a symbol of his journey, was readied for the road. The 90-mile distance loomed ahead, a path too long to traverse before nightfall, necessitating a stop along the way.

Janet's figure at the gate was a poignant image, her gaze following him as he set off, the hum of the generator a steady companion. The road stretched before him, a ribbon of possibilities, and though the thought of this being the end saddened him, there was a sense of rightness to it—a fitting close to a chapter that had run its course.

***

Janet's voice trembled with urgency as she reached out to Annabella. "Annabella, he's becoming more unreasonable. I may have lost him," she confessed, the fear of losing control palpable in her tone.

Annabella's response was measured, and her mind was already calculating the next move. "Transport is on the way; delay his progress," she instructed with a calm that belied the gravity of the situation. "I'd rather hoped we'd have had more cooperation. Nevertheless, abduction will have to suffice; otherwise, the 12 will lose confidence in our ability, Janet, to resolve issues."

The conversation was a stark reminder of the stakes at play, a game of chess in which human lives were the pieces and the board a landscape of power and secrecy. The mention of the 12 hinted at a larger conspiracy, a group whose confidence was not easily earned nor retained.

Janet was left to grapple with the reality of the task at hand, the weight of expectations heavy on her shoulders. The word 'abduction' echoed in her mind, a drastic measure for desperate times. The path ahead was fraught with moral and ethical dilemmas, but the wheels of their plan were already in motion, unstoppable and ominous.

***

As the twilight settled over Ravensdale, Zachariah found solace in the simplicity of his makeshift camp. The large verge on the side road became his refuge, a place where the stars watched over him and the gentle hum of the night was his lullaby.

His provisions may have been forgotten in the rush of departure, but necessity is the mother of invention. An old cattle trough provided water, and a boiled kettle was enough for a cup of black tea—a small comfort in the quiet of the evening. The absence of sugar and milk was a choice, a nod to health and a testament to his willpower.

The fish and chips from lunchtime lingered, a satisfying memory that kept hunger at bay. Then came Janet's text, a beacon of concern in the digital darkness: "Would you like something to eat, Zachariah?"

His response was a reflection of his current state: "No, thanks; I'm fine." Self-sufficient and content, even in the face of scarcity.

Janet's offer to join him was a warmth he could feel even through the cold screen of his phone: "Would you like me to come and stay with you for the night?" But Zachariah's reply was a mix of humour and stoicism: "It resembles a pigsty. I wouldn't bother; stay in your warm house. I'll survive; thank you for the offer."

In that exchange, the distance between them was both physical and emotional, a gap filled with unspoken words and unshared experiences. Yet, there was a connection, undeniable and strong, surviving despite the silence of the night and the solitude.

As Zachariah sat within the confines of his teepee, the question of tolerance weighed heavily on his mind. "Do I need to be?" he pondered, the scent of his surroundings a stark reminder of his current state. The machete, once a tool of utility, now bore the marks of neglect, its surface marred by rust.

It was then that his phone buzzed with the arrival of a new message. Expecting it to be Janet, he was surprised to find Agnes' name on the screen. Her words were a burst of light in the dimness of his thoughts: "Zachariah, boy and girl confirmed today; we are over the moon. See you soon. Love Agnes."

The news of twins, a boy and a girl, was a beacon of hope, a reminder that life was ever-sprouting, ever-surprising. It was a moment that transcended the trivialities of daily squabbles and the imperfections of one's living space. In that instant, Zachariah was connected to something larger—a cycle of life that continued to turn, bringing with it new beginnings and reasons to celebrate.

In the quiet of the teepee, illuminated by the soft glow of the light, Zachariah and Janet faced each other. Their conversation was a crossroads of emotions and futures intertwined.

"Janet," Zachariah began, his voice a blend of weariness and sincerity, "I may be set in my ways, but that doesn't mean I'm incapable of caring. It's true, I'm an old bugger, and maybe I am stubborn, but I've lived long enough to know that caring is about more than just the present moment."

He reached for her hand, a gesture of connection. "I care, Janet. More than you might realise. It's not about being a 'quick screw' or finding someone else. It's about understanding that we're two people from different walks of life trying to navigate this path together."

Janet's eyes searched his, looking for the truth in his words. "And the future?" she asked, her voice a whisper of hope and fear.

"The future is uncertain for all of us," he admitted, "but that doesn't mean we give up on it. We make the best of the time we have, and we do it together. I may not have many years left, but I want to make them count. With you, with our child, and with every moment that life gives us."

The air between them was charged with the weight of decisions yet to be made, of lives yet to be lived. But at that moment, there was a shared understanding, a recognition that whatever the future held, they would face it as one.

The tension in the air was palpable as Annabella commanded the scene with an air of authority. "When you two have finished bickering, collapse the teepee. We have a lorry waiting for your equipment; you're coming with us, Zachariah," she declared, her tone brooking no argument.

Zachariah's instincts kicked in, his grip on the machete tightening, but Annabella was prepared. The dart that struck his arm was a clear message: resistance was futile. "That will calm you down, Zachariah," she said, a note of triumph in her voice as Janet swiftly disarmed him.

Weakened by the tranquilizer, Zachariah could only comply as they navigated the logistical challenge posed by the Tissington Trail railway bridge. His belongings, his past, were being loaded onto a lorry, a symbol of the transition he was being forced to undergo.

The interior of the luxury compartment starkly contrasts with the rustic simplicity of his teepee. As he sank into the plush sofa, the reality of his situation began to sink in. Annabella's words to Janet were a revelation, hinting at a deeper history, a lineage that Zachariah had only suspected: "You know his suspected ancestry. I'm surprised he never executed you."

The pieces of the puzzle were slowly coming together, each revelation adding depth to the mystery that enveloped Zachariah's life. What lay ahead was unknown, but it was clear that his journey was taking a turn into uncharted territory, with Janet and Annabella as enigmatic guides.

Annabella's presence was commanding, her every move calculated and precise. The casualness of tea being served belied the seriousness of their mission. Zachariah, still under the influence of the tranquiliser, could only observe, his mind a foggy landscape where reason and emotion blended into a surreal tableau.

Janet's care for him, even in his compromised state, was a small comfort. Her question to Annabella about the timescale to their destination revealed a sense of urgency and a need to understand the framework of their plan. "What is the timescale, Annabella, to the Castle of Mey?"

Annabella's response was a mixture of practicality and foreboding. "Probably a good eight hours; we can't afford to be stopped for speeding, not as you can with the lorry very often. Once we reach better roads, travelling should be far more comfortable; a bed next door if you wish to sleep."

The mention of Zachariah's alleged ancestor adds a sparkle of intrigue. "I don't think Zachariah will be much of a problem for the next three or four hours, mind you, if he's anything like Blackbeard, his ancestor; although not well documented, he was renowned when he used the title Zachariah Black for his skills."

As the lorry continued its journey, the past and the present were on a collision course, with Zachariah at the centre, a man whose history was as mysterious as the road ahead.

"Are you in the same condition as me, Annabella?" Janet asked, her voice barely above a whisper as if the walls themselves were eavesdropping on the sordid conversation.

Annabella paused, her eyes reflecting a turmoil that matched the storm brewing in her heart. "Perhaps," she began, her words measured and heavy with reluctance. "I must confess, the very notion was repellent from the outset. Upon our first encounter, he inspired nothing but revulsion within me. The mere thought of his aged hands, calloused and unyielding, tracing the contours of my skin ... sent shivers down my spine. And that beard—unkempt, bristling with neglect—it seemed a nest for vermin rather than a man's face. The idea of such a person laying claim to even a sliver of my being was enough to make my flesh crawl. Agnes, of all people, was the revelation. Her appetite for his presence was insatiable. Close your eyes and think of Scotland, she'd say, a whimsical mantra for enduring the unendurable. But now, I find myself ensnared in the same web of paradoxical desire. Like Agnes, like you, I'm drawn to him, a moth to a flame, against all reason. They caution to never judge a book by its cover, and he embodies that adage. His exterior belies the complexity within; he's become my singular craving. Since our paths crossed, no other's touch holds meaning—it's ludicrous, the power he wields over one's senses."

"I've borne the weight of his memory longer than you have," she confessed, the words tumbling out with a mix of nostalgia and sorrow. "I was but a child when he first entered our lives, an all-too-frequent shadow in our home, sharing whispered nights with my mother on the old settee downstairs. Their affair was a silent spectacle until infidelity severed their clandestine bond. I thought him gone forever, a ghost from a chapter best forgotten. Yet, fate has a peculiar sense of humour. Our paths crossed again, quite by chance, amidst the quaint streets of Hope. He was merely a day-tripper then, arm-in-arm with his wife, blissfully unaware of the history he'd left behind. It wasn't until two years on, as he glided past on his electric bike, that the past rekindled its ember. Following your directives became a secret delight, a guilty pleasure that you now witness before you."

There I was, perched on the edge of reality, a foolish grin plastered across my face. Did they know I could decipher their veiled words, or had my presence faded into insignificance? The truth, a spectre hovering on the horizon, beckoned me closer—its revelation promised liberation from the shackles of uncertainty.

The notion that my lineage could be entwined with that of a pirate's was laughable, a flight of fancy best reserved for the pages of adventure novels. The dead hold no claims over the living, or so I mused. Yet, whispers of Oak Island and its buried secrets seemed to cast a long shadow over their perceptions of me. A chuckle escaped my lips, a defence against the absurdity of my musings.

My laughter, however, did not go unnoticed. Janet and Annabella turned their gazes upon me, eyes narrowed with suspicion as if my mirth had betrayed a hidden truth I myself had yet to uncover.

A sudden consciousness gripped me; my eyes flickered open to the stark glow of my wristwatch, its hands marking the early hour of 5 a.m. A headache pounded within my skull, a foul reminder of the night's escapades. Janet and Annabella were nowhere to be seen—likely, they had found a corner to rest, assuming I'd remain dormant.

The lorry's brakes groaned in protest, signalling an approaching junction. Stealthily, I edged towards the side door, easing it open with a gentle pull. As the vehicle resumed its journey, I seized the moment and leapt, tumbling down an embankment as the lorry trundled on without me.

A Scottish downpour greeted me, relentless and familiar. My anorak, a shield against the deluge, clung to me with sodden comfort. Grasping my wallet, a lifeline in leather, I felt a flicker of hope. Helmsdale was within reach, a beacon of potential salvation.

My mobile, a silent companion, rested securely in my pocket. The railway was not an option—they would anticipate that route. Hitchhiking was a gamble in these parts; the likelihood of a passing car stopping was as slim as the morning light. No, I had to be cunning and chart a path untraced and unexpected.

With each step, I battled the relentless Scottish tempest, my arms flailing in a futile attempt to ward off the deluge. The cliffside loomed in the distance, where the sea churned violently under the moon's watchful gaze. The absurdity of being linked to a pirate gnawed at my thoughts. Seasickness was my faithful companion on even the calmest of voyages; the mere idea of crossing to France without losing my supper was laughable.

Regret crept in, whispering that the dubious shelter of the lorry might have been a wiser choice. The threat of pneumonia seemed a more tangible fate than the romanticised demise of a swashbuckler. I halted, chiding myself for the folly. The sting of the vaccine against the new variant was still fresh—a modern-day armour with no promise of invincibility.

The rumble of an approaching vehicle broke through my reverie. It was the distinct growl of a lorry, likely making its way from Wick. As it roared past, a sudden pain lanced through my arm. The lorry screeched to a halt, and the truth dawned on me as cold as the rain—Annabella had found me, and her dart had hit its mark once more.

I could only watch in a dazed stupor as Annabella and Janet briskly manoeuvred me back into the lorry from which I had so desperately fled. My limbs were leaden, devoid of the vigour needed to resist; any attempt at struggle would have been futile, likely leaving me in a far worse state than mere defeat.

With a swift efficiency that spoke of routine, Annabella stripped away my trainers, while Janet peeled off my anorak with a clinical detachment. "Tempt fate once more, Zachariah, and you'll rouse my ire," Janet warned, her tone laced with a chilling positivity. "Your lineage is not in question—you bear the blood of Blackbeard himself. The dose that should have felled a beast of great size barely tames your spirit. We're but a mere two hours from our destination, traffic willing. Patience, for what lies ahead will eclipse your wildest imaginings," Annabella chimed in, her assurance doing little to quell the unease in my gut.

The weight of the sedative dragged me down into darkness, and when awareness next graced me, I found myself in a place out of time—a cave aglow with an ethereal light. The rhythmic cadence of the sea against stone reached my ears, a natural lullaby against the backdrop of a grand fire that danced in the heart of the cavern. Warmth enveloped me, a stark contrast to the chill of my shackled ankles—a clear message that my captors would brook no further attempts at escape.

Anxiety clawed at my chest as twelve enigmatic figures emerged from the shadows, their faces obscured by masks that reflected the flickering flames. They stood in solemn formation across the fire, draped in gold robes adorned with a crimson cross—a stark symbol against the gilded fabric.

A thirteenth figure joined them, his presence commanding attention. Clad in a black robe with the same red cross, his mask was a mirror to theirs, a barrier to his true self. His voice, clear and devoid of any discernible accent, cut through the silence. "You hail from the lineage of the notorious Blackbeard or the elusive Jack Ward. Both pirates once served the Crown in secret; we have brought you here to ascertain your heritage and safeguard it from the brink of oblivion."

I remained silent, my mind racing for an escape that my voice could not articulate. A plea for help hung unspoken in the air. A sidelong glance revealed Annabella, transformed into a vision from the past, her gown a tapestry of sixteenth-century elegance. Agnes and Janet, her twins in time, flanked me, their gazes fixed on the twelve. The man in black issued a command that resonated with foreboding, "Agnes Montague, step forward."

Agnes advanced with a serene certainty, her gaze unwavering as she addressed the assembly. "I bear a dual blessing within me—a son and a daughter," she declared, her voice resonating with pride. "Zachariah Black alone has sired them, and no other's touch has marred my sanctity."

A wave of applause erupted from the twelve, their cheers echoing like a chorus of triumph, celebrating the perpetuation of their esteemed bloodline.

The man in black turned his attention to another. "Janet Simpson, of Calico Jack's lineage, present your gift to the brethren."

With a grace befitting her heritage, Janet stepped forth. "A son grows within me, his future written in the stars. Zachariah Black is his progenitor; since our fateful union, I have known no other man."

Once more, the twelve heralded the news with fervent acclamation, as if the very act of procreation was a divine event.

Finally, Annabella stood before the expectant eyes. "I stand before you, a descendant of Andre de Montbard, Grand Master of the Templar Knights. Yet, I bring no tidings of fruition—my mission remains unfulfilled. With your leave, my Lords, I shall endeavour once more."

"Annabella," the man in black intoned, his voice a harbinger of gravity, "you must grasp the gravity of your shortfall. The twelve and I shall deliberate upon this matter."

Her eyes, brimming with unshed tears, met mine across the flickering flames. In their depths, I read a silent plea for understanding. What drives the fervour to preserve a lineage etched in the annals of history? I pondered the purity of such a quest, likely diluted by the passage of time.

Agnes drew near her presence, a comforting warmth amidst the chill of the cavern. Our embrace was a sanctuary, a momentary reprieve from the ritualistic proceedings. "You've sown the seeds of life twice over, Zachariah," she whispered, her voice tinged with pride. "Once I've brought our twins into this world, I'll seek you out. My heart yearns for more of what only you can give."

Laughter bubbled up from within me, a defiant sound against the throbbing ache the drugs left in their wake. The man in the black robe resumed his solemn vigil, his gaze piercing through the masquerade of his disguise.

"Annabella," he began, his voice echoing with a stern finality, "the deficiency lies with you. Zachariah's virility is proven—twice over. Your father's grace affords you another chance. Test not his patience, for failure will bring dishonour upon your name. Behold, the twelve titans of wealth stand before you, their coffers emptied in pursuit of our brotherhood's vision—a vision aligned with the Royal decree."

"Forgive the oversight," the man in black replied, his voice betraying a hint of deference. "Your involvement is not only desired but essential. The fortunes of Blackbeard and Jack Ward, though shrouded in legend, are very much real. The twelve have nurtured these legacies, awaiting the rightful heir. Your stake in this is nothing less than a claim to history—a chance to revive a lineage of formidable renown."

I nodded, the weight of centuries bearing down upon me. "And what of my own desires? Am I to be a mere vessel for your ambitions?" I challenged, my gaze unwavering.

Annabella stepped forward, her eyes meeting mine with an intensity that belied her earlier vulnerability. "The blood has been drawn, the past poised to reveal its secrets. Your fate, and ours, hangs in the balance," she said, handing over a vial to the man in black.

He held it aloft, the crimson liquid catching the firelight. "Let the analysis commence. For today, we stand on the precipice of a new era—one that will either confirm our deepest beliefs or unravel the threads of our grand design."

"Your acumen does not go unnoticed, Zachariah," the man in black remarked, a hint of admiration lacing his words. "Your handling of those unfortunate necessities was nothing short of masterful. And your counsel to Agnes—ingenious, ensuring the end of a blight within her own family."

Annabella's expression shifted, a realisation dawning upon her. Her parents had been orchestrating a solution to their son's rebellious streak, one that would ensure he never tarnished the fellowship's esteemed ranks. It was Annabella who, unbeknownst to her, reached out to a descendant of the realm's most formidable assassin—a lineage that served the crown with silent, deadly efficiency.

"There are depths to our history that remain shrouded in shadows, Zachariah," the man continued. "Secrets so profound and closely guarded that they are whispered only within these hallowed walls."

Annabella, momentarily taken aback, hesitantly stepped toward me. I wrapped her in a comforting embrace, a silent message of solidarity amidst the unfolding revelations. It was a gesture of reassurance, a recognition of the burdens she bore.

From the shadows, a voice resonated with a paternal timbre. "We comprehend the gravity of your actions,

Annabella," he spoke, a blend of empathy and authority in his tone. "Desperation led us to the brink, and you, our daughter, faced the tempest alone. You may have perceived our silence as indifference, but it was a quiet storm of concern. Your choice, though fraught with darkness, was made in the name of preserving our legacy and safeguarding the fellowship."

The chamber fell into a hushed reverence as the women, garbed in the finery of the sixteenth century, made their solemn procession. Each took her place beside her partner, their united front a testament to the enduring strength of the fellowship. In unison, their voices rose, a pledge of unity and protection, "We are one family."

The man in black addressed me once more, his tone imbued with a newfound respect. "Zachariah, the lineage of each woman here is known to us, as yours will soon be. Your ancestry, whether it be Blackbeard or Jack Ward, holds a mastery that we honour. We offer you freedom from these chains, on the condition of your sacred oath."

Janet, Bible in hand, approached with solemn grace. My left hand found its place upon the ancient text, eliciting a collective intake of breath from the assembly. "I'm left-handed," I explained, a simple truth that seemed to hold deeper meaning for those gathered.

"Blackbeard, too, favoured his left," came the murmured realisation. "You may proceed."

With the weight of history pressing upon my palm, I spoke the words that would bind me to this enigmatic brotherhood. "I vow not to forsake these grounds without consent, so help me God, Amen."

Annabella's gaze softened, a hint of empathy breaking through her composed exterior. "You will not be caged,

Zachariah," she assured her voice a gentle contrast to the grandeur of our surroundings. "You shall have quarters befitting your status—a comfortable space where you can rest and reflect. As for your meals, they will be provided with care and consideration for your preferences. This period of transition is necessary, but it is not without its comforts. Patience, Zachariah. Once your lineage is confirmed, the doors of this fellowship will open to you fully, and the life that awaits is one of privilege and purpose."

With that, she led me down a corridor lined with portraits of stern-faced ancestors, their eyes following our passage through time. We stopped before a door, its wood carved with intricate designs. "This will be your sanctuary," she said, pushing the door open to reveal a room bathed in the warm glow of lamplight, its furnishings a blend of comfort and antiquity.

"I will leave you to settle in. Should you need anything, do not hesitate to call upon me," Annabella offered before closing the door with a soft click, leaving me alone with my thoughts and the weight of an uncertain future.

Zachariah's resolve was a flickering flame in the twilight of his confinement. The balcony, with its view of the sprawling gardens, whispered promises of freedom. The wisteria, with its stubborn grip and intoxicating scent, was a familiar adversary from his days as an estate manager—a symbol of nature's tenacious will.

He descended from his lofty perch, a smile gracing his lips despite the height that challenged his comfort. The gardens welcomed him, a labyrinth of beauty and secrecy. The sea's breath caressed his face, yet its song remained elusive, perhaps muffled by the clandestine tunnels he suspected snaked beneath the estate.

The notion of the fellowship entangled in illicit trades flickered through his mind—a stark contrast to their regal pretensions. But such thoughts were fleeting shadows, for the organisation, bound by royal edicts, would surely not dabble in such sordid affairs. Or so he hoped, as he wandered through the gardens, a captive yet free within their walls.

The garden, once a silent witness to Zachariah's clandestine stroll, now burst into life with the illumination of security lights and the emergence of figures from the shadows.

Laughter rippled through the air, a chorus of amusement at the sight of the fruit thief at play. "Indeed, he must share the blood of Blackbeard," they jested, "bold as brass and fearing nought, pilfering produce as if it were a treasure."

The man in the black robe, his identity still veiled, stepped forward with a chuckle. "It was the humble apple and pear that betrayed your absence, Zachariah. The moment you plucked them from their cold sanctuary, the house was alerted to your adventure."

In that moment, Zachariah stood—not as a prisoner caught in flight, but as a man whose spirit echoed that of his legendary forebear, his actions sparking a camaraderie among those who watched on with delight.

Zachariah's declaration resonated with the firmness of his conviction, a reminder of the freedoms promised to him. The applause that followed was a cacophony of madness to his ears, a testament to the absurdity of the situation.

The man in black's decree, however, sliced through the merriment with the sharpness of a command. Annabella's compliance, marked by a curtsy, seemed at odds with the fiery spirit Zachariah believed she possessed. The notion of such an order was anathema to him, a violation of will he could not abide.

"Wait," Zachariah interjected with authority, halting the proceedings. Annabella faced him; her smile was a beacon in the garden's luminescence. His concern for her feelings was genuine, rooted in the memory of her words that spoke of repulsion.

Yet, her response was a revelation, a shift from initial revulsion to something more complex. "You misheard," she confessed, her admission painting a different picture of their encounter. Her resolve to fulfil her role within the fellowship was unwavering, a decision made for the greater good, yet it left Zachariah pondering the true nature of freedom and choice within the gilded cage they both inhabited.

The man in the black robe's proximity did little to unsettle Zachariah; his resolve was as steadfast as the ancient trees that lined the estate. "Annabella's worth is not for me to judge, nor is it my place to decide her fate," he stated with quiet conviction. "A week of solitude will grant us both time for reflection—a respite from the weight of expectations."

The man nodded, his voice a calm ripple in the sea of decisions. "Very well. Annabella, inform the Buxton branch of Janet's indisposition. Agnes, take this time to rest; the journey ahead demands it. As for the rest of you, the morrow calls for your departure. Be ready to reconvene should the ceremony beckon."

He turned to Zachariah, a hint of anticipation in his tone. "In a fortnight, we shall unravel the mystery of your heritage, Zachariah Black. The DNA will speak of your past and, perhaps, dictate your future within our fellowship."

With that, the assembly dispersed, leaving Zachariah to ponder the path that lay before him—a path veiled in history and bound by blood. The coming days would reveal much, not just about his lineage but about the very essence of the fellowship and the role he was destined to play within it.

Zachariah's defiance hung in the air, a challenge that could not be taken lightly. Malcolm's retreat was not one of fear, but of calculation, his laughter a dark omen of the power he wielded within the fellowship.

Annabella's concern was etched upon her face, and her grip on Zachariah's arm was both a restraint and a silent plea. "You must understand, Zachariah," she implored, "Malcolm is not a man to be trifled with. His influence runs deep, and his connections are vast. A threat made against him is a threat against the very pillars of our society."

The gravity of the situation settled upon Zachariah like a shroud. His journey had brought him to the heart of a labyrinth, where each turn held the promise of danger or destiny. As the night enveloped the estate, he knew that the choices he made henceforth would seal his fate, for better or worse, in the annals of the fellowship's storied history.

Zachariah's jest, though light-hearted, carried an edge of truth—a month of close quarters with Annabella, a prospect that stirred a complex blend of emotions. Her response was a dance of amusement and complicity, her kiss a seal on the unspoken pact between them.

Hand in hand, they traversed the castle's ancient corridors, arriving at the kitchen—a chamber of abundance where the air was thick with the promise of feasts to come. The sight of meat suspended in the cool air conjured memories of a more sombre place, a reminder of life's fragile balance.

As they stood amidst the bounty, Zachariah felt the weight of his lineage, the pull of destiny yet to be claimed, and the warmth of a hand that held his own—a hand that could either lead him to salvation or to the end of all he knew.

Zachariah settled into the quietude of the kitchen, the bounty on his plate a stark contrast to the solitude of his dining. Annabella's words, though spoken with a smile, were a decree of patience—a waiting game that he was bound to play.

As she departed, leaving him to the company of his thoughts and the feast before him, he turned his attention to the wine. The pop of the cork was a small celebration, a solitary toast to his circumstances. The rich aroma promised a reprieve from the day's tensions, a luxury to be savoured.

He poured the wine, its crimson hue a reminder of the bloodline that had brought him here, to this moment of indulgence amidst a web of intrigue. If enjoyment eluded him, it would not be for lack of provision. The sedation, an unwelcome chapter in his journey, was but a shadow now—overpowered by the warmth of the meal and the comfort of the wine.

The morning greeted Zachariah with a quiet absence, Agnes' warmth replaced by the cool, crisp sheets. Fresh attire chosen from the wardrobe's offerings, he caught a glimpse of his electric trike and generator outside—a sight that sparked a sense of familiarity in this grand, unfamiliar world.

Descending the staircase, his smile was a silent testament to the night's comfort. Janet's voice, a soft herald of the new day, guided him to a side room where breakfast lay in wait. The transformation from historical garb to a modern floral dress and blazer marked the passage of time, a blend of the fellowship's ancient lineage with the present moment.

Before him, a spread of morning fare invited indulgence. He chose the classic combination of eggs, bacon, and tomatoes, accompanied by golden toast—a hearty start to a day shrouded in mystery and anticipation. Janet, mirroring his choice with a more modest portion, joined him in breaking the fast, and their shared meal gave a moment of normalcy in the midst of the fellowship's intricate dance.

Zachariah pondered Janet's question, his gaze steady. "Anger is a luxury I can't afford at the moment," he replied. "I'm suspended between truth and deception, waiting for clarity. As for living together, it's a thought that requires careful consideration."

Janet's eyes sparkled with a mix of hope and mischief. "Imagine it, Zachariah—a new beginning. We could roam the highlands in the motorhome, free from the past's shadows. With Annabella's father's blessing, we'd have the world at our fingertips, and I could leave the work to others. A life of leisure could be ours, should you choose it."

Her words painted a picture of a future unburdened by the fellowship's machinations—a future where choice and freedom could truly flourish. Zachariah's heart dared to hope, even as the wheels of fate continued to turn, unseen.

Janet's response was laced with a camaraderie that transcended personal entanglements. "Our bond as sisters in this endeavour supersedes any potential rift," she assured him. "The anticipation of discovering your lineage adds an element of excitement to our relationship. I look forward to the mischievous adventures that await us, regardless of whether you descend from Blackbeard or Jack Ward."

Her playful demeanour suggested a light-hearted approach to the fellowship's intricate dynamics. The interruption by the waiter did little to dampen her spirits. "It seems I have a morning of discovery ahead," she said with a twinkle in her eye. "Let's take the trikes for a spin, Zachariah. You can show me the ropes, and we'll enjoy the freedom of the open paths."

The prospect of a leisurely ride, coupled with the chance to bond over a shared activity, offered a brief respite from the weighty matters at hand—a moment of normalcy amidst the grand tapestry of their intertwined fates.

Zachariah's laughter echoed in the vastness of the castle, a sound of lightness amidst the labyrinth of corridors and secrets. Janet's kiss was a seal of their shared moment, a brief interlude of affection before the day's adventures.

Following her directions, he found himself outside, where the trikes stood ready, silent steeds awaiting their riders. The hum of the generator filled the air as he connected the batteries, a symphony of preparation for the journey ahead.

Janet reappeared the embodiment of practicality in her jeans and coat, her hands offering warmth against the morning's chill. "The castle's walls may shield us from the elements, but beyond them, the Scottish air is brisk," she said, her voice carrying the care of a companion well-versed in the whims of the highlands.

The Scottish landscape unfolded before them, a tapestry of green and gold under the expansive sky. Janet, with newfound zeal, took to her trike like a natural, the pedal-assist mechanism propelling her forward with an ease that belied the strength of her will.

Zachariah, ever the guardian, kept a watchful eye, ensuring she was never without support. Together, they ventured towards John O'Groats, where memories lingered in the salty kiss of the wind. Side by side, they shared the road, a pair of explorers on a journey that was as much about discovery as it was a flight from the intricate web they were entwined in.

Janet's laughter was carried away by the breeze, a sound of pure delight that rose above the whispering grasses. The comfort of her saddle was a small mercy, a gentle reminder that amidst the grand designs of fate, it was the simple pleasures that often meant the most.

The journey to John O'Groats, a mere five miles on the electric trikes, was a brief escape from the castle's confines. The car park, now a quiet expanse, echoed with the absence of the usual tourist bustle, the closed shops standing as silent sentinels to a time before.

Janet's embrace was a celebration of the simple joy they had shared. "It's a different kind of thrill," she mused, her voice tinged with the exhilaration of their ride. "Once this little one arrives, I'll be back on these trails, chasing the wind and reclaiming myself. And you, Zachariah, will be my partner in crime."

Her laughter was a melody that danced with the sea breeze, a sound that softened the rugged landscape. Hand in hand, they stood by the water's edge, the waves performing their timeless ballet before them. The signpost, a marker of journeys taken and those yet to come, stood witness to their moment of respite—a brief interlude in a life that was anything but ordinary.

The return trip was a blend of caution and carefree abandon. Zachariah's attentiveness to Janet's well-being was evident in his pre-emptive battery swap—a small act of tenderness amidst the uncertainty of their situation. Janet's sudden burst of speed, her laughter trailing behind her like a comet's tail, was a spark of spontaneity that ignited Zachariah's curiosity and concern in equal measure.

The narrow lanes they traversed were a maze of possibilities; each turn a question left unanswered until they found themselves on familiar ground, the A836 leading them back to the Castle of Mey. Their arrival was marked not by fanfare but by the quiet presence of Malcolm, a sentinel at the threshold of the estate.

The underground passage to the sea was a clandestine corridor, a remnant of an era when the fellowship's forebears might have engaged in similar secretive exchanges. Malcolm's revelation of the incoming boat, laden with brandy and Bacardi for the fellowship's personal use, was a wink to their indulgent traditions.

Zachariah's laughter rang out, a joyful acknowledgement of the fellowship's roguish undertones. "A bunch of crooks," he declared, his jest met with Malcolm's headshake and an amused grin.

As they moved deeper into the earth, the echoes of their steps were a reminder of the cave's storied past. The place where Zachariah's ankles had once been shackled now served as a path to new introductions and camaraderie among the fellowship's members.

The cave's illumination cast away any shadows, guiding their way to the sea's edge. The daylight at the end of the tunnel was a beacon, a symbol of the fellowship's ability to navigate the fine line between the hidden and the revealed, the illicit and the luxurious.

The vessel's approach was a delicate dance with danger, navigated with the precision of a seasoned sailor. Malcolm's device, a beacon in the dim, cast a laser beam that sliced through the darkness, signalling the boat's safe passage. His smile hinted at more than just cargo—there was a hint of intrigue in the air.

Perched on a rock, Zachariah observed the transformation of the small craft into a robust fishing boat, its arrival at the cave a ballet of nautical skill. The ladder clattered down, and crates of spirits began their journey ashore—twenty cases of brandy, five of Bacardi, and six of champagne, not to mention ten truckles of cheese—a veritable treasure trove.

Malcolm's exchange with the crew, a flurry of French and currency, was the transaction of smugglers' lore. Then, from the vessel emerged Gabrielle, a vision of allure, who declared her intent with a playful tug of Zachariah's beard. "You are Blackbeard," she proclaimed, "and I am your future lover."

Zachariah's glare was met with Malcolm's nonchalant smile, a casual revelation of the contingency plan involving Gabrielle. "It's all in the bloodline," Malcolm seemed to suggest, implying that either woman's ancestry would serve the fellowship's purpose. "And if you 'serve' both, even better," he added with a shrug.

"Wonderful," Zachariah replied dryly, the sarcasm barely veiled. He trailed behind Malcolm and Gabrielle, the latter's casual attire a stark contrast to the gravity of the situation. As their French conversation floated back to him, Zachariah mused on the universality of attraction, a language unto itself that needed no translation.

Zachariah returned to his room with a retreat into introspection, the walls around him holding the echoes of a plan he still struggled to comprehend. The fellowship's motives, entangled in wealth and ancient lineage, were a puzzle that left him feeling like a pawn in a game of kings.

As he lay on his bed, the drone of the television offered a mundane escape, a slice of normalcy in a world that had become anything but. The phone call to order lunch was a lifeline to the outside, a reminder that life continued beyond the machinations of the powerful.

In the solitude of his room, with a meal on its way, Zachariah allowed himself the luxury of peace—a momentary respite to gather his thoughts. The challenge before him was daunting: to outmanoeuvre the influence and resources of the twelve. Creativity would be his weapon, cunning his shield, as he navigated the treacherous waters of wealth and power that sought to claim him.

Zachariah's lunch arrived with the quiet efficiency of the castle's staff, a silent exchange that left him alone with his thoughts and a fresh salad. As he gazed out at the moorland, a subtle movement caught his eye—a picture above the bookcase that seemed to stir with a life of its own.

The possibility of secret passages sparked a sense of intrigue in Zachariah. He approached the bookcase, fingers tracing the spines of the books, searching for the mechanism that would reveal the hidden pathways he was certain lay beyond. The movies had taught him that a single book could be the key, but reality proved more elusive.

Time ticked away as he probed and pondered, the waiter's return a brief interruption to his quest. With the tray gone and his act of casual perusal maintained, Zachariah's determination to uncover the castle's secrets only grew. The answer was there, somewhere among the leather-bound tomes and the silent whispers of history.

Zachariah's discovery of the secret passage was a moment straight out of an adventure film, the bookcase sliding away to reveal a hidden world beneath the castle. The descent down the cobweb-laden staircase was a journey back in time, each step taking him deeper into the bowels of the earth.

As the tunnel opened into a larger space, he found himself an unseen observer of a clandestine operation. The lab before him was a hive of activity, the white-coated figures engrossed in their work. The mention of a lethal formula and the unfortunate fate of the rats sent a chill down his spine. The implications of such experiments were ominous, and the casual mention of moving on to chimpanzees suggested a disregard for the well-being of more than just rodents.

Concealed in the shadows, Zachariah was a witness to the darker side of the fellowship's quest for power—a quest that seemed to extend beyond wealth and bloodlines into the realm of science, with unknown and potentially dangerous intentions.

Zachariah returned to his room in a silent rush, the evidence of his secret exploration clinging to him in the form of cobwebs and dust. With a nudge, the bookcase slid into place, concealing the passage once more. A swift shower washed away the physical remnants of his journey, but the mental impressions were not so easily cleansed.

Finding a hiding spot for his soiled garments became a new mission. The space behind the bookcase, now familiar to him, served as a makeshift wardrobe, the rocks providing a ledge just out of sight. His clothes were tucked away, and he emerged from the hidden passage, ensuring the bookcase was secure before examining his reflection for any lingering signs of his escapade.

Zachariah Black's Quest for Truth

The mirror revealed a man outwardly composed, the full-length glass reflecting no hint of the secrets he had uncovered. Yet behind his eyes lay the knowledge of what lay beneath the castle—a knowledge that set him apart from the other inhabitants of this grand and mysterious estate

Zachariah stood on the balcony, the wisteria scent a natural reprieve from the castle's oppressive secrets. The thought of contacting the police flickered through his mind, but the web of influence he'd seen spun doubts about who could be trusted. The risk of exposure, both for himself and against the fellowship's reach, was too great.

The realisation that every word might be monitored sent a shiver down his spine. He retreated to his room, eyes darting over every surface, searching for signs of surveillance. But the fellowship's expertise in concealment left him empty-handed. They were masters of their craft, and Zachariah knew that if they had hidden something within these walls, it would remain unseen to the untrained eye.

Zachariah's solitude was interrupted by Gabrielle's entrance, her presence a stark contrast to the quiet contemplation he had been immersed in. The coffee she brought was a gesture of camaraderie or perhaps an attempt at diplomacy, but her attire and the pungent scent of garlic were off-putting to him, his eyes fixed upon her attributes plain to see.

His blunt assumption about her profession as a prostitute and suggestion that she seek fashion advice from Annabella was met with a fiery response—a cup of hot coffee flung in his direction, soaking his face and beard, a clear rejection of his commentary. Gabrielle's swift departure, marked by the slamming door, left Zachariah in a mix of shock and amusement.

In the bathroom, he cleansed himself of the coffee's residue, his laughter echoing off the tiles—laughter tinged with the absurdity of the situation and the realisation that navigating the fellowship's social intricacies would be as challenging as unravelling its secrets.

Zachariah's fleeting moment of amusement was brutally cut short as two men barged in, their intent clear as they delivered a ruthless beating. His attempts at defence were futile against their aggression. The room, once a place of solitude, became a stage for violence and a reminder of the power dynamics at play within the fellowship.

As the staff cleaned the remnants of Gabrielle's outburst, Malcolm's presence loomed over Zachariah, his words a stark warning. "Don't insult Gabrielle," he cautioned with a cold authority that left no room for a retort. "Her father's influence is vast, and your cleverness is no match for it."

With a final, painful reminder of his vulnerability—a kick to the ribs—Malcolm departed, leaving Zachariah to contemplate the precariousness of his position. Lying there, the desire for his machete was more than a wish for self-defence; it was a yearning for the power to stand against the forces that sought to control him.

CHAPTER 5

Must be more discreet

Gritting through the pain, Zachariah steadied himself on the bed, his ribs aching with each breath. He donned his thick coat, a layer of armour against the chill and a shield for his battered body. Wallet in tow, he descended the stairs, each step a testament to his resolve.

The garden was a sanctuary of sorts, and the potting shed within it held the promise of retribution. The sight of the old machete brought a grim smile to his face. Hours passed as he worked, the blade's transformation from a neglected tool to a gleaming instrument of defence mirroring his own sharpening purpose.

With the sheath now cleaned and secured to his belt, Zachariah felt a semblance of control return. The weight of the machete at his side was a comforting presence, a silent vow that he would not be taken unawares again.

Zachariah's stride was unwavering as he approached Malcolm, the weight of the machete in his hand a familiar comfort. The moon hung low, casting elongated shadows that danced around them like spectres of the night. The laughter from Malcolm's men had ceased; their lifeless forms were a testament to Zachariah's swift retribution.

Malcolm's face was a mask of feigned composure, but his voice betrayed a hint of desperation. "Zachariah, let's not be hasty. We can settle this without further violence."

Zachariah's response was a cold chuckle. "Hasty? My actions are deliberate, Malcolm. You preyed on me when I was vulnerable, but I am no longer that person."

Malcolm's hand trembled as he drew the revolver, the metallic glint in the dim light betraying his sudden move. But Zachariah was quicker, his machete flying through the air with deadly precision. The blade struck Malcolm's arm, the force of the throw driving it deep into the wood of the door frame, effectively pinning him in place.

Malcolm's scream shattered the night's silence, a visceral sound of pain and shock. Zachariah advanced, his steps measured and silent. With a swift motion, he retrieved his machete, the sound of steel sliding against wood echoing ominously. Malcolm's revolver clattered to the ground, and Zachariah stooped to pick it up, his movements deliberate.

He stood before Malcolm, the revolver now in his grasp, its barrel cold against Malcolm's temple. "Russian roulette, Malcolm?" Zachariah's voice was calm, almost serene, in stark contrast to the situation. "A game of chance seems fitting for you—a gamble at every turn of your life."

Malcolm's eyes were wide with fear, his breaths coming in ragged gasps as he realised the gravity of his predicament. Zachariah's finger toyed with the trigger, a dark dance between life and death. "But you see, I don't leave things to chance," he continued, his tone unwavering. "I make my own fate."

Malcolm clutched his arm tightly, the dark fabric of his shirt slowly blooming with red. I watched him for a moment, the revolver now a heavy presence in my pocket. Through the window, Annabella's eyes met mine, her expression a mix of horror and awe. Agnes and Gabrielle stood behind her, their faces pale in the moonlight.

As Malcolm disappeared into the house, the sound of his pain echoing behind him, I turned my back on the scene. The trike lay forgotten; my only thought was to put distance between myself and this place of violence. Each step down the gravel drive was measured, and my senses heightened for the telltale sound of a trigger being pulled.

The sudden rush of paws on the ground had me spinning, machete in hand, ready to defend myself against new attackers. But it was the German shepherds, their powerful bodies barrelling towards me with lethal speed. I braced myself, but Annabella's sharp whistle cut through the tension. The dogs halted, sitting obediently as she approached.

Annabella's run was swift, her breath coming in quick gasps as she reached me. I kept my distance, aware of her skill and the threat it posed. "Zachariah," she panted, "you don't have to do this alone."

Her words hung between us, an offer of alliance or perhaps a plea for peace. I weighed my options, the machete's handle slick in my grasp. Trust was a luxury I couldn't afford, not yet. But in her stance, there was an earnestness that gave me pause.

Zachariah's stance was wary, the machete an extension of his arm as he maintained a cautious distance. "It's not about being horrible, Annabella. It's about survival," he said, his voice steady despite the tension that crackled in the air between them.

Annabella's hand fluttered to her mouth, a gesture of mock surprise. "Oh, Zachariah, such harsh words for Gabrielle. But I suppose we all have our ... preferences," she replied, her tone laced with sarcasm.

Zachariah's gaze didn't waver. "Preferences or not, it's about respect. And that lab," he gestured vaguely towards the ground, "it's a whole other level of disrespect. To nature, to life."

Annabella's shock seemed genuine, her eyes widening at the mention of the underground passageway. "DNA sequencing? Rats? That's one thing, but chimpanzees ... " She trailed off, her expression troubled.

Zachariah nodded, his jaw set. "Exactly. It's illegal and immoral. And I won't stand for it. Not anymore."

The air was thick with unspoken words as Annabella took a step forward, only to be met with Zachariah's defensive posture. "What's the matter?" she asked, her voice a mix of concern and challenge.

Zachariah's reply was a cold reminder of their respective skills. "You're a black belt, and I'm not exactly holding a bouquet of flowers here. Let's just say, it's for the best if we keep this distance."

Annabella paused, considering his words. Then, slowly, she nodded. "Fair enough, Zachariah. But remember, not everyone is your enemy." Her eyes held his for a moment longer before she turned, her silhouette fading into the darkness as Zachariah stood alone, the weight of his decisions heavy in his hands.

Annabella's words hung in the air, a challenge to Zachariah's heated emotions. "Think logically? That's rich, coming from you," Zachariah spat back, his voice laced with contempt. "Those dogs are just another tool in your twisted game."

He paused, taking a deep, steadying breath. "Where do we go from here? Nowhere. I'm done playing your games, Annabella. You and your ilk are worse than any villain I've ever written."

Annabella's laugh was light, almost musical, but it did nothing to ease the tension. "Take a walk, Zachariah. Mull over your next move. But remember, running is futile. You're in this too deep."

Zachariah's response was a sneer. "And you think I'd stoop so low as to be with Gabrielle? She's not my concern. My concern is getting out of this nightmare."

With a final, disdainful glance at Annabella's smug expression, Zachariah turned and sprinted away. The sound of her calling the dogs back to the castle was a distant echo in his ears. He ran until the estate was a mere speck behind him, the sense of liberation growing with each stride.

As he reached the end of the drive, the sight of the drone brought him back to reality. It hovered there, an unblinking eye in the sky. Zachariah stopped, looked up, and raised his middle finger defiantly. "I'm not your pawn," he declared, his voice a whisper against the vastness of the sky. "And I won't be pushed around."

With that gesture of defiance, Zachariah turned and walked away, his silhouette a lone figure against the sprawling landscape. The drone remained.

His revolver felt heavy in Zachariah's grasp, a stark reminder of the path he had chosen. With a steady hand, he aimed and fired. The drone, once a silent observer, spiralled down, crashing into the earth with a satisfying thud. Zachariah's smile was one of triumph as he crushed the camera underfoot, the lens shattering with a crunch.

He turned his back on the wreckage and made his way to Loch Mey, the serenity of the water a stark contrast to the chaos he had left behind. Sitting at the water's edge, he sent pebbles skimming across the surface, each bounce a momentary escape from his troubles.

The sound of footsteps drew his attention, and he glanced to his left. A man approached, his attire marking him as a gamekeeper, his smile warm and genuine. "Hello there," the man greeted in a rich Scottish accent, confirming Zachariah's suspicions.

"Hi, estate gamekeeper, I presume?" Zachariah responded, his tone cautious yet polite. The game warden's presence was unexpected, but perhaps it was just another twist in the ever-complicated game he found himself in. Zachariah was ready for whatever came next, his resolve as unyielding as the Scottish landscape that surrounded him

The game warden, Rory, offered a knowing nod, his presence a calm contrast to the turmoil Zachariah felt. "Caused a bit of a stir, have you?" Rory's smirk suggested he was no stranger to the castle's dramas.

Zachariah's annoyance was palpable. "I'm not some pawn in their games," he said tersely. "Tell me about the fish here. Something peaceful for a change."

"Ah, the loch's full of life," Rory replied, his gaze drifting over the calm waters. "Salmon and trout, mostly. They're thriving, especially with the bugs this season."

As Rory spoke, Zachariah's attention was drawn to the approaching horses. Gabrielle, astride one of them, seemed to bring the castle's shadow with her. Zachariah's heart raced, a mix of anger and anticipation surging within him.

Rory stood, sensing the shift in the air. "I'm Rory, by the way," he said, extending a brief moment of camaraderie before adding, "Looks like you might have company. The ladies seem keen on fly fishing. Maybe you'll get lucky and catch more than just fish today." With a pat on Zachariah's shoulder, Rory departed, leaving him to face whatever came next on the shores of Loch Mey. Zachariah watched him go, the weight of the revolver in his pocket a silent reminder of the day's earlier events. He turned his attention back to the water, the skimming pebbles a momentary distraction from the approaching figure of Gabrielle.

Gabrielle secured the horses to a young tree, then proceeded to unpack a fishing box and assemble two rods. She glanced over with a playful smile. "I've brought an extra fly rod. You can give it a try if you're up for it, or just watch and learn. Or would you rather just sit and brood?" Her grin held a hint of mystery.

It had been ages since I'd last fished, and my skills with a fly rod were rusty at best. Yet, the thought of being outdone by Gabrielle was intolerable. "Thanks," I said, picking up the spare rod and attempting to set it up. Gabrielle watched, her grin never fading, but she mercifully kept any comments about my clumsiness to herself. "Here, take mine," she offered after a moment. "You'll still be fumbling with that when night falls." I took her rod; my pride stung, but I was grateful for the shortcut.

Gabrielle's expertise with the rod was evident, her movements refined by years of experience. She seemed at one with the loch, her casts smooth and precise, effortlessly pulling trout from the water. I observed and learned, and soon enough, I felt the tug of success on my own line. With Gabrielle's help, the fish was quickly dispatched.

As the evening wore on, our collection grew—eight for Gabrielle, three for me. But the midges were relentless, feasting upon me with a voracity that rivalled the fish we caught. Together, we packed up, the fruits of our labour secured in a bag destined for the castle's kitchen.

Gabrielle's offer of dinner was unexpected, a gesture of peace amidst the chaos of recent events. "We can have dinner together, Zachariah," she proposed a hint of camaraderie in her voice. "Let's enjoy the fruits of our fishing. I'd like to be friends."

Her words were a balm to the sting of the midges and the sting of isolation. "Annabella told me what you said," she continued, her tone light. "No garlic when I'm around you, I promise. And don't worry, I had no expectations of being swept off my feet—literally or figuratively. You Brits are an enigma."

Her laughter was a melody that danced across the loch, and for a moment, Zachariah allowed himself to consider the possibility of friendship in this strange, new world.

The castle loomed in the distance as Zachariah hesitantly mounted the horse, its size daunting. Gabrielle's encouragement did little to ease his nerves. "He's gentle," she assured, but Zachariah couldn't shake the feeling that he was one wrong move away from a bruising encounter with the earth.

As they rode, Gabrielle's words floated over to him, carrying the weight of others' opinions. "Annabella and Agnes think the world of you," she said, a note of sincerity in her voice. "And Janet—there's a story there, isn't there?"

Zachariah let out a heavy sigh, the past and present colliding within him. "I sometimes wish I'd stayed in my own little world," he confessed, the admission hanging between them like a delicate mist.

Gabrielle nodded, understanding more than she let on. "Loss is a shadow that clings to us all," she murmured. "But they say time brings healing. Here, in this place, there's a chance for something new, something better. Your lineage, your bloodline—it could change everything."

Her words were a balm, and as they continued their ride, the castle's imposing walls became less of a prison and more of a gateway to possibilities yet to be explored. Zachariah's grip on the reins loosened slightly, a tentative peace settling in his heart.

Zachariah's defiance was unwavering, and his words were a clear declaration of his intent to survive, no matter the cost. "Over my dead body," he proclaimed, the revolver a cold weight in his pocket, a symbol of his determination to fight until the very end.

"You're like Blackbeard reincarnated," Gabrielle remarked, half in jest, half in awe. "Fearless even when the odds are against you."

"Why fear?" Zachariah retorted with a shrug. "At my age, death is a constant companion. And what use is fortune if one has nothing to spend it on?"

The standoff escalated as Malcolm's voice cut through the tension. "Zachariah, surrender the revolver or face execution," he demanded, the threat of a rifle from the battlements looming over them.

Zachariah's response was swift and cunning. "Malcolm, take a good look," he said, revealing the barrel of the revolver hidden up his sleeve. "Call off your sniper, or it'll be the last thing you do."

Malcolm's hand waved, a signal of defeat, and the gunmen retreated. With a swift kick, Zachariah ensured Malcolm would remember their encounter, the man crumpling to the ground in pain.

"I'm glad we're friends," Zachariah said with a sardonic smile, stepping over Malcolm's prone form and making his way to the sanctuary of his room, the castle's walls echoing with the tale of his daring.

Zachariah's room was a sanctuary of sorts, a place where the chaos of the outside world seemed to fade into the background. Annabella's entrance was like a whirlwind, her concern for his recent actions written all over her face. "Zachariah, have you lost your mind? Malcolm is S.A.S.," she exclaimed, her voice a mixture of worry and disbelief.

He lay there, nonchalant, on the bed, an island of calm in the storm. Her figure was indeed striking, and he couldn't help but acknowledge it with a wry comment. Her grin was infectious, and as she leaned in to kiss him, the tension in the room seemed to dissipate, if only for a moment.

The cold steel of the machete was a stark contrast to the warmth of her lips. "Don't move, Annabella," he warned, though his tone was soft, almost playful. She complied, and their lips met again, a dangerous dance between desire and danger.

As she stepped back, the grin returned to her face, a sign that she was impressed despite herself. "You may act the part of the decrepit old man, but you're sharper than most," she teased. "Before long, I might just find myself sharing this bed with you."

Zachariah's quip about his offspring and his aversion to adding a French-speaking child to the mix drew a grin from Annabella as she departed. Alone again, he observed the waiters meticulously setting the table, the silverware gleaming in the soft light, the view of the gardens adding a touch of serenity to the room.

Gabrielle's entrance was nothing short of cinematic; her evening dresses a cascade of blue velvet that seemed to capture the twilight itself. Zachariah, still in his day clothes, felt a twinge of regret for not dressing for the occasion. Yet, as he stood and offered Gabrielle a seat, his manners were impeccable.

"You look magnificent," he said, his compliment genuine as he surrendered to change, returning moments later, and he took his place across from her. The table between them was a small island of civility in a sea of uncertainty, and for a moment, as they began their meal, the outside world, with all its intrigue and danger, seemed a world away. Zachariah allowed himself this respite, a gentleman in the company of a lady, under the watchful eyes of the castle's ancient walls.

Zachariah's response was a mix of amusement and mock indignation. "Well, Gabrielle, I can assure you that the only thing I plan to rip into tonight is this excellent meal," he said with a chuckle, his gaze shifting from her cleavage to meet her eyes with a twinkle of mirth.

The dinner progressed with light-hearted banter and the clinking of cutlery. The fish was exquisite, and the company was unexpectedly pleasant. As they dined, the tension that had defined their earlier interactions seemed to melt away, replaced by a camaraderie that Zachariah hadn't realised he'd been craving.

"Your eyes tell quite the tale themselves," Zachariah quipped, raising his glass in a toast. "To an evening free from danger and full of surprises." The night was still young, and for the first time in a long while, Zachariah felt a sense of ease settle over him.

Zachariah's comment drew a blush from Gabrielle, a silent acknowledgement of the boldness of his words about her cleavage. As the soft strains of music filled the room, it seemed to transport them to another time, a world of swashbuckling pirates and grand balls.

Gabrielle's invitation to dance was met with a roguish grin from Zachariah. "Dance? With a lady as fair as yourself? It would be my honour," he declared, rising from his seat with a flourish. He extended his hand, the pirate costume adding to the charm of the moment.

As they took to the makeshift dance floor, Zachariah found that the rhythm of the music matched the newfound rhythm in his heart. The evening had turned into a scene straight out of a storybook, and for once, he allowed himself to enjoy the narrative unfolding around him. The dance was a celebration, a momentary escape from the intrigue that awaited them beyond the castle walls.

Zachariah Black's Quest for Truth

Zachariah's hand rested on the hilt of his cutlass, the tension in the room palpable. Malcolm's entrance had cast a shadow over the evening's festivities, yet his smile suggested a truce, if only temporary.

"I appreciate the compliment, Gabrielle," Zachariah said, his voice steady despite the interruption. "And Malcolm, your concern for my attire is noted. I assure you, the decision to don these clothes was mine alone, inspired by the company and the spirit of the evening."

He glanced at Gabrielle, whose concern had shifted to curiosity. "We were indeed enjoying ourselves," he continued, addressing Malcolm directly. "I trust we can return to our evening without further ... surprises?"

The bedroom, once a stage for the evening's light-hearted jests, had quickly become a theatre of the unexpected. Annabella, Agnes, and Janet's entrance were met with Zachariah's wry humour, diffusing the tension with a quip about his inability to entertain such a crowd. Malcolm's laughter echoed, a brief respite from the undercurrent of power plays at work.

Annabella's whisper was a mix of threat and flirtation, her words a reminder of the delicate balance between desire and allegiance. Malcolm's command for privacy was a clear directive, yet it was his request for Zachariah to don the pirate's attire once more that hinted at deeper machinations.

Zachariah's query about his fate was met with Malcolm's blunt assurance of his safety—for now. The room emptied, leaving Zachariah and Gabrielle in a bubble of intimacy, briefly punctured by Malcolm's presence. Gabrielle's kiss was a bittersweet end to an evening that had promised so much more.

Alone, Zachariah shed the pirate's facade, returning to the comfort of his jeans. The descent into the castle's bowels was a journey into darkness, the candlelight a guide through the webbed corridors of secrets. The burning cobwebs, a grim reminder of the castle's age and mysteries, did little to deter him.

Hidden behind crates, Zachariah became an unseen observer, the whispers around him weaving a narrative he was only beginning to understand. The stakes were high, and in the shadows, he listened, the pieces of the puzzle slowly coming together in the flickering candlelight.

In the quiet of his room, Zachariah lay in bed, the echoes of the conversation he had overheard mingling with his own thoughts. The idea of being part of an experiment was unsettling, yet there was a part of him that couldn't help but be intrigued by the possibility of turning back the clock.

The notion of reclaiming years lost to time brought a wry smile to his face. "To be twenty-five again," he mused, the idea as alluring as it was impossible. The chuckle that escaped him was a mix of disbelief and whimsy, a sound that seemed out of place in the stillness of the night.

As sleep claimed him, his last conscious thought was a playful wish to the universe—to wake up with the vigour of youth, to face the challenges ahead with the fearlessness of a man who had been given a second chance at life.

The morning light crept in, accompanied by the call of a cock pheasant, a natural alarm that stirred Zachariah from his slumber. The open balcony windows invited the new day, and with it, the reality of what Saturday might bring. But for now, he was content to lie there a moment longer, wrapped in the quiet comfort of his room, the cobwebs of the past night's adventure a mere memory.

Gabrielle's arrival with breakfast was a pleasant surprise, her smile brightening the room as much as the morning sun. "The staff run away?"

"No, I just thought it'd be nice to start the day together," she replied to Zachariah's playful inquiry.

As he joined her by the window, the view of the gardens provided a serene backdrop to their impromptu meal. Gabrielle's flimsy dressing gown and see-through negligee left no surprises. "Thank you, Gabrielle. This is quite the spread," Zachariah said, accepting the plate of bacon and eggs. The table was set perfectly, the toast rack and tea completing the ensemble.

The weight of the tray did suggest strength or perhaps the assistance of a waiter at the door. It was hard to imagine Gabrielle navigating the castle's corridors in her night attire, yet here she was, the very picture of grace and ease.

They settled into a comfortable silence, the kind that only a shared meal can bring. The morning's tranquillity was a stark contrast to the intrigue of the previous night, and for a moment, Zachariah allowed himself to simply enjoy the company and the simple pleasure of a shared breakfast.

"Have you ever married, Gabrielle?"

"No, far too young to venture into marriage. I haven't lived; I'm still a virgin!"

I choked. I'd heard some porkies in my time, but that one was beyond comprehension. Gabrielle rose to her feet, patting my back. I dashed to the bathroom, drinking a glass of water; how I believed that remark, I don't know. I returned to the table with a grin.

Zachariah's morning took a dramatic turn with Gabrielle's outburst. Her question hung in the air, met with his blunt honesty about her behaviour. The result was a splash of tea and a flurry of French, leaving Zachariah alone, his breakfast afloat in a pool of Earl Grey.

Despite the unexpected shower, he remained seated, a wry smile on his face as he continued with his meal. The incident was just another ripple in the castle's ongoing saga, a story that seemed to thrive on the unpredictable. And as he sat there, the morning light streaming in, Zachariah couldn't help but savour the peculiar start to his day.

Zachariah's stroll to the shoreline was a moment of reflection, the revolver and machete at his side a reminder of the ever-present undercurrent of danger. The castle, with all its intrigue and mystery, seemed a world away as he gazed out over the water.

Gabrielle's claim of innocence lingered in his mind, a puzzle yet to be solved. "Don't judge a book by its cover," he mused, considering the possibility that appearances could be deceiving. Perhaps Gabrielle was, as she claimed, her outward behaviour a facade masking the truth.

Yet, the question remained—why would she choose him, a self-proclaimed "old codger," over someone more fitting of her youth and vitality? The answer was as elusive as the horizon where the sky met the sea, and Zachariah knew that some mysteries were not meant to be unravelled in a day. For now, he would watch the waves and wait for the tide to bring in new revelations.

Zachariah's contemplation by the loch was a solitary affair, the stones skipping across the water mirroring the ripples of his thoughts. The drone overhead was a stark reminder of the constant surveillance, a silent guardian tracking his every move. Janet's arrival, with her Range Rover as a symbol of the outside world, was a jarring contrast to his solitude.

Her kiss was a mix of affection and warning, a plea for caution in a world where provocations could lead to dire consequences. "I know, Janet," Zachariah replied, his voice heavy with the weight of decisions yet to be made. "But sometimes, stirring the pot is the only way to see what rises to the top."

As he settled into the passenger seat, the prospect of donning a pirate's costume seemed increasingly ludicrous. The lure of a simpler life, one where his pension and savings could fund adventures on an electric bicycle, was a tempting escape from the castle's machinations.

The drive away from the loch was a journey back to reality, and the castle's spires were a reminder of the role he was expected to play. Yet, the open road whispered promises of freedom, and Zachariah found himself yearning for the wind in his hair and the open sky above—a pirate of the road, charting his own course.

"That's a fair point, Janet," Zachariah acknowledged, his tone reflecting a newfound understanding. "I'll make sure to apologise to Gabrielle. It was out of line for me to comment on her personal matters."

With a plan to make amends, Zachariah felt a sense of resolve. It was time to navigate the social intricacies of the castle with the same care he would tread through a minefield. An apology was due, and he was prepared to offer it sincerely, hoping to restore some semblance of peace—or at least a ceasefire—in the ongoing drama of castle life.

Zachariah's swift apology to Gabrielle was a gesture of good faith, an attempt to smooth over the ruffled feathers without lingering for a potentially heated exchange. As he retreated to the sanctuary of his room, the castle's walls provided a silent backdrop to his thoughts. The apology hung in the air, a testament to his willingness to admit a misstep and move forward. Now, with the quiet of his room enveloping him, Zachariah could reflect on the day's events and brace himself for whatever lay ahead in the castle's ever-unfolding drama.

Annabella knocked and came in. Her presence on the balcony was a mix of comfort and complexity. Her candidness about Gabrielle's claim to be a virgin and her own desires revealed the intricate web of personal agendas within the castle. Zachariah listened, his own glass of sherry in hand, as she laid bare her plans for the future—a future she envisioned on her own terms.

"I understand your desire for independence, Annabella," Zachariah said, his voice steady. "And I respect your decision to choose your own path. If you're certain this is what you want, then I'll support you in any way I can."

The evening air was cool, the sherry warm, and the conversation laden with implications of choices made and yet to be made. In the quiet of the balcony, with the castle's walls around them, they were two individuals navigating the complexities of life, each seeking a semblance of control over their destiny. Zachariah's role in Annabella's plan was clear, and as the night deepened, so did his understanding of the delicate balance between freedom and obligation.

Zachariah's actions and Annabella's readiness marked a significant moment, one that was both intimate and laden with the weight of future implications. The pill, a silent witness to the gravity of their decision, was a small but potent symbol of the complexities of their relationship.

As the night unfolded, the castle's walls stood silent around them, the stories they held a testament to the many lives and secrets that had passed through its halls. In the privacy of Zachariah's room, the two of them navigated the delicate dance of personal desires and the overarching schemes that seemed to govern the castle's inhabitants.

The softness in Annabella's voice belied the strength of her resolve, and as Zachariah joined her, the outside world—with its drones, its intrigues, and its watchful eyes—faded into the background, leaving only the immediacy of the moment and the shared understanding of the path they were choosing to walk together.

Zachariah's encounter with Annabella was a passionate interlude, a moment of intense connection that transcended their differences in status. The pill, a catalyst for their fervour, reminded them of the physicality of their relationship, but it was Annabella's affection that truly marked the depth of their bond.

As she left the room with a simple "Later," her smile lingered in the air, a promise of more to come. Zachariah was left to reflect on the unexpected turns his life had taken within the castle's walls, the lines between commoner and nobility blurred by shared moments of intimacy and vulnerability.

In the quiet aftermath, Zachariah could only wonder at the future, at the paths they would walk—both together and apart—and at the role he would play in the unfolding drama of the castle and its inhabitants. For now, he was content to rest, his heart still racing from the encounter, his mind alive with the possibilities that lay ahead.

Zachariah's time in the shower was interrupted by an unexpected visit from Gabrielle, her actions adding another layer of complexity to the already intricate web of relationships within the castle. Her sudden departure left Zachariah with more questions than answers, pondering the motivations behind her actions and the role he was playing in the silent dance of courtship and power.

As he stepped out of the shower, the room felt emptier for her absence, the steam dissipating into the air just as quickly as she had vanished. Zachariah was left to consider the games being played around him, the unspoken rules and the potential consequences of each move. The castle's walls were silent observers of the drama unfolding within, and Zachariah knew that every choice he made could tip the scales in this delicate balance of desire and strategy.

As the evening settled and the stars began to dot the sky, Zachariah found himself in a reflective state. Alone on his balcony, he considered the gravity of the coming day. "Tomorrow is Saturday," he mused, the uncertainty of the future weighing heavily on his mind. "Will the truth finally come to light, or is this the end of the road for me?"

The thought of his late wife brought a bittersweet comfort. "If my time comes, perhaps it's not such a dire fate," he contemplated. "To be reunited with her, wherever she may be, wouldn't be the worst outcome."

Yet, the prospect of wealth and continued adventure still held a certain allure. "Or maybe," he pondered, "I'll find myself with the means to carry on, to see and experience more of what life has to offer."

The notion of ageing, of reaching a point where the joys of life might no longer be within reach, was a sobering one. "In five years, will I still be able to savour the journey?" he questioned, the night air wrapping around him like a cloak of solitude.

With these thoughts swirling in his head, Zachariah retired for the night, the castle's silence a stark contrast to the turmoil within. Tomorrow's dawn would bring answers, for better or worse, and all he could do was wait and see what fate had in store.

Zachariah's morning began with a tinge of surprise. Annabella's absence left him with a sense of relief mingled with concern. Her decision, whether intentional or not, seemed to align with his own thoughts on the matter. As he enjoyed his breakfast on the balcony, the tranquillity of nature provided a stark contrast to the complexities of life within the castle.

Dressed in his Blackbeard attire, Zachariah felt a mix of anticipation and discomfort. The outfit was a costume of obligation rather than choice, a symbol of the role he was expected to play in the day's events. Descending the stairs, he found himself amidst a scene from the past, the women adorned in dresses that spoke of a bygone era.

Gabrielle's approach was unexpected; her kiss was a declaration of intent that left Zachariah both bewildered and intrigued. "Blackbeard, you will be mine soon," she whispered her words a promise or perhaps a premonition. As the assembly gathered, Zachariah stood ready, his pirate's garb a fitting metaphor for the day ahead—a day of revelations, of truths unveiled, and perhaps, of new paths forged.

Zachariah stood silently, the gravity of the situation pressing down on him like the weight of the earth above. The armed guards, the masked assembly, and Malcolm's words were components of a ritual that felt both ancient and terrifyingly real.

As Malcolm's question hung in the air, Zachariah knew that his fate was being decided at this very moment. The eyes of the assembly were upon him, their judgment obscured by the masks they wore. It was a moment of truth, a test of his resolve and his ability to navigate the treacherous waters he found himself in.

With no shackles to bind him, Zachariah's freedom was a cruel illusion, his life hanging in the balance of a single collective decision. The fire crackled, a beacon of light in the darkness, and Zachariah stood ready to face whatever verdict would come from the shadows.

The unanimous "I" echoed through the chamber, a chorus of consent that sealed Zachariah's fate. The rifles trained on him were a stark reminder of the high stakes of this clandestine gathering. As Malcolm unveiled the purpose of the assembly—the introduction of a life-extending vaccine—Zachariah became the unwilling centrepiece of a historic moment.

The two figures in white approached, their presence clinical and detached. Zachariah stood resolute, his options limited, his defiance conveyed only through his piercing glare. The concern etched on the faces of Annabella, Agnes, Janet, and even Gabrielle offered little comfort as he braced himself for the unknown.

The vaccine, a marvel of science shrouded in secrecy, was now his burden to bear. As the needle neared, Zachariah's thoughts raced—thoughts of life, of mortality, and of the strange journey that had led him to this point. Whatever the outcome, he knew that his life would never be the same again.

Zachariah's awakening was a rebirth of sorts, the fear of death replaced by the relief of survival. Annabella's presence was a comfort, her words a balm to the confusion that clouded his mind. "I'm alive," he whispered, the reality of the situation settling in. "And the chimpanzees...they deserve freedom."

The castle, with all its secrets and shadows, had become a place of transformation for Zachariah. The vaccine, a gamble with his life, had proven to be a risk that he had unwillingly taken. Now, as he lay in his bed, the future was an open book, the pages yet to be written.

Annabella's father's actions, driven by a mix of guilt and responsibility, were a small step towards righting the wrongs that had been committed in the name of science. For Zachariah, the experience was a stark reminder of the value of life—his own and that of the creatures who had been unwilling participants in the castle's dark experiments.

As he recovered, surrounded by the familiar walls of his room, Zachariah knew that his journey was far from over. There were choices to be made, paths to be chosen, and a life to be lived—freely and on his own terms

Gabrielle's entrance was a blend of concern and determination, the aroma of coffee a subtle reminder of life's simple pleasures amidst the castle's complexities. She handed out the coffees, her firm stance on the vaccine echoing Zachariah's own sentiments. "They must perfect it," she insisted. "No one should suffer as you did, Zachariah. The risk is too great."

Annabella nodded in agreement, her eyes meeting Zachariah's over the rim of her cup. "Absolutely," she affirmed.

"We have time on our side. There's no need to rush into uncertainty."

The three of them sat in quiet solidarity, the morning light casting a soft glow on the room. The vaccine, once a beacon of hope, now cast a long shadow of doubt. But in this moment, with the warmth of the coffee and the shared resolve to demand safety and assurance, they found a common ground. Zachariah's ordeal had united them in a way that the castle's walls never could—through empathy, understanding, and a mutual desire to protect one another from harm.

Zachariah absorbed Malcolm's words, the revelation of his lineage casting a new light on his presence in the castle. "A descendant of Blackbeard," he repeated, the notion both surreal and oddly fitting. The weapons in Malcolm's hands, once tools of defence, now felt like relics of a past that was intimately connected to his own blood.

"So, the tales of Blackbeard's demise were just that—tales," Zachariah mused aloud. "And now, it seems, his legacy is mine."

The room was charged with a sense of history rewritten, the air thick with the implications of this newfound identity. "What does this mean for my future here, Malcolm?" Zachariah inquired, his mind racing with questions about his role in the castle's secretive affairs.

Malcolm's gaze was unwavering, his stance authoritative. "It means, Zachariah, that you are more than a mere guest within these walls. You are part of a legacy that predates the stones themselves. And with that comes a duty, a purpose that we believe you are destined to fulfil."

The revelation was a turning point, a moment that would define Zachariah's path forward. As he grappled with the weight of his heritage, he knew that his journey had taken an unexpected turn, one that would lead him deeper into the heart of the castle's enigmas and, perhaps, to the discovery of his true purpose within its storied halls.

Zachariah sat alone, the echo of Malcolm's chilling words and Annabella's frustration fading into the silence of the room. The finality of the ultimatum left him with a sense of foreboding. Tomorrow's ceremony would be the culmination of his time in the castle—a decisive moment that would seal his fate.

The choice was stark: join the fellowship's enigmatic ranks or face the end. It was a gamble with the highest stakes, and as the night crept in, Zachariah knew he had to prepare for what might be his last stand. The fellowship, shrouded in secrecy and power, was an unknown that both intrigued and terrified him.

As the door clicked shut behind Annabella, Zachariah felt the solitude of his room more acutely than ever. The night ahead would be a long one, filled with contemplation and resolve. He had to decide whether to embrace the legacy of Blackbeard and the fellowship or to stand against them, knowing it could cost him everything. The dawn would bring answers, but until then, Zachariah was left with his thoughts, the silent castle, and the ticking clock of destiny.

Gabrielle removed the tray with purpose, removing her clothes. She slid into bed, watching my gaze; she spoke softly, "Please, me, you will feel I wasn't lying." She lay waiting. I hadn't had a Viagra; nevertheless, her gorgeous figure, equal to Annabella's, awaited. She let out a gasp, speaking in French. I couldn't understand a word; I guessed I was pleasing her by the pain in my back as her nails left their mark. Gabrielle lay grinning, cuddling me, trying to encourage me to perform again. I opened the side draw, took a Viagra pill and sipped the remainder of my coffee. Now I'm turbocharged; it wasn't long before I was ready and loaded for action. I thought if she screamed any louder, the windows would crack.

As Gabrielle's words echoed in my mind, I couldn't help but feel a mix of excitement and trepidation. Blackbeard, the notorious pirate, was a figure shrouded in legend, and now I was to be his descendant. The thought was as intoxicating as it was daunting.

While Gabrielle showered, I pondered over the tales of Blackbeard. Did he enjoy the simple pleasures like a cigarette, or was his life filled with nothing but the pursuit of treasure and adventure? My own experiences in France were far from adventurous, marked by mundane trips to hypermarkets and the unfortunate incident in Holland.

Gabrielle emerged, her presence pulling me from my reverie. "We have much to prepare," she said, her tone serious yet tinged with a hint of excitement. "Your heritage is not just a title; it's a legacy that comes with responsibilities."

The slap from Annabella was a jolt back to reality, a stark contrast to the gentle kiss I had shared with Gabrielle. The room was thick with tension, the air charged with the electricity of unspoken words and broken expectations.

"Annabella," I said, my voice a mix of hurt and resolve, "our time together was a chapter in my life I'll always cherish. But if your heart isn't in this—if I am not the one you see standing beside you in the eyes of your friends—then it's time we close this book."

Her eyes, once filled with anger, now glistened with the onset of tears. "Zachariah, it's not that simple. You know the world we live in, the expectations, the ..."

I interrupted, "I know, Annabella. But I also know that love doesn't bow to age or peer pressure. It's a treasure far greater than any Blackbeard ever sought. And if we can't share that treasure together, then perhaps it's best we seek our fortunes apart."

She took a step back, her hand touching the cheek she had struck. "I ... I need to think," she whispered.

The night had unfolded like a dream, one that I could scarcely believe was real. Annabella's departure had left a silence in its wake, a void that was quickly filled by Gabrielle's unexpected presence. Her arrival was like a scene from a film, the kind that plays out in the hazy glow of a dimly lit room, where every movement is charged with intention.

As we lay there, the afterglow of our passion surrounding us like a warm blanket, I posed the question that had been lingering in my mind. "How would you like to live with me in a small house in England?" It was a simple proposition, yet it carried the weight of a thousand unspoken dreams.

Gabrielle's surprise was evident, her eyes wide as she processed the thought. "What's wrong with France? We have better weather," she countered, her voice a mix of curiosity and challenge. "I would live there with you, not here."

Her response was not what I had expected, but it was one I understood. France, with its sun-kissed vineyards and languid afternoons, held a certain allure that the English countryside, for all its charm, could not match.

The morning light crept through the curtains, casting a soft glow on the remnants of a night that had defied expectations. Gabrielle's presence lingered in the air, a sweet perfume that spoke of passion and whispered promises.

As she left, the reality of our situation settled in. Long-distance lovers—a term that carried with it the weight of absence and the ache of longing. Yet, there was a certain romance to it, a testament to the strength of our connection that could span miles and oceans.

I lay back, the sheets still warm from her touch, and allowed myself a moment to imagine our future. Conversations over the phone, letters filled with longing, visits that burned bright and fast—fuel for the fire that would keep our love alive across the distance.

Dressed in the garb of Blackbeard, I felt a part of me slip into the role of the legendary pirate. The window framed a scene devoid of the familiar trikes, and Janet's Range Rover, now sporting a trailer, hinted at movements and plans set into motion.

Descending the stairs to the dining room, the atmosphere was one of casual normality, as if the events of the night had been nothing more than a dream. The twelve and their wives gathered around the grand oak table, which seemed untouched by the undercurrents of change.

Malcolm's invitation to join them was a beacon of camaraderie in the sea of stoic faces. I took my place between Agnes and Janet, the polished wood cool beneath my hands. Malcolm's words, delivered with a nonchalant grin, carried the weight of Gabrielle's absence. "Gabrielle has caught the morning tide. She's on her way to France; she said she would consider your proposal."

The news was both a relief and a cliffhanger, leaving the future of our relationship hanging in the balance like a ship on the horizon. Yet, there was a promise in his words, a possibility that she might yet return to my side.

I nodded, acknowledging the update with a mix of hope and resignation. "Then we shall let the tide carry her thoughts to a safe harbour," I replied, my voice steady. "And in the meantime, we'll navigate the waters here, with or without the guidance of the stars."

The meal passed in a blur of conversation and clinking cutlery, the mundane actions belying the tumultuous emotions within me. As the day unfolded, I found myself gazing often at the horizon, wondering if Gabrielle's thoughts were drifting back to me with the ebb and flow of the sea.

The breakfast before me was a feast fit for a seafaring captain of old, yet the bustling silence from my companions made the meal feel less hearty. As the waiter poured my coffee, the rich aroma did little to mask the sense of isolation that hung over the table like a dense fog.

I took a bite of the crispy bacon, the savoury flavour a stark contrast to the blandness of the company. It seemed that in the wake of Gabrielle's departure and the unresolved tensions, I had become an island unto myself.

With each mouthful, I resolved not to let their indifference dictate my mood. I was, after all, the descendant of Blackbeard, and if the tales were true, he would have never allowed the sentiments of others to steer his ship.

So, I savoured my breakfast; each bites a silent rebellion against the cold shoulders around me. And as I finished my coffee, I decided that their neglect would not mar the taste of my day.

I would set my own course and navigate my own destiny, and perhaps in time, the tide would bring back not just

Gabrielle but also the camaraderie that seemed to have sailed away with her.

The descent into the bowels of the castle was a journey from the light into the shadowy depths of uncertainty. The clinking of the shackles around my ankles was a grim symphony, accompanying the silent march of the marksmen lining the cave. The fire's glow, a barrier of light in the darkness, cast long shadows that danced upon the walls.

As I took my place, the warmth of the flames was a stark contrast to the chill of the situation. The faces around me were a mix of beauty and stoicism, a gallery of expressions that spoke volumes without uttering a single word.

The arrival of the lab-coated duo was silent but charged with an air of clinical detachment. Their syringe, a vessel of unknown intent, was a cold intrusion into the flesh of my arm. As the liquid entered my bloodstream, I braced for an onslaught that never came. This time, my body accepted the foreign substance without protest, leaving me with a sense of eerie calm.

At that moment, I was both participant and observer, a man shackled not just by metal but by the unfolding narrative of which I was an unwilling protagonist. Yet, within me, a resolve began to stir—a determination not to be defined by these trials, to rise above the role of a lab rat and reclaim the narrative as my own.

The man in the golden robe regarded me with a mixture of surprise and respect. "Zachariah Black, your point is well made. As the first to undergo this trial, you bear the brunt of the risk. It is only fair that your compensation reflects your unique contribution to our cause."

He turned to confer with the others, their heads bowed in hushed conversation. After a moment, he faced me again, his expression resolute. "We have reached a decision. In addition to the two million pounds and the annual allowance, we will grant you a bonus of one million pounds. This is in recognition of your bravery and the pivotal role you play in this venture."

I nodded, the gravity of the situation not lost on me. "Very well," I replied, "I accept your terms, and I will fulfil my part in this grand experiment. But let it be known that my cooperation is not born of greed, but of a desire to see this through to the end, for better or worse."

The man in the golden robe extended his hand, and I shook it firmly. "Then it is agreed. Welcome aboard, Zachariah Black. May the winds be ever in your favour, and may the legacy of Blackbeard live on through you."

As the meeting adjourned, I felt the weight of history on my shoulders, a lineage reborn through science and ambition. The future was uncertain, but one thing was clear: I was no longer just a man; I was a symbol of hope, a beacon for those daring enough to chase immortality. And with that, my new life as Zachariah Black, heir to a pirate's fortune and a pioneer of science, began

The laughter of the spokesman rang out, a chilling reminder of the power he wielded. "You are delusional, Zachariah!" he exclaimed with a cold mirth. "With the snap of my fingers, you will have more bullet holes in you than a colander."

The threat hung in the air, a stark warning that underscored the gravity of my situation. Yet, it was his next words that truly set the course of my new reality.

"To a more serious matter," he continued, his tone shifting to one of solemnity, "you will become a member of the twelve in a lower capacity until you prove your loyalty and are finally permitted to wear the golden robe."

The weight of the golden robe's significance was not lost on me. It was a symbol of power, of inclusion, and now, a goal to which I must aspire.

"If you ever speak of any member present, or the castle, anything related to a member, you will be executed without hesitation," he declared. The rules were clear, and the consequences were dire. Secrecy was the linchpin of this clandestine assembly, and my silence was the price of entry.

"Release his bondage, Annabella," he commanded, and with those words, the shackles that bound me were undone.

As the cold metal fell away, I felt a surge of resolve. I was Zachariah Black, bound by blood to a legacy of shadows and secrets. My journey had taken an unexpected turn, but I was determined to navigate these treacherous waters with the cunning and daring of my infamous ancestor.

And so, with a cautious step forward, I accepted my place among the twelve, my eyes set on the golden robe and the mysteries it concealed. The path ahead was fraught with peril, but I was ready to walk it, for in my veins flowed the blood of Blackbeard and, in my heart, the courage to face whatever lay ahead.

Freedom, at last, came with a set of conditions, but it was freedom nonetheless. Malcolm's words were a reminder of the bond I now had with the twelve, a monthly pilgrimage back to the castle to confirm the effects of the vaccine coursing through my veins.

Agnes's kiss was a balm to the soul, her words a mix of admiration and concern. "You're a brave fool, Zachariah." Her affection was a fleeting comfort, a momentary light in the shadow of the grand scheme I was now part of.

The silence of Annabella was a stark contrast; her wordless exit was a chapter closing without fanfare. Then there was Janet, who was pragmatic and ready to move forward. "Grab your things. Leave your Blackbeard clothes here, Zachariah."

The journey back to Long Marston was a quiet one, punctuated only by the hum of the engine and the occasional whisper of the wind. The roads were mercifully clear, the world seemingly oblivious to the drama that had unfolded.

As I took the wheel at Gretna Green, Janet's trust in me was evident as she succumbed to sleep. The miles rolled by, each one a step further from the castle and closer to the semblance of a normal life.

Parking outside my house in the early hours, the stillness of Long Marston welcomed me home. It was here, in the quiet embrace of the familiar, that I could reflect on the odyssey I had embarked upon—an odyssey that promised to be as challenging as it was extraordinary.

For now, though, I would rest, gather my thoughts, and prepare for the days ahead. Zachariah Black's journey was far from over, and the road ahead was sure to be as winding as the one that had led me here.

The morning light filtered through the curtains, casting a gentle glow on the remnants of yesterday's journey. Janet's confusion was understandable; the exhaustion had claimed us both, leaving little room for memory's grasp.

"You were out the moment we hit the motorway," I reassured her, my voice still heavy with fatigue. "I've done the long haul to Tain and back before, one thousand and twenty miles in a single stretch. It's a feat I'm not eager to tackle again."

Janet nodded, the gears of recollection slowly turning. "Well, I'm grateful you got us home safely," she said, a soft smile touching her lips.

I returned the smile, feeling the weight of the previous day's events settle around us like a cloak. "Let's take it easy today," I suggested. "We've earned a bit of rest, and there's no rush for anything else."

The aroma of a hearty breakfast and the warmth of a freshly brewed pot of tea were welcome comforts after the tumultuous events we had endured. Susan's kindness was a reminder of the simple joys that friendship can bring, a stark contrast to the complex web of secrets and legacies I was now entwined in.

Janet's words brought a smile to my face. "Yes, Susan is a gem," I agreed. "And as for my notorious ancestor, well, let's just say that some stories are best kept within the pages of history books."

Her mention of the motorhome sparked a realisation. "Ah, you're right. The motorhome would have been a more direct route to rest and recovery. But I suppose after everything, a little detour is nothing to fret over," I said with a chuckle.

Janet's grin was infectious, and I found myself echoing it. "Well played, Janet. Your foresight is as sharp as ever. Let's enjoy this breakfast, and then we can make our way to your place. After all, we've got a new day ahead of us, and who knows what adventures it might bring for Zachariah Black and his trusty companion."

With that, we settled into the comfort of the breakfast bar, the morning's light casting a golden hue over the start of a day that promised a semblance of normalcy, at least for now.

Janet's laughter faded as the gravity of her words settled between us. "Three dead chimpanzees and two bodyguards," she repeated, her voice a whisper of disbelief. "Someone cut their throats; to be buried at sea weighted down with a few Scottish rocks."

The room grew silent; the earlier banter gave way to a sombre reality. The mention of Gabrielle and her departure on a fishing boat now took on a darker tone, one that cast a long shadow over our light-hearted sparring.

I processed the information, the pieces of a macabre puzzle falling into place. "It seems the waters we navigate are more treacherous than I thought," I said quietly. "And the secrets we keep are more dangerous."

Janet nodded, her eyes reflecting a mix of fear and resolve. "We tread a fine line, Zachariah," she agreed. "But we do so together. Whatever comes, we'll face it side by side."

And with that, we understood the unspoken pact between us. Our lives were intertwined with mysteries and legacies that stretched beyond the horizon, and we would need each other to weather the storms ahead.

For now, though, the immediate concern was practical. "Let's focus on the day-to-day," I suggested, trying to steer us back to safer waters. "A change of clothes, a new car, and a fresh start. We'll handle the rest as it comes, one wave at a time."

Janet smiled, a small but defiant act of courage. "One wave at a time," she echoed. And with that, we began to plan our next steps, ready to face whatever the tide might bring.

Janet's actions were a dance of normalcy in the midst of our chaotic world. As she tidied up with practised ease, her movements spoke of a desire to maintain a semblance of order. Yet, a question lingered in the air, a thread of doubt pulling at the fabric of trust we had woven.

"You know, Janet," I began, my tone light but probing, "in a world where truth is more valuable than gold, it's hard not to question what's presented before us."

She paused at the door, the weight of the fifty pounds under the cup a symbol of gratitude and, perhaps, a small price for the secrets we kept. Her kiss was a sweet punctuation, a moment of tenderness in the midst of uncertainty.

As she thanked Susan, her words carried the warmth of genuine appreciation, a reminder of the bonds we form with those who step into our lives, however briefly.

When Janet returned, the question hung between us, unanswered but acknowledged. "We all have our reasons for the truths we tell," I said, meeting her gaze. "And sometimes, the full story is a tapestry too complex to unravel at once."

With a nod, we agreed to let the moment pass, to focus on the here and now, and to navigate the waters of truth and secrecy as best we could. For in the end, it was not just the legacy of Blackbeard that bound us, but the shared journey of discovery, wherever it might lead.

The spontaneity of the moment caught Janet off-guard, her surprise melting into a smile as I kissed her. "Come along, you, home to my place. We can argue on the way home, and I'm driving," I said with a playful assertiveness that seemed to brighten the mood further.

Susan's interruption was a testament to her honesty, her shock genuine at the sight of the fifty pounds. Janet's response was gracious, a reflection of her appreciation for Susan's kindness. "With my compliments, thank you for a lovely breakfast and for looking after Zachariah's property. You have Zachariah's number. Give him a ring if you have any problems; bye for now," she said, her generosity leaving a lasting impression as we drove away.

I watched Susan's astonished expression through the rearview mirror, a reminder of the simple, honest interactions that form the fabric of our daily lives. As we left, the world outside seemed oblivious to the complex web of secrets and legacies we were entangled in, and for a brief moment, everything felt disarmingly normal.

The journey ahead promised to be filled with debates and laughter, a welcome change from the high-stakes drama that had enveloped us. As we drove on, I couldn't help but feel a sense of anticipation for what lay ahead, both the challenges and the quiet moments of connection that make life such an unpredictable adventure.

Janet's concern was evident, her eyes scanning mine for signs of distress. "Zachariah, we can't take any chances," she insisted. "The effects of the experiment are unknown, and we need to be cautious."

I could feel the rush of adrenaline, the strange elixir they had injected me with, igniting a fire within. "Janet, I assure you, death is not on the agenda today," I said with a wry smile, trying to ease her worry.

She hesitated, then nodded, her hand squeezing mine in a silent promise of support. "All right, but we're keeping an eye on you. Any change, and we're calling for help," she declared, her tone brooking no argument.

I agreed, standing up slowly and steadying myself against the table. "Let's just take it one step at a time," I suggested. "And as for what's beneath your jumper, well, perhaps that's a mystery best left for another time."

With a shared laugh, we moved past the moment; the bond between us strengthened by the trials we faced. As I lay down to rest, I couldn't help but wonder what other effects the mysterious elixir might unveil.

The energy that surged through me was a mystery, a potent force that seemed to defy the very laws of nature. Janet's words, a mix of admiration and concern, were a testament to the intensity of the moment. "You're not old, Zachariah, you are wonderful," she said, her breathlessness matching my own.

As we rose from the bed, the darkness outside was a stark contrast to the passion that had illuminated the room. Her playful accusation, "You are crazy and dangerous," was a reminder of the unpredictable journey we were on.

I chuckled, watching her dash to the bathroom. The experiment had indeed changed something within me, but whether it was a blessing or a curse remained to be seen. For now, I was content to bask in the afterglow of our connection, a connection that seemed to grow stronger with each passing day.

"Careful is my middle name," I called out to her, a grin on my face. "But sometimes, a little bit of crazy is just what life calls for."

And with that, I settled into the quiet of the room, waiting for Janet's return, ready for whatever the next chapter might bring for Zachariah Black and his indomitable spirit.

Janet's concern was palpable, her voice tinged with a mix of awe and apprehension. "The scientists are right to be cautious," she said, taking a sip of the tea. "This elixir, whatever it is, has certainly stirred the waters."

I pondered the situation; the scientist in me was intrigued by the unexpected results, while the man in me was wary of the unknowns. "I suppose it's best to follow their request," I continued. "If there are side effects, it's important to understand them fully, not just for my sake, but for the sake of the experiment itself."

Janet's practicality was always a grounding force, her foresight a counterbalance to my sometimes whimsical nature. "Malcolm's foresight is impressive," I acknowledged. "Royal trade plates should make the journey smoother."

Her reminder of the stakes involved brought a more sombre tone to our conversation. "I understand the importance of the trial," I said, the gravity of the situation settling in. "The potential to reverse ageing is...staggering."

I paused, considering the implications. "If this experiment can truly turn back time, it's not just a personal victory; it's a scientific breakthrough. I'm committed to seeing this through, for all those who have invested in this venture."

With a promise to spend wisely, I watched Janet disappear into the bank, her final kiss still warm on my lips. The key to her house was a symbol of trust and a reminder of the new responsibilities I now shouldered.

The taxi driver nodded, "Sure, the nearest Porsche dealership is in Wilmslow, about twenty miles from here." With a sense of anticipation, Zachariah climbed into the taxi, the prospect of a new Porsche adding a spring to Zachariah's step. The journey to the dealership was a blur, Zachariah's mind already racing through the sleek lines and powerful engine of the Porsche Cayenne Turbo S E-Hybrid Coupe.

Arriving at the dealership, Zachariah paid the taxi driver and stepped out. The dealership's facade was impressive, a testament to the luxury and performance housed within. Zachariah walked in, his attire casual, but Zachariah's intent serious. The salesperson approached, his initial scepticism fading as Zachariah clarified his intentions.

"I want this one," he said, pointing to the black Porsche with tinted windows, "I don't mind waiting a couple of hours. I'm sure you can provide a suitable insurance company."

The salesperson, now fully attentive, nodded and began the process. As Zachariah waited, the thrill of the purchase settled in. This was more than just a car; it was a statement, a piece of the new life Zachariah was carving out, a descendant of Blackbeard.

With the thrill of the purchase still fresh, Zachariah handled the practicalities with efficiency. The bank transfer went through without a hitch, and despite the sting of the insurance and road tax costs, he couldn't help but feel a sense of excitement. After all, as Zachariah rightly thought, you only live once.

The dealership's team was a flurry of activity, their movements swift and precise as they prepared the new Porsche Cayenne Turbo S E-Hybrid Coupe. The number plate fitting was the final touch, a tangible sign that the car was now ready.

Zachariah watched them work, and the reality of it all began to sink in. This was no ordinary day, and that was no ordinary car. It was a symbol of a new chapter, a powerful machine that would carry you forward into a future filled with unknowns.

Soon enough, the keys were in Zachariah's hand and sliding into the driver's seat, the leather hugging like a second skin. The engine roared to life at the touch of a button, a symphony of engineering that promised adventure at every turn.

Driving off the lot, the world outside seemed to blur into the background. Zachariah Black, a man with a legacy as mysterious as it was thrilling, and now, with a car to match. The road ahead was open and ready to meet it head-on.

By lunchtime, I'm driving away in my matte-black Porsche; this beast certainly does not hang around. I arrived home just in time to receive a parcel from a courier, a detail that had slipped my mind. After signing for the delivery, I enter Janet's house, make some tea, and sit down. My mobile rings with Janet's name on the display; I answer on speakerphone, sipping my tea as we speak: "Hello, my true love."

"What have you bought now? Please don't bother lying. I know the company you purchased from. I've seen the money transferred to their account; it could have been worse. You could have bought a Ferrari, and then I would be annoyed."

"Are you picking on me even though we're not married?"

Janet ended the call abruptly. I methodically placed the trade plates—one in the front window and another in the rear—ensuring they were visible. To my astonishment, Janet pulled up behind my Porsche in her Range Rover. Stepping out, she flashed a smile and said, "At least it has four seats for the baby seat. I must dash; even a bank manager must adhere to time, lest I set a poor example. I presume you're off to Scotland, Zachariah; take care. I love you loads." After a tender kiss, she climbed back into her Range Rover, driving away with a playful blow of a kiss.

After ensuring Janet's house was securely locked, I didn't bother to pack any clothes; I had a stash in the wardrobe at the castle. Stopping at the nearest garage, I filled my Porsche with fuel before setting off for Edinburgh. Despite the variable speed restrictions, I planned to take the M-90 and A9 after crossing the road bridge. With cruise control engaged, I found myself wishing for autopilot—the thought of dozing off was tempting. Fortunately, I avoided the rush-hour traffic and arrived at the Castle of Mey by 8 o'clock.

Malcolm greeted me at the back door, his expression a mix of amusement and curiosity at the sight of my car. "You didn't go completely overboard, Zachariah. As expensive as it is, it wouldn't be much use off-road," he mused. "You'll be in the same room as before. The scientists are eager to examine you first thing in the morning after you've rested." He extended his hand in a gesture of camaraderie, which I gladly accepted. "We're on the same team, Zachariah; let's be friends. It'll be less painful for both of us," he added with a warm smile, ushering me inside.

"I'll second that," I respond with a light-hearted tone, hastening to my designated bedroom. No sooner had I crossed the threshold than two evening meals were ushered in by the staff and set on the table near the window. The security lights flickered on as dusk settled, casting a protective glow around the garden's edge.

My next surprise came in the form of Annabella, who entered in an elegant evening gown. I rose from my chair, pulling hers out for her. She took her seat with a simple, "Thanks," and I returned to mine.

"You're the last person I expected to see, Annabella. I thought we had made our positions clear during our last meeting."

"Indeed, it wasn't the conclusion I had envisioned for our relationship. You must understand where I'm coming from."

"In plain terms, you're superficial and pretentious, seeking the best of both worlds. You crave a bit of excitement, then you parade around like royalty for the remainder of your days."

"This is the issue when I associate with those of lesser breeding and manners. What Agnes ever saw in you is beyond me!"

"You've imposed yourself, Annabella; my presence here is solely for the tests."

"My reasons for being here are strictly professional. I require a descendant of Blackbeard to inherit my parents' estate upon their passing. As I've stated, marriage isn't in my plans; I can acquire what I need without it."

"So, I'm to father your child to fulfil your scheme?"

"Our medical team could certainly arrange for artificial insemination, which would spare us any unpleasant interactions."

"Whatever you prefer, madam. At this moment, your intentions are quite transparent, Annabella. Heaven help the person who ends up marrying you. If you can plot against your own brother, dealing with a husband should be trivial for you."

Annabella stormed out, the slam of the bedroom door echoing behind her. I savoured the last bites of my meal before pouring myself a glass of sherry from the crystal decanter. A knock at the door preceded the entrance of a distinguished gentleman. With impeccable manners, he began, "Please excuse the intrusion. I am Mr Goldstone, Annabella's father, and a member of the twelve. I fully grasp why you might wish to cast Annabella from the balcony; she has inherited her mother's less endearing traits. Alas, my wife and I are beyond the years of producing a healthy son to succeed the one whose life you claimed at Annabella's behest. Might I implore you, for the sake of our peace and her mother's, to consider Annabella? So, she may Conceive an heir for our estate and fortune. Think of England, close your eyes, do whatever is necessary."

I was perplexed. "I fail to see, sir, why I am the chosen one. Countless men would leap at the opportunity to be with such a captivating woman, despite her challenging demeanour at times."

Mr Goldstone replied with a solemn air, "It's quite simple, Zachariah. Your lineage traces back to Blackbeard. History has often painted him as a fearsome brute, a narrative that sells books. Yet, few have recorded his benevolence and generosity. You've demonstrated similar traits—your kindness and your formidable prowess. Like any man, you've erred, but more often than not, you've aided others akin to your forebears. It may surprise you, but in times of crisis, he was held in high regard by the Royals. I desire to leave my estate in the hands of such a man."

"I will do my best; that's all I can promise," I replied with a nod of acknowledgement. "Thank you for speaking with me directly, Mr Goldstone. May I offer you refreshment before you depart? A glass of sherry, perhaps, or whisky?"

"No, thank you, Zachariah," he declined with a hint of respect in his voice. "You exhibit more gentlemanly qualities than many I encounter. I'm aware of your proposal to Annabella and her refusal—she's a fool. You possess a sophistication that far exceeds the standards of those she deems suitable."

With a firm handshake, I bid him farewell and closed the door behind him. After a refreshing shower, I settled in for an early night with the television for company. As the night deepened, Annabella made her entrance, her silhouette pausing before she let her nightgown fall to the floor. Slipping under the duvet, she cast a glance upward, then fixed a scowl on me. "Well? What are you waiting for? A written invitation?"

I obliged positively; within minutes, she was kissing me frantically. She had succumbed to my wild charm. I had no idea what was in that injection, but my enthusiasm was faultless. I would make sure she'd remember this night for the rest of her life. Annabella picked up her night dress and walked to the shower. I lay in bed smiling; she came out a short while later, sliding into bed with me, kissing my neck and lips. When I awoke, she was still in bed with me.

A gentle knock echoed at the door as breakfast awaited on the sunlit balcony. The August sun bathed the morning in a brilliant glow, with not a single cloud to mar the azure sky. The air was alive with the melodious chorus of birds. With a smile, I stepped into the refreshing cascade of the shower. When I emerged, Annabella was already seated at the table, her presence inviting me to join in the morning's repast.

"My father's right! I should have said yes to your proposal, Zachariah. I've never had a night like that before; if I'm not pregnant now, I never will be. It must be the vaccine Janet reported that you are different; she wasn't joking."

I suggested with caution, "Let's see what unfolds after breakfast. I'm off to the lab now." With a gentle kiss on Annabella's forehead, I activated the bookcase, revealing the staircase on which I descended. As I navigated through the unfamiliar equipment, an elderly gentleman approached me with a warm greeting, "Good morning, Zachariah. You're looking quite well today. Please, take a seat over there; we need to draw some blood for tests.' I obliged, seating myself in a chair reminiscent of a dentist's, and allowed him to proceed. 'By the way, my name is Peter,' he added. 'We'll be seeing quite a bit of each other in the coming months as we monitor the efficacy of our genetic enhancer. The preliminary results, informed by Janet and Annabella's data, are quite promising."

Flashing a grin, I shared, "I've never felt better, almost as if I've turned back the clock to my thirties. Remarkably, my hair is regaining its youthful black, and it seems to be sprouting even in areas that had gone bald."

Peter nodded, "Zachariah, after two injections, we're ready to proceed with a third. This could potentially revitalise other parts of your body and awaken dormant brain cells. Your body was on the brink, gearing up for its final chapter. We believe we've halted that process. However, we're charting new territory here—it's a matter of trial."

With a light-hearted chuckle, I replied, "As long as I don't meet an early demise, I'm all for it. Life's becoming an adventure once more."

Peter carefully retrieved a syringe from the cold storage, meticulously ensuring it was air-free before administering the injection into my arm. He then monitored my blood pressure for any immediate effects of the injection, which, to our relief, remained stable. With an encouraging smile, Peter said, "Zachariah, I'd like you to come back around the 30th. By then, we should be able to observe any physical enhancements. Don't be surprised if your hair regains its colour and your beard shifts from grey to black. I'm also expecting a further boost in your vitality." With a final note, he added, "We're done for today; you're free to go."

I stood up, returning his smile, "I'll see you in a few weeks, Peter. And if these tests pan out, maybe you should consider a dose or two for yourself," I quipped, eliciting a hearty laugh from him as I made my way up the stone steps to my bedroom. After securing the bookcase, I slipped into fresh attire, snatched my Porsche keys, and descended the grand staircase. Stepping out the back kitchen door, I paused to admire my splendid new vehicle. Suddenly, Annabella appeared, concern etched on her face, "Zachariah, you're not heading home, are you?"

"Yes, I don't need to see Peter until the 30th," I reassured Annabella. Her face lit up with a playful smile, "I was looking forward to tonight." Taking her hand, I led her towards the stables. She giggled, "What are you up to, Blackbeard?" We found ourselves in an empty stall, away from prying eyes.

We reclined amidst the sawdust, our passions entwined. As we parted, Annabella rose; her efforts to dislodge the sawdust from her hair and floral dress were endearing. She bestowed upon me a tender kiss, her voice soft but earnest, "Drive safely." With a graceful sprint, she disappeared towards the house.

In solitude, I dusted off the remnants of our interlude and ventured into the tack room. A glance in the mirror was prudent—ensuring no trace of sawdust accompanied me; after all, it had no place in my Porsche.

After ensuring no trace of the stable lingered on me, I stepped outside to find Annabella comfortably seated in my Porsche, deep in conversation on her mobile. Sliding into the driver's seat, I was greeted by her mischievous grin. "You might as well tell him yourself, because he'll never take my word for it, Janet," she said, her eyes twinkling with amusement.

With a flick of her wrist, Annabella switched the call to speaker mode. "Zachariah, Annabella will be our guest for a few days; her chauffeur will escort her to London thereafter. Please, extend your courtesies. Farewell."

As the call ended, I couldn't help but chuckle. "I trust you've packed a suitcase?"

Her grin widened. "It's already in the boot. Besides, I have a couple of these cars back in London."

At that moment, a sudden pang gripped my chest, and instinctively, my hand flew to my heart.

CHAPTER 6

Recovery

My eyelids fluttered open, revealing the familiar grandeur of the castle's bedroom. A dull ache throbbed in my chest, and upon drawing back the duvet, I was met with a row of neat stitches—a stark reminder of an ordeal I had yet to recall. Beside me, the steady drip of an IV punctuated the silence.

The door creaked open, and Peter emerged from the shadows of the corridor, his smile a beacon of relief. "You're alive, Zachariah. A welcome sight, indeed. You must be brimming with questions."

A slight nod was all I could muster. "It appears quite grave?"

"Indeed," he confirmed, his tone sobering. "A blood clot in your heart, obstructing a valve. It's nothing short of a miracle that you're here. Annabella's swift actions saved your life."

The weight of his words settled over me. "How long have I been unconscious?"

"A fortnight," he replied, his gaze never leaving mine. "There were moments we feared you might not awaken, or worse, be lost to us in mind."

A defiant clarity surged within me. "I am far from a vegetable, Peter. My mind is intact. How soon can this drip be removed? I yearn to rise from this bed and be rid of this infernal catheter."

Peter's smile was a gentle reassurance as he spoke. "You're in possession of your faculties, Zachariah. I'll have the nurse attend to you shortly to remove the drip and catheter. Now that you're conscious, there's no longer a need for intravenous nutrition."

He paused, a hint of concern in his eyes. "However, there's something you should be aware of. The treatment we administered had some...unexpected results. You might notice some changes when you look in the mirror. We're hopeful these effects will stabilise soon. After all, this is all part of the experimental process, and you've become an unwitting participant."

With that, Peter left the room, his footsteps echoing down the hall. Moments later, a nurse briskly entered, her movements efficient and silent. She swiftly removed the catheter, and I V then departed without a word.

Feeling a bit unsteady, I made my way to the bathroom. My reflection in the mirror confirmed Peter's words: my physique had undergone a remarkable transformation, with a noticeable increase in muscle mass. My face, however, remained unchanged, framed by a beard that, curiously, seemed darker than before.

Clad in the only jeans and shirts that could accommodate my altered physique, I made my way to the serenity of the garden. The birds' melodies and the scent of ripe fruit were a balm to my senses. I indulged in a stolen pear and apple, their sweetness a contrast to the recent bitterness of life, as I swung gently, lost in thought.

Annabella's presence soon pierced my solitude. Her smile radiated relief as she approached. "Zachariah, you had me terrified," she confessed, dabbing at my beard with her handkerchief to remove the remnants of pear juice. Her lips met mine in a gentle interruption of my snack.

Without preamble, she inspected my stitches, her grin unwavering. "Do you think you'll recover by next week? There's something I need from you..." Her suggestive arch of the brow left little to the imagination.

I sighed a mix of frustration and affection in my voice. "Annabella, this isn't the time for such thoughts. You should seek a life with someone you can cherish, not this... obsession."

Her declaration caught me off guard. "I'll marry you, Zachariah. I've been a fool, chasing after fair-weather friends when it's your steadfast love I need."

The mention of Janet brought a frown to my face. "And what of her feelings?"

"She'll understand. I'll ensure she's well cared for."

I shook my head. "It's not that simple. We can't just dismiss her emotions."

Annabella's expression softened. "I regret not accepting your proposal before. Please, consider it, Zachariah. We make a good team."

"Okay," I replied, as Annabella's kiss lingered before she hurried up the garden path. Her determination was clear, but I couldn't help but wonder if her resolve would falter under the scrutiny of her London peers.

Retreating to my bedroom, I welcomed the solitude. The room had been tidied during my absence, with fresh linens inviting me to rest. As I settled in to watch some television, a soft knock heralded the arrival of lunch courtesy of a silent waiter.

The ping of my mobile interrupted my meal. It was a message from Janet: "How are you? I heard what happened. I love you terribly."

I paused, regretting my lack of communication. Quickly, I responded: "I miss you too. Don't worry; I'll come to you as soon as I'm able."

After finishing my meal, I set the tray aside and must have dozed off, as I awoke to the early morning light. A quick glance at my wristwatch showed it was 5:30 a.m. Dressing swiftly, I grabbed my car keys and descended the stairs, moving silently through the house without a word to anyone. My destination was clear: Buxton.

Janet deserved better, and I couldn't shake the feeling that I was responsible for her current predicament. Despite her involvement with the organisation and her willingness to play her part, my concern for her well-being was paramount. The influence and power wielded by others could easily complicate matters, but I trusted that common sense and decency would prevail, preventing any unnecessary conflicts.

By the time the clock struck 3:30 p.m., I found myself outside Janet's residence, my eyes catching the sight of a familiar black Mini. With a sense of urgency, I entered the house to find Annabella and Janet seated at the kitchen table, their expressions a blend of surprise and concern at my sudden appearance.

"Zachariah, please, take a moment to breathe," Janet said, her voice steady and reassuring as she prepared a cup of coffee for me. "Annabella and I have had a thorough discussion. There's no conspiracy here; no one is trying to mislead you."

I took a deep breath, accepting the coffee. "All right, I'm listening. But just so we're clear, I'll decide whether I'm on board after I've heard everything. I'm growing tired of feeling like I'm not in control of my own life."

Annabella and Janet exchanged knowing smiles. Janet's hand gently patted mine, her voice calm and sincere. "Zachariah, I knew you'd rush back, fearing Annabella might disrupt what we have."

I couldn't hide my confusion. "It's rather odd to find Annabella here, isn't it?"

Annabella's smile was wry. "You'll need to be an early bird to stay ahead of us. Your suspicion puzzles me. You're about to become part of something extraordinary, but your current attitude..." She trailed off, her raised eyebrows conveying a silent admonition.

Janet's next words caught me completely off guard. "Your keys have been returned to the Housing Association. Your belongings are safely packed away, and the storage costs will be taken care of—courtesy of Annabella's facilities. You won't be going back to Long Marston, Zachariah."

Stunned, I managed to articulate my disbelief. "That's quite presumptuous, and why?"

"The transformation you've undergone would raise too many questions," Janet explained. "We can't risk drawing attention to our work. Rest assured, your presence here—or in Scotland—is known only to a select few. Any further changes will be closely monitored by our team alone."

"Thank you for sharing your plans," I said, my tone firm yet composed. "Now, if you'll excuse me." With that, I departed swiftly, sliding into my Porsche and driving away before either Janet or Annabella could respond. Alone with my thoughts, I parked at the end of the lane, considering my next move.

The world was bustling, and solitude was scarce. My options were limited to my trike or motorhome, but the latter would attract too much attention. The trike, with its trailer and teepee, had served me well on a previous journey to Scotland, unnoticed and unbothered.

Deciding on the trike, I parked the Porsche, retrieved my gear from the garage, and embarked on an unexpected journey. As I reached the lane's end and started the generator, a twinge of pain reminded me to be cautious with my recent stitches.

My route was undecided, perhaps towards Wales, avoiding the busy roads where police were vigilant. If I could navigate through Congleton and Nantwich, I'd be heading in the right direction. Despite the frustration of having my belongings packed without my consent, I focused on the path ahead, ready for whatever lay before me.

I hoped my departure sent a clear message: "I need space." The thought of Annabella possibly being pregnant crossed my mind, but I quickly dismissed it, my thoughts drifting to Agnes, who seemed kinder in comparison. The more I reflected on the recent events, the more I realised how much I had been swayed by others. Despite the enjoyable aspects and the financial rewards, including a substantial treasure and my pension, I couldn't shake the feeling of being used.

At a service station, I took a break to refuel and stock up on supplies. I found a quiet spot to park for the night just outside Congleton. As I settled in, I was surprised by the silence of my phone—no messages, no disturbances. I prepared a simple meal, grilling a steak and opening a tin of peas. With a makeshift plate piled high, I couldn't help but laugh at the indulgence, determined to savour every bite of the hearty feast.

I'd barely finished my meal when a distressed girl approached, begging for protection. I guided her to my teepee and closed the flap. Minutes later, a man, I presumed her father, approached.

"No, I haven't seen anyone around," I replied. "She might have taken a shortcut across the field or doubled back to hide inside. It's getting dark; I doubt she'd stay out in the twilight by choice. Did you manage to deal with the boy appropriately?"

He shook his head, a mix of frustration and resignation in his voice. "I wish I could have, but these days, you can't lay a finger on them without facing assault charges. Kids seem to have all the power now."

I nodded in understanding. "I'm just glad my own children are grown and have left the nest. I'm just trying to enjoy retirement and stay clear of this new virus that's going around."

He glanced towards the road, worry etching his features. "There's a police station a few miles from here. If she doesn't turn up soon, I'll have to report her missing. Her mother is beside herself with worry." With that, he turned and retraced his steps.

As I watched him leave, I couldn't help but wonder about the girl's story. My mother always said there's no smoke without fire, and there might be a grain of truth in what the girl said. It's a sad reality that sometimes one parent might harm a child while the other turns a blind eye. I sighed, feeling the weight of uncertainty, unsure of the right thing to do.

I opened the flap on my teepee, looking at the young girl's expression in the light. She stayed reticent, listening to my conversation with her father. I closed the flap, sitting on my sleeping bag, "What is your side of the story, and what is your name?"

"My name is Margaret Paxton. He's my stepfather, not my real father; he died in an accident some years ago."

I realised he'd never mentioned that to me, but why should he, I surmised: "You are implying he's attempting to assault you? And where is your mother when this is supposedly taking place?"

"I think she knows I've suggested what's taking place. She said it's probably my imagination and my age; I should think myself lucky I have a stepfather who is prepared to spend money on me."

I sighed heavily, somewhat suspicious.

The only way I could think of helping was to contact Janet. She may have some idea of how to deal with the situation. This is way out of my league: "I'll phone a friend," I smiled, trying to be reassuring and surprised Margaret displayed so much flesh exposing her bruises to a stranger. She was too trusting for my liking.

I was about to ring Janet's number when the flap opened on the teepee. Janet entered, glaring at Margaret, tidying her

T-shirt, and adjusting her bra. Janet Expressing earnestly: "I think there's an explanation needed here, Zachariah!"

"Better still, I will make everyone a coffee. Margaret, please explain the situation to Janet; she will advise you and probably help if she can." Janet looked at me, somewhat puzzled by my remark, sitting comfortably in her pregnant state, starting to talk to Margaret. I went outside, starting the generator to make three coffees; rather pleased to escape the situation, I found it challenging to deal with. I'd have no problem decapitating her stepfather. Would that be the solution in my book? Yes? The immediate concern is Margaret; I hope Janet will help her.

Janet and Margaret appeared from the teepee, Janet holding Margaret's hands and smiling at me. The pair stepped into my Porsche, which Janet had arrived in. I watched them both smile. Janet drove away, so much for three coffees, emptying two and stepping inside my teepee.

A horrible thought crossed my mind: what would I do if Margaret's stepfather phoned the police and they came to question me, examine my teepee and find traces of Margaret's DNA? Only one place I'd be heading to prison.

I have never collapsed my teepee in such a hurry before. The problem is if the police started searching for me wherever I was with the teepee, Margaret's DNA would be with me unless I scrubbed the teepee thoroughly. No guarantees: it would only need one of her hairs to be found; I will be hung, drawn, and quartered.

I started cycling towards Buxton; thank God I had lights fitted to the trike, including the trailer. I parked on the side of the road, noticing the remains of a fire in a field. I had no choice but to carry my teepee sleeping bag and set fire to them. The material vanished in minutes, leaving no trace apart from the zips. I returned to my trike, realising I was asking for trouble entering Buxton tonight. Unfortunately, I will have to rough it somewhere; in some respects, I had travelled miles with that old teepee and now vanished into thin air; another piece of history disappeared into the clouds of my life.

I started laughing, watching the motorhome park on the side of the road. Janet opened the side door, "I have room for one. Are you interested?" she smiled encouragingly. "You realise, Zachariah, you're becoming a pain in the arse?"

As I stepped into the motorhome, my mind was consumed with thoughts of Margaret. "Where is she? Where's Margaret?" I asked with urgency.

"Zachariah, you're still weak from the surgery, and it's not wise to exert yourself," came the reply, tinged with concern. "I don't know who you're talking about."

Changing the subject, Janet shed her jumper with a hopeful smile. "You haven't paid any attention to these two in over two weeks," she said, gesturing to herself. "There's still time, but only if you're gentle." Taking her hand, I led her to the rear of the motorhome, my touch gentle and reassuring.

The next couple of hours were spent in laughter and light-hearted banter on the bed. Yet, the loss of my house still gnawed at me. Upon reflection, I realized that with my means, I could choose any house, anywhere. So, what was there to worry about? I was leaving behind a trail of bittersweet memories—few joyful, many sorrowful.

Our laughter was cut short by a sudden knock on the motorhome door. Hastily, we dressed, still chuckling at the interruption. With a mix of curiosity and concern, I swung the door open to find a police officer eyeing us with suspicion.

"Good evening, Sir. May I inquire about your origins and the reason for parking your motorhome here?" he asked.

Janet stepped forward, gently nudging me aside as she addressed the officer with confidence. "Officer, I'm a key worker, and this motorhome belongs to my fiancé. We live together, and I work in Buxton. Our home is merely six miles from here. We simply sought a change of scenery for the evening, without violating any restrictions or risking contamination," she explained.

Her tone took on a more assertive edge as she continued, "Tomorrow, I'll be at the bank, reviewing your overdraft facilities, Peter Jameson. Let's leave it at that, shall we?"

The officer's expression remained stern. "We'll need to verify that. You're pushing the boundaries of acceptable conduct. Please vacate the area at dawn. We can't have other motorists following suit; it's not permissible. Consider this a final warning," he stated before briskly walking away, hopping into his patrol car, and driving off into the night.

"More trouble, Zachariah. First, the pregnancy, now this brush with the law," Janet chided with a mix of frustration and affection. "Let's not waste the night, though," she added, her voice softening as she made her way to the bedroom.

By the break of dawn at 5 a.m., Janet was already on the road with the motorhome, and I followed suit on my trike, the trailer and generator in tow. As I navigated past the cement works on the outskirts of Buxton, I caught sight of Janet driving in the opposite direction in her Range Rover, heading to the office. Her smile and wave were a brief but warm exchange in the early morning light.

Upon reaching Janet's home, 'Rose Cottage' greeted me, the name elegantly etched into the stone—a detail Janet had never shared. My phone buzzed with her message: "Did you notice we didn't have a single argument last night? Love you. See you later."

Margaret's absence was like a shadow that had passed silently; she seemed to have disappeared without a trace. It was perhaps for the best, I mused, sipping hastily made tea. The thought of venturing out to Buxton crossed my mind—maybe to look for a new teepee with ample headroom, one where standing tall wasn't an issue. I chuckled at the irony; why pine for a teepee when I had the luxury of a motorhome? With the fading of the new variant, the open road beckoned, ready to be explored with my trailer and trike in tow.

Annabella's entrance broke my contemplation, the epitome of elegance in her grey ensemble. Without waiting for her to speak, I declared, "Annabella, we're off to London."

Her surprise was evident. "Why, may I ask?"

"It's a test," I said firmly. "You claim to want me as your husband, indifferent to the opinions of others."

She responded with a hint of challenge, "It's your choice, Zachariah. If you wish to embarrass yourself, so be it. We could be married without ever setting foot in London—a place you'd hardly relish. I imagined our life together would be in Scotland or somewhere close by."

"I'd like to see the damage from the bomb Annabella."

Annabella's reply was tinged with disdain. "Where the explosion took place is a part of London I'd rather avoid, where the less desirable congregate."

As we approached London, Annabella's restlessness grew. She proposed a detour, "Why not a hotel stay? Claridge's is lovely—we could dine and spend the night there," she said, her grin infectious.

I had other plans. "Let's start with a stroll instead. Oxford Street beckons with its shop windows. A wedding dress hunt seems fitting, though perhaps not in white," I said, my smile broadening at the thought of her reaction.

Annabella's silence was palpable as I navigated the congested streets, searching for a parking spot. She offered no help, stepping out of the Porsche with a deep breath that, sans makeup, would have revealed a flushed face. Our stroll down Oxford Street was leisurely, the shop windows reflecting our images back at us. My transformation had been profound; my youthful visage belied my years, save for the jet-black hair and the odd sensation in my gums—perhaps a side effect of the mysterious concoction I'd been given.

The call of "Annabella, Annabella!" pierced the air, drawing our attention to a young Asian woman crossing the street towards us. I braced myself for an interesting encounter, eager to hear Annabella's explanation of my altered appearance. With a welcoming smile, Annabella greeted her friend, "It's wonderful to see you, Tasmin. What a coincidence to find you here!"

Tasmin's words were a mix of excitement and secrecy, "Didn't you get the text, Annabella? There's a party at number six, just for a select few. Jeremy will be there—you wouldn't want to miss that. Sorry, Grandpa, this is girl talk." I couldn't help but laugh as I walked back to my Porsche, leaving Annabella with her friend. It seemed the truth had a way of revealing itself; perhaps today had been a lesson for Annabella.

Despite my rejuvenation, I still bore the marks of age, at least to the younger generation for whom even the thirties seem ancient.

The drive back to Rose Cottage was serene, a moment of tranquillity as the motorway stretched out before me. The sting of betrayal lingered, yet it served as a jarring reminder to embrace the present, witch's brew or not.

The abrupt ring of the phone shattered the silence. "Yes, Annabella," I answered, the speakerphone carrying her voice through the car.

Her words were laced with regret. "Zachariah, I'm truly sorry. I should've defended you, but I found myself speechless."

My response was resolute. "You've made your stance clear, Annabella. That's all I needed to know. Live well, for our paths shall not cross again. As for your advice, I'll leave that to your discretion. Farewell." With that, I ended the call, the finality of the gesture echoing in the quiet.

Ignoring the persistent calls from Annabella, I blocked her number and retreated upstairs. Stripping down, I confronted my reflection in the full-length mirror. The changes were subtle but undeniable: tighter skin and more defined muscles, yet my face remained untouched, betraying no signs of the elixir's promise. The thought of resorting to cosmetic creams crossed my mind, a laughable shift from my usual pragmatism.

A shower seemed like the next logical step, a simple pleasure that grounded me as I grappled with my changing physique. Dressed in fresh clothes that now felt snug against my skin, I was interrupted by Janet's arrival. Her ascent up the stairs was swift, her breaths short and quick with concern.

"What's happening, Zachariah?" she asked, her eyes searching mine for answers. "Annabella's father is furious, threatening to disown her. I've never heard her so distressed."

The weight of her words hung in the air, a stark reminder of the chaos that had unfolded. The fallout from my encounter with Annabella was more severe than I had anticipated, and now, it seemed, the consequences were just beginning to surface.

"Janet, it was about integrity, not just a whim," I explained, my voice steady despite the turmoil. "Annabella's true colours needed to be revealed, not just to me, but to herself as well. It's one thing to claim indifference to public opinion, quite another to stand by it when faced with the reality."

Janet seemed to ponder this for a moment before speaking. "I understand, but at what cost, Zachariah? You've stirred up a storm that might take a while to settle."

I shrugged, a wry smile crossing my lips. "As for Jeremy, let's just say I'm not in the business of sharing, especially not with someone who can't decide where her loyalties lie. It's better to face the truth now than to live a lie indefinitely."

Janet nodded, her expression softening. "You're right, of course. It's just a shame it had to come to this."

We stood in silence, the weight of the situation settling around us like dust after a storm. The path forward was unclear, but one thing was certain: the facade had crumbled, and from here on out, it was about moving forward with eyes wide open.

Janet's shock was evident as she absorbed the gravity of the situation. "Annabella's father's wrath could strip her of her inheritance. And Jeremy, well, he fancies himself a charmer, though I've only heard of him through Annabella's occasional mentions. She seemed more invested in her future and the organisation than in any dalliance with him."

I pondered Janet's words and then posed a hypothetical question to gauge her reaction: "So if I chose Annabella over you, would you accept it because of your commitment to the organisation?"

Janet's response was pragmatic, yet tinged with resignation. "In our circle, personal desires often yield to the greater ambitions of the organisation."

Her admission surprised me. "But Agnes wanted an heir, not a partner. She never laid claim to me."

With a shrug, Janet revealed her own disappointment. "I've been candid about my feelings for you, but I knew Agnes or Annabella's higher standing in the organisation meant I'd likely have to step aside."

The revelation hit me with clarity. Janet was prepared to sacrifice her feelings for the sake of the organisation's hierarchy. I resolved then that I wouldn't let her make such a sacrifice. Pulling her close, I affirmed our bond with a kiss. "It's you and me, or it's nobody."

Janet's gaze met mine, a mix of concern and realisation dawning on her. "You mean it, don't you? I always thought Annabella or Agnes sway you at a moment's notice."

As we prepared to eat, a sudden pang of discomfort in my chest gave me pause. I tried to ignore it, focusing instead on the simple pleasure of the salad sandwiches Janet and I made together. Her smile was a balm to the unease that had settled within me.

Sitting at the kitchen table, the warmth of the teacup in my hands contrasted sharply with the cold realisation that something was wrong. The dampness on my shirt was not from sweat but from blood seeping through the fabric. Janet's alarm was immediate, her actions swift as she uncovered the source of the bleeding—the stitches that were supposed to be healing me were now betraying me.

The urgency in her voice as she called Peter was matched by the severity of the situation. "Peter, Janet! Zachariah's stitches are bleeding. What do we do?"

Peter's instructions were clear, his voice steady through the speakerphone. "Don't panic. I'm sending a helicopter. Drive to the edge of the village and wait. Zachariah, you should've rested more. We'll fix this."

Apologies were pointless; the priority was to get to the helicopter. As Janet and I hurried out, the gravity of my condition weighed heavily. The hope was to make it back in time, to reverse the consequences of my impatience. "I'll see you soon, Peter," I said, a promise I intended to keep.

Janet's care was meticulous as she assisted me into her Range Rover. I settled into the passenger seat with caution, each movement a silent prayer for the stitches to hold, for life to cling on a little longer. The irony of mortality's edge wasn't lost on me; the once distant concept of death now loomed uncomfortably close, its reality far less romantic than any notion I had entertained before.

The drive was a testament to Janet's attentiveness; she navigated the roads with a precision that spared me from further discomfort. Upon reaching a suitable expanse of grass, she parked and sent a signal that would guide our aerial saviours to our precise location. "The helicopter will find us easily now. Just stay calm, Zachariah," she reassured me.

I remained silent, conserving my strength, pressing the handkerchief to my chest in a feeble attempt to stem the bleeding. The prospect of enduring hours in flight to reach the safety of the Castle of Mey was daunting. Yet, as I monitored the crimson stain on my shirt, a small relief washed over me—the bleeding was slowing. Clinging to the fragment of medical trivia that a person could lose up to 40% of their blood before succumbing to unconsciousness, I willed time to hasten its pace, to bring the rescue that seemed to crawl towards us with agonising slowness.

The roar of the helicopter's blades must have echoed through the village, a stark contrast to the usual tranquillity. As I was ushered into the back seat, the weight of the helmet felt like a tangible reminder of the gravity of my situation. Janet's figure, receding as the helicopter lifted off, was the last familiar sight before embarking on this unexpected journey.

The flight, an experience far removed from my preferences, was a testament to the organisation's resources and their vested interest in my recovery. It was a peculiar thought, considering their primary goal had been met with the securing of an heir. Yet here I was, the focus of a costly and urgent medical evacuation to the Castle of Mey. The potential expense of such an endeavour was a fleeting concern, overshadowed by the more pressing matter of survival.

As the landscape passed below, a patchwork of life and land, I couldn't help but reflect on the strange turns my life had taken. From the intrigue of the organisation's machinations to the personal revelations with Janet, each moment had led to this—a flight for life, with hope waiting on the distant horizon.

The hum of the helicopter's engine was a distant lullaby, lulling me into a fitful rest. It was the pilot's voice, crisp and clear through the headset, that roused me. "Fifteen minutes, Zachariah, we'll land." The sight that greeted me—a pool of blood at my feet—was a stark reminder of my vulnerability. Yet, strangely, I felt a semblance of calm.

As we descended towards the castle, a team clad in white awaited my arrival, their presence a silent promise of care. The moment the helicopter's skids grazed the ground, the flurry of activity began. The door swung open, and I was swiftly transitioned to a wheelchair. Peter's voice, attempting reassurance, couldn't mask the urgency of the situation.

The lab was a blur of motion as I was settled onto the operating table. Peter's "Don't worry" echoed in my ears as the world faded to black, the last vestige of consciousness slipping away.

Awakening in the castle's familiar embrace, I was greeted by the sight of Margaret, her smile a beacon of relief. Her joy at my consciousness was a silent testament to the bond we shared. The ensuing chaos, a cacophony of concern from the science team, was both overwhelming and oddly comforting. My protest, a declaration of my resilience, brought a collective laughter that echoed through the room.

Peter's reprimand, though stern, was laced with an undercurrent of care. "Zachariah, your impulsive departure nearly cost you dearly. You're confined here for a month—no arguments," he declared. His words painted a stark picture: my recklessness had not only jeopardised my own life but had also ruffled the feathers of the organisation's hierarchy.

The revelation of my blood loss, a staggering 20%, was a sobering fact. It was a stark reminder of mortality's fragile thread and the narrow escape facilitated by the fortuitous availability of a helicopter. As Peter's words sank in, the reality of my situation became clear: I was to remain within these walls, under the watchful eyes of those who had saved me, until I was fully restored to health.

Peter's acknowledgement of my motives brought a semblance of solace. "I appreciate your understanding, Peter. My departure wasn't taken lightly. If you could extend my apologies to the council, I'd be grateful. My reasons were personal, and I hope they can be respected."

His response was firm, yet not without empathy. "The situation with Janet and Annabella has been addressed. Rest assured, Annabella's father is taking the matter seriously. She won't be manipulating sentiments or relationships any further."

The revelation was a bittersweet vindication of my actions. It seemed the organisation valued the sanctity of personal choices, after all. As I lay there, the pieces of a complex puzzle falling into place, I knew the road to recovery would be long, but perhaps, in the end, it would lead to a future where choices were honoured and deceptions laid bare.

Margaret's presence in the room, now not just as a familiar face but as my caretaker, brought a sense of comfort despite the circumstances. Her smile was a silent reassurance that I was in good hands. Peter's instructions were clear, and Margaret's nod was all the confirmation I needed that she was up to the task.

The balcony and the garden called to me a reminder of life beyond these walls. Peter's cautious approval gave me hope, a small yet significant liberty in the face of my convalescence.

"I understand the stakes, Peter. I won't take any risks," I assured him.

As Peter departed, the reality of my condition was underscored by the catheter—a necessary intrusion. Margaret's vigilant gaze was both a deterrent and a promise of diligent care. "I appreciate your vigilance, Margaret. And I owe you a debt of gratitude for your help," I said, acknowledging the role reversal. Her commitment to my recovery was a debt repaid, a cycle of aid and gratitude that had come full circle.

Margaret's reassurance was a small comfort in the grand scheme of things. "I'm glad you've found kindness here, and Annabella's gesture was indeed thoughtful," I acknowledged; the intention to express my gratitude was already forming in my mind.

As she brought the orange juice to my bedside, her care was evident in the simple act. "Thank you, Margaret. The vitamin C will do me good," I said, managing a smile despite the dryness of my throat.

Her swift response to assist me in drinking was a testament to her nurturing instincts. "You have a natural talent for this, Margaret. Perhaps nursing is in your future," I mused, appreciating the ease with which she had stepped into the role of caregiver. Her presence, a constant in the ebb and flow of the castle's life, was now a source of healing in its own right.

The morning light filtered through the curtains, casting a soft glow on the walls of my old room at the castle. I awoke with a start, the hands of my wristwatch pointing to 9 a.m. The room was quiet, and Margaret's absence was noticeable. I imagined her downstairs, perhaps enjoying a well-deserved breakfast when the door opened.

Annabella stepped in, her face etched with concern. She perched on the edge of the bed, her voice a whisper of regret. "Zachariah, I'm sorry. Seeing Tasmin, I realised how much I wanted to distance myself from you. My father's threat to disown me has shaken me to the core."

I offered her a wry smile, trying to lighten the mood. "Your father's threats are just that—threats. Besides, accidents do happen," I said, the grin not quite reaching my eyes.

Annabella returned from the bathroom with dental essentials in hand. The act of brushing my teeth, though mundane, felt like a victory. Her towel dabbed at my mouth before she planted a kiss filled with desperation. "I must be with you, Zachariah, until we have a child. Janet understands this," she declared, her words echoing the agreement made in the heat of a moment at Rose Cottage.

Annabella's resolve was clear, her voice firm. "The lineage is crucial, Zachariah. It's not just about the child; it's about the integrity of the bloodline for the organisation. And as for Jeremy, he's not an option. I need someone I can trust, not someone who flits from one dalliance to another."

I sighed, the tension easing from my shoulders. "I understand, and I apologise for my earlier words. They were spoken in anger. And thank you for aiding Margaret—that was a kindness I won't forget."

Her lips pressed into a thin line, a silent acknowledgement of my gratitude. "Margaret's situation is her own to share. I've given her my word, and I won't break it, not even for you."

The frustration bubbled within me, a desperate need to know. "Annabella, please," I implored, my voice rising despite my efforts to remain calm.

She reached out, and her touch was a gentle reminder. "Patience, Zachariah. All will be revealed in time. For now, focus on your recovery. That's what truly matters."

Annabella's words were a mix of caution and revelation, her grip on my hand a physical anchor as she urged me to remain calm. "You must focus on healing, Zachariah. Margaret is safe, and that's what's important. But I can see you need some answers."

I nodded, taking a sip of the lemon juice, its tartness a sharp contrast to the previous day's orange. Annabella settled beside me; her posture relaxed against the headboard as she prepared to share what she knew.

"The situation with Margaret isn't dire, but it's delicate. He took photos, nothing more. She's young, only thirteen, and could have sought help. Yet, she's complicated, perhaps her own adversary in ways we don't fully understand."

I pondered her words, considering the nuances of the situation. "It's easy to pass judgment without knowing the whole story. Maybe Margaret was playing a dangerous game, or maybe she was just being a teenager."

Annabella sighed, a hint of concern in her eyes. "Time will tell. She's integrating with the estate's children at our private school. We'll see how she adapts and how she interacts with everyone. It's a fresh start for her."

The room's atmosphere shifted with Annabella's departure, leaving behind a silence that was soon filled by the waiter's arrival. The tray he placed before me held a modest salad, a stark reminder of my current state and the need for a light diet. As he left, I turned my attention to the meal, the greens a pale comparison to the rich flavours I longed for.

My attempt at lunch was interrupted by Malcolm's booming laughter as he entered the room. "Zachariah, you truly are one of a kind," he said, shaking his head with a mix of exasperation and amusement. "I've just received word from France. Gabrielle is expecting, and you, my friend, are the father. Her father has kept her secluded since her return, ensuring that there's no question of paternity."

The news was as unexpected as it was significant, adding another layer to the intricate web of my life's recent events. Gabrielle's condition and her father's subsequent actions were a testament to the old-world values still held by many within our organisation. As I processed this information, the salad in front of me seemed even less appealing, yet I knew that each bite was a step towards regaining my strength—for myself and now, it seemed, for Gabrielle and the child we would share.

Malcolm's words hung in the air, a stark reminder of the power wielded by Mr Goldstone and the twelve. "It seems my fate, and now Gabrielle's, is a matter of strategic importance to them," I mused, the gravity of the situation not lost on me.

Annabella's entrance, her face a canvas of emotions, signalled another twist in the tale. "Yes, Annabella, Gabrielle is expecting. Her father's decision is... perplexing," I admitted, sharing in Malcolm's confusion.

The plan laid out for Gabrielle felt like a chess game, with moves and countermoves dictated by her father's will. "It's a strange predicament," I continued, "to be so valued by someone I've never met, for reasons beyond my understanding."

Annabella's concern was evident, and her involvement in this intricate dance of destinies was clear. "We're all pawns in a larger game, it seems," I said, a wry smile touching my lips.

"But for now, we play our parts and wait to see how the board changes with each move." The room was filled with a sense of anticipation, the next chapter of our stories yet to be written.

The castle's drama continued to unfold like a scene from a play, each character vividly portraying their part. Annabella's frustration was palpable, her outburst echoing off the walls before she exited with a stormy flourish. Malcolm's laughter served as a counterpoint, a moment of levity amidst the tension.

Left alone with my thoughts, I turned to the escapades of Indiana Jones on the television, finding a strange kinship with the fictional adventurer. The mysteries of my own life seemed to rival those on the screen. The question of my numerous progeny and the organisation's plans for them lingered in my mind, unanswered.

Hunger piqued my curiosity about the evening's meal, hoping for something more satisfying than the day's light fare. But for now, rest beckoned. As I settled into the bed, the prospect of freedom from the catheter and the confines of the room was a hopeful thought for tomorrow. Despite the day's revelations and the lack of clarity they brought, I allowed myself a moment of respite, closing my eyes to the complexities of the world outside.

The scent of perfume lingered in the air, a subtle hint of change as Margaret tended to my needs with a newfound grace. The meal she brought was a welcome reprieve from the lighter fare I had grown accustomed to during my recovery. The rich flavours of the roast venison and the hearty accompaniments were a reminder of the life I was eager to return to—a life of robust experiences and tangible pleasures.

As I savoured the last sip of my coffee, the room felt a bit emptier without the tray, a silent testament to the satisfaction of a good meal. Margaret's return, marked by the delicate fragrance and the careful touch as she adjusted my pillow, was a gentle intrusion into my convalescence. It seemed Annabella's influence extended beyond mere apologies, perhaps in an attempt to provide comfort through these small luxuries.

The day's events had unfolded like chapters in a novel, each moment leading to the next with a sense of inevitability. As I settled back against the freshly fluffed pillows, the castle's walls seemed to hold not just secrets, but also the promise of recovery and the complexities of intertwined lives.

The evening brought an unexpected visitor to my bedside. Agnes entered the room, her pregnancy unmistakable, and greeted me with a kiss that spoke volumes of her concern. As Margaret discreetly exited, Agnes shared her relief at my narrow escape from death's door; her voice tinged with a mix of frustration and affection.

"Zachariah, your antics never cease to amaze me," she said, a smile breaking through her worry. "But I'm glad you're still with us."

In response, I couldn't resist making a cheeky request. "Agnes, would you mind helping me get rid of this catheter? I'm tired of being tethered to this bed. Plus, a shower with you sounds like the perfect remedy," I said, hoping my grin would convey the light-heartedness of my proposition.

Her laughter was the answer I expected, a gentle reminder of the protocols we had to follow

Agnes' decision to remove the catheter against medical advice was a risky move, driven by a mix of concern and desire to see me regain my independence. The shower was a moment of vulnerability and connection, a shared space where the worries of the outside world were washed away, if only temporarily.

Her refusal to stay the night was a reminder of the delicate balance between my health and our emotions. "I understand, Agnes. Your caution is as appreciated as your company," I said, watching her leave with a mixture of disappointment and respect for her judgment.

Peter's entrance and his stern reprimand were not unexpected. His concern for my well-being was evident, even as he administered a sedative to ensure I would not further endanger my recovery. As the room faded to black, I was left with the realisation that my actions had consequences and that the path to healing would require not just physical care but also the discipline to follow the guidance of those tasked with my care.

Waking up disoriented, I realised I had lost track of time—two days, then a whole week had slipped by. The medical equipment that I thought I had been freed from was once again part of me. Margaret, ever the vigilant caretaker, was there, ready to administer another injection. But this time, she surprised me by removing the catheter and drip, signalling a significant step towards normalcy.

"Peter has given the green light for a bit of freedom, Zachariah. Take it slow, and you can enjoy breakfast on the balcony," Margaret informed me, her tone professional yet caring.

Grateful for the progress, I didn't protest. The shower was a refreshing escape, the water a cascade of renewal over my weary body. Dressed in the clothes Margaret had laid out, I felt a semblance of my old self returning.

Margaret's next gesture, serving a hearty breakfast of bacon and eggs on the balcony, was a luxury I hadn't realised I'd missed so much. Her refusal to join me was understandable, but the offer stood as a token of my appreciation for her care.

Alone with my meal and the morning breeze, I turned to my phone, where messages from Janet awaited. Her concern was a warm thread in the fabric of my convalescence. Using my mobile, I greeted her with a playful familiarity. "Hello, sexy Janet," I balanced the call with the pleasure of my breakfast, the simple joys of life slowly returning to my world.

Janet's voice, warm and filled with concern, was a reminder of the life that awaited beyond the castle's walls. "I'm not disappointed at all, Janet. A son is a blessing, and I'm eager for his birth," I replied, the joy in my voice genuine.

Her words were a balm, soothing the frustration of confinement. "I'll follow Peter's instructions to the letter. I have too much to live for now, especially with our son," I assured her, the promise of fatherhood igniting a newfound resolve within me.

As I ended the call, the balcony's solitude gave way to a sense of connection. Despite the physical distance, Janet's presence was felt, a comforting constant as I navigated the path to recovery. "I'll be back before you know it," I said, the promise hanging in the air as I disconnected, the future with Janet and our child a beacon guiding me forward.

The morning's tranquillity was briefly pierced by the sight of a stag in distress, but nature's drama resolved itself without my intervention. The garden, a tableau of life at the castle, offered up a private moment between Margaret and a young man—a glimpse of a budding romance or perhaps just a fleeting connection.

Margaret's reaction to being observed was one of alarm, a testament to the castle's atmosphere where privacy is a rare commodity. Her rush to explain was unnecessary, yet it spoke volumes of her perception of the boundaries within these walls.

"Margaret, there's no need for explanations. Your life is your own," I reassured her, hoping to ease any concerns about judgment or reprimand. "And I'm grateful for your care. Let's look forward to that walk in the garden, a step towards normalcy for us both," I added, offering a smile to cement my sincerity.

As she departed, the promise of tomorrow's walk lingered in the air, a shared experience to come that would further distance us from the roles of patient and caretaker to simply two individuals enjoying the beauty of the estate.

Turning off the television, I felt a pull towards the garden's tranquillity. The sun was out, and with a bit of caution, what harm could a gentle stroll do? I ventured to the garden's cold store, selecting an apple and pear for a snack. Settling on the swinging bench, I became an unintended attraction for the garden's bees. In a bid for peace, I surrendered the pear to the lawn, finishing my apple with minimal buzzing company.

As I sat there, a figure caught my eye—Gabrielle, her smile radiant as the sun above approached me. We met halfway, and our embrace was a silent exchange of relief and affection. "Zachariah, my father thought it best for me to stay with you at the castle for a while," she shared, her voice filled with warmth. "I've been told of your recent ordeal; it's been quite distressing. Please, take care—you have so much more to live for now."

Her presence was a vivid reminder of the life growing within her, a life connected to mine, and the responsibility I now carried. Her concern was a gentle admonition to tread more carefully on the path ahead.

Gabrielle's visit to the castle was a pleasant surprise, her conservative attire and fresh breath a stark contrast to our first encounter. Her affectionate greeting and her father's insistence on her visit filled me with warmth. As we strolled through the garden, arm in arm, the sight of Margaret with a young man brought back memories of my own youth.

However, the reality of Margaret's situation—a young girl in a precarious position—cast a shadow over the idyllic scene. When Gabrielle and I stumbled upon the couple in a compromising situation, her quick thinking spared them further embarrassment. Malcolm's timely arrival assured me that he would handle the matter with discretion.

Reflecting on my past, I recognised the folly of youth and the importance of guidance. As Gabrielle and I resumed our walk, I was grateful for her presence and the future we would soon share with our child. The garden, with its hidden corners and blooming life, was a fitting backdrop for the contemplation of life's ongoing cycle and the roles we play within it.

The lounge's warmth was a stark contrast to the gathering clouds outside as I settled by the fire, the flickering flames casting a soft glow on the faces of Annabella and Gabrielle. Their shared glances hinted at secrets about to be unveiled, and I braced myself for the revelations to come.

Annabella's announcement was as swift as it was surprising. "I'm pregnant," she declared, her voice a mix of astonishment and disbelief. The news seemed to hang in the air; a new life silently acknowledged in the quiet of the room. Her swift departure left a trail of emotions in her wake, the door closing softly behind her.

Gabrielle's laughter filled the space left by Annabella's absence, and her declaration of companionship and care was a comforting promise. "You're my lover; I will be gentle with you; I'm sleeping with you," she said, her words a blend of humour and sincerity.

As the evening settled around us, the castle became a vessel for our intertwined stories, each of us navigating the complexities of relationships and the unexpected turns of life. The fire's warmth was a reminder that, despite the chill of the coming rain, we were sheltered here together, bound by the ties of affection and the shared anticipation of what the future would bring.

Malcolm's words were a sobering reminder of the responsibilities that come with overseeing the estate and its inhabitants. "I understand, Malcolm. It's a delicate situation, but I trust your judgment on the best course of action for Margaret," I replied, acknowledging the complexity of the matter.

The use of surveillance was a necessary precaution in managing such a vast property and ensuring the well-being of everyone on the grounds. "I appreciate you being on top of things. It's important that we maintain a certain order here," I added, recognising the importance of Malcolm's role.

As I returned to Gabrielle, I carried with me the weight of the conversation, a renewed awareness of the intricate web of lives within the castle's walls. The decisions made here, in these rooms and gardens, shaped not just our own futures but those of everyone connected to this place. It was a burden we bore collectively, each playing our part in the grand scheme of the estate's legacy.

Malcolm's light-hearted comment about his past marriage brought a moment of levity to the room. After he left, I turned my attention back to Gabrielle, who had thoughtfully prepared drinks for us both. Her question about our future hung in the air, weighted with her father's expectations and our own desires.

"Gabrielle, there's no rush for us to make such a life-altering decision. You're safe here with me, and that's what matters most right now," I reassured her, hoping to ease the pressure she felt.

Her inquiry about Janet was poignant, reflecting her own insecurities. "Janet and I have a unique connection, but that doesn't diminish what you and I share," I explained gently.

Gabrielle's concern for my health and the treatments I was undergoing was touching. "I value every moment we have together, Gabrielle. Let's focus on the present and cherish our time," I said, offering her a comforting smile as we sat together, contemplating the complexities of life and love.

Malcolm re-entered the lounge with a grave look on his face. He declared, "The twelve are convening tonight, Zachariah. Your presence is requested, along with Annabella, Gabrielle, and Agnes. Janet will arrive with a special escort. Let's meet here at 7 pm." With those words, he disappeared as abruptly as he had arrived.

Gabrielle's demeanour shifted from her usual warmth to something more sombre—Malcolm's message had clearly affected her. Taking my hand, she led me upstairs. In the quiet sanctuary of my bedroom, Gabrielle undressed with deliberate slowness and settled into bed, gesturing for me to join her under the duvet. We lay together in silence until Gabrielle began to whisper sweet nothings in French, her voice soft and tender. She was mindful of my healing wounds, offering herself to me with a gentleness that spoke volumes. As she murmured in French, I longed to grasp the meaning of her words, feeling in my heart that they were profound. The thought crossed my mind that if her words held the sentiment I imagined, it was a declaration of a depth of intimacy reserved only for me.

Gabrielle's shriek pierced the air as she tumbled next to me, her kisses fervent, her French whispers fleeting. I must admit, it was a moment of pure bliss, the first in what felt like forever. We succumbed to sleep's embrace, finding solace in each other's presence. Our peace was soon interrupted by a knock at the door, a voice commanding, "Zachariah, Gabrielle, you're needed in five minutes." Hastily, we sprang into action, sharing a quick shower. Gabrielle dressed with urgency and departed. I donned my pirate attire and descended the stairs, only to be ushered by Malcolm into the caverns. It was then I noticed the shackles around my ankles. Malcolm's breath was heavy with regret as he said, "Forgive me, Zachariah, but we can't afford any mishaps tonight."

His words hung heavy in the air. "What are you implying, Malcolm? Will there be more of your potions in my veins, or is it a bullet this time?" I asked, a sense of foreboding settling over me.

Malcolm's voice was cold and distant as he uttered, "Under these circumstances, shooting you might be the lesser pain." He left without another word. Shackled; I could only watch as logs were cast into the fire, the flames growing ever higher. The twelve emerged, robed and solemn, their wives beside them in gowns that whispered of the sixteenth century. Agnes and Annabella stood nearby, tears streaming down their faces. To my left, Gabrielle was equally distraught, and I immobilised, could offer no comfort to anyone.

Malcolm, clad in his black robe, took his place beside the fiercely burning fire. The intensity of the flames was unlike anything I had witnessed before, and the heat was palpable. A part of me wondered if I was to be their next offering to the fire. Suddenly, the cavern's ceiling lit up, revealing a coffin draped in a pirate flag. As it was lowered into the heart of the flames, the flag caught fire, the coffin suspended by a thick rope. With a calculated move, Malcolm fired his revolver twice, severing the rope. The coffin descended gracefully into the inferno.

I could only assume this was part of a ritual, the details of which were unknown to me. The sound of gunfire filled the air as each member of the organisation fired a single shot skyward. I hoped the rounds were blanks; the thought of bullets ricocheting in this enclosed space was unnerving. The echo of the shots was nearly overwhelming. In a final act of ceremony, the women each cast a rose into the flames before retreating to their partners' sides.

Malcolm's voice cut through the silence, clear and resolute: "We share in your grief, Zachariah, for Janet's untimely departure, taken from us in yesterday's bank raid. We honour her memory and send her spirit to soar with her forebears in the celestial realms."

Overcome with disbelief, I collapsed, my heart refusing to accept the truth. The thought of enduring another loss, so soon after the first, and the future of my unborn child, was unbearable. My anguish erupted in a visceral cry, "Janet, your death will not go unavenged!" Rising unsteadily, I drew my cutlass, its blade striking against my chains in a shower of sparks. Fuelled by the legacy of Blackbeard, vengeance became my vow. With each swing, my resolve deepened until, at last, a shackle gave way. As I turned to the remaining chain, the cavern fell silent, save for the crackle of pine in the fire and the resonant clang of my cutlass against the iron, echoing my fierce determination.

Gasping for air, I halted, my gaze fixed on the flames that now consumed Janet. The others had retreated into the darkness, leaving me alone with the fire as the sole illumination in the cavern. I resumed my assault on the chain that bound me, fuelled by a promise that I was determined to fulfil. Life and death seemed inconsequential at that moment—my only focus was on the blood that had begun to seep from my chest. In a frantic motion, I tore at my cotton shirt, revealing that my stitches had burst open, and I was bleeding heavily. That overwhelming sight is the last memory I have.

The ensuing three weeks passed in a haze. As September began, I felt nothing short of mechanical. Margaret was the sole companion permitted to visit during my convalescence, tasked with the care of my surgical wounds. Sedatives kept my turmoil at bay, while Peter worked tirelessly to salvage what he deemed an undeserving soul on the brink of ruin. One day, Margaret revealed a chilling update: the trio implicated in Janet's murder had met their end within the confines of their cell. Yet whispers of an elusive puppeteer persisted—his identity shielded by the silence of his cohorts. Over a freshly poured cup of tea, Margaret shared this grim news.

No sooner had Margaret exited than Malcolm made his presence known. "Upon your return to strength, Zachariah, the puppet master's name shall be yours to know," he proclaimed. "His fate, and that of his kin, will rest in your hands. As for the others, the twelve have seen to their justice through an ally within the prison walls."

CHAPTER 7

Dancing with the Devil

Fighting back tears, I inhaled deeply. "Thank you. It's hard to grasp that this is reality, Malcolm; it feels like a nightmare."

Malcolm nodded, his voice tinged with empathy. "I understand. I've lost close colleagues during my time in government service. When you've worked side by side for years, you become more than just a team—you're family."

"I'm at a loss, Malcolm. Taking a life would be simple, but it won't undo the past. It won't bring her back, nor the child she carried."

Malcolm's expression softened. "Janet might have had a premonition. She had her affairs in order, leaving her estate to you. Your Porsche has been retrieved by Annabella, and she's made sure your house is secure. I've also arranged for a security firm to monitor the property daily."

As Malcolm exited, my emotions overwhelmed me, and I wept openly. Peter then stepped in, offering a reassuring smile as he inspected my stitches. "You're healing well, no signs of infection. It's good to let it out, Zachariah. Mourning is necessary. But remember, revenge can wait until you're fully recovered. I won't let you out of my sight until you're indestructible." With a supportive pat on the shoulder, he left me to my thoughts.

My room felt like a revolving door of visitors. Annabella approached my bed with a smile that didn't quite reach her eyes. "You can't just lie there wallowing, Zachariah," she said, her tone firm yet caring. "You need to heal, and staying in bed won't help." With a swift motion, she whisked away the duvet and removed my catheter with an efficiency that belied her gentle nature. Despite my protests, she coaxed me out of bed and guided me toward the shower.

Annabella joined me after disrobing, and we let the warm water wash over us for what seemed like an eternity. When we emerged, the bed had been refreshed with crisp linens and two robes lay waiting for us. We wrapped ourselves in the soft fabric and sat side by side, watching a waiter set a tray on the balcony table. Together, we stepped out into the sunlight, savouring the warmth that would soon give way to winter's chill. As Annabella poured the tea, a question hung heavily in the air. "Where's Gabrielle? Is she all right?" I asked, concern lacing my words.

"Gabrielle has flown back to France; she needed to speak with her father directly," Annabella explained. "She's decided to make England her home with you. It's a change of heart from her initial insistence on living in France. Your actions in the cavern moved her deeply. The sight of sparks flying from your cutlass, the way you severed the bolt—it was something none of us had ever witnessed. I'll admit, it was terrifying. Had you broken free, I believe only a bullet could have halted your rampage."

I could only respond with a dazed acknowledgement. "To be honest, I don't recall much of anything from that night."

Annabella spoke with an icy detachment: "You need to understand that the twelve have not only dealt with the three responsible for Janet's death but have also eradicated their entire lineage. Our policy is clear-cut; upon your release, when you confront the mastermind, we expect you to act with the same decisiveness. The lives of all cohabitants are forfeit. Janet was an integral part of our organisation, and her loss will not be without repercussions. Those at fault will face severe consequences.'"

"Does that imply they will be subjected to torture prior to their execution?"

"We prefer that they fully comprehend the agony they've inflicted. On a different note, a new cutlass, a replica of Blackbeard's own, is being crafted for you. It will be completed within a week, utilising only the highest quality steel. The previous one you wielded was shattered, compromised by the severity of the punishment you meted out."

"Such fury was unfamiliar to me; even Hazel's passing, which I had anticipated, didn't evoke this intensity. I fear that without universal inoculation, none will withstand the onslaught of these new strains." With a heavy heart, I dressed alongside Annabella. We embraced tenderly, exchanging soft kisses for a lingering moment. "I must go, Zachariah; otherwise, I risk staying here, in your bed—and we cannot have that. You're still recovering; please, refrain from any exertion." With those final words, Annabella hastened to the door, securing it as she departed.

Armed with my binoculars, I settled on the balcony, basking in the warmth of the sun. My gaze wandered over the gardens, following the Canadian geese as they made their way toward the lake. Compelled by the beauty of the day,

I decided to explore the grounds. As I circled the castle's perimeter—a path previously untraveled by me—I stumbled upon an unassuming door. Beyond it, I believed, lay the staff quarters. A voice, strangely familiar, beckoned me to a particular door. A discreet glance through the keyhole revealed more than enough: Margaret was entwined in an intimate encounter. Silently, I retreated outdoors, only to find my Porsche being attentively detailed by one of the staff.

Further afield, Rory, our steadfast gamekeeper, was accompanied by his loyal dogs, rifle in hand. They seemed poised for a hunt, perhaps after a stag, or maybe for a more sinister purpose—removing an unwelcome presence. A pang of solitude struck me, a feeling I hadn't experienced in days. My thoughts were singular, fixated on one thing alone: bringing the architect of the bank heist to justice.

Malcolm approached with a purposeful stride. 'Follow me, Zachariah,' he said, handing me a key. 'You've earned the trust of the twelve. They're certain you'll keep our secrets and fulfil your duties without faltering. You have my unwavering support. Despite your lack of training as an assassin, I have no doubt you'll succeed in every task."

I couldn't help but smile at his words, trailing behind him into the cavernous depths. We arrived at a door that could easily be mistaken for a bank vault. Malcolm deftly inserted his key, turned it with a deliberate force, and the door swung open, revealing its formidable six-inch thick steel construction. Inside, the lights flickered on, illuminating an arsenal vast enough to wage a war—grenades, assault rifles, rocket launchers capable of decimating a tank, and night vision goggles—all at the ready.

Malcolm unexpectedly handed me a handgun and a shoulder holster with two magazines of ammunition. His voice was steady as he said, "These are now yours. Given that you're licensed to carry a firearm, I'll provide you with an identification card upstairs. It will mark you as a Royal armed guard, part of an elite group whose authority is unquestionable by the police. Present this card if you're ever stopped. To ensure your actions remain untraceable, your gun will be replaced and destroyed after each mission, and you'll be issued a new one. Our influence extends further than you can imagine."

I was taken aback by the sudden weight of responsibility. "And Janet's ashes?" I asked.

"They'll be scattered in the vegetable garden and amongst the rose bushes," Malcolm replied. "That way, she'll always be a part of this place."

Dabbing away tears from beneath my glasses with a handkerchief, I stepped out of the armoury as Malcolm secured the door behind us. Together, we made our way up the castle stairs. At the top, Malcolm opened a drawer and presented me with an identification card. It bore my photograph, my designated position, and a unique coded number to verify my identity. "You'll be back in form within a couple of weeks, Zachariah," he said with a reassuring smile. "Then, we'll ensure your targets are isolated, ready for you to handle." With a final pat on my shoulder, he departed.

Ascending the remaining stairs to my bedroom, I found Agnes on the balcony, a salad awaiting me for lunch. Observing me as I placed my new gun and holster on the balcony's edge, she offered a knowing smile. "You're truly one of us now," she remarked. "The intensity of your desire for vengeance is unparalleled. I fully support your quest."

The mention of Janet always reopens a deep wound within me. I hold onto the hope that time will mend the heartache. Maybe, just maybe, once I've dealt with the mastermind, I'll find some solace. I quickly ate my simple salad. Agnes then said softly, "Zachariah, they're scattering Janet's ashes among the roses."

I watched as two gardeners carefully distributed the ashes around the rose beds. Completing their task, they paused and bowed their heads in respect. At the far end of the garden, a priest, Bible in hand, offered words I couldn't hear, but the solemnity of the moment spoke volumes. It was, indeed, a fitting resting place for Janet.

Agnes added, "There's one more thing, Zachariah. This room, with its view over the roses, is now yours."

Overwhelmed, I abruptly left the table, tears streaming down my face. I seized a bottle of Bacardi and Coke, pouring a glass to the top and drinking hastily, trying to numb the searing pain. After three glasses, the sharpness of my grief began to dull. Agnes, ever watchful, handed me another glass and led me to an armchair. She took a seat opposite me, her eyes full of empathy. "I'm so sorry, Zachariah," she whispered. "I wish I could ease your pain."

After draining my fourth glass, I continued to pour more, seeking oblivion. Agnes watched silently, understanding the depth of my grief; she left me to my sorrow. I recall staggering to my bed, the world spinning as I succumbed to a troubled sleep, the pain momentarily forgotten.

Dawn brought clarity and a shocking discovery—Margaret was beside me. As she emerged from the duvet and walked towards the shower, I buried my face, unable to reconcile the fragmented memories. The click of the door signalled her departure, and panic set in. I rushed after her, fearing the consequences of my inebriated actions—actions that would betray my intent to protect, not harm.

Once composed, I stepped out to the balcony with a coffee in hand, the roses in view, stirring a longing to be reunited with Janet. My gaze fell upon my gun and holster, left untouched on the wall—fortunately spared by the weather. Malcolm would have disapproved, no doubt; moisture is no friend to firearms.

"Zachariah, we'll soon remove those stitches. You're nearly healed," he said, his smile brimming with assurance. "Have you seen your reflection lately? I recommend you do. And prepare yourself for another injection tomorrow—I doubt you'll object," Peter added with a playful grin.

I stood and faced the full-length mirror, my remark tinged with sarcasm, "Ah, more of the witch's brew—marvellous." The reflection required a double-take; my beard had darkened to black, and my hair was regrowing. My gums had been sore, a sign of new teeth emerging. As I examined my naked form, I noted a youthful vigour, the body of a man in his mid-thirties, though my face still bore the marks of time. Yet, I had no grievances; I was starting to understand the ambitions of the twelve, both for themselves and for me.

Margaret entered, her gaze lingering on my figure. "I half-wished you'd take your chances with me while you were inebriated, but you only snored," she said with a hint of disappointment. She placed a towel by the shower and exited. A profound relief washed over me—I had not crossed that line with her.

Peter walked into my room just as I was unbuttoning my shirt to show him the stitches. "They're ready to come out," he observed. "We double-stitched this area; the rest will dissolve on their own. See me in the lab tomorrow morning."

At that moment, Annabella entered, pausing to take in my changed appearance. "The formula is indeed effective," she remarked with a smile, shedding her garments and joining me in bed. The grief of losing Janet seemed distant now, almost understandable. Annabella spoke with a mix of seriousness and affection, "Take care, Zachariah Black. I can't bear the thought of losing our child. It took me longer to conceive than anyone else—probably because you desired me more than any other," she said, her grin playful and teasing.

My heart is racing, and I can't tell if it's the same heart I've always had. Annabella's teeth gently press into my skin. She whispers, "I'm so glad I stopped by before heading home, Zachariah. You've truly brightened my day; that's why I love you."

We step into the shower, laughter echoing between us. Annabella declares, "We've come to a decision, Blackbeard. Agnes and I have agreed to let Gabrielle be with you. We'll seek our thrills with you when the mood strikes us. Both Agnes and I are busy managing our businesses. Gabrielle, meanwhile, remains under her father's care. He has two sons who are showing great promise and may soon join the organisation, pending the twelve's approval."

"Absolutely not! I won't move to France for you or anyone else. True, Gabrielle is as stunning as you are, Annabella, but living in France is out of the question for me."

Annabella's laughter filled the room as we stepped out of the shower and dried each other off. "You won't have to," she clarified. "Gabrielle will be moving into the house you inherited from Janet."

The idea didn't sit well with me. "Janet's memory is still fresh; how can Gabrielle adapt to life here without her beloved garlic?"

Annabella responded with a hint of amusement, "It's about compromise, Zachariah. You'll learn. If things don't work out, she'll go back to France, child in tow. She's planning to give birth there to ensure French citizenship for the baby."

I couldn't help but express my frustration. "I find it remarkable how you all make decisions about my life without consulting me. One moment, Annabella, you're eager to marry me, and the next, you're not. The only one who's been consistent is Agnes. She never wanted marriage, just children—and perhaps the occasional tryst."

Annabella grabbed my arm, taking me into another room. She said, "Here's our window into your target's world," her voice a mix of determination and disdain. This man, the architect of Janet's demise, has shielded himself and his family with luxury and distance. But we've pierced that veil. Observe closely, Zachariah. The footage you're about to study could unravel their facade and expose their guilt."

As the images on the screen began to move, the voices from the yacht's past whispered secrets into the present. Each frame framed a piece of the puzzle that Zachariah was tasked to solve. The mission was clear: to bring justice for Janet, no matter the cost.

For several minutes, I observed the two daughters and sons lounging on the yacht's deck alongside their mother. The crew had just finished setting the table for a meal. Seated with them was Mr Jamieson, a man whose presence dominated the scene. Annabella and I listened intently to their conversation. One daughter commented, "Father, we must hire more competent people; after all, a mere million in the bank hardly justifies a robbery, not to mention the foolishness of shooting the bank manager."

"I'm aware that not every plan is foolproof," he replied.

As he munched on his salad, one of the sons added coldly, "The bank manager was pregnant. We've prevented another nuisance from coming into the world."

Their knowledge of the events was undeniable, sealing their fate in my eyes. I would devise a flawless plan. Annabella, sensing my growing fury, squeezed my hand reassuringly and switched off the projector.

Malcolm entered, flooding the room with light. "Apologies for the delay. Have you finished watching, Zachariah?" he asked.

I gave a nod of confirmation. "Yes, I've seen what I needed. Now, about the castle's underground tunnels—can they be used? They need to be soundproof; we can't risk any noise escaping."

"Ah, the old prison cells within the cave system," Malcolm mused. "There are quite a few—eight in total if memory serves."

I couldn't help but smile at the thought. "What are the odds you could arrange for the Jamiesons to be sedated and brought here to be confined in those cells?"

Annabella's excitement was palpable as she clapped her hands. "Oh, Malcolm, you must install cameras in the cells. Agnes, Gabrielle, and I wouldn't miss watching their downfall."

Malcolm nodded. "I can set up a meeting with them at John O'Groats under the guise of transporting a large sum of money. It's deserted there, making it simple to manage the

Jamiesons. We'll bring them here, lock them in the dungeons, and then, Zachariah, they're your responsibility."

Gratitude filled my voice. "You have my thanks, Malcolm. This way, their reckoning can be ... extended."

Zachariah, before anything else, I need to discuss your plan with the twelve, it's risky, but I foresee no issues getting approval for your request. Once I have their decision, I'll inform you later tonight.

Malcolm hurried out, clearly on another urgent task. Suddenly, Annabella's arms were around me, her kisses fervent, betraying her excitement. Panting, she exclaimed, "The thought of you dealing with the Jamiesons thrills me, Zachariah! It'll be like watching a live drama unfold, every detail visible. How thrilling! As soon as Malcolm confirms our travel arrangements, I'll let Agnes know. Could you give me a hint about how you plan to handle them?"

I cautioned her, "We don't have the twelve's consent yet, Annabella. Don't jump to conclusions. I doubt they'd want such trouble near the Castle of Mey."

After Annabella hurried away, I retreated to the solitude of my bedroom. A deep breath filled my lungs; the idea of the twelve sanctioning a massacre here seemed unfathomable. My gaze drifted across the room, landing on the familiar shape of my old machete, now adorned with a fresh sheath. It coaxed a rare smile from me.

The quiet was broken by a waiter, who silently placed two steaming coffees on the balcony table before making a discreet exit. I settled into a chair, the presence of a second cup suggesting an impending company. It wasn't long before Malcolm burst in, taking his seat across from me. He wasted no time, "Zachariah, patience is key. The twelve are adamant about keeping the assassination off these grounds. I've argued that our dungeons serve a specific purpose and should be used as such. Yes, dispatching an assassin or a distant gunshot would be simpler, but such swift ends don't seem fitting retribution for what you've endured."

"I'm not taken aback, Malcolm. The last thing we—or the twelve—need is the police prying into our affairs. I take it the Jamieson's yacht is moored in Guernsey?"

"That's correct. The yacht is currently anchored there. Jamieson was scheduled to fly into Birmingham airport within three hours, but the rest of the family planned to remain in Guernsey," Malcolm replied, just as his mobile began to ring. After a brief conversation, he hung up and turned to me with an update. "Change of plans. They're not flying after all. The entire family will be sailing back to England. They're heading for Poole Harbour, which should make our task easier. You caught all that, Zachariah?"

I simply nodded in acknowledgement.

Malcolm's phone rang once more, and he answered with a look of concern. His voice was reverent as he spoke, "Yes, Sir, absolutely, Sir. No errors, thank you." He ended the call and turned to me, his expression one of disbelief. "Zachariah, that was unexpected. Louis, Gabrielle's father, has ordered his fishing vessel to intercept the Jamieson's yacht. They're to capture the family and eliminate any other passengers, then bring them here. He's managed to persuade the rest of the council with his influence—I guess his wealth speaks volumes. His ship, the one that ferries Gabrielle and other...cargo, is equipped with advanced radar and signal jammers." Malcolm chuckled, "He's what you'd call a true pirate, Zachariah."

I expressed my gratitude for his assistance: "Thank you, Malcolm. Do you have any idea when they might arrive?"

"Give it three days," he replied, standing up with both coffee cups in hand. "We'll need to keep them sedated until they're secured in the dungeons. I should also prepare the cameras; Annabella would be quite upset if she missed out, and the council, along with their spouses, are eager to witness your expertise. They say Blackbeard was a terror when provoked. After witnessing your actions at Janet's funeral, I believe you share that trait." With that, Malcolm left my room.

I hurried after him, catching up as he descended the stairs. "Malcolm, could we discreetly procure six portable toilets and the necessary supplies? I assume we have them in stock?"

His brow furrowed in confusion, "Why the sudden need for toilets?"

"It's a crucial part of my plan. I'll cover the cost if it's an issue. I want this to be thorough. Only one needs to be...civilised," I said with a sly grin.

Malcolm's laughter filled the air. "You've piqued my curiosity, Zachariah. Consider it done; each dungeon will have its own toilet. Should I also look into showers?" he quipped with a hint of sarcasm.

I gave Malcolm a reassuring pat on the shoulder before wandering off to the garden. There, amidst the rose bushes, lay Janet's final resting place. The mere thought of her untimely departure sent a surge of anger through me. Seeking solace, I entered the cold store, picked a pear and an apple, and settled on the swing, sheltered from the biting wind.

Margaret approached her steps light on the lawn. She joined me on the swing, playfully snatching the pear and taking a hearty bite. With a cheeky pat and a carefree laugh, she flashed a mischievous grin, lifted her jumper in a bold display, and darted away. I could only shake my head in bemusement—some aspects of the younger generation were truly beyond my grasp.

Malcolm's laughter echoed across the gardens as he approached me, still chuckling. "I've managed to source the toilets from various suppliers. They'll all be delivered within the next two days. And I've also ordered buckets—can't have your captives dying of thirst, can we? Plus, I've thrown in some plastic cups for good measure."

I couldn't help but grin at his enthusiasm. "You seem to be quite enjoying this, aren't you, Malcolm?"

"Whatever gave you that impression, Zachariah?" he replied with a smile, then walked off.

The distant whir of helicopter blades grew louder, signalling an arrival or departure nearby. I lay back on the swing, basking in the warmth of the sun, and must have dozed off. I was jolted awake by raindrops pelting my face as the sky opened up. I sprinted towards the castle, rushing upstairs to change and take a shower.

To my dismay, Margaret walked in as I was showering. "Out!" I demanded.

She stood her ground. "No," she said firmly.

I hurried past her, drying off and dressing quickly. Margaret emerged from the shower, looking puzzled. "What's wrong with me?"

"You're thirteen, Margaret. You don't want to be labelled inappropriately," I cautioned her.

She dressed silently, deep in thought, and left without a word. She was attractive, no doubt, but I couldn't entertain such thoughts. Malcolm entered with the news. "The Jamiesons will arrive Saturday morning, early hours. They'll stay sedated until noon, giving you plenty of time to plan."

"Thank you, Malcolm. I'll need about a month to handle them. There's no rush, right?"

"No rush at all. You're after a thorough reckoning, aren't you, Zachariah?"

"Indeed. And I'm glad it's being recorded. It's important that the message is clear: never cross me again." I watched Malcolm leave, anticipation for Saturday building. I planned to set my alarm for 3:00 a.m. I needed time to assess each one and decide their fate.

As I sit on the balcony, my sanctuary, the twilight gently wraps around the garden. I can almost see Janet there, amidst the roses. The thought of her brings a pang of sorrow, and my dinner—a plate of venison and greens—sits untouched. Her absence is a void I'm learning to navigate; those responsible will soon be nothing more than compost or deep-sea drift, a fitting end, I muse. Hatred, a foreign sensation, now courses through me with an intensity that's startling.

Dinner concludes with a heavy heart. I retreat to the solace of my bed and flick on the television. A news report draws a rare smile; the Jamieson's yacht has been claimed by the sea, leaving no survivors. The search will resume with the morning light. This is just the beginning. They will come to understand true suffering. As for forgiveness, it's a concept that eludes me, and mercy is not in my vocabulary.

Leaping from my bed, I push aside the bookcase to reveal the hidden passage leading to the laboratories and beyond. In hand, a single candle casts flickering shadows as I descend into the depths of the dungeons. The doors stand ajar, swept clean in anticipation, yet cobwebs lace the ceiling—a detail that brings a smirk to my face. Malcolm has been here; buckets of water sit in the corner, a stark contrast to the pitch-black cells. The oak doors are solid, punctuated by barred windows and trapdoors for passing meals. It's all more perfect than I'd dared to dream.

As I explore further, I stumble upon a room dominated by a massive oak table, its presence almost oppressive. The walls are adorned with shears and an array of instruments designed to inflict pain. A camera, an unblinking eye in the corner, catches my attention. I wave mockingly, my laughter echoing off the stone walls.

Exiting the room, I'm met with Annabella's grin, her news sending a thrill through me. "The Jamiesons will be early," she says, her voice tinged with excitement. We retreat to the castle, to my chambers, where she slips into bed with a mischievous glint in her eye. "You press my buttons, Zachariah—or should I say, Blackbeard! Do your worst. I'll take it," she teases, her laughter youthful and carefree.

Our moment is interrupted by Malcolm's urgent entrance and swift exit. "Zachariah," he announces, barely containing his glee, "we're ahead of schedule. The Jamiesons will arrive at 9 a.m., a full day early. Louis's boat is swift, even against the storm. They're desperate to distance themselves from the sunken yacht, to avoid suspicion." His message is clear: "Do your worst, Blackbeard. Gabrielle awaits your invitation."

"Please pass along my invitation, Malcolm. And Louis, my gratitude for your timely aid," I say, extending an official summons to Gabrielle for September, once my current troubles are settled.

Malcolm's laughter echoes as he departs, and Annabella, fierce as ever, confronts me with a tempestuous passion. "Another blunder on my part," she seethes, "I should have been your bride, you devil." Yet, her anger doesn't keep her from claiming what she desires, and she remains until the morning light creeps in.

Adorned in Blackbeard's garb, cutlass at my side, I descend to the dungeons, where the lights blaze a welcome. Malcolm, ever vigilant, peers through his binoculars. "An hour, perhaps, given the storm," he estimates. He gestures to a collection of medieval torches and ropes. "For your special room," he says with a knowing smile.

Gabrielle's message arrives unexpectedly—she won't wait until September. She yearns to be by my side now.

With a nod, I take in the sight of the newly installed porta-potties in the cells. Ascending to the castle's heart, I enter the dining room, where a hearty breakfast awaits. Annabella greets me with an eager kiss, her presence a stark contrast to the dungeon's gloom. In my haste, I neglect to remove my tricorn—a lapse in manners. I set it aside and delve into a feast of sausages, bacon, eggs, and beans, all complemented by toast and rich coffee.

The delightful Breakfast finished. I descended to the cells, grabbed the garden shears, lit the torch, and entered one of the cells. This must be Mrs Jamieson. She's no spring chicken; I suspect a plastic surgeon had spent some time on her face. I clipped off her peroxide-blonde hair, leaving it in a pile beside her, cutting her wrist and ankle ties. She's now free to move around once she regains consciousness, minus her hair, she would soon discover. I entered the other cells, clipping off the two daughters' hair.

Regarding the two boys, I put my torch against their heads, watching their hair burn. Finally, Mr Jamieson himself lay on the stone floor. I dragged him from the cell into my little room, struggling to lift him onto the oak table, tying his hands above his head, stretching to a ring in the wall and his feet with another piece of rope to a ring in the other wall, no way could he escape.

I piled more wood on the fire. The beautiful pine fragrance filled the room, and I left him. I wanted him to be fully conscious and enjoy what happened next. I returned to Mrs Jamieson's dungeon, deciding to remove her clothes using my machete. I carefully cut her garments away, removing the clothes outside the cell.

I ran back to my little room, checking on Mr Jamieson. He's still unconscious. I grabbed three pieces of rope; Malcolm had kindly left, dashing to enter one boy's cell, tying his hands, and hoisting him to the ceiling, leaving him balancing on tiptoe. I shot him in both feet. I administered the same to his brother, leaving the daughters alone. I checked that the cells were locked, returning to Mr Jamieson, watching him slowly regaining consciousness. He focused on my face, horrified, trying to move and couldn't. Panicked, he shouted: "What do you want? I have money. Where are my family? Release me now!" Realising he couldn't move. He went quiet, hearing his wife shouting, "Help, help," along with his two daughters—finally, the two boys shouting, screaming for help and in pain.

"Who are you."

"Do you remember an attempted bank robbery? Discuss with your family while you enjoy a lavish meal aboard your yacht. Your family enjoyed the thought of the bank manager, my future wife dying pregnant; I think your son said good riddance or something along those lines and your daughter advised you should hire better help, Mr Jamieson."

Grabbing a rag, I removed a red-hot steel rod from the fire, burning out both his eyes and ramming the piece of steel in his mouth. I removed placing back in the fire to reheat. Mr Jamieson had passed out. I picked up my shears, cutting off his tongue. I carried to Mrs Jamieson's dungeon. Seeing her try to look through the small hole, I pushed the tongue through: "I thought you might enjoy part of your husband."

She screams.

While I waited for Mr Jamieson to regain consciousness, I opened one of the sons' cells, hearing a load of abuse. "Release me, you bastard; my dad will kill you!"

I returned to my little room, lighting another torch and returning to the foul-mouthed young man, "This should improve your manners." I set fire to his jeans, watching him burn alive, screaming in agony. He finally passed out. I wondered how long he would survive after my barbecue attempt. I opened Mrs Jamieson's cell door. She's passed out on the floor. I singed her pubic hair with my torch, ensuring I hadn't missed any of the hair on her head, and ignited what was left with my torch. I locked her cell door, hearing the two daughters crying, begging to be released. I opened one cell door, holding my torch and cutlass in the other, "This way and don't try to run; there is no escape." She gingerly exited her cell, guiding her into my little room. She ran to see her father, looking at his face, realising his eyes were no longer there; she fainted.

I drag her back to her cell, locking the door. I unlock the cell. Her sister is feistier: "You wait until my friends find you.

You better release my family. You're on borrowed time; look what you've done to my hair! You'll pay!"

I could see she's trouble; I'd ensure she suffers for the privilege. I removed my gun, watching her eyes enlarge when she realised what was in my hand; she immediately went silent. I indicated where to go. I pushed her into my tiny room; she dashed to her father like her sister, staring at me in disbelief and violently sick, "What you want, I can pay; I don't want to die. What's this all over?"

"A bank robbery that went wrong in Buxton. Do you remember the bank manager died pregnant?"

"Nothing to do with me, my father's business. I only deal with prostitution, giving these bloody immigrants something to do. I might as well make money out of them; it's my taxes pay for their bloody welfare."

"Strip," I ordered firmly.

I watched her folder arms. "No!"

"How old are you?"

"Seventeen! Why none of your bloody business? Why are you masquerading in a stupid pirate costume? Honestly, you must be desperate," she sneered, trying to be forthright.

I shot her father in the kneecap; I thought she'd jump out of her skin. I ordered: "Strip last chance."

"No, wrong time of the month," she grinned smugly.

"What a shame," I pointed the gun at her head. She immediately started removing her clothes,

"You're just a dirty old bastard." She proclaimed.

I shot her in the foot, and she fell to the floor screaming. I realised the bullet had gone straight through. I grabbed my hot piece of steel from the fire. She glared at me with a terrified expression. I placed my foot on her leg, my gun pointed at her head; using the red-hot rod of steel, I cauterised her wound. She screamed, passing out. To save any further arguing, I cut away her clothes with my machete, and I dragged her back to her cell, locking the door.

I could hear weeping for the one remaining son I hadn't bothered with apart from shooting in the foot. I grabbed my lit torch and opened his cell door. I shot him in each kneecap and between the eyes, setting fire to his clothes. I returned to my little room, grabbing a red-hot rod of steel. I skewered Mr Jamieson's heart, smelling the flesh burning, watching him stop breathing. I removed my cutlass from the leather scabbard and decapitated his head, observing it roll onto the stone floor.

I realised I'd inflicted pain on them all. What's the point in prolonging the outcome, inflicting more suffering, maybe? Even I must show compassion; I grabbed my last torch, lighting unlocking Mrs Jamieson's cell, thrusting my torch in her face, decapitating her head. I repeated the same process with the two daughters. I cut down the sons; they suffered the same fate. It's over!

Malcolm and two others emerged, methodically removing bodies. They tossed them onto a pinewood fire that crackled further along the cave. The corpses would either nourish the earth as fertiliser or be cast into the sea.

I sat momentarily, tears streaming down, my body shaking with a mix of relief and sorrow. It was finally over. I navigated through the laboratory's sterile silence to the sanctuary of my bedroom. There, I hastily changed, snatched my Porsche keys, and fled. The drive was a blur, an attempt to outrun the horrors etched in my mind.

Hours later, I reached Buxton. Janet's Range Rover greeted me, a silent sentinel to the life we once shared. I parked behind it and, with a heavy heart, entered the house. Overwhelmed, I succumbed to tears at the breakfast bar.

Twenty minutes passed before I mustered the strength to rise. I brewed a cup of tea, its warmth a small comfort, and added a splash of whisky. The liquid courage did little to steady my trembling hands.

Shoes discarded, I slipped into my slippers and ascended the stairs. The task ahead loomed over me—erasing Janet's presence from our home. But upon entering the bedroom, I was met with emptiness. Her drawers were bare, the closet hollow save for my own garments. Janet had vanished, leaving no trace behind.

Perplexed, I sat on the bed, grappling with the nonsensical turn of events. My journey began with Hazel, a promise of leisurely retirement days that were abruptly snatched away. In seeking solace from my grief, I embarked on what I believed would be my final adventure. Yet, fate had other plans, breathing new life into my weary soul.

As I lay in bed, I yearned for the day's end. Restless, I spent the night tossing in the vast emptiness that Janet's absence had left.

With the waning days of August, I imposed rules to maintain the pristine condition of Janet's house. Her decision to leave everything to me remained an enigma. Our acquaintance was brief, yet here I was, a year later, transitioning from a terraced house to affluence, overwhelmed by a fortune I scarcely knew how to manage.

After tidying the breakfast remnants, I gazed out the kitchen window. The cows grazed contentedly under a sombre sky, oblivious to human sorrows. A heavy sigh escaped me as I ventured to the garage. There, memories flooded back at the sight of the trikes and baby carrier. Overcome, I wept, then hastily shut the doors, as if to contain the past.

Wiping away tears, I met the postman at the front. His words, "A tragic loss," echoed the sentiment of the letters he handed me—bank confirmations of Janet's legacy now in my name and condolences from those who remained.

Sitting at the kitchen table, the reality sank in. Janet's wealth was mine, but I would trade it all in a heartbeat for her presence. The money was a hollow consolation for a life cut tragically short.

The kitchen door swung open abruptly, and in walked Gabrielle, suitcase in tow. Her sudden entrance startled me, and my heart raced. She dropped her luggage and rushed over, her arms enveloping me in a much-needed embrace. I was on the brink, emotions fraying at the edges.

Without hesitation, Gabrielle retrieved a bottle of Scotch from the cupboard and poured a generous measure. I gulped it down, the liquid fire barely quelling the turmoil within—sorrow and anger vying for dominance.

She then busied herself at the sink, brewing strong coffee for us both. Her coat found its place on the back door, and she offered a silent, comforting presence. With a practised hand, she organised the letters from the post, tucking them away neatly.

It was only then that Gabrielle broke the silence, her voice a gentle whisper. "Grieving is necessary, Zachariah. Let go of the anger and pain," she urged. A look of pride washed over her face as she continued, "I've seen how you handled those villains. My father is honoured that I bear your child."

Laughter broke through the tension, catching Gabrielle off guard. She gave me a puzzled look as I quipped, "I can't smell any garlic." A soft kiss sealed our bond; she was my anchor in a stormy sea. Understanding her motives was beyond me, but her presence was undeniable.

I lingered over the last drops of coffee before lifting Gabrielle's suitcase. We moved to the main bedroom, where she began to unpack with purpose. "I keep another set of clothes at the castle, for when we travel," she mentioned casually, as if our lives were a series of grand escapades.

Gabrielle entered the new situation with an air of confidence, seemingly unfazed. Her assurance was unshakable, knowing that as the daughter of a trillionaire, financial worries were foreign to her. I observed her smile warmly, then turn and gracefully slip into bed. "You need to release your stress, Zachariah," she whispered.

Gabrielle's beauty was undeniable. After we both showered, we donned our dressing gowns and made our way downstairs. A light dinner preceded our evening in the front room, where we settled in to watch television. Gabrielle's resolve to demonstrate her love was palpable as she voiced her fears, "I need to be loved before my condition limits us, Zachariah."

I responded without a second thought. It had been a long time since I felt this relaxed, and Gabrielle was intent on maintaining this tranquil state. As we prepared for bed, she mused, "Sleep is for the dead. I'm very much alive. Show me that you are too, Zachariah." Her words lingered in the air, allowing me a peaceful slumber eventually. Yet, despite the youthful reflection staring back at me in the mirror, I couldn't shake the feeling that my mind wasn't quite in agreement.

Awakening to Gabrielle's gentle kiss on my cheek was a delightful surprise. As my eyes fluttered open, I saw her balancing a tray with care. I sat up eagerly, ready to savour the bacon and eggs on toast she had prepared. After she quickly returned to the kitchen and came back with her own tray, we shared a cosy breakfast.

Post-shower, Gabrielle's smile was radiant as she proposed, "Teach me to ride Janet's trike, Zachariah. She said it was great fun. We can explore; the weather is inviting, though it might not last much longer at this time of year."

"Sure," I agreed, "but let's take our waterproofs, just in case." Watching Gabrielle slip into jeans and a thick jumper brought a smile to my face. The thought of confronting the contents of the garage, especially the two trikes and the baby trailer, was daunting. Yet, it was a reality I needed to embrace, making practical use of what was available.

As I swung the garage doors open, Gabrielle peered into the baby trailer with a bold declaration, "Your son will ride in this and smell the cowshit!" Her grin turned sheepish as she corrected herself, "I mean, manure," and we both erupted into laughter. It was a side of Gabrielle I hadn't anticipated. She continued, her voice filled with nostalgia, "My father owns two dairy farms in France. I adore the scent of the parlours. I have fond memories of petting the cows and enjoying fresh milk with my nanny."

My head shook with a mix of wonder and amusement, marvelling at the day's unexpected turns. I prepared my trike, attaching the trailer and generator, ensuring the spare batteries would charge as we journeyed. Janet's new trike was then rolled out onto the lane, where I adjusted the seat for Gabrielle and briefed her on the controls. She took to it instantly, pedalling up the lane with a look of pure bliss.

"You take the lead, Gabrielle," I encouraged with a smile. "I'll be right behind you. That way, if anything goes awry, I'll be there. And remember, we stick to the left side of the road here," I added with a chuckle. She shot me a playful glance, "As if I'd forget, Zachariah!"

Gabrielle's pace was steady and cautious, perfect for the winding country lanes where a hasty driver might lurk around any bend. As we neared Castleton, descending the steep hill past the Blue John mines, I was taken aback by Gabrielle's eagerness for such vigorous activity, given her condition. And there, to my disbelief, stood a burger bar just outside the village.

With a beaming smile, Gabrielle parked her trike and fetched her purse. She returned with two colossal cheeseburgers, heaped with onions. "Thankfully, it's not garlic," I mused silently. I liberally applied tomato sauce to mine, while Gabrielle opted for mustard on hers. We sat on an aged bench, guarding our clothes from the dripping fat, though Gabrielle seemed indifferent to the mess—a small testament to her carefree spirit.

Reflecting on the day, I realised that Gabrielle and I had managed to avoid any arguments, a stark contrast to my past with Janet. After enjoying our coffees, Gabrielle made a quick stop at the public restroom while I contemplated the looming clouds, hinting at an imminent downpour. Gabrielle's effortless ascent past the Blue John mines was a sight to behold. Her strength seemed boundless while I laboured slightly under the added weight of the trailer and generator.

Yet, together, we conquered the hill, coasting down the homeward lane.

The joy of the ride lingered; it felt like the beginning of a well-deserved retirement, a chance to relish life's offerings. Arriving home, I was taken aback by the absence of Janet's Range Rover, now replaced by a sleek black sports model bearing the registration BB1. A ping from my mobile broke the silence, revealing a message that read, "A gift from the 12; please return to the Castle with Gabrielle Friday."

I shared the cryptic message with Gabrielle, who offered a brief smile before continuing to stow her trike, undeterred by the raindrops. It seemed my input mattered little, despite my status as a member of this enigmatic group. Driving Janet's old Range Rover would have been a painful reminder of what was lost, yet her memory would always remain. As I stepped through the side door into the kitchen, a note and a set of keys greeted me on the floor. Gabrielle, meanwhile, had hurried upstairs, likely to change out of her damp clothes. The day's events left me with a sense of intrigue and a newfound appreciation for the unexpected turns life can take.

The new Range Rover's interior was the epitome of luxury, its mirror-like black finish reflecting our anticipation for the journey ahead. As I secured the vehicle, the rain began to fall, prompting a swift retreat indoors. The sound of Gabrielle's singing—or perhaps an attempt at feline harmony—drifted from the shower, adding a touch of levity to the moment.

Post-shower, the aroma of fresh coffee filled the air. Gabrielle descended, her attire casual yet elegant, and her soft kiss was an invitation to refresh and change. I obliged, trading the familiar scent of adventure for the comfort of clean clothes. Returning downstairs, I found Gabrielle engrossed in messages, their French content a mystery to me. Her affectionate kiss was a prelude to her own preparations.

With Friday's dawn, a 500-mile trek to the castle awaited us. The Range Rover, a symbol of new beginnings, seemed the fitting chariot for our expedition. Gabrielle's practicality shone through as she proposed an early departure, mindful of the notorious travel conditions.

I offered an alternative, driving through the night to avoid the congestion, ensuring a smoother passage. Gabrielle's playful banter about avoiding speeding tickets brought a smile to my face, and her candid admission of past driving escapades in France revealed a rebellious streak.

Her jest about the police elicited a chuckle, though it was a reminder of the cultural nuances that colour our perceptions. As we prepared for the morrow, the anticipation of the journey mingled with the comfort of companionship, setting the stage for an adventure as unpredictable as it was promising.

Gabrielle's playful spirit was infectious, her laughter and light-heartedness filling the room. "You truly are a delight," I said, appreciating her vivacious energy. Her response was as carefree as her demeanour, prioritising the joy of the moment over mundane concerns. With a shared smile, we embraced the evening's promise of relaxation and intimacy, a fitting end to a day of simple pleasures and newfound connections.

CHAPTER 8

Trusts no one

The evening was set in motion with the chiming of the alarm at 8 pm, signalling the end of our brief respite. We rose with ease, the anticipation of the journey lending us energy. With a flask of coffee in hand and toast warming our bellies, we ensured Rose Cottage was secure before venturing into the night.

The M6 greeted us with its usual fanfare of traffic and repairs, a slow-moving procession under the watchful eyes of speed cameras. Gabrielle, succumbing to the lull of the road, dozed off beside me, her soft snores a comforting soundtrack to our progress.

Edinburgh's lights faded behind us as we ventured onto the A9. A brief stop in a lay-by, a ritual shared by many a traveller, and I was back in the driver's seat, the familiar scent of coffee a welcome companion.

Inverness marked our next pause, and fuel quenched the Range Rover's thirst. The castle loomed ahead, a beacon in the darkness, as Gabrielle continued her peaceful slumber.

Upon arrival, I couldn't help but wonder if Gabrielle's nocturnal symphony had always been this pronounced or if my hearing was waning. Gently, I unbuckled her seatbelt and lifted her with care, her pregnancy adding a delicate weight to my arms. The task, daunting in thought, proved tender in action, as I carried her safely to the comfort of the castle's embrace.

The castle's security was prompt, opening the door as I carried Gabrielle through the threshold. The room, a sanctuary prepared for our arrival, welcomed us with its warmth. I nestled Gabrielle under the duvet with care before joining her, the fabric whispering against my skin as I settled in.

Morning's light brought a sudden start from Gabrielle, her scream piercing the silence. My eyes, heavy with sleep, struggled to adjust to the commotion. Malcolm, ever the protector, burst in with his weapon at the ready, only to retreat with a chuckle at Gabrielle's animated French reprimand.

"English, please, Gabrielle," I requested, a calm anchor amidst the flurry of French and laughter.

Her fear, a remnant of a dream's grip, was evident as she questioned the unfamiliarity of her surroundings. I confirmed her query with a nod, watching her silhouette against the morning light as she retreated to the loo.

The balcony beckoned, offering a view of rose beds that stirred a deep emotion within me. I withdrew, a battle against the swell of feelings raging inside.

Dressed and composed, a knock at the door announced the waiter's presence. "Breakfast in your room, Sir, or downstairs in the dining room?" he inquired.

From the shower's steamy veil, Gabrielle's voice emerged, decisive, "We'll have breakfast downstairs in five minutes."

The day awaited, a canvas ready for the brushstrokes of new memories and experiences, starting with the simple pleasure of a shared meal.

As Gabrielle readied herself, she playfully attributed her changing figure to me, her affectionate tease of 'Blackbeard' lightening the mood. Hand in hand, we approached the breakfast table, a veritable feast that promised indulgence at every turn. Our morning coffee was nearing its end when Mr Montague, Agnes's father, entered with a smile that seemed to herald good news. I rose to greet him, a gesture of respect and anticipation.

He joined us, sharing the news of Agnes's early labour—a tense moment that gave way to joy with the birth of twins, both healthy despite their early arrival. My relief was palpable as I settled back into my chair, the waiter's timely service a quiet presence in the room. Gabrielle's smile was radiant, reflecting the happiness that filled the space.

Mr Montague, settling into the conversation, broached the subject of meeting the newborns once Agnes was ready, an invitation that filled me with honour. I had not anticipated such a privilege.

The discussion took a turn towards the future, with Mr Montague revealing a change in plans regarding my involvement with the children. His candidness about our shared mortality lent a sobering note to the morning's levity.

I mentioned the experimental treatment that had rejuvenated me, suggesting it might offer him similar benefits. His revelation that he was to be part of the upcoming trials, albeit with a more cautious approach, was met with a shared smile and a sense of camaraderie. With a final sip of coffee,

Mr Montague departed, leaving behind a sense of hopeful anticipation for the future.

Gabrielle's touch was gentle, her concern evident as she held my hand. Her kiss was a soft punctuation to her words, a reminder of the life we were nurturing together. "I must see the doctor," she said, her voice tinged with the responsibility that love brings. "To ensure our little pirate is well."

I watched her leave, her figure a retreating promise, and turned to face my own obligations. The scientist awaited with another injection, a sharp hope for continued vitality. Our paths diverged, hers to preservation, mine to endurance.

In the caves, Peter's professional gaze swept over me, his verdict delivered with clinical precision. "One more jab," he declared, a sentinel guarding the gates of time. I thanked him, a simple acknowledgement of the complex dance between science and mortality.

The sea called to me then, its waves a rhythmic testament to nature's indifference to human affairs. I stood at the edge, the water's fury a mirror to my own turbulent thoughts. Annabella's silence loomed large, a chapter closed, perhaps, in the book of my life.

Time slipped by, marked only by the ebb and flow of the tide, until Malcolm's hand on my shoulder anchored me back to reality. "Gabrielle's worried," he said, his voice a lighthouse in the gathering dusk. "It's nearly 6 o'clock."

The day was fading, just as some connections do, but others—like the bond with Gabrielle—only grew stronger with the passing hours. As I followed Malcolm back, I knew that no matter how dark the night, the dawn would always hold new beginnings.

With a nod, I ascended from the sea's embrace, traversing the shadowed caves to the staircase that led to my bedroom—a place steeped in the essence of my days. Gabrielle's reproach for my silent mobile was swift, yet my apology flowed easily, a small sacrifice for tranquillity's sake. She detailed her imminent return to France, a decision driven by the desire to bestow citizenship upon our unborn child. As I sat on the bed, her words washed over me, but it was the undercurrent of unease that held me captive, its source eluding my grasp.

The sudden trill of Gabrielle's phone shattered the stillness. Her animated French filled the room, a crescendo of excitement that culminated in a fleeting kiss and her rapid departure. I remained, bemusement of my solitary companion, until the distant whir of helicopter blades signalled her swift exit. My mobile, once silent, now vibrated with urgency. Gabrielle's voice, laced with tears, reached out across the miles: "Zachariah, my mother has suffered a heart attack; I'm on my way to France." Her words, once foreign, now carried a clear message of distress.

My response was immediate, a calm amidst her storm. "Take care, Gabrielle," I offered, "and convey my wishes for your mother's swift recovery. We'll be reunited soon." The line went dead, leaving me in the quiet company of flickering television scenes—scenes as familiar as the memories they evoked. I turned away, drawn to the garden's glow, where Janet's memory lay in eternal repose. A longing stirred within me, a yearning for the authenticity of a love defined by passionate discourse—a love that, in its own tumultuous way, felt profoundly genuine.

The evening's weight settled heavily upon me as I descended the stairs, the hands of my wristwatch marking the passage of time. In the kitchen, the staff had prepared a meal, and to their surprise, I joined them. We shared dinner and wine, our conversation as light as the air, though the specifics eluded my memory.

Scotland's charm was undeniable, yet the pull of home beckoned stronger. The rose garden, once a symbol of beauty, now cast a shadow over my heart; its blooms are a vivid reminder of Janet and the memories I longed to escape.

After a courteous farewell to my companions, I retreated to my room. The keys to my Range Rover felt cool and heavy in my hand. On the balcony, I offered a silent tribute to Janet, my emotions spilling forth unchecked—a stark contrast to the stoicism that had marked Hazel's passing.

With a shake of my head, I left the castle behind, the Range Rover carrying me towards the familiarity of home. The night's journey was punctuated by a stop at Tesco's garage, the mundane act of refuelling grounding me in the present.

Then, as if summoned by thought alone, Annabella's voice came through the hands-free system, a sudden intrusion into the night's solitude. "Hi, stranger," she greeted, her instructions curt and mysterious. "Pull into the next lay-by."

The line went dead, leaving me with a sense of intrigue and the echo of her words guiding me to an unexpected rendezvous. The journey continued, each mile a step towards resolution and perhaps, a new chapter waiting to unfold.

Annabella's sudden appearance and her command to drive were unexpected, but I complied, steering the Range Rover back onto the road. Her agitation was palpable, her words sharp with indignation. "My father should be castrated, stupid man!" she exclaimed.

I urged her to explain, maintaining a calm demeanour despite the tension. "Annabella, what's the issue? You know I'm on my way to Rose Cottage," I reminded her.

She was curt in her response, revealing the scandal that had unfolded. "My father has been involved with a young member of his staff, barely 18. My mother is furious, to the point of wanting drastic measures taken against him."

Her anger was a live wire, sparking with every word. I couldn't help but react with laughter, which only earned me a sharp punch on the shoulder. "It's not funny, Zachariah!" she snapped.

I realised the gravity of the situation, but my offhand remark slipped out before I could stop it. "So, your father has admitted to being with an 18-year-old. That's quite the revelation," I said, trying to lighten the mood, though I knew this was no laughing matter.

The drive continued, the car filled with a tense silence as we both contemplated the implications of her father's actions and the turmoil it had caused. The road stretched before us, leading towards Rose Cottage and away from the chaos of Annabella's family drama.

Annabella's accusation stung, her words slicing through the air like a cold wind. I couldn't contain my reaction, pulling into the lay-by with a jolt. "There's the door," I said, my voice a mix of anger and disbelief. "If you want me to take such drastic action against your father, I need proof. And if you're lying..." I trailed off, the threat hanging between us.

She exited the Range Rover, her usual poise replaced by shock. As I drove off, the door slammed with a finality that echoed my frustration. I was certain she would find another way; her resources were vast, after all. Her silence on her pregnancy only added to the complexity of her character, a puzzle I was no longer sure I wanted to solve.

Gossip could be a venomous thing, and I was not one to act without evidence. The phone rang, and it was Annabella again, her sobs breaking through the line. Despite my better judgment, I found myself saying, "I'm turning around. I'll be there in five minutes."

True to my word, I returned to find her waiting. She slipped back into the passenger seat, her demeanour softened, her apology a whisper. "I'm sorry, Zachariah. I'm just so angry."

As we resumed our journey, the silence was filled with the weight of unspoken thoughts and the faint hope that understanding might still be within reach.

"All right, Annabella," I said, my tone even and focused. "Finding the truth is the only way forward. We can't act on hearsay alone. I'll look into the matter discreetly and gather the facts. Once we have a clear picture, we'll decide how to proceed. It's important to handle this sensitively and legally."

Annabella's smile, a mix of relief and gratitude, told me I had made the right choice. The drive continued, the night around us a cloak of secrecy as we navigated the complexities of truth and justice in the dim glow of the dashboard lights.

"I assume you'll be staying with me tonight, Annabella. We'll head to London in the morning. The Porsche is more suited for the city's traffic. You'll drive; you're familiar with the hustle and bustle, unlike me."

"That's a sensible plan. In the office, let's keep a low profile, Zachariah. It's a diverse workplace, so it's crucial to be considerate of our words."

"Have you warmed up to the idea of being seen with me in London, or are you still worried about appearances?"

"Given that you've played a part in my changing figure, I'm not concerned about others' opinions. My family's well-being is my priority. Everyone else's views are secondary," she replied, her voice firm and resolve.

The journey to Rose Cottage was uneventful, and upon arrival, we shared a brief moment of respite over coffee before retiring. The night passed quietly, with sleep coming easily to us both, undisturbed by desires or expectations.

The morning brought with it the reality of Annabella's family crisis. After a shared shower, she descended the stairs with a preoccupied air, her thoughts undoubtedly with her family as she prepared breakfast. The lack of foresight in her hurried departure for London was evident; she had no change of clothes for the unexpected stay.

By nine, we were on the road again, Annabella at the wheel of the Porsche. Her driving was assertive, to say the least, darting through the London traffic with a confidence that left me grappling with a touch of motion sickness. Relief washed over me as she finally parked the car, my senses grateful for the respite from her whirlwind navigation. The day ahead loomed with the promise of resolution and, perhaps, a return to equilibrium.

Stepping into the grandeur of J. Goldstone Ltd., the building's opulence was immediately apparent, with a large gold nameplate marking our entrance. Inside, the hustle of activity was evident, with around 20 staff members intently focused on their monitors. We made our way across the striking black-and-white chequered floor toward her father's office.

A mature lady, identified by her nametag as Miss Savage, stood to greet us, her position allowing her a clear view of the office's comings and goings. "Miss Goldstone, your father is not in his office at the moment," she informed Annabella in a hushed tone.

I offered Miss Savage a reassuring smile. "I'm here in support of Miss Goldstone," I explained. "It seems there have been some unfortunate rumours circulating. As someone of your discernment, I'm sure you understand the importance of addressing such matters swiftly and discreetly."

Annabella then stepped forward, her voice carrying a note of formality. "Miss Savage, allow me to introduce Zachariah Black, a private investigator. He's here to help us get to the bottom of this situation." The introduction set the stage for the delicate task ahead, as we sought to navigate the murky waters of office politics and family drama.

"Mr Black, we have a team of 20 here, with another 20 upstairs. Gossip is inevitable, though I do my best to curb it," Miss Savage began as we followed her from the office. The elevator carried us to the next level, where I seized the moment to inquire about her insights.

"Miss Savage, given your keen observation skills, do you suspect anyone in particular?" I asked.

She nodded, her expression serious. "There is one individual who's been quite forward about her ambitions to become Mr Goldstone's PA. Regrettably, her qualifications are lacking; her physical appearance seems to be her main leverage. Mr Goldstone had previously confided in me to limit her access to his office. He's wary of the repercussions that might follow if he were to dismiss her outright, so he's opted for a strategy of patience, hoping she'll choose to leave on her own."

Annabella's reaction was one of surprise, her hand covering her mouth as she whispered, "Father never mentioned Miss Savage."

With a strategy in mind, I turned to Miss Savage and said, "Could you identify the individual in question and leave the rest to me? I assure you, she'll be inclined to leave within the next 15 minutes."

Miss Savage led us through the office, its layout mirroring the floor below. My gaze swept over the staff, instinctively narrowing down the possibilities. Miss Savage's confirmation came quietly, "The blonde-haired girl, peroxide blonde—her name is Samantha Stevens."

Approaching the front, I raised my voice for all to hear, "Could Samantha Stevens please join me?" Annabella's eyes were shut tight, bracing for what was to come, yet she remained silent. I continued, "I trust you're all aware of the terms of your employment here. Gossip, particularly of a malicious nature, is strictly prohibited. It's time for someone to come forward regarding the rumours about Miss Stevens and Mr Goldstone. Denial is futile at this point. I'm prepared to take legal action if necessary, and it might be prudent to conduct drug tests while we're at it."

The room fell into a tense silence, the gravity of the situation settling over the staff as they awaited the unfolding drama.

Samantha Stevens' reaction was immediate and heated. "You have no right to test for drugs. You're not the police. I'm leaving; I don't need this hypocrisy!" she declared loudly.

I seized the moment to clarify her intentions. "Is that your resignation, Miss Stevens?" I inquired.

Her response was as swift as it was defiant—a two-fingered salute. "Yes, stuff the job," she retorted. As she stormed past Miss Savage and Annabella, the latter struggled to contain her amusement, while Miss Savage remained unamused, a testament to her traditional values.

Seeking to uncover the origin of the rumours, I posed a question to the room. "Who started the rumour about Mr Goldstone and Miss Stevens? Can anyone shed some light on this?"

A young man at the back of the office stood up, his voice shaky with nerves. "Miss Stevens would boast about securing the PA position over coffee breaks. She claimed to have Mr Goldstone wrapped around her finger. But we all knew it was just talk—Mr Goldstone wouldn't touch her with a barge pole, sir."

Gratitude and relief were the order of the day as the truth came to light. "Thank you for your honesty," I said to the staff. "Let's put this matter behind us and move forward." Annabella, still on her phone, seemed to be sharing the good news, her face a canvas of relief.

Miss Savage's admission was a testament to the tension of the moment. "You gave me quite the scare, Mr Black," she confessed. "I feared a mass exodus and a media circus, but your instincts were spot on. She left too easily, hiding something, no doubt. Thank you."

As Annabella and I descended into the elevator, her hand found mine—a gesture I hadn't anticipated. Her public display of affection was unexpected as she kissed me, her words filled with admiration. "Brilliant, Zachariah. You had me worried, but you were right—as usual. Now, let me treat you to lunch at one of my favourite spots before we head home."

The day's events solidified our bond, and as we stepped out into the street, it was clear that our partnership was stronger than ever. A celebratory lunch awaited, a fitting end to a morning filled with tension and triumph.

Annabella took the wheel of my Porsche, guiding us through a part of London that glittered with an unfamiliar glamour. As we stepped out, the valet whisked the car away, leaving its fate uncertain. The doorman, with a discerning eye, handed me a tie, his gaze suggesting I was out of place in such opulence.

Inside, the head waiter, Rogers, greeted us with familiarity, and Annabella ordered champagne, mindful of her pregnancy. When questioned about the tie, she deftly looped it around my neck, reminding me that standards were to be upheld, regardless of her father's ownership.

Seated at a prominent table, we attracted curious glances from other patrons. The arrival of Annabella's father brought a familial warmth to the table. His playful chiding about marriage and his swift departure to meet Mrs Goldstone left us in good spirits.

After a sumptuous lunch of strawberries and cream, I returned the tie with a grin, and we found the Porsche awaiting us, ready to carry us onward from the grandeur of the restaurant to the comfort of home. Annabella slid into the driver's seat, her confidence unshaken by the day's events.

After a rapid two-hour drive, we reached Rose Cottage. Annabella's urgency was palpable as she handed me the keys to my car, her Rolls-Royce ready to whisk her away to attend to urgent matters. Her departure left me contemplating my role—was I merely a cleaner for the messes left by the 12?

The house, though mine by law, felt more like Janet's legacy than a home to me. With a glance at my watch, I began preparing for my solitary journey. The motorhome was backed onto the road, the trailer attached, and my trike loaded and secured. Essentials packed, I set off for Elan Valley without haste, finding solace in the stillness of the Aberystwyth Mountain Road.

As I settled in, the realisation that I had missed my own birthday in September, now in late October, crossed my mind, yet no one had reminded me. The motorhome, with its water tank filled and the cassette toilet emptied by Janet—a task I should have taken on—reminded me of my imperfections as a husband. Alone with my thoughts, I faced the truth of my past relationships, the motorhome a silent witness to the introspection of a man who had never quite been the perfect partner.

The comfort of the motorhome, rocked by the breeze, was a welcome respite after the day's events. As darkness enveloped Elan Valley, I discovered forgotten items and braced against the strengthening wind. The simple pleasure of a hot coffee was marred only by my lack of foresight in packing—typical, indeed.

The journey to Crossgates was uneventful, a routine refuelling and restocking before indulging in a hearty breakfast that left me feeling content, if not a bit overfull. The familiar campsite offered a sense of continuity with the past, a place once shared with Hazel now a solitary spot for reflection and recharge.

The cycle to Elan Valley, though challenging, was a testament to the changing seasons and the courtesy of fellow travellers. The return to the motorhome was a relief, my exertions evident in my fatigue.

But it was Gabrielle's unexpected arrival, with her warm smile and the offering of soup, that brought a new sense of comfort. Her presence was a balm to the solitude of the road. "How is your mother?" I inquired, eager for news and grateful for the company.

Gabrielle's revelation about her mother's flair for the dramatic brought a light chuckle to my lips. "It's a relief to hear it's nothing serious. She must indeed miss your presence," I replied, sharing in the humour of the situation.

Gabrielle's expression shifted to a slight frown as she mentioned her father's relief at her return, hinting at her mother's penchant for extravagance. "Well, it's good to have you back, regardless of the reason," I said, offering a comforting smile.

The sight of the trike in the boot of the Range Rover was unexpected, and I couldn't help but appreciate Gabrielle's foresight. As I set about reassembling it, I gently admonished her, "You should be taking it easy, Gabrielle. But I'm grateful for your thoughtfulness." Her smug grin in response to the farmer's assistance was endearing, and I finished my soup with a contented sigh.

Gabrielle's invitation to dine at a local pub was welcome, and as we linked arms, I felt a sense of camaraderie. "A stroll sounds perfect, and I could certainly use a good meal," I agreed, ready to enjoy the simple pleasures of the town with her company.

The walk to town was a pleasant one, with the river providing a serene soundtrack to our stroll. Gabrielle's attire, casual yet chic, contrasted with my more utilitarian garb. Her presence by my side was a mystery, her life of affluence a stark contrast to my simplicity. Yet, there she was, seemingly content.

As we navigated the footpath, I caught the curious glances of passersby. Their silent judgments were of no consequence to me; I was content in the company I kept.

The restaurant's exterior belied the luxury within. Its Edwardian facade opened up to a lavish interior that spoke of expense and exclusivity. It seemed I had inadvertently chosen one of Rhayader's finest dining experiences. But as we settled into the opulence, I realised that the true luxury was not the setting, but the shared experience with Gabrielle. It was a moment to savour, regardless of the cost.

The atmosphere in the restaurant was charged with a blend of elegance and a touch of comedy. As I pulled out the chair for Gabrielle, her beauty, accentuated by her pregnancy, was undeniable. The room seemed to pause, taking in the scene before us.

The attempt at a French accent from a nearby patron was a stark contrast to Gabrielle's authentic tones. Her order, placed in flawless French, seemed to catch the waiter off-guard, his facade crumbling under the weight of authenticity. Gabrielle's gracious smile as she switched to English was a balm to the waiter's flustered state, though I couldn't help but feel a twinge of second-hand embarrassment.

As the waiter hurried away, only to return with a bottle of wine, I felt the eyes of the other guests upon us. It was a moment that would have driven me to seek refuge under the table if not for the composure of my companion. Gabrielle's presence, her ease in such situations, was a guiding force, and

I found myself drawing confidence from her poise. The meal ahead promised to be as memorable as the company.

Gabrielle's assertiveness with the wine left a distinct impression on the waiter, and her discerning palate ensured we would enjoy a better vintage. As the waiter retreated, a local man approached our table with a grin, his comment directed at Gabrielle both rude and unwarranted.

I met his gaze steadily, my voice calm but firm. "I believe you're mistaken, sir. Gabrielle's company is her choice, and your opinion is neither solicited nor appreciated." I removed my gun from the inside of my jacket in seconds without thinking of the consequences, placing the barrel against his head. The restaurant went silent. Gabrielle grabbed my wrist: "Don't Zachariah, I will deal with him," Gabrielle launched her fist, hitting him under the jaw. He collapsed to the floor, unconscious. I placed my gun in my shoulder holster. Gabrielle stood, calmly lifting the bottle of wine. She emptied it over the table, smashing the bottle on the flagstone floor, saying something in French that I suspected was not favourable.

As we approached the door, armed police confronted us and swiftly confiscated my gun. They rifled through my wallet and found the card Malcolm had given to me. The officer's face drained of colour upon seeing it. With a salute, he handed back my weapon and card and then hurried into the restaurant. Moments later, the proprietor emerged, pleading with Gabrielle and me to reconsider leaving. Gabrielle's response was curt: "I'll seek out a finer venue—one without the risk of food poisoning. Rest assured, the King will hear about tonight's fiasco." With a firm tug, she led me away. Her parting words to the proprietor echoed in my mind, stirring unease. As we departed, I caught sight of the man Gabrielle had struck being escorted into a police vehicle. Compelled by concern, I turned to her and asked, "Were you serious, Gabrielle? Are you acquainted with King Charles?"

"Absolutely," Gabrielle affirmed, her voice laced with determination. "Through my father's influence, that contemptible restaurant will soon be ours, and its owner will find himself without a business."

Gabrielle's fierce temperament was something I dared not provoke. With caution, I inquired, "You're skilled in martial arts, I take it?"

She nodded, her tone serious. "And beyond. My father made certain I knew how to defend myself, even to the point of taking a life if needed."

I let out a sigh. "Good heavens. Gabrielle, I must admit, the fellow who called me an 'old fossil' wasn't entirely mistaken. What's your interest in me, aside from wanting a child? Now that you're expecting, do I serve any purpose?"

Stopping mid-stride, Gabrielle turned to face me, her deep brown eyes searching mine. With a swift motion, she playfully slapped my cheek. "You're quite the fool, Black Beard. Are you implying you no longer desire me?"

"That's not what I meant at all! But consider our age gap. You're breathtakingly beautiful, while I could give a wrinkly old cabbage a run for its money in terms of looks."

Her lips curved into a smile, and she let out a soft sigh. "But you're my beloved wrinkly old cabbage. That's all that matters, Zachariah Black. You're the one I've chosen. If your feelings aren't the same, speak now."

A playful pinch on Gabrielle's backside and a kiss on her cheek elicited a chuckle from her. She had made her feelings clear, and I saw no reason to contest them. We bought fish and chips, settling on a bench shielded from the wind at the campsite, while a magpie kept a hopeful eye on us for any stray chips.

The next morning, Gabrielle was adamant about taking the trikes for a spin around Elan Valley, despite the dubious weather. Thankfully, I had charged the batteries overnight. To ward off the chill and dampness, I insisted Gabrielle don her waterproof gear. Our day began with breakfast at the Elan Centre, where we were among the early birds, and thankfully, the restrooms were open.

Once we set out again, Gabrielle chose the gated track, requiring us to open gates along the way. It didn't bother her since I took care of the gates, ensuring our trikes remained unscathed. The decision to have her in waterproofs paid off as the wind whipped fiercely off the reservoir. Upon reaching the final reservoir, complete with another restroom facility, we could have ventured along an old, nearly vanished track through the gorse bushes leading back to the Elan Valley Centre.

I had attempted that route once before, only to be defeated by the harsh conditions and forced to retreat. Knowing the trikes wouldn't stand a chance, we stuck to the tarmac, crossing the dam to the main road. Before tackling the steep climb to rejoin the Aberystwyth Mountain Road, we stopped at a picnic area to swap batteries, ensuring we had ample power for the ascent.

Gabrielle was in high spirits, captivated by the sight of water cascading down the hillside into the reservoir. My biannual visits to this place over the last four decades have never dulled its wonder; the scenery remains breathtaking.

We began our ascent, coaxing the trikes up the steep incline that even cars find challenging. Inspired by Gabrielle's unwavering determination, despite her pregnancy, I felt a surge of energy. She pressed on until the junction was reached, her smile unwavering. I dismounted and walked my trike to the top, joining her in her triumph.

The journey continued, and the gradient was now more forgiving. But as we reached the mountain's summit, the descent loomed ominously—a brake failure here would be disastrous. I cautioned Gabrielle, advising her to keep the trike's speed in check; once a certain velocity was reached, the brakes would be futile. Heeding my words, she navigated the descent with care, and together, we safely made our way to Rhayader. The relief of returning to the motorhome was unparalleled.

The Warden glanced at her wristwatch as she approached. "You have 20 minutes to vacate the site, or would you prefer to extend your stay?" she inquired.

Gabrielle and I exchanged a look before she replied, "We'll be leaving on time, thank you."

I quickly hitched the trailer to the motorhome, secured the trikes, and made sure everything was in place. Meanwhile, Gabrielle brewed a swift cup of coffee. Once changed, she came to me, her voice filled with affection, "Let's head home, Zachariah. A more comfortable bed awaits your future wife and your son."

With a smile and a tender kiss, I watched Gabrielle drive off in my Range Rover. I then meticulously manoeuvred the motorhome and trailer out of the campsite, setting a course for Buxton and the quaint Rose Cottage—a mere two-hour drive in the current light traffic.

Upon arrival, I backed the trailer into the driveway, positioning the motorhome neatly. Gabrielle had already parked the Range Rover at the front, with my Porsche to the side. She left me to store the trikes in the garage while she prepared a meal. It was surprising, really, how a woman of her youth and wealth could adapt so seamlessly to domestic life. I half-expected her to demand a staff of servants or to transport her entire entourage from France, perhaps even to suggest selling Rose Cottage for a grander estate.

Upon securing the garage, I stepped into the kitchen to find Gabrielle; her face lit up with a smile as she read a message on her phone. She looked up at me, her eyes shining with excitement. "We're invited to the castle. Agnes is bringing her son and daughter to meet their father. It's wonderful news, isn't it, Zachariah?"

My response was a noncommittal shrug, which in hindsight, wasn't the most sensitive reaction. Gabrielle's smile faded into a look of disapproval. "A shrug? What's your reaction to meeting your son and daughter? I hope you won't be so indifferent to our own child!"

I sighed, the weight of the situation settling in. "Gabrielle, how can I form a bond with children I'll only see a handful of times in my life? We need to be realistic about this."

She paused, pondering my words before responding with a softened gaze. "I see your point. You're guarding your heart to avoid unnecessary pain, and you don't want the stress. But remember, our son will be there for you to cherish for the rest of your days."

I let out a deep sigh. Gabrielle has a way of casting a shadow over one's spirits. I ascended the stairs to shower, her words echoing in my mind. She was right, after all. I might be fortunate to witness our child's fifth birthday. Gabrielle is still shy at 25, and I would be 70 if not for the rejuvenating elixir that keeps me looking 35. Sometimes, I long for Janet's presence, for our shared past. Maybe it's time to sell Rose Cottage and seek a fresh start elsewhere. Long Marston is now just a faint memory.

Gabrielle's voice broke through my reverie, "Dinner's ready, Zachariah." I quickly donned my jeans and descended to find a fresh salad and a tempting pork pie at the table's centre, which Gabrielle divided with precision. "Don't lose yourself in 'what I said,' Zachariah. The future is a mystery to us all," she said, noticing my sombre mood. "I didn't mean to upset you. Who's to say? You might have another two decades ahead."

Her words hung in the air as I pondered the uncertainty of life. "It's strange, isn't it? That you're not troubled by the thought of my death. But as you said, it's all unknown. After all, I'm part of an experiment."

Gabrielle set down her utensils, her voice carrying a reflective tone. "At first, I had no say in the matter, and the idea of an older man's touch was unsettling to me. I yearned for a vibrant, young man full of flair. When my father showed me your picture, it didn't exactly warm me to the idea, to be frank. However, the offer of 2 million francs certainly changed the equation. As a member of the organisation, I understood the urgency of preserving the Blackbeard lineage with suitable partners. Given my virginity and noble heritage, I was the prime candidate. Once I've had my child, there is no reason I can't sample younger men."

I let out a weary sigh and reclined in my chair, the situation's absurdity washing over me. "Gabrielle, why insist on marriage? We could simply cohabit until the baby's born, and then you're free to leave. If there's no love, this is all futile—you're squandering your youth." I said, feeling hurt by her remark.

Gabrielle's response was clinical, devoid of warmth. "The transformation you underwent and our ... encounters have been satisfactory. Marriage is a necessity—for the child's legitimacy and to solidify the Black lineage. Once you're gone, I can remarry or seek other companions. It's only fair, considering your liaisons with Agnes and Annabella."

Her words stung, a bitter reminder of the transactional nature of our relationship. "If that's how you feel, you can walk away now. Annabella might have retracted her proposal, and Agnes has always been clear about wanting only children. But you, Gabrielle, you're an enigma to me."

"Their focus is on the estate, not sentiment. Your selection was based on your compliant nature, akin to that of a loyal hound. Your lineage as a Blackbeard descendant is merely an added perk. I possess the genuine bloodline, granting our son entitlement to your fortune upon your demise."

A frown flickered across my face. "The council of twelve restricts my access to the wealth. How will my son fare any differently?"

"He won't, not inherently. Any appeal for funds will have to be approved by the twelve. They will judge the merit of his petition."

The realisation settled in, bitter and cold. "Then let's not drag this out. A simple civil marriage will suffice. You can return to France, and I'll resume my life of solitude," I declared, the sting of exploitation lingering in my voice.

Gabrielle remained silent, briefly lifting her phone from the table to send a rapid text. I poked at the unappetising salad before me, my hunger gone. Rising from the table, I seized my Porsche keys and stormed out, a mix of hurt and anger boiling within me. The thought that Gabrielle might actually care had been a deception.

I slipped into my car, the cool evening air a stark contrast to my inner turmoil. I drove aimlessly, needing to flee the cold, calculating nature of Gabrielle, which mirrored that of the others. I had just passed Buxton when Gabrielle's call came through the hands-free. I cut her off before she could speak, "If you're still in my house when I return, you'll be shipped back to France, but not as you might expect." I ended the call, and she didn't attempt another. Any hope for reconciliation seemed futile; perhaps Gabrielle, too, yearned for an escape. I pulled over at Snake Pass, seeking solace in the solitude.

The elixir's influence on my body and mind was undeniable. To fend off the chill, I occasionally ran the car's engine, watching the night turn to early morning. At nearly 6 am, I began the slow drive back to Rose Cottage. The absence of my Range Rover was the first thing I noticed, but it was of little consequence. I could replace it without a second thought; it hadn't been a personal purchase, after all.

Entering through the side door, a note in the kitchen caught my eye. "Your Range Rover is at the castle. My father's helicopter is booked to take me home. Goodbye." Unsigned, the message was as cold as the air outside. Perhaps my earlier threat had spurred her swift departure. Yet, she had left the house in immaculate condition—a surprising act of consideration.

Zachariah Black's Quest for Truth

Doubt crept in as I pondered my recent actions. Was I too rash? The question lingered, but Gabrielle was already gone. My phone buzzed with Malcolm's name, bringing me back to the present. With trepidation, I answered. "Zachariah, the council requests your presence at the castle. Gabrielle is expected to return, and her father's helicopter will arrive in the morning," Malcolm informed me, his voice betraying no emotion.

"I've had enough, Malcolm," I declared with finality, cutting the call short. As I sat at the breakfast bar sipping tea, it dawned on me that I should have been more mindful of Gabrielle's condition. Hormones can wreak havoc, yet that doesn't excuse the things she said or how she said them. In need of solitude, I powered down my phone and unplugged the landline, pondering my rash suggestion for the council to take a proverbial leap.

Regret nipping at my conscience, I found Gabrielle's number and dialled. Her voice was icy as she picked up. "Zachariah, have you cooled off?" she asked, devoid of any warmth.

"Yes, I'm calling to apologise. Your earlier remarks caught me off guard," I replied.

Her response came in rapid French—a sure sign she was upset—and then the line went dead. I wondered if the police had stopped her or if she'd neglected to use hands-free. Concerned, I called Malcolm back. "I was in the middle of apologising to Gabrielle when she switched to French, and the call dropped. I'm worried about her," I confessed.

Malcolm's voice was urgent. "Your Range Rover's stopped. Wait, it's moving again, but not under its own power. It could be on a transporter. She might be kidnapped, and if so, it's on you, Zachariah Black!" The line went dead.

Adrenaline surging, I armed myself with my machete and gun from the motorhome, ready for confrontation. I sped off in the Porsche, pushing it to the legal limit. On hands-free, I called Malcolm. "Can you send a signal to track her vehicle?"

"I can, but we've got a team on it. You're 20 miles behind her. We're launching a chopper with a team."

"Please, Malcolm."

Reluctantly, he agreed. "Fine. I'll send the coordinates to your monitor. You'll have her location."

I watched my display show me the map, whatever Gabrielle was transported in, and its location. I realised I knew that road. I quickly left the motorway, watching the bleep on my screen. I was wishing I was 007 with all the gadgets he possessed attached to his car. I realised I was behind a low-loader transporter similar to the one I was kidnapped in.

I removed my handgun, lowering the passenger window. I overtook the lorry, firing four shots and hitting the tractor unit tyres. The lorry swerved violently, steering into a lay-by and removing the bark on an oak tree. I skidded to a halt, running back, immobilising the driver. I opened the back of the transporter, and with two men attacking me, I put them to sleep permanently, hearing cars blasting horns as they overtook, not realising what was taking place.

There was my Range Rover, and thankfully, Gabrielle strapped to the back seat. I released her bondage; she held me for a few seconds, crying. I released what was keeping the Range Rover secure to the trailer bed, asking Gabrielle to stand to one side. I started the Range Rover, reversing as fast as possible; the vehicle dropped to the floor with a jolt.

I banged my head against the car roof as the car landed, but that didn't matter. I quickly assisted Gabrielle from the back of the trailer, asking: "Can you drive!"

She nodded and climbed into the driver's seat. "Park at the next service station; we'll have coffee." She smiled, spinning the vehicle around on a sixpence dodging oncoming motorists. I open the driver's door, set fire to the newspaper on the floor, and close the door. I jumped in my Porsche, tyres burning, and chased Gabrielle, finally catching up with her. She was driving at a steady pace. I contacted Malcolm: "I've rescued Gabrielle, Malcolm. We are calling in at a service station for a coffee. I set fire to the truck; there should be no evidence, providing it burns."

Malcolm chuckled, expressing, "For an old bugger, you're okay. I'll convey the information to the 12."

Gabrielle eased the Range Rover into a spot at the service station, and I pulled up beside her. Climbing out, she was visibly rattled, her nerves frayed by the ordeal. I marvelled inwardly at the unexpected courage that had surged through me. When Gabrielle wrapped me in a heartfelt embrace, I couldn't help but quip with a smile, "Do you realise where we are, Gabrielle? This is near Gretna Green."

She looked puzzled. "Gretna Green?"

"It's a place famous for eloping couples to wed," I explained with a playful raise of my eyebrows.

A knowing smile crossed Gabrielle's face. "Ah, I've heard tales of such a place."

Inside the cafe, I couldn't help but notice the bruise marring Gabrielle's cheek, a testament to her struggle. Her attire bore the marks of the fray. Concerned, I asked, "Would you care for something to eat, Gabrielle?"

She shook her head, the bruise a stark contrast to her resolve. "No, thank you, Zachariah. I wish to return to the castle and then back to France. I need the safety of home. The UK isn't for me; it's just not possible."

Her words hung between us, a mix of vulnerability and determination. It was clear that the events had taken their toll, and all she yearned for now was the comfort of familiar surroundings.

Reflecting on the day's tumultuous events, I sat in silence, acknowledging my overreaction to Gabrielle's earlier comments. After finishing our drinks, we stepped outside, only to find Malcolm efficiently overseeing the loading of my Range Rover onto a transporter. A dark stain of oil marked the spot where it had been parked, a reminder of the vehicle's rough descent from the kidnapper's lorry.

Malcolm's voice cut through the air with authority. "Your father's helicopter has arrived ahead of schedule. However, before you leave, you must marry Zachariah Black to ensure your son's lineage is formally recognised."

Gabrielle, with a resigned nod, accepted Malcolm's arm. He then turned to me, his gaze sharp. "Gabrielle will accompany me to the castle for a medical evaluation. As for you, your Porsche is in good condition—I've made sure of it."

The weight of Malcolm's words settled over me. The urgency of the situation was clear, and the next steps were laid out with precision. It was time to move forward, to address the consequences and the future that awaited us all.

I never bothered to answer. I realised I was as popular as a rattlesnake, which was my fault. I filled my Porsche with petrol and drove toward the castle more sensibly. I wouldn't reach the castle until 8 a.m. I realised my gun and machete were missing from my Porsche. I presume they needed to be changed because I'd use them to rescue Gabrielle, although I would have preferred to keep my machete. We'd had a long love affair. I barely passed Inverness when I could smell burning, wondering if it was from outside. I continued, not realising my engine was on fire until I saw the flames. I pulled over to the roadside and jumped out of the vehicle. I had the horrible feeling that Malcolm may have placed a device in my car to dispose of me. Perhaps I'd become more of a problem than they wanted to deal with, especially my attitude.

Watching the flames consume the Porsche, I couldn't help but feel a sense of relief. The car had been more of a statement than a beloved possession. Contacting Malcolm, I couldn't resist a jab: "Next time, remind me to skip your car service."

Malcolm's voice was sharp. "What are you talking about?"

"The car's ablaze on the outskirts of Inverness. Firefighters are on the scene," I explained.

A curse slipped from Malcolm, and I pressed on, suspicion lacing my words. "Was I not meant to make it, Malcolm? Is this a blunder?"

His retort was swift. "Ridiculous, Zachariah. If I wanted you gone, you'd be at the bottom of the ocean, not roadside-attracting attention. Stay put; I'm sending someone."

Concern for Gabrielle crept in. "And Gabrielle? She's not injured, is she?"

"She's rattled but will recover. Just some bruises," he assured me before the call dropped.

A sleek black Rolls-Royce pulled up, and I couldn't suppress a smirk. The chauffeur hastened to open the door, and I slid in beside Annabella, who greeted me with a mix of exasperation and disbelief. "Zachariah Black, trouble seems to follow you."

Taking a deep breath, I acknowledged Annabella's presence with a slight nod. "Annabella, despite the early hour, you're looking quite radiant."

Her grin was a mix of amusement and reprimand. "Zachariah, you're in for quite the apology session. Gabrielle's ordeal was a direct result of your heated words. Her father is furious. Shall I continue?"

I shook my head in a slow, deliberate motion. "There's been a colossal misunderstanding. If you had heard Gabrielle's words to me, you'd understand why I thought she wanted to leave."

Curiosity piqued, Annabella urged me to recount the tale. As I detailed the events, her expression shifted from scepticism to surprise. After a brief call to the castle, she turned to me, phone in hand. "It appears Gabrielle has admitted to saying those things, corroborating your account of the story."

As I sat there, the weight of the day's chaos pressing down on me, Annabella's touch brought a moment of warmth. "He's hungry," she said with a gentle smile, her hand guiding mine to feel the life within her. Her kiss was a balm, her words a reminder of the man I strive to be—the Blackbeard known for bravery and heart.

I couldn't shake the gloom, though. "It doesn't feel like enough," I admitted. "Maybe Gabrielle was just looking for a way out, back to France."

Annabella's smile didn't waver. "Don't fret. Her father suspected she might rethink her hasty choice. Let's wait and see what awaits us at the castle."

Her reassurance offered a glimmer of hope that perhaps not all was lost—that there might be a chance to mend the tattered threads of the day's events.

Malcolm greeted me, his grip firm on my arm as he led me into the cavernous depths where the council awaited. The dim firelight cast long shadows, and I noticed Annabella's attire harkening back to an earlier era. Agnes stood by her side, and Gabrielle, looking forlorn, completed our quartet.

The council emerged from the shadows, their presence commanding even in the subdued light. Gabrielle's father, having flown in from France, addressed her in stern French. She knelt, bowing her head in silence.

Turning to me, he presented a cat-o'-nine-tails, a traditional instrument of punishment. "Gabrielle has dishonoured you, Blackbeard," he declared, devoid of empathy. "You have the right to correct her."

The council's spouses echoed their agreement, turning away from Gabrielle, who was now in tears.

The scene was surreal, a tableau from a bygone era. Despite the hurt Gabrielle had caused, the thought of retribution was abhorrent to me. I stepped forward, helping her to her feet as she clung to me, her sobs filling the silence.

Addressing the council, I made my intentions clear. "Gabrielle wishes to return to France, and I respect her decision. I couldn't live abroad either, though I've never tried. We will marry here, and then she may go home."

To my surprise, the council and their spouses showed their respect with a bow before departing. Agnes and Annabella approached, ready to support Gabrielle and me in whatever came next.

Malcolm's smile was a stark contrast to the turmoil I felt inside. "A wise decision, Zachariah Black," he said, his arm reassuring on my shoulder. "It was indeed peculiar for Gabrielle to suddenly wish to return to the UK. Rest assured, I've taken care of the formalities. The marriage certificate will be arranged, and Gabrielle will have her child in France, named Zachariah Black Jr., in honour of his father."

I let out a deep breath, my emotions a tangle of disappointment and confusion. "You always have a solution, Malcolm. But right now, I'm not sure how to feel," I admitted, my voice trailing off as I retreated to the solitude of my room.

Ascending the stone steps, the distant sound of a helicopter hinted at Gabrielle's departure. Margaret's brief visit, marked by the delivery of coffee and a comforting kiss, was a small solace. Alone on the balcony, the view of the rose garden prompted reflections on how different life could have been with Janet still here.

Agnes and Annabella's presence was a silent acknowledgement of my grief. They noticed the tears I couldn't hide, and with a silent exchange of glances, they left me to my thoughts, the untouched coffee growing cold beside me.

***

I am Zachariah Black Jr., the son of Zachariah Black. I am on a quest to piece together the latter years of my father's life. Following my mother's departure back to France, he led a solitary existence at Rose Cottage. From the information I've gathered, he never revisited the castle and ultimately vanished, leaving no trace. Our paths have never crossed, but I cling to the hope that if he is still alive, I may one day find him.

What happens next is another story.

By Robert S Baker

Printed in Great Britain
by Amazon